MERRY FANGIN' CHRISTMAS
Twice Bitten: Book Six

CRYSTAL-RAIN LOVE

Copyright © 2021 Crystal-Rain Love

All rights reserved.

ISBN: 9798787058628

DEDICATION AND ACKNOWLEDGEMENTS

This was possibly the most fun I've ever had writing a book, primarily because I have such great friends who allow me to put them in books and do hilarious, yet awful things to them.

Thank you so much Greg Bennett for letting me pick on ya, and for being my editor.

Thank you Christle Gray for dealing with my "OMG I SUCCCCKKKKKKKKK" hissy fits I have during every single flippin' book I write.

Thank you Danielle Muething for bringing Danni and the gang to life in audio, and cracking me up as you do. Also, for allowing me to have some fun with you in this book.

Thank you Manuela Serra for creating such beautiful covers. This is the first series of mine to truly take off and I know your art is a big part of that.

Thank you Rome Kimbrough for allowing me to create a character after you and put him through all sorts of crazy scenarios. I appreciate the fact you haven't killed me yet. Ha ha!

To TL Macon and Sharon Pence: Y'all get me through the days at the day job. I would go crazy without y'all! And TL, you're just the writing drill sergeant I need!

To my wonderful readers: THANK YOU. I wish I could put you all in a book for Christmas and give you the world. There are, however, only so many pages… so I did put some of you in here! Please don't hate me. I tried to only kill off the ones who wanted to be killed (some of y'all are weird like that, but I suppose that's why you get me) but it's a Twice Bitten book. Y'all know there's gonna be blood and death mixed in with Christmas cheer. ;)

Merry Fangin' Christmas, Y'all! Hope you enjoy!

CHAPTER ONE

Every child has that one Christmas present they long for with every ounce of their heart and soul, that one gift they think of night and day, beg and plead for, just knowing deep within his or her little heart, it must be acquired or else they will simply die.

My childhood ultimate dream present was the African-American version of the Midnight Tuxedo Barbie doll. I begged. I pleaded. I wrote letters directly to Santa Claus, kept my room meticulously clean despite the fact I shared it with Shana, the world's messiest child, got straight A's, and on Christmas Eve I left out the most delicious homemade chocolate chip cookies for Santa to bribe my beloved gift from him in case my parents hadn't bought it. When Christmas morning finally came, I ran to the living room as fast as my little eight-year-old legs would take me, and came to an abrupt stop in the doorway.

There, propped in front of the wrapped gifts under the tree, were the Santa gifts. The special gifts. The gifts our parents left unwrapped so we'd believe Santa had brought them to us directly from The North Pole. Shana squealed with the pure joy of a child who'd gotten exactly what they wanted for Christmas as she zoomed around me to scoop up the three Bratz dolls she'd made sure to ask for every day for the past three months. I didn't squeal with joy. I didn't zoom. My feet planted themselves into the carpet as I stared at the glamourous blonde, blue-eyed Barbie doll staring back at me, her painted facial expression seeming as unimpressed with me as I was with her.

"Merry Christmas!" my father said. He stepped into the room with a big smile, my less cheerful mother at his side, still wiping sleep from her eyes. He looked down at me with a frown, looked toward the tree, and I saw the brightness fade from his eyes as he turned them on my mother to deliver a dark look her way.

She shrugged her shoulders in response and prodded me forward. "Look what Santa brought you, Danni. See, even Santa Claus knew which Barbie was the prettiest and you can't argue with Santa Claus."

My father squeezed my shoulder and walked me over to the tree. "Come on, kiddo," he said in a soft voice a lot less cheery than he'd greeted us with. "You've got some good stuff left under there."

I sensed an angry undertone to his voice, which was rare. My father was slow to anger, unlike my mother who got her underwear in knots over pretty much anything, and I realized Shana was ripping open packages and fawning over every gift while I… I was acting like a spoiled brat.

I dropped to my knees beside the tree and opened my gifts. I made sure to thank my parents for every single one I received, and I did receive wonderful gifts. I'd been given other Barbie dolls, clothes, shoes, earrings for my newly pierced ears and many of the books I'd wanted off my 'To Be Read' list, which even back then, was pretty long. But I didn't get my African-American Midnight Tuxedo Barbie and all I could think as I looked over at the plate of crumbs Santa had left on the coffee table was, "I hope they give you diarrhea, you fat fart-faced jerk-head."

Hey, I was only eight years old. The F-bombs and witty yet wildly inappropriate names for slimeballs came years later when I was less likely to get my mouth washed out with soap.

I didn't know then that my mother had been in charge of the Santa gifts and had purchased the white Barbie because she refused to get me the black one, or that she'd done it without my father's knowledge, but snippets I heard from their arguing later that night clued me in. Long after Shana had fallen asleep clutching her favorite fish-faced Bratz doll to her chest and the arguing had died down, I crawled out of my bed and tip-toed to the tiny little room off the kitchen my father used as an office, drawn by the light and the sound of typing and clicking.

The door was ajar, so I tried to peek in unnoticed, but the old door squeaked with the slightest movement. My father's hands froze over his keyboard, and he swung his head around to see who had intruded. I saw the alarm in his eyes before he raised his hand to cover the computer screen, which I could see clearly from where I stood. He realized this and sighed. "Ah, hell. Come here, kiddo."

"I'm sorry," I whispered as I approached.

"You haven't done anything wrong." He smiled down at me as I climbed onto his lap and snuggled against the warmth of his flannel shirt. He hadn't showered or changed into bedclothes yet, despite the late hour, and smelled of Old Spice, Christmas cookies, and the hint of motor oil he could never seem to get completely off his hands. "With all the sugar you ate today, I'd be surprised if you were asleep."

That wasn't what I was apologizing for, or why I was sorry. The doll I wanted, the beautiful brown-skinned Barbie with the prettiest doll face I'd ever seen was on his screen. I was still pretty young back then, but I was old enough to see a three-figure dollar amount next to it and know I was never getting her. The only thing worse than knowing that was knowing my father was just as disappointed.

"I'm sorry, honey. She's sold out and I've searched all

over the internet. I can only find her on reseller sites for way more than we can afford."

"It's okay, Daddy." I forced my disappointment down and faked a smile as I looked up at him. "The one Santa Claus brought me is pretty too, and you got me some other Barbies I can play with. I would have never taken her out of the box anyway. She's too pretty to mess up."

My parents had argued a lot that week when they thought we weren't listening, but I was a curious child and could always sense when something wasn't quite right, so I was always listening. That was how I learned Santa Claus wasn't real and that the African-American Midnight Tuxedo Barbie had sold out quickly, but still not until after my mother had purchased the Caucasian version. I could have had her at the regular price, which was still high because she was a collector's Barbie, not the kind anyone with sense would allow a child to play with, but my mother's racism had ensured I'd never have her. So I learned what racism was too.

It was my worst Christmas and that blonde, blue-eyed doll sitting in its mint condition box on my dresser was a constant reminder of it and how horrible my mother could be, and how sad my father was because he knew how badly I'd wanted the other doll and felt inadequate for not being able to afford to get her for me. I hated that fucking blonde doll.

I hated her shiny hair and her pouty pink lips. I hated her round boobs and her tiny waist. I hated her blue eyes that mocked me every day of my life growing up in my parents' home and I hated her stupid peach skin which didn't make her prettier than the doll I'd really wanted no matter what my mother said to the contrary. I hated that plastic bitch and what she constantly reminded me of so much that the day my father died and I no longer had to pretend I liked her, I took that doll outside, poured gasoline over her, lit a match, and watched her burn into a blackened puddle of goo.

MERRY FANGIN' CHRISTMAS

Blood was my white Midnight Tuxedo Barbie now. Cupcakes, brownies, and pretty much anything delicious were my African-American Midnight Tuxedo Barbie. My stomach practically cramped with the desire for moist cake and rich, chocolate frosting as I watched the women sitting in a booth across the room take dainty bites out of the sweet treats they'd brought into The Midnight Rider.

"That is not the Christmas spirit I see on your face, sweetcheeks."

"Huh?" I tore my hungry gaze away from the cute cupcakes with little Christmas tree sprinkles to look over at the slender vampire who'd just slid onto the bar stool next to mine. Ginger's short, dark, spiky hair sported green tips the same color as her heavy eyeliner. She wore her usual attire of cropped black leather jacket with metal studs, ripped jeans, and black leather shit-kickers, but her T-shirt was more on the festive side, if you considered a gangster Santa Claus with a machine gun and a huge blunt hanging out the side of his mouth festive. "I see you're in the spirit. I'm not quite sure if that spirit is of the Christmas or demonic variety, however."

Ginger laughed and flagged Tony for a drink. The tiger-shifter placed a fresh bottle of warm blood in front of her a moment later before returning to his real customers, ones who weren't on Rider's payroll and actually paid for drinks, and tipped. "Definitely Christmas. I count the days every year until I can wear this shirt. It's bitchin'."

"It's something." I nodded toward her glittery red lips. "I do like the lipstick. I've never noticed your lips sparkle before. New shade?"

"Yep, just for the Christmas season. It's called Ho Ho Skank-Ho."

I barked out a laugh so unexpected I was very thankful my depression over not being able to enjoy all the yummy, wonderful treats of the season had put me off my drink because spitting or snorting out blood would have been way more Halloween than Christmas and would have freaked the human patrons out.

Ginger raised her drink, waited for me to do the same, then clinked her dark glass bottle against mine before taking a hearty and very enthusiastic gulp. I didn't bother, opting instead to set my bottle back down on the bar top and glare daggers into the happy laughing women still working on their cupcakes.

"I know you get by with a lot because you're sleeping with the boss and all, but glaring at the customers isn't good for business."

I redirected my dark glare to Ginger. "Those twits have been pecking at those cupcakes for like ten minutes already. They don't even have the decency to devour them in the way they deserve to be devoured. No appreciation for their chocolatey goodness whatsoever. It's a fucking insult."

"I know, sweetie, I know." Ginger gave my hand a squeeze, but immediately withdrew as she caught my grimace.

"Sorry." The stupid succubus side of me could be so finicky about touch, repulsed by females and way too happy with males.

"No big." She took another drink. "I know it sucks wanting to eat all your comfort foods and having to settle for bland, flavorless crap or blood instead, but letting that grow cold isn't going to make it any more appetizing and you know you have to stay on top of your diet."

Yep, I had to stay on top of my special blood diet or else I'd end up on top of random men or I'd just go really psycho-violent. In my opinion, neither option were cute looks, so I picked up the dark glass bottle and forced myself to drink down its coppery contents. I didn't think the blood tasted bad. I was half vampire after all, but I wanted chocolate cake, damn it. "It's white Midnight Tuxedo Barbie all over again," I muttered.

"What?"

"Nothing."

MERRY FANGIN' CHRISTMAS

Ginger stared at me for a moment, her brow knit in concern, then looked over at the two women still too busy gabbing to finish shoving the small cakes into their face holes and put me out of my misery, and cracked her knuckles. "All right. That's outside food and technically they're not supposed to bring it in here, so I'll go over there and toss them and their pecked-over cupcakes out."

"No, don't." I sighed. "Let them enjoy it, even if they don't know how to properly enjoy a cupcake. Somebody should have a merry Christmas season."

"Okay, seriously, what is up with you, girlfriend? You have been way too doom and gloom lately. You're the newest vampire here, the least removed from humanity. You should be the most festive bitch out of all of us and you're moping around plotting murder with your eyes and muttering about Barbies in tuxedos. What is your problem?"

"Problem? *Problems*." I picked up my drink and forced the remainder of the blood down my throat before setting the bottle down hard enough to earn a raised eyebrow from Tony, where he stood on the other side of the bar taking a young couple's drink order. I pulled an "oopsy" face, earning a little headshake from the quiet shifter who I was pretty sure thought I was a complete trial, and let out another sigh.

"Enough sighing. You're starting to sound like a deflating tire. Spill. Who pissed in your Christmas cookies? Please tell me you're not upset over *that*."

I followed her line of sight to where Daniel sat in a corner booth across from a long-haired brunette. I'd noticed them earlier, their heads bowed close as the woman in the festive sweater showed him something on her cell phone and seemed to jot notes into a small notebook. Sensing us staring, Daniel glanced up and narrowed his eyes. I quickly averted my gaze.

"What? Daniel talking to a woman? Why would I be upset about that? It's a slow night. He can take a break."

Ginger gave me a look that suggested she knew I was full of shit and being deliberately coy. "I can't think of any reason why it should upset you. Not one single good reason."

I picked up on her warning undertone and squelched the sigh that nearly erupted in reflex. Ginger was right. I was starting to sound like a deflating tire and I was annoying myself. "Do you know who the woman is? She puts out that Imortian vibe, but she doesn't work for Rider."

"Yeah, I noticed, but no, I don't know who she is. I imagine she might be someone Daniel knew from his time in his home realm. Why?" Again, she gave me a warning look.

I shrugged and stayed quiet. There was no reason to admit I was wondering if the attractive woman was someone Daniel had known romantically or confess the way that thought seemed to eat at my stomach lining. Nope, not while under Ginger's glare, a glare she directed my way because despite how much they teased each other, she liked Daniel and didn't want Rider to kill him, which he definitely would if he thought I gave a damn about the dragon-shifter's love life, especially given the sad state of ours.

"So how are you and Rider doing?" Ginger asked, careful to keep her voice down. "If I'm not pushing too far to ask. I'm not prying, it's just I've noticed some, uh, tension between you two since we returned from Pigeon Forge."

"You're my friend, Ginger. You should be able to ask me how I'm doing without sounding like you're afraid of risking losing your own damn head if my boyfriend overhears you," I said with far more bitterness than I'd intended. The image of Rider covered in Trixell's blood flashed before me, along with the sound of the witch screaming, and I shuddered.

"So there *is* trouble in paradise. Well, I guess that

would ruin the whole Christmas mood."

"It's not just Rider." I sighed again, unable to stop myself. "I have no Christmas spirit whatsoever. The holidays in my family have been rough for years, especially after I lost my father. You know how my family is, and now with everything going on with Shana and that letter from my mother…"

"You two still haven't had that talk, huh?"

"You'd know if I had. Rider has you and Daniel practically joined at each of my hips."

Ginger had been taking a drink from her bottle of blood and choked on a laugh. She quickly pinched her nose with her fingers to keep from snorting out blood and grabbed a napkin to discreetly wipe it. "Sorry, but that hit me funny. You know the last place Rider would want Daniel is anywhere near your hips. That whole region is a big No-Go."

I rolled my eyes. "It's not quite as funny when you know his jealousy isn't just an inconvenience."

"Believe me, I know what he's capable of. I've fought with him." She shot a look Daniel's way. "That's why it may seem I'm always watching you two a little too close, spying on you. I know you have to be irritated by it, but think of me as a double agent. I'm not waiting for something to happen so I can run tattling to Rider, even if that is part of my job. I'm watching, trying to make sure nothing *does* happen because I've seen the way that dragon looks at you and I saw the way it hit you when he almost died. I don't like a whole lot of people enough to call them friends, but I'd take bullets for you two idiots, so what I'm saying is… I guess…"

"I know. I feel the same way and I know he does too. I've never had friends like you two before. Honestly, I never really had friends at all."

"Same." Ginger took another drink. "That's why we've got to cheer you up. I can't have my bestie all sulky during the merriest season of all."

"Why are you so into Christmas? I wouldn't think our community would be into it. Rider certainly doesn't seem to care about it at all." I looked around at the pitiful excuse for Christmas décor, just a bit of gold garland here and there.

"Rider's busy trying to find whatever hole that rodent, Pacitti, has burrowed his ass into so he can yank him out and gut the sneaky bastard, and deal with the possible ramifications of what he saw. Not your fault," Ginger quickly added. "I was right there with you. So were Rome and Daniel. None of us saw a security camera, none of us knew we were being recorded or followed. We all are to blame for that series of fuckups."

"Yeah, but if I hadn't lost my mind when I saw Daniel's hand get shot off—"

"He still would have been on camera shifting shape to heal the damage, and don't blame yourself for the tracking device or, for that matter, the jackass private eye either. How many mothers actually hire goons like that to follow their own daughters, and how many jerks are big enough assholes to even think of planting a tracking device on a person's dog? No, on second thought, fuck this. We're not taking the blame for *any* of that mess."

"Any of what mess?" Daniel leaned his hip against the bar next to me and grabbed a handful of beer nuts to toss into his mouth. He'd been careful to distance himself enough our bodies didn't touch, but I still felt the warmth coming off of him. The man seemed to exude heat.

"The presumably dickless private dick," Ginger answered.

"Nice." Daniel shared a fist bump with the vampire and glanced toward the front door as his companion left the bar.

"So, what was up with your little meeting in the corner?" Ginger asked. Bless her undead heart, she knew it would eat me up not knowing.

Daniel shrugged and threw back another handful of

beer nuts.

"Oh, come on. You can't have a private discussion with someone throwing off Imortian vibes and not tell us *something*." She leaned toward him, which meant she leaned toward me, and my succubus side did not like it, but I fought the cringe in an effort to not appear insulting. "What was she? Did we finally have a wereunicorn in our presence and not know it?"

"I wasn't aware a conversation in a public bar was viewed as some sort of covert meeting," Daniel said, "and no. Her name is Donna Jordison, and I was put in touch with her through The Moonlight Agency."

"The agency that you and other Imortians went through to come to this realm?" I said. "The one that assigns Imortians security jobs."

"Mostly security jobs," Daniel said, "but some get other jobs, and yes, that's the agency that handles our training on this realm and helps us acclimate."

"So…" I frowned. "Did Rider ask you to check out a new hire or something?"

"If you two busybodies must know, Donna is helping me to acquire a gift that's not so easy to find here in the local gift shops."

"Aww," Ginger said. "See, now he has the right spirit. Who is this special gift for, as if we didn't already know?"

"I've told you all I'm going to tell you," he replied while I squirmed a little in my seat, skin warm at the thought of Daniel giving me a special gift. I hoped it wasn't anything too special and worried mine might not be good enough.

"Hey, you can't bring some strange woman here, tell us she's helping you with a gift, and not have us dig for more," Ginger told him. "If you didn't want us to pry, you should have gone to her or handled things over the phone or internet."

"For one, neither of us can leave Danni until we get things handled with Selander Ryan and now that damn detective, and for another, no way was I going to her. Because of the type of shifter she is, The Moonlight Agency thought it best to place her in Australia. I'm not going to Australia."

Ginger's eyes widened. "Ohmigawd, was she a werekangaroo?"

"No."

"Werekoala?" I asked.

"Werewallaby," Daniel answered.

Ginger and I looked at each other and I was pretty sure I wore the same confused look as she did. "Is that the thing that throws its babies at prey?"

"Geez, I thought my mother-daughter relationship had issues," I said.

"I don't think so," Daniel said. "Whatever a wallaby is, it looks like a kangaroo to me, but apparently it's another kind of animal, still indigenous to Australia, so that's where Donna was sent to fit in."

"If this agency assigns Imortian shifters to places their animal forms naturally fit in, explain to me again why they sent your dragon ass here," Ginger said.

"They weren't renting out a lot of rooms at Hogwarts," Daniel replied deadpan. "Basically, I'm SOL on finding a place in this realm to really fit in."

"Do you have wallabies in Imortia?" I asked.

"No."

"But you said Imortian shifters were created through a spell that killed the original animal to bind its soul with the cursed Imortian. Where did the queen get the animals if they weren't from Imortia?"

Daniel shrugged. "Fairuza was an evil bitch. A little animal-napping from different realms certainly wasn't out of her range."

"Okay, well this has all been very interesting," Ginger said, pointing toward Lana and Juan, the two shifters who'd just walked through the back door, dressed identical to Daniel and me in black long-sleeved shirts and pants, "but I do believe I see your replacements for the night and our girl here needs some holiday spirit so let's get out of here and go find that Christmas décor Rider said we could get."

"Works for me," Daniel said, sharing a nod of greeting with Lana.

My stomach did the little clench thing it did when the two shifters appeared friendly despite the fact I liked Lana and Daniel was just my friend, and I didn't need much more than that to get my rear off the bar stool and in motion. "I guess we're all going in Daniel's truck."

"There's no way I'm fitting a couple of Christmas trees in my 'stang," Ginger said as we moved toward the front door.

As we neared the door, I saw a tan woman with purple hair showing something on her cell phone to Marty, the burly, loveable yet dimwitted troll on front door duty. I could tell by the crease lines running the length of his low forehead, he wasn't going to be much help to the woman, whatever she wanted, and something in my gut told me she needed help.

"Is there a problem?" I stopped next to the pair, bringing my two bodyguards to a stop with me.

The woman turned toward me, which was when I saw the Bobby Singer T-shirt peeking out of her open coat. I liked her already, and even if she wasn't a fellow *Supernatural* lover, I'd have felt compelled to help her based on the worry I saw in her eyes. She took in Daniel's hair, then my attire. "You're security. I was here the night you kicked out some handsy woman for groping this guy here."

I recalled the incident and nodded.

"My name is Tina Sweeney. I come here pretty often with my cousin and some work friends. My cousin is missing, and I was checking if she's been around here the last few nights." She stepped away from Marty and held out her phone to show me a picture.

I looked at the blonde woman in the picture and felt a sudden onset of alarm in my chest. The woman in the picture was dressed in a *The Walking Dead* T-shirt and smiled as she posed with Tina next to a life-sized cardboard cutout of Jensen Ackles in character as Dean Winchester. I didn't know her, didn't recall ever seeing her before, even if she was a frequent bar patron, but I knew she was dead and whatever had killed her wasn't finished hunting.

CHAPTER TWO

"Drink this." Daniel forced a mug of blood into my hands while angling himself in a way that blocked Tina Sweeney's view of the dark red liquid inside, and gave me a look when I started to protest. "You just nearly passed out. Drink it all down right now, or we can go see what Rider thinks."

I lifted the mug to my mouth and gulped the liquid down, but kept my glare on the pushy dragon-shifter. Still, as bossy as he could be, no one was as bossy as Rider, and with the mood my sire-slash-boyfriend had been in since Pacitti had dropped his bomb on us, I didn't want him disturbed, let alone informed of an incident I knew would send him into protective overdrive.

"That's a good girl," Daniel drawled and winked as I drank down the last drop of blood, then took the mug from my hands. "Now you may carry on."

I licked my lips, ensuring no telltale blood was there to give away my ghoulish nature and shot eye-daggers into his back as he walked the mug back to the bar.

"Are you all right now?" Tina asked from where she sat to my right at the table we'd grabbed after I'd apparently nearly fainted from the enormity of whatever had happened to me when I'd looked at the picture of her cousin. Genuine concern showed in her eyes, which touched me, considering the poor woman was already worried about her cousin.

"I'm fine." I gave a little dismissive wave and forced on a bright smile. "I just have this blood sugar thing."

Ginger snorted where she sat on my left and quickly faked a short coughing spell to cover it up. "Sorry," she said, the twinkle of amusement still in her eyes. "Go on."

"Anyway," I continued, "back to what's important. You said your cousin… I'm sorry. I don't think I got her name."

"Angela," she said and glanced up at Daniel as he returned and dropped his tall form down into the chair directly across the table from me. "Angela LaRoche. We usually sat at that table."

I looked at the table she pointed toward and vaguely remembered a group of women sitting there the night Daniel had been propositioned by some woman with a thing for sharing men with her sister. That particular group of women had been well-behaved, however, and I thought I recalled them sending up a loud cheer when I'd declared the next person to put their hands on anyone else would be knocked the hell out. Angela LaRoche wasn't a troublemaker, at least not in my book, and I felt bad for not remembering her.

"I wish I could say I remembered her given you say you've been here often, but if it's any consolation, I generally only pay attention to the jerks I end up having to kick out."

Tina smiled. "We could be a little rowdy, especially when *Carry On Wayward Son* came on the jukebox, but we kept it to an acceptable level. This is the one bar we know jackasses will be kicked out of without question if they can't take no for an answer, so it's easily our favorite place to go after a rough day at work."

"Tell me more about Angela. What brought you here

tonight?" I asked, the same feeling in my gut that told me the woman was long gone from this world telling me that on some level, Tina knew it just as well as I did.

The woman's sorrow-filled eyes peeked out at me from behind a fringe of purple bangs before they blinked away a line of tears she wouldn't allow to fall. "Angela didn't meet me at Starbucks this morning. We always meet there the same time every morning without fail, especially this season when they have their holiday blends. I called her cell phone three times and she didn't answer, so I thought she overslept. I went on to work and tried her phone on my breaks but she still wasn't answering so after I got off work I went to her house and…"

I ached to reach over and take Tina's hand when she hiccupped on a sob, but the demon inside me couldn't stand the thought.

Seeming to pick up on what I was feeling, or just being his decent, kind self, Daniel reached out instead and took one of Tina's hands between his own and encouraged her to continue. "What happened, Tina?"

"She didn't answer the door, so I… I used the spare key she kept in the zombie gnome's ass."

"I'm sorry, the what's what?" Daniel asked as Ginger and I sat blinking at the woman.

"Oh." Her eyes widened as if just realizing what she'd said and she laughed. "Sorry. She has this hideously ugly zombie gnome that no one in their right mind would ever want, but that's Angela. She loves zombies, the uglier and more ridiculous, the better, and she has the sense of humor of a twelve-year-old boy, so when she saw this zombie gnome with a secret compartment that opens when you spread its—"

"Okay, I think we get it now," I said, cutting her off before she finished the sentence I knew would cause Ginger to lose the battle with silent laughter that currently had water pooling in her eyes. I shot her a look that warned a discreet under-the-table shin-kick was headed her way if she didn't get it together. "So, you used a spare key and entered the house?"

"Yes," Tina continued without missing a beat, seemingly oblivious to Ginger's struggle. "I called out for her but didn't get any answer. There were boxes in the foyer and I could tell she'd been putting up Christmas decorations like she'd said she planned to do a couple nights ago. I heard the radio on in the living room, so I headed that way, expecting to find her up to her ears in garlands and ornaments since she tends to overdo things, but …"

"But what?" I prompted, as a haunted look settled in Tina's eyes. "What did you find?"

"Blood," she said and shuddered. "The tree was up and boxes of ornaments were open. A long string of garland hung halfway off the tree as if she'd been in the process of hanging it and just dropped it there and at the end of it, right in front of the fireplace was … so much blood."

I shared a look with Daniel. "Tina, why would you see that and come here? Did you call the police?"

"No." She shook her head. "I searched the house and the garage. I searched everywhere she normally would go, and I thought of here. She's had some trouble with her ex and usually after a rough bout with him, she comes here to have a drink."

"By rough bout, you mean…"

"Things could get pretty heated. To my knowledge, he never hit her, but he was very possessive, and I know he threatened her the last time they got into it. I didn't call the police because… I don't know if the blood was hers or his. She said she'd kill him if he ever put his hands on her and she'd said his temper had gotten worse the longer she refused to go back to him… so I didn't call the police. I hoped I would find her here and get an explanation for what happened."

"Tina, if she was attacked and taken somewhere, allowing this much time to elapse is not what you want to do," Daniel told her. "You really need to call the police right now."

"Wait," I said, my gut picking up on something in the way Tina averted her gaze and chewed her lip as if wanting to say more. As if she knew more. "There's something you're not telling us, Tina, some other reason you didn't call the police instead of coming here to look for Angela."

She let out a mirthless laugh. "You'll think I'm crazy."

"Believe me, Tina, the three of us have seen some crazy things. Try us."

She looked over at me, met my gaze. "I saw wrong. There's no way I saw what I thought I saw. She has to be here or out shopping or somewhere. She couldn't have… It doesn't make any sense."

"What did you see, Tina?"

"The blood. It was only there in front of the fireplace and… up the fireplace."

"Up the…" The feeling in my gut warning me something dark and evil was dangerously close intensified. "Are you saying the blood went up the chimney?"

Tina nodded slowly, then barked out a sharp, near-hysterical laugh that brought tears to her eyes. "You see? Crazy. If she were dead, who killed her? Krampus?" She wiped her eyes. "Angela likes to play pranks. It's a prank. She knows I love *Supernatural,* so she's pranking me. I've wasted your time."

Despite the aversion my succubus side had to female touch, I gripped Tina's forearm when she made to stand, and forced her to remain sitting. "If you thought your cousin was pranking you, you wouldn't have looked so scared when you came through that door looking for her earlier and you wouldn't have allowed yourself to think her ex might have had something to do with what you found either while trying to come up with stories to tell yourself because you don't want to face the truth of what happened to her."

"Danni!" Daniel said sharply. I looked up to see him

and Ginger both staring at me with their mouths dropped open and was aware of how incredibly insensitive I'd just sounded.

I jerked my hand back from her arm. "I'm so sorry, Tina. I didn't mean to say that like that."

"No, you're right." She angled her head to the side and looked at me as if trying to search inside my head. "You're exactly right. How are you right?"

"Call it a hunch," I said, knowing in the pit of my stomach that I had to find out what had killed Angela LaRoche and stop it before it killed again. "Do you still have that spare key?"

***

"Are you sure we should be doing this without getting Rider's approval first?" Daniel asked as we followed Tina Sweeney's Kia Forte in his new truck. It was still a Ford F-150 and still black, but he'd upgraded to an extended cab to accommodate Kutya, who spent a lot of time with us. The only reason we didn't have the big guy at the moment was because Rider had been under the impression our plans only involved shopping and Kutya couldn't go into stores with us.

"We're not officially working any kind of job," I answered. "We're simply helping someone out."

"By checking out the big murder stains in her cousin's living room," Ginger pointed out from where she sat in the backseat. "I couldn't possibly imagine anything bad coming from this."

I turned and shot her a look. "If the blood has been there long enough to stain, I think it's safe to say the murderer has left the building."

"More reason the cops should be called," Daniel suggested.

"This isn't the type of killer that can be caught by the cops," I said. "I don't expect you to understand how I know that—"

"You feel it in your gut?"

I nodded.

"The same way you felt all that stuff when Eliza was missing?"

"Yes."

"Well, then, that's good enough for me. Your gut instincts haven't failed us yet, but what exactly do you think happened to this woman? What's a Krampus?"

"Evil Santa Claus," Ginger answered for me.

"Seriously? Evil Santa?" Daniel let out a laugh and shook his head. "That's not a real thing."

"I'm sorry, but were you not with us when we killed Cupid after weakening him with a piece of mythical tree?"

"Or when we chopped up a bunch of zombies," Ginger chimed in.

"Okay, but those zombies weren't actually real zombies," he argued.

"They were solid and smelled like wide open ass which was real enough for me," Ginger said, "and do I really need to point out how ridiculous it is that you're questioning the validity of anything when you can shift into a dragon and you're driving around two women who drink blood?"

"Fine, but still? Evil Santa?"

"I don't know if there's such a thing as Evil Santa or Krampus or whatever," I told him. "All I know is I took one look at the woman in that picture and I instinctually knew she was dead and whatever killed her was not human, and it was not stopping at just that one kill."

"Did you get any sense of what killed her? *Not human* is a pretty vague description."

"Is anything in my life ever that easy, Daniel?"

He grinned. "Nah, I guess not. Man, when I pictured my very first Christmas, I sure didn't see us investigating Evil Santa."

"Ya know, it could be a shifter or a vampire," I pointed

out. "All I know at this point is it's evil and not human."

"I guess we'll find out soon enough," Daniel said as he pulled into a driveway behind Tina's car and we all stepped out of our vehicles.

Angela LaRoche lived in a two-story house with white paneling and a small porch. Large bushes I didn't know the names of lined the front of the house and an assortment of ugly gnomes peeked out from among them. They'd also been decorated with multicolor Christmas lights. Icicle lights hung from the edge of the roof, but none were turned on.

Tina walked past the porch and bent over to retrieve a hideously ugly ceramic zombie gnome that appeared to be losing its grayish-green skin. She looked around and, after seeing no one appeared to be spying, she turned the gnome over in her hands and cracked open its ass cheeks. Daniel and Ginger choked down laughter, and even I had to turn my head and bite the inside of my cheek.

Tina replaced the gnome and unlocked the front door, which had already been decorated with a very festive wreath. We stepped into a foyer with a staircase leading to the second floor. Seeing the red and green plaid ribbon wrapped around the railing and the open boxes of garland, stockings, and other décor, I expected to be met with the smell of hot cocoa, pumpkin pie, and baking cookies, and the coppery scent of blood my vampire nose could pick up a mile away, even if it was nearly dry since I'd been warned it would be there. What I didn't expect to hit me was the hint of sulfur.

I turned toward Daniel and Ginger to see them staring at me, having picked up on the smell too.

"I know it smells bad in here," Tina said, having stopped in the foyer, her back to the archway I assumed led to the living room based on the fact I could see a huge half-decorated Christmas tree over her shoulder. "I think it's the blood. I thought something might be rotten, so I took out the garbage earlier, but it's still here. Maybe blood gets stinkier when it dries, and there's so much of it."

"It's fine," I assured her, picking up on the way she shifted her feet and fiddled with her hands. She didn't want to see the bloody remainder of her cousin again and if I were in her place, I wouldn't either. "Ginger, why don't you take Tina into the kitchen and see if you can find anything rotting while Daniel and I check out the living room?"

Ginger's brow furrowed in confusion, knowing damn well what we smelled wasn't a case of rotten eggs. Then her eyes widened a little as it clicked that I wanted Tina out of the way while Daniel and I investigated. "Sure. You know, Tina, I once had a mouse die in a wall and it left that smell. Does Angela have a pantry or a mudroom? They like those kinds of places and can wedge their furry little butts into the tiniest cracks."

"You thinking demon?" Daniel asked as Ginger and Tina disappeared into a room at the far end of the foyer.

"Aren't you?" I jerked my head toward the archway to our left and we stepped into the living room.

The overwhelming smell of blood hit me harder as I stepped fully into the room, the sulfur stronger as well, but neither hit me with quite the same punch as the shock of what I saw.

"Uh, Tina failed to properly describe this setting," Daniel said, his mouth agape as he scanned the room and all its gory detail.

I nodded, needing a moment to find words again. "Yeah, *so much blood* doesn't quite cut it, does it?"

"Nope. Not really."

Angela LaRoche's living room was spacious. A three-piece light green living room suit surrounded an oak coffee table and despite the framed prints of *The Walking Dead* posters adorning the walls and all the collectible toys and busts lining the mantle and filling the shelves that took up an entire wall, it felt warm and homey. The Christmas tree to the right of the fireplace was enormous and decorated with round red ornaments interspersed among various *The Walking Dead* and *Supernatural*-themed ornaments. I saw a Dean Winchester ornament I'd love to have just above the spot where a red boa of garland hung haphazardly from the branches, as if the decorator had just stopped mid-decorating and left her unfinished work hanging there.

Other than the boxes stacked on the table, a recliner, and floor still containing Christmas décor that had yet to be placed, the only other thing that stood out in the otherwise well-kept room was that hanging piece of garland that dropped down to the outer edge of an enormous puddle of blood, except puddle wasn't exactly the right word. It was more an explosion of blood that had splashed onto the tree, the nearby boxes, the fireplace and halfway up the wall around it. If that blood belonged to Angela LaRoche, she either exploded or was ripped apart.

"Well, it's red, but not exactly festive, huh?"

I shot a withering look Daniel's way. "Seriously?"

"Sorry." He had the decency to look genuinely apologetic. "Way too soon for jokes, I see."

"Ya think?" I looked around the room, noting the lack of bloody footprints leading away. "Whatever happened here, what was left of a body didn't get taken out this way. There'd be smears or blood splatter leading out."

We both crouched and looked across the big puddle to the fireplace, where smears in the blood covering the hearth and going up the logs and back wall suggested if Angela LaRoche had been taken from her home, that was the way she'd gone out.

"You want me to go up that chimney, don't you?"

"Somebody has to go up it and unless you have some crime scene coveralls and booties stashed somewhere, it's not going to be me, not in these new Merrell boots."

"That's about what I figured." He crouched down lower, getting as close to the fireplace as he could without stepping into the blood, and sniffed. He frowned and sniffed again. "You smell that?"

I took in a big whiff and my mouth wet in response. "Other than the hint of sulfur, which is definitely stronger here, I'm pretty much overwhelmed by the blood, but there is something else there. Something kind of sweet and spicy… almost cinnamon-like."

"Allspice." He sniffed again. "A little cocoa, peppermint… nutmeg. Smells like that plate of Christmas cookies Jadyn brought in this morning."

I sniffed, but again was too overwhelmed by the coppery scent of blood to notice more than a hint of anything else. "Okay, well, your dragon nose beats my vampire one which is only getting thirstier with each whiff, so up you go."

He looked up at me and frowned. "You had two whole bottles of blood today and a mug of the freshest stuff right before we came here. Even standing over this little lake of blood shouldn't make you so thirsty right now. Have you been meeting all of your blood requirements?"

"Yes, Mom," I lied.

His eyes narrowed and I could tell he doubted my honesty, then he stood, disappeared in a shower of rainbow sparkles and those glittering colors zipped up the chimney, leaving me to stand all alone if the middle of a crime scene.

"Unholy cow," Ginger said, stepping into the room from the foyer. "I appreciate the use of color, but so not the right aesthetic for the season."

I directed the same look I'd given Daniel for his ill-timed humor her way, but she was too busy looking up to notice. I followed her line of sight to the ceiling. "What are you looking at?"

"Someone clearly burst or got ripped apart in this room. I was just looking to see if any ended up on the ceiling," she answered with a shrug before looking back into the area of the foyer she'd come from. "Tina's in the bathroom, so just checking in. You still want me to keep her busy?"

"Yeah, I think it best she not see this again."

"An image like this has a way of sticking in one's brain, so I don't think it could get any worse if she did, but I'll keep her occupied." She looked at the fireplace and let her gaze roam up the wall to the ceiling. "Did Daniel go up the chimney?"

"Somebody had to."

She looked at the grotesque hearth and shuddered before glancing over at a group of décor boxes sitting on the floor. "Just a reminder, if we don't return to The Midnight Rider with Christmas decorations, Rider's going to know we weren't out shopping, so you might not want to spend too much time here playing detective."

A storm of rainbow sparkles blew out of the fireplace and accumulated on the side of the blood puddle across from me before Daniel appeared. "Well, that was fucking gross, but based on what I could see, Evil Santa doesn't seem like such a crazy concept anymore. Also, I'm never going to be able to eat Christmas cookies again."

"What, did you find a sleigh with eight flying hellhounds up there?" Ginger asked.

"No, but I found chunks of Angela LaRoche that were scraped off her body as whatever-the-hell killed her yanked her up the chimney," Daniel answered just as Tina appeared behind Ginger in the doorway.

CHAPTER THREE

"I think she slipped into a coma," Ginger whispered as we stood in front of the staircase we'd moved Tina over to, afraid she'd pass out right there on the foyer floor if we hadn't. She sat there on the step with her mouth hanging open and eyes glossed over. Her body was rigid, completely frozen, and if not for the sound of her racing heart, I wouldn't think she was breathing. Ginger reached out to poke the woman with her index finger, but I smacked it away before she could connect her fingertip to the poor woman's shoulder. "Ow! Geez, it's not like I was about to poke her with a stick. I was just checking for signs of life."

"You can hear signs of life," I told her and shooed her back a step before I crouched down in front of the staircase to put myself at Tina's eye level. "Tina, hey, I know this has been quite a shock, but I need you to snap out of this."

Tina's eyelashes fluttered a little, but that was about all the reaction it seemed I was going to get.

"Yep, her brain's fizzled out. We're going to have to slap her back to the here and now."

Tina's eyes fluttered faster, and she directed a shocked

look Ginger's way before taking a loud gulp. I'd already sent a glare Ginger's way, but she only grinned and gestured toward Tina as if to say, "See? Intimidation works."

"Ignore her, Tina. She means well. We just wanted to snap you out of this shock."

The woman blinked a bit more while she nodded, seeming to clear her head of the last remnants of fog, then raised her glossy eyes to where Daniel stood at my side. "You said you found ch…ch…"

"I said something I wouldn't have ever intentionally said in front of you had I not been too distracted to notice you were within earshot," Daniel said, "and I'm sorry. You shouldn't have had to hear something like that."

"But it's the truth. You found…" She covered her mouth with a trembling hand until she pulled herself together well enough to speak again. "You said it looked like something dragged her up the chimney. Not someone. Something."

Daniel and I shared a look, neither wanting to tell the woman what we thought.

"I guess I need to call the police."

"No," I said. "We're not just bar security. We work investigations like this too."

Ginger took a card out of her inner jacket pocket and handed it to the woman. I read it as Tina looked it over and, despite it being upside down, I made out the bat and moon design of Rider's MidKnight Enterprises logo.

Tina studied the card. "So the bar thing is your day job?"

"Exactly," Daniel said. "Cases like these don't pop up every day and we have to do the bar thing to pay rent."

Alarm filled her eyes. "Oh. Of course. I don't have a lot of money, but I can probably get something from my credit cards."

"You misunderstood," I told her. "We have the bar job to pay rent because we do these jobs for free."

"Oh." Her shoulders slumped a little in relief as she pocketed the card. "And you're sure I don't need to call the police?"

"We'll call the police," I assured her, and nodded at Ginger. She took out her cell phone and walked toward the back of the foyer for a bit more privacy. "We know the perfect detective to do the official report on this, but, uh, Tina, it's best you don't tell a lot of people what happened here."

"That someone made bloody soup of my cousin and dragged her up the chimney like Krampus?" she managed to get out before hiccupping on a sob. "Who would I tell that to, Sam and Dean Winchester?"

Daniel laughed silently next to me until I discreetly elbowed him in his side. *Sorry*, he said through our mind-link.

"Grissom was close by, so he'll be here in about ten minutes," Ginger said, returning to us. She looked down at Tina. "Answer any questions he has as honestly as you can. I know what happened here seems crazy, but I assure you he's seen crazier, as have we. We help him out from time to time, so if you remember anything later, you can call the number on the card I gave you and just ask for Ginger, Daniel, or Danni. You'll be put through to one of us."

Tina took a moment to study each of us, seeming to wonder if she could trust us. Apparently, trust won out because she nodded and released a pent-up breath. "Do you guys think whatever took her knew her? Do you think it knows I was here? Will it come for me?"

Daniel and Ginger both looked at me expectantly, which made me a little nervous. I was trusting Jon's declaration that I had some sort of special gift, but I didn't like the thought of being some all-seeing eye. I had hunches. I didn't know everything, and I didn't want to tell anyone something wrong, especially in matters of life or death.

I took a deep breath to relax my mind and opened my

senses, similar to how I did when casting out my paranormal energy to seek if others of the paranormal community were within close proximity. This time I didn't search for others. I simply allowed my mind to clear and sense for ... I wasn't sure exactly what I searched for, but I didn't get any sense that Tina Sweeney was in any immediate danger. Whatever had dragged her cousin up the chimney was long gone. "I think you'll be fine. Will you be all right here until the detective arrives?"

She straightened her shoulders and nodded. "I'm not going back in that living room ever again, but I'll be all right until the detective arrives, and I have family at home. I won't be alone there."

"That's good," I said and started to give her shoulder a reassuring squeeze, but my stomach revolted at the thought of touching her. I really needed to drink some live male blood. As if on cue, Daniel's warm scent reached out and enveloped me, making my mouth water. "We have to go now. Grissom's a great detective. You'll be perfectly fine in his hands."

I jerked my head toward the door, ignoring Daniel's concerned look, and turned to leave.

"Wait," Tina said, as I was just a few steps away from freedom. "You're not normal, are you?"

I sensed my friends' hearts stutter just like mine, as we all turned to look at where Tina still sat on the staircase.

"I mean, you knew to come here. You knew this wasn't a prank or some normal burglary gone wrong. You're a psychic, aren't you?"

Breath left my lungs in a whoosh of relief. "Something like that. I have hunches. It's not something I really share with people."

"I won't tell anyone." She covered her heart with her hand. "I had an aunt who saw ghosts, conversed with them. I know people have gifts. Thank you, even if you don't find what... *who* did this... thank you for using your gift to help."

MERRY FANGIN' CHRISTMAS

Unable to speak as emotion clogged my throat, I gave a sharp nod and damn near fled the house before tears could drip from my eyes. They dried up as the harsh December wind whipped across my face and I trudged over the snow-dusted sidewalk toward the truck. "Ginger, you can ride up front with Daniel."

I didn't even have to look at them to know they were sharing a look that said "Oh shit."

***

"How about these?"

"Fabulous. Grab it all."

Ginger set down the box of blue and white glass Christmas ornaments and frowned at me. "You've said that about everything. You have to have an opinion."

I glanced at the boxes of ornaments and blew out a breath. We'd picked up Angel after leaving Angela LaRoche's house so she could grab some things for the apartment, then headed to Wal-Mart since it was the only place that would stay open late enough for us after our crime scene detour. "Rider didn't have a preference for how we decorate the bar."

"That's because Rider's a stuffy old vampire who was probably turned before Saint Nick sprouted his first dingus hair," Ginger replied. "To my knowledge, The Midnight Rider has never done any kind of holiday décor. I don't think any of Rider's directly owned businesses have. It's clear he's allowing it this year because he's trying to please you. What the hell happened between you two? You were just fine when we returned from Pigeon Forge. Then the next time I saw you two together, there was a chill in the air so frigid it made my nips tighten hard enough to cut glass."

"Thanks for that picture."

"Anytime, sweetcheeks. Now spill. You haven't even

drank from him, have you? I can tell because your aversion to females is headed toward off the chart territory and you're starting to do that thing where you salivate in Daniel's presence. At least it's his blood I hope you're salivating for, but if you're not drinking from Rider, I highly doubt you and he are—"

"Enough!" I snapped and looked around, thankful to find it was just the two of us in the ornament aisle at the late hour. Most of the shoppers were there for gifts, having already purchased all their décor, and Daniel had stayed back in the aisle with Christmas trees with Angel, waiting for her to decide which she wanted. No doubt he picked up on the same thing Ginger had and knew it was best to give me a little space, despite his tendency to be protective. "I'm sorry. I didn't mean to snap. I just really don't want to talk about it. I'm fine."

"Fair enough," she muttered and returned her attention to the ornaments.

"We should do traditional decorations if the bar has never been decorated for Christmas before. Give everyone that sense of nostalgia."

"All right." Ginger grabbed a set of ornaments that included traditional designs primarily in red and green. "It would be kind of funny, though, if we could find something like vampire bats with little Santa hats."

I grinned at the image. "It would, and Rider certainly enjoys the whole vampire shtick, but we don't want to be too obvious. There's only so many times we can wave bats in front of human's faces and they not catch on to us, no matter how out there the idea of us being real might be to them."

"Vampire shtick? Rider?" Ginger arched her eyebrow.

"The man once told my mother he'd impale himself if I didn't dance with him," I replied, unable to hold back a smile at the memory, "and hello, he has bats in both his MidKnight Enterprises and The Midnight Rider logos, not to mention the part of the sublevel he calls The Bat Cave."

"Oh, right. I guess he does have more of a sense of humor than I give him credit for. I'm used to being at the end of sharply barked orders or fighting alongside him, so I don't really get to see that side. I imagine very few actually see that side." She glanced back at me as she pushed the shopping cart toward the shelves of garland and tinsel. "Judging from that look on your face, I have to ask if you're sure you don't want to talk about it. I'm a good listener, and let's face it, Eliza's dealing with her own issues these days."

I sighed. It was very true the few sessions I'd had with Eliza since she'd started up counseling again were not the same as they used to be. She still hadn't fully recovered from what had happened in Pigeon Forge, and I couldn't help feeling like a bitter reminder when I dropped in for my sessions. It probably didn't help at all that Daniel was my escort for those sessions and if I wasn't a bitter reminder, he definitely was. He'd almost died, something that could have been entirely prevented had she acted sooner. Not that we blamed Eliza, but we didn't have to. She blamed herself enough for the lot of us.

Either way, going to the sessions were more a way of helping her dip her toes back into the water than a real therapy session for me. I didn't feel right dumping my personal issues on her while she was still dealing with her own stuff, and as for my sessions with Nannette… I no longer thought the woman hated me, we'd grown our own odd brand of friendship, but the things bothering me weren't things I felt comfortable discussing with her. Rider's people were loyal to him, but Nannette's feelings went beyond loyal. She was devoted to him and I instinctually knew that no matter what he did, she would never see him as anything but the savior who freed her from her horrible sire, and a man she owed, and would willingly give her life for.

"I know most of the vampires in Rider's nest joined him after he killed their sires and that those sires were vile masters, many treating their fledglings like slaves. Is that how you came to know Rider?" I asked. "You don't have to tell me if it's uncomfortable."

"Nah, it's cool." She looked through the different colors of garland and selected red. "My sire was an asshole, but not old enough or powerful enough to be as terrible as some of the others I've heard horror stories of. Bastard didn't even have a place to keep us. We were basically a small gang, a homeless gang at that. We were squatters in the nastiest places."

She tossed a few more boxes of garland into our cart and pushed it down the aisle toward the stockings and Santa hats. "He didn't make us sex slaves or anything like that, but he stole us. I was twenty-one when I was turned and already all alone in the world, so it wasn't so bad for me, but he liked kids. The nest he built included a lot of teenagers. Yeah, most were runaways but still… they had their lives ahead of them, time to change direction, go back home, go to school, time to make a life, you know?"

I nodded.

"That bastard robbed them. Worse, he started making us gather for him. I'd had enough when he started watching this field where school-aged kids would play youth sports at night. It was soccer season, and he had his eye on this girl who couldn't have been any older than twelve at most. She wasn't a runaway. She wasn't even a teenager. She was just some kid he liked the look of and wanted to make part of his messed-up family. He wanted me to lure her, and I told him to fuck himself."

"I can imagine how that went over," I said, knowing the control a sire had over fledglings.

"Yeah." She chuckled. "I always was a rebel though, and I didn't stop at telling him what he could do to himself either, not even after he backhanded me so hard my teeth were loosened. I had the audacity, or ignorance, depending on how you look at it, to try to fight my own damn sire."

I felt my eyes widen. "No fledgling can fight his or her

own sire and win."

"Yeah, I know, but what can I say? I've always had this thing; tell me I can't do something and I'm going to do it just because, no matter how stupid or dangerous." She shrugged. "He could have just frozen me in place, made a joke of me in front of the others in our nest, but he chose to make an example out of me instead. Once done, he left me in a bloody heap in an alley, expecting the sun to fry me first thing in the morning. My legs were broken, but my arms weren't so I managed to drag myself to the street and it was in an area near bars, so fortunately two decent guys who'd been drinking late found me on their way to where they'd parked their car."

I grimaced.

"They wanted to take me to the hospital, but I'd heard of this vampire who ran a bar, a real badass who'd taken out whole nests. I had no reason to trust him. All I knew was if I couldn't stop my sire and the other fledglings who had no problem taking orders from him, maybe he could, and a human hospital wasn't in my best interest. I told the guys to go to the bar, ask for him. I told them he was my brother and would take care of me. Hell, I didn't know how old he physically looked or what his race was, or if any of that mattered. I didn't know if the guys would even be allowed to see him long enough to question the familial bond."

"You really took a risk."

"There was no way I could go to a hospital and let humans try to take care of me, and I couldn't make it to the bar myself. My best shot was hoping the things I'd heard about this badass vampire who didn't take too kindly to women being abused were true and that he'd give a shit about my predicament. The bar was close enough. One guy stayed with me while the other ran the two blocks to get this man he believed was my brother. Two huge shifters returned with him, thanked the guys for their help, and carried me to the bar. That's when and where I met

Rider. He took out my sire the next night and gave me a job."

"After seeing to it, you healed."

"Oh yeah. He hooked me up with Nannette like two minutes after meeting me, gave me blood and a room to rest in."

"Wait. The bar wasn't The Midnight Rider, was it?"

"No, this was another bar in another state, long before The Midnight Rider. It's probably best I don't tell you the where or how long before."

I nodded my head, understanding. Good friends or not, vampire code was vampire code. We didn't ask each other's age or try to find out too much detail about each other's origins, even though there were slips and loopholes. Pretty much everyone in Rider's nest knew the where and when of my turning because he'd been the one to turn me, and I had a decent idea of Nannette's age because of something she'd shared with me and I now had to take to my grave. Then there was Rider and the accidental tumbling into his memories the night he'd killed his own half-brother to save my life. I found it hard to swallow with that memory in mind.

"Sometimes people do terrible things for the right reasons," I murmured, not meaning to say the thought out loud. I looked at Ginger to see her watching me.

"Sometimes people do terrible things because they have to in order to stop even worse things from happening," she said softly. "Is that what's wrong between you and Rider? Did he do something?"

I bit my lip. Hell, she was probably going to badger me until I spilled anyway, so I might as well. "He killed Trixell the morning after we returned from Pigeon Forge."

"Yeah, I know." She frowned. "You're not upset about that, are you? Correct me if I'm wrong, but that's the same evil bitch who helped your sister lure you into a deathtrap and had been helping Selander Ryan screw with you from the grave or wherever his evil ass is haunting you from."

"I know." I raked my hand through my hair and struggled for words to adequately describe the problem, only I didn't really know myself. All I knew was since that morning, I couldn't get the image of Rider stepping into his room covered in blood out of my mind. I'd seen him rip out a man's spine and behead a werewolf with his own bare hands and wasn't nearly as bothered by those incidents as I was by the way he'd looked that morning after killing Trixell. I couldn't get that image of all her blood on him or worse, her horrific screams out of my brain.

"So, what's the problem?"

I shook my head, the words not there. Maybe I was the problem. I knew Rider was a killer. I'd always known it just like I knew I was a killer too. So was Ginger. So was Daniel. Even Angel had killed a man, and she was just a human teenager. Hell, I'd killed a man just for asking me to go down on him in an alley, hadn't made it one week as a vampire before I'd taken a life due to a mixture of being thirsty and offended.

"Hey." Fingers snapped in front of my face and I realized Ginger had moved to stand right in front of me, and we'd been joined by Angel and Daniel, the latter of which gave me a look so knowing I immediately averted my eyes. Sometimes I really thought the dragon-shifter could read my mind. "Sorry. My mind drifted. We got everything?"

"I'm just going to grab a few more things," Ginger said, and started filling the cart. "We'll figure it all out later."

"I got the trees waiting up front," Daniel said, still eyeing me pretty hard. "One Angel picked out for the apartment and one for The Midnight Rider."

"We're going to check out now so you don't see what we got," Angel said, eyes lit with excitement. "I grabbed your present, but you can't see until Christmas. Hurry up," she called over to Ginger as she wheeled the cart she and

Daniel had filled around. "I got stuff for brownies and fudge and Christmas cookies, and I want to make some tonight."

"Ugh. Christmas cookies." Daniel groaned and covered his stomach with his hand before following Angel toward the front of the store.

Ginger zoomed our cart up the opposite side of the aisle, snatching bows and ribbons and wreaths.

"We're only decorating the actual part of the bar customers see, right?"

"Maybe," she said, and dumped some more stuff into the cart. "If all this décor doesn't work to get you out of your mood, Rider might not let it happen again next year, and I, for one, want to be festive, so we are doing it up while we have the chance."

"Why are you so obsessed with me being festive this year? Christmas is for kids and families. Why are you so into it?"

She'd been pushing the cart toward the front, having grabbed all she could grab from our aisle, and stopped to look back at me with a look that instantly made me regret asking my question. "I imagine for the same reason Angel is so into it. I never had a real Christmas, either before or after I was turned, and I want to share it with the people I consider family, even if some of those people seem to have a peppermint stick stuck up their ass."

***

"Merry Smexy Christmas, loves and lovers, this is Danielle Muething—"

"Shut uppp," I groaned and closed out the WDNI radio station's app on Angel's phone before setting it back on the table in front of me.

"Hey!" she said, looking up from the mixing bowl Ginger had just dipped her finger into. "We were listening to that."

"Look, I'm trying to do the festive thing here and I can take the all day, all night Christmas music station, but I cannot take that particular DJ and her fake-ass sexy voice."

"It's *smexy*," Ginger corrected me before popping her chocolate-covered fingertip into her mouth. "It's her *smexy* voice."

"Whatever. It sounds like she's trying to orgasm in the middle of an asthma attack and you've already got the Christmas channel going on the television."

"I want Christmas music too," Angel complained. "You can't have Christmas baking without Christmas music."

"Yeah, bring on the tunes!" Ginger winked at me. "You heard the girl."

"It's not Christmas yet. That's Christmas practice baking."

"It still needs music." The teen narrowed her eyes. Standing there in the kitchen in her ugly Christmas sweater (the hideous thing showed the giant rear end of a cat with an ornament dangling off its raised tail in a way that made it impossible to look at it without staring straight into its butthole) with flour in her dark brown hair and food coloring stained into her fingers, she was too cute to refuse.

"Fine, but we're not listening to that station until Danielle Ewwww-thing and her asthma-porn voice go off the air." I opened up Angel's laptop, pulled up Pandora, and set up a Christmas station to play. "Here. These guys sound really good, and damn, look at this one with the muscles. He looks like Rome, or what Rome will look like in another decade or so."

I turned the laptop around so they could see the album cover showing on the screen.

"Oh wow, that does look like Rome," Ginger said. "Who is that?"

"Linkin' Bridge."

"That's the guy's name?"

"No, that's the group. I have no idea what the guy's name is." I stared at the guy a little longer, amazed by how much he looked like Rome, then shrugged. I supposed we all had doppelgangers out there somewhere.

"They sound good too," Angel said, bobbing her head to the Christmas melody. "You should take some brownies for Rome with you when you leave. He loves to eat."

"I don't think Rome can eat anything like that right now, maybe not for a while," I told her. "He has to have surgery."

Angel's jaw dropped open. "Surgery? What happened to him?"

"Ooh! Ooh!" Ginger jumped up and down. "Can I tell her?"

"Knock yourself out." I rolled my eyes.

Ginger laughed so hard she could barely tell Angel anything, but finally managed to say, "Rome finally produced a monster turd even he couldn't pass."

"Oh, ew!" Angel pulled a face, giving the impression she wished she hadn't asked.

The oven timer dinged and Ginger removed a sheet of gingerbread men while Angel continued stirring her brownie batter. The aroma of cinnamon, ginger, allspice, and nutmeg floated across the room to sucker-punch me where I sat at the table.

"Too much?" Ginger asked, pulling a yikes face.

I closed my eyes and inhaled the heavenly aroma, and wanted to shed a tear when I reopened them. "I swear the day I can eat whatever I want without getting sick, I'm going to be the biggest pig you've ever seen. I mean disgusting. I'm going to swim naked in chocolate cake batter."

"Okay, I know you mean for that image to come off gross, but it's coming off really sexy to me," Ginger said.

I barked out a laugh and rose from the chair. "I'm going to go check on Daniel."

"You sure you want to do that without nose plugs? He

was looking pretty green."

"If we had nose plugs, I would have already used them to block out the torturous smells of delicious things I'm not allowed to eat," I said as I crossed the living room and pushed open my bedroom door.

The shower ran in the bathroom and the strong scent of one of the Mountain Energy-scented bath bombs I kept a supply of wafted out from the barely open door. I closed the bedroom door to block out as much of the overwhelming cookie aroma as I could and crept over to the bathroom.

"Daniel?" I knocked on the door, and it swung open a little, revealing a lot of steam.

"I'm decent," he said.

I pushed the door open farther to see Daniel leaning back against the wall next to the small window he'd raised halfway to let in fresh air. Beside him, the shower ran, the warm water reacting with the bath bomb he'd placed at the bottom, causing the citrusy scent to fill the air. His head rested back against the wall and his eyes were closed.

"I'll replace the bath bomb. I needed something strong to cover the smell of all that shit they're baking."

"I bought the bath bombs, not Angel, and you don't have to replace it. The smell of that chimney really got to you, huh?"

"The scent of blood, sulfur, and fleshy chunks should never be mixed with cinnamon and allspice." He almost choked on the last word and I stepped back, pressing my backside completely against the sink, afraid he might spew, but he covered his stomach with his hand, took in a deep breath through his mouth, and released it nice and slow. "I'm all right."

"Good," I said, but unfortunately I was not. Placing his large hand over his stomach had dragged my gaze there, and I was having a hard time lifting it away. I'd seen those abs bare and knew how hard and muscular they were. That had been soon after meeting, but Daniel had gotten bigger since then. Thicker. Stronger. Seeing those abs the first time had been a surprise, but now he stretched out his shirts in a way that made it very clear what treasure hid beneath the fabric.

My gaze drifted up his chest to his throat. He swallowed and my fangs pressed against my gums. My mouth watered with the pressure. His warm, spicy scent cut through the citrusy steam surrounding us and aroused my thirst to a degree that quickly became almost painful. I imagined the kick that always came with his blood, could almost taste the hot liquid spill over my tongue and coat my throat as I swallowed it down. His heartbeat quickened. I could see it in his pulse point, hear it beat within my own ears as it throbbed. I forced my gaze down, allowed it to latch on to where else he throbbed. My palms sweat.

Rider had fed me well the night he'd left to help Seta, with his blood and his body, but I hadn't taken either from him since, and Daniel was right there, looking delicious in every possible way.

"Get the hell out of here, Danni."

My heart stopped and air left my lungs on a whoosh as my gaze shot back up to the source of that growled order to see Daniel's eyes open, fixed on me in a molten glare. "What?"

"Get. Out." His body trembled as he took a loud gulp. "I can feel your thirst and we both know there's no way I can let you drink from me right now, but damn it, I'm not made of steel. Get. Out. Now."

I staggered out of the room with tears in my eyes. Reprimanded. Humiliated. Ashamed. I turned to put together an apology, only to jump as the door closed in my face.

CHAPTER FOUR

"Danni." I turned just as Ginger grabbed my arm and pulled me back toward the living room, closing the bedroom door behind her before pinning me in place with a warning look. "Why don't you help us get the rest of the ornaments on the tree?"

I looked over at the five-foot-tall tree we'd gotten at Wal-Mart and nodded. Heat filled my face as I walked over and randomly picked out a box of ornaments. Angel had just finished plugging in the tree and stared up at the multi-color twinkling lights with a big smile.

I ripped open the box in my hand and went to work, trying to push down the embarrassment of being rejected, then felt worse for seeing what had happened as a rejection. I was with Rider. No matter what we were going through, I was with Rider, and I shouldn't have been looking at Daniel that way, thirsting for him like the demon I was.

The glass ornament in my shaking hand dropped, tumbled through the branches, and hit the carpet just as the oven timer went off. "Fuck!"

I looked at Ginger and Angel in time to see them share a concerned look before the teenager excused herself from the tree decorating to check on her brownies. I crouched down to pick up the ornament that had slipped from my fingers and caught myself sucking in air, holding a storm of tears at bay.

"Hey." Ginger crouched in front of me. "It's all right. Nothing broke."

"Not yet," I whispered.

The bedroom door opened and Daniel emerged. He kept his eyes on the front door as he headed toward it. "I need air."

"You need live male blood, girlfriend, and you need it soon," Ginger said as the front door closed behind Daniel. She took the ornament from my hand as we stood together, placed it on the tree, and walked me over to the couch. She sat next to me, started to take my hands, then thought better of it. "You absolutely, positively cannot take it from Daniel. That man is barely holding on to his willpower."

"Hey, he slammed a door in my face pretty well."

"He saved his life by slamming that door," Ginger said, "and the really messed up thing is I don't think that was even his reason. He did it to protect you."

"I can finish decorating the tree myself if you guys need to go now," Angel called over to us from the kitchen. "It's getting late and I don't think this cookie smell is going to get out of here anytime soon, so Daniel probably isn't going to want to come back in here anyway. I really thought he was being overdramatic when he complained about the smell, but I guess it really is bothering him."

"Yeah, I think we should go," Ginger told her. "Don't eat all that stuff by yourself. I want some when we come back."

"I make no promises." Angel winked as she grabbed a gingerbread cookie and took a big bite.

"Maybe we should take my car," I suggested. "It's just been sitting in the lot since Daniel was assigned as my guard. We can meet him back at The Midnight Rider."

Ginger stared at me for a moment, seeming to study my face, searching for clues as to what the hell was wrong with me. Good luck, I thought. I'd sure like to pinpoint my problem myself. "We could do that, but Rider will be curious why you'd choose to drive your own car when there's plenty of room in Daniel's truck. Do you think now is a good time to make that man curious?"

No. No, I didn't. I blew out a breath and shook my head.

"I'll sit up front again," Ginger said, voice low so Angel couldn't hear. "I don't know what's going on between you and Rider and you don't have to tell me, but if you care about Daniel, you need to let Rider feed you… in all the ways you need to feed. You know that succubus side of yours is a hard bitch to control when she goes all wonky."

"Yeah. Yeah, I know." I took a deep breath and stood. "Thanks, Ginge."

"Anytime, sweetcheeks." She grabbed her leather jacket off the couch as she stood and walked over to the kitchen area to snag a cookie before she met me at the front door.

I paused with my hand on the doorknob and looked back toward the kitchen where Angel cleaned the bowls she'd used for the treats she'd baked. She danced a little to the Christmas music as she moved about. The blood stain in Angela LaRoche's carpet flashed through my mind.

"What?" Ginger followed my gaze toward Angel, then looked back at me with raised eyebrows. "What's wrong?"

I shook my head. "Nothing. For a moment there, I thought maybe we should bring Angel to The Midnight Rider, but she should be fine. She has guards."

And she would probably be far more comfortable in my old apartment than in a room in the sublevels of The Midnight Rider, where the dark cloud of whatever my damn problem was polluted the atmosphere.

As we stepped outside, Ginger stretched her hand out toward the corner of the hallway, offering one of those guards I'd mentioned the gingerbread cookie she'd pilfered.

"About time one of you assholes came bearing gifts," Carlos muttered as he cast off the shadows around him and took the cookie. "Do you know how annoying and near maddening it is standing guard out here while that girl bakes for hours, filling this hallway with the smell of cookies and cakes?"

"Probably not as rough as being in there smelling it when you can't eat any of it," I replied, and grinned as Carlos froze mid-bite and uttered an apology. I sniffed the air. "It's cool, and I can feel where you're coming from. It is smelling pretty delicious out here."

I unlocked the apartment door again and stuck my head in to find Angel still standing in the kitchen, wiping her hands dry on a reindeer dish towel. "Hey, Angel, can you set a plate of cookies out here in the hall for Carlos?"

She frowned a little, understandable since she'd never seen Carlos due to the shadows he wrapped himself in, but knew there was always a guard stationed outside, and shrugged. "Sure thing."

"Appreciated. Good night." I pulled the door closed again. "There you go. One plate of cookies coming your way. Merry Christmas."

"Merry Christmas." Carlos smiled as he stepped back into the corner and, for the first time ever, I noticed the dimples in his cheeks. I wanted to think I'd never noticed them before because he didn't smile often, but that wasn't true. I'd seen the vampire smile before. I hadn't noticed dimples then. I noticed them now because they'd set off a flare in my belly. Shit. I turned away before that flare turned into a full-blown fire and destroyed everything within its path.

"Aw, that was nice," Ginger said as we took the stairs down. "You feel a little merrier now?"

"I feel something, but it's definitely not merry."

"Huh? What do…" Ginger's lips rounded into an O-shape as she glanced back up the stairs and muttered a very creative string of curse words.

"Yep," I said and pushed through the big thick door that allowed me to escape the building, which was suddenly feeling very claustrophobic. I breathed in the frigid twilight air and shoved my hands into my pockets. I hadn't bothered to grab my coat before leaving the apartment and had no intention of going back to get it, not with a warm male body standing just outside the door. A lusty moment for Daniel was one thing, but when I started doing the belly butterflies for Carlos, I had to admit I was in serious trouble.

We reached the parking lot and froze to stare at the space where Daniel had parked his truck when we'd arrived at the apartment after our shopping trip, the now empty parking space. "What the hell?"

"Where's the truck?" Ginger asked, turning. "Where's Daniel?"

"Did it get stolen?"

"No, the wolves on street duty were watching it because we had stuff in it," Ginger said. "They would have let us known if someone was messing with the truck and handled it."

We shared puzzled looks and turned toward the street to locate the shifter guards assigned to watch the building from the outside and ask them what had happened, and where had Daniel gone, when a sleek black car rolled to a slow stop along the edge of the parking lot and the passenger side window rolled down to reveal Lana at the wheel. "Rider sent me to pick you two up," she called out. "Daniel went ahead."

"Oh, fuck, that can't be good," Ginger said, putting my own fear into words.

***

I would have had better luck getting gold out of Fort Knox than I had getting information out of Lana. After her tenth, "Danni, I really don't know…" I started imagining my claws in her throat. Ginger must have picked up on it because she sent me a look so quelling I spent the last ten minutes of the ride staring out the window and reminding myself Lana wasn't my enemy while biting my thumbnail, and I wasn't even a nail-biter.

The black Ford F-150 sat in the parking lot when we finally reached The Midnight Rider and appeared to have been emptied of all the Christmas loot we'd purchased at Wal-Mart. Daniel wasn't in it and I wasn't sure if that was something that should cause me to feel relief or dread.

I was the first one out of the car and immediately cast my senses out, searching for Daniel. I picked up on his unique signature as well as Rider's and knew they were both inside, within close proximity.

The three of us were nearly to the front door when a wave of Rider's power washed over us and his voice snapped, *My office. Now*, into my head.

I could tell by the look Ginger sent my way she'd received the same order. Lana, however, had come to a complete stop. "Well, I'll see you two later," she said and turned back toward the car we'd just left, her duties clearly finished until her next shift.

"How does he feel to you?" Ginger whispered as we pushed through the front door and stepped inside. The door immediately locked behind us. It was close to dawn, and the bar was empty of people, human and non. The shopping bags from Wal-Mart were piled near the bar, the big box containing the Christmas tree we'd bought standing next to them.

I shook my head, unsure how to answer. Rider wasn't putting out a clear emotion, but whatever it was I picked up from him, it was dark.

We continued on in silence, pushing through the door at the back of the room to gain entry to the narrow hallway that ran the length of the bar. We turned left and took it to the end. I took a deep breath and braced myself before pushing the door to Rider's office open.

Kutya jumped up from his plush doggy bed and raced over to shove his head into my thigh, demanding pets and scratches. I obliged and took the moment to survey the situation. Daniel stood in the corner of the room, leaning back against one of Rider's bookshelves, hands shoved in his pants pockets. He appeared to be studying the books, but I could tell by the set of his jaw, that was a front. However, he didn't look as if he'd been in any type of altercation with Rider, and I was thankful for that.

Rider sat behind his desk dressed in a dark blue button-down shirt, sleeves rolled to reveal his wrists. His ebony hair was pulled back into a ponytail at the nape of his neck, his usual style, and his eyes matched the color of his shirt as they bore into me. I noticed then they missed their usual sparkle, instead carrying the darkness of two stormy seas. Rider ran his hand over them, rubbing them, and I saw in that action how tired he was. It didn't detract from how mouthwatering handsome he was, but still I felt something in me recoil. Kutya whined, seeming to pick up on my reaction.

"Sit, Kutya. You two as well." Rider motioned toward the two chairs in front of his desk. "I've spoken with Grissom, and Daniel just finished filling me in on how you spent your evening."

Kutya trotted back over to his doggy bed and plopped down, and I shot a look at Daniel as Ginger and I took the seats we'd been directed to, but he didn't look my way. "What did Grissom say?" I asked.

"He said it looked like someone exploded or got gutted really good in their living room," Rider said. "He had to call it in to the department, but he's the lead on the case which is fortunate since whatever took that woman's life is clearly not a killer of the human variety, but you already know that since you were the first on the scene."

I met his gaze dead-on for the first time since I'd stepped into the office, and probably for the first time that entire day, and saw his disapproval loud and clear a second before I had to look away, nightmare images that had haunted me since my return making the simple act of looking at him too hard. "I felt something when I looked at that woman's picture," I told him. "I looked into that woman's eyes and knew she was dead, and whatever killed her wasn't human and wasn't done hunting. I knew... I *know* I have to help put a stop to it, so I went. If you don't believe in my gut, you can track Jon down and ask him. Or ask Grey. He seemed to believe in my gut too."

I felt Rider's gaze as it burned into me. His jaw clenched as the rest of his body went deathly still and tension filled the room like a thick smog. I looked up as something in his eyes shifted, darkened, and I saw him covered in blood, standing in the middle of his room like he had the morning he'd killed Trixell, and I couldn't hold his gaze any longer. Kutya whined again.

"You two can leave," Rider said, voice firm but devoid of emotion.

Please drink from him, Ginger said through our mind-link as she rose from the chair next to mine and moved behind me. *Someone's going to get hurt soon if you don't and I'm not even sure which one of you is going to do the hurting.*

The door opened and closed behind me, and they were both gone. Daniel hadn't said a word, not even a goodbye through our mind-link.

"You think I don't believe in you?" Rider said. "You think I have no faith in you?"

"You're clearly upset about me looking into the missing woman. You couldn't even wait for me to come back here after talking to Grissom. You called Daniel in and sent Lana to come fetch me. Going to that woman's house was my call. If you're going to be mad about it, be mad at me, not Daniel and Ginger."

"Grissom called me hours ago. I had no intention of sending anyone out to fetch you, even though, let's be honest, I had no reason to assume you were coming back here to sleep. You certainly don't seem to enjoy my company lately."

I flinched, his words hitting me like a slap. Tears burned the backs of my eyes as the hurt undertone of his voice cut through me. I didn't want to be the reason for that hurt. I loved him. I could barely look at him, for reasons I couldn't fully understand myself, but I loved him. "I always come back. We were on our way when we discovered Daniel gone and Lana there to get us. Why did you send Lana for us instead of waiting for Daniel to bring us back? That was so unnecessary."

"Then tell Daniel that. He's the one who told me to send her before he left your apartment."

That brought my gaze up, my blood pressure too. "What? Why would he do that?"

"Because he has a hell of a lot more honor than most men," Rider growled. He pushed away from the desk and stood. Kutya rose with him, but whined, picking up on his master's anger. "It's time for bed and you need to drink. Apparently, you'd prefer to drink from Daniel, but we both agree that's not going to happen."

He crossed the room in quick strides, opened the door and slipped out, Kutya on his heels, and I knew I was supposed to follow. I had a hard time getting my feet to move, however, his last statement hanging in the air like a threat. Of all the thoughts that had run through my mind when I'd left my apartment building to find Daniel missing and Lana sent to retrieve me, all the terrifying scenarios that could have played out, I never thought of a single one where Rider and Daniel would talk about me behind my back, where Daniel would tattle that I'd sized him up for a blood meal, or worse… that Daniel would have left me to run straight to Rider and do the tattling. I'd always known my succubus side could make me desperate, but until then I'd never realized it could make me repulsive.

I should leave, I thought, and mentally calculated how much money I had, then had to laugh. Money wasn't any of my many worries. I'd had some built up in savings when I'd quit working for Prince Advertising, and now I worked for Rider. He paid very well, but it wouldn't have mattered if he didn't because he acted personally offended if I wanted to spend anything I'd earned. He paid for everything, including my apartment I didn't really live in anymore. He said as my blood donor, Angel was under the umbrella of business expenses he paid for, and those expenses included her food and shelter, but I doubted that. He paid everything for me because he wanted to ensure my security. I'd thought it was because he cared. Now I had to wonder if it was because he didn't think I could take care of myself on my own, if he feared what I would become without his monitoring. If I would become something shameful. Maybe the monster I saw in him the morning he killed Trixell was just as horrific as the monster he saw in me when my succubus side bared its fangs.

Maybe that was part of why I couldn't meet his gaze for any length of time anymore. Maybe it was too hard seeing what was reflected there when I did. Maybe I saw truth I didn't have the strength to bear.

I sensed the sun break through the final remnants of twilight, snatching away my energy as it started its ascent, and the thought of leaving the bar to find somewhere to be alone seemed a lot harder. My special sunscreen was upstairs in Rider's room, where he waited. All my belongings were there, and I knew he wouldn't let me leave, not while my succubus side thirsted for live male blood. Not while I was a danger to any male that breathed in my vicinity.

My stomach rolled with an equal mix of hunger and nausea as I forced myself to my feet and left the office. I had to go to him. I had to drink from him, take in the blood of my sire and the living warm nectar of what the nightmare inside me craved before I lost control of it. Before I lost control of myself.

That particular thought hit me as I reached the top of the stairs, just outside Rider's room, and nearly sent me tumbling back down the steps. I grabbed the railing and let the waves of dizziness wash over me until the lightheadedness dissipated and my limbs stopped trembling. Then I took a deep breath and opened the door, only to have all that air leave my lungs on a whoosh as Rider stepped out of the bathroom in nothing but a towel slung low over his hips.

Kutya perked up from where he'd been resting on the chaise, looked between the two of us, let out a whine, and zipped past me right out the door.

"Your eyes are red."

I wasn't surprised, given he looked like a Christmas package ready for the unwrapping, and I hadn't treated myself to a gift of that particular nature in what now felt like ages, although it had only been about four weeks. My body burned with aching need and my mouth filled with moisture as I closed the door behind me and moved across the room, only to come to a slamming halt three feet away from the damp, rock hard body calling out to the demon inside me.

I saw him covered in blood, drenched in it as if he'd torn through Trixell's body and rolled around in the mess. He hadn't even bothered to wash it away before entering the bedroom we shared, hadn't thought twice about hiding what he'd done. He'd spilled that much blood and strolled right up to the room I waited for him in as if it were nothing, as if it were acceptable... because I had accepted it. All of it. Why wouldn't I have? It was what we were.

"Danni. You need to feed." He stepped in front of me, gingerly lifted my chin. I got the sense he feared I might bite. Feared it and wanted it at the same time. Exactly how I felt as I looked into his perfectly sculpted face framed by the long, dark hair dripping beads of water over his shoulders.

I felt myself nodding, the fire deep inside my belly

growing, charring everything in its path as the bloodthirsty sex-craved demon inside me champed at the bit, but the small part of me still human enough to be haunted by the nightmare image that refused to vacate my mind held it back. Then Rider bit his lip, drew a bubble of blood, and the demon tore out of me.

I drank at his lip, growling deep in my throat as the warm, powerful yet thin stream of blood teased my desire, but flowed far too slowly. My saliva healed the small wound while I pulled on it, enraging the beast his blood had awakened, and with an animalistic sound I didn't think my body capable of making, I plunged my fangs into his throat and tore a wide, gaping wound as I pushed him down on the bed and straddled him.

I buried my face in his throat, feeding off the scent of his blood as well as the taste. Power I'd deprived myself of roared to life as I pulled the source from his veins and slurped it down, impatient for it to fill me. I drank from the fount I'd created until the blood lust turned into pure carnal hunger and the hard part of him pressing between the juncture of my thighs couldn't be denied any longer.

I lifted my face from his throat to tear away the towel hiding what I needed, and Rider licked the blood that had dribbled down my chin. He growled low in his throat, ripped my shirt in half and rolled me under him before treating my jeans to the same violation and plunging his body inside mine.

I lifted my lower body off the bed and grabbed his hips with both hands forcing him in as deep as he could possibly go while he pumped back and forth and still it wasn't enough, not even as the first orgasm hit, taking my breath with it. I needed the blood too. I needed to drain him of everything I could take.

With that in mind, I wrapped my legs around his and forced him onto his back, never allowing his body to escape mine, and took over. I rode him hard enough to break a mortal man, and when he lifted his upper body off the bed, I grabbed a handful of his long hair, yanked his head back to expose his throat, sank my fangs into the side I hadn't mauled yet, and blacked out on the third massive gulp.

CHAPTER FIVE

"That's my girl. Nice and slow. Doesn't that feel good? Breathe."

I blinked, aware time had escaped me and my heart was racing as if I'd just finished running a marathon… as a human. I sensed the sun, knew it was morning and I should be asleep, but I'd needed something else more than I'd needed sleep and that something had left me deeply sated. My limbs felt boneless, my body free of the tension that had been coiled inside me, where it had festered almost painfully.

"I love you," Rider whispered against my ear as he moved in and out of me, and reality brought me completely back to the present. I'd lost myself to the bloodlust and the hunger for sex I'd denied my succubus half. I'd mauled Rider, tore into him like an animal and despite the fact I was still sorting out my issues with what had happened with Trixell, and had shamefully hungered for Daniel's blood, and if I were truly being honest, more than Daniel's blood, I'd still given my body to Rider. No, that sounded far too tame for what had happened. I'd used my body to take what I'd craved from his, and I'd done so to feed something dark and hideous inside of me.

"You're all right now," he whispered as he continued moving in and out in a smooth, slow motion, my breathing slowing to match the rhythm. "You're fine. I've got you. Everything's all right now."

I smelled the coppery scent of blood and looked down to see where it had dried over my chest and stomach and recalled that blood spilling from gashes I'd made in Rider's flesh as I'd ripped into him with my teeth, how I'd wanted to bathe in it and had tried my damnedest to before he'd finally managed to take control, to slow me down and tame the demonic entity that had taken over, forced it back into its cage to wait until I weakened again. I was not fine and everything most definitely was not all right. Warm liquid spilled from the corners of my eyes to roll down the sides of my face as I gasped on a sob.

Rider instantly stopped moving, even his breath froze in place. A moment later, he eased out of me and used the pad of his thumb to wipe the wetness from my face as I turned my head, not wanting to look at him and see whatever emotion filled his eyes. Hurt? Anger? Disgust? I didn't know and didn't desire to know.

"Are you hurt?"

I sniffed, willed back the tears steadily filling my eyes. "No."

He moved his body away from mine and sat up, covering me with the bedsheet which had become completely tangled at some point while I'd been consumed by the raging hunger inside me. He swung his legs over the side of the bed and bent forward, elbows rested on his knees, head bowed. He sat like that for a while before taking a deep breath. "Danni, do you still love me?"

My heart hitched painfully, the fear in his voice unbearable. My fingertips ached to reach for him, but the blood marring his back and shoulders, evidence that I had at some point tore open his flesh, stopped them. "Yes. I think I always will."

Silence again. Another deep breath. He turned his head

toward me. He didn't look at me, maybe as afraid to look into my eyes as I was to look into his. He kept his gaze down and asked, "Do you *want* to love me?"

I blinked, freeing another warm stream of tears, and looked up at the ceiling. *No* came with a rush, but I held it inside. How did you tell the man you loved that you didn't want to love him? That on some level deep down you were afraid of him, of the thing inside him he'd given you a glimpse of, the thing he'd allowed you to see, had even told you about, because he was that confident you'd stay with him, because you would. Because he knew that deep down inside of you lived a monster too. I didn't want to love him, but I did. I didn't want to be like him… but I was. Only I was worse.

He stood from the bed and went into the bathroom. The shower turned on. I kept my gaze locked onto the ceiling, even when the shower cut off and he returned to root through the closet. *Stay*, I thought. *I don't want to hurt you. I don't want to hurt anyone.* But I didn't say anything, not even when he opened the bedroom door where Kutya waited for him, whining with the same sadness I felt in my chest as the door closed behind them and I gave myself to the day sleep just to escape having to feel anything at all.

***

I entered the bar and froze as what looked like a million strings of lights glowed around the room. Mariah Carey's voice spilled out of the jukebox to fill the air, and the Christmas tree we'd picked out the night before was standing proudly beside the entrance door, fully decorated and topped with a golden-haired angel. Marty the troll looked a lot more like Marty the giant elf in his green elf hat and pointy-toed shoes, complete with jingle bells. In fact, the entire staff looked more like North Pole workers than employees of The Midnight Rider. My jaw dropped open as I caught sight of Tony in a Santa hat, filling bowls with miniature candy canes.

"Laugh and it's a stocking full of coal for you," he warned as I reached the bar.

"Wouldn't think of it." I made a cross my heart and hope to die gesture, which was when I noticed I was wearing a long red cable-knit sweater over black leggings and high-heeled boots far too fancy for a night working security at the bar. "I guess I'm not working security tonight."

"Working security? My sweet girl?"

My breath hitched in my throat as I turned, sure I hadn't just heard who I thought I'd heard. The bar was full of customers decked out in holiday colors and ugly Christmas sweaters. Clearly I'd heard someone who sounded like—"Daddy?"

My father stood before me in blue jeans and a U of K sweatshirt featuring the Kentucky Wildcats mascot in a Santa hat roasting the U of L Cardinal mascot over an open fire. He opened his arms, and I dove inside, wrapped my arms around his shoulders, and held him tight as something niggled at the back of my mind.

"Are you all right, baby girl? You're squeezing pretty tight there."

"Sorry." I pulled back but not completely away, unable to let go of him, that niggling sensation still there in the back of my mind, telling me something was off. "Why are you here?"

"I can't come see my daughter and give her a Christmas present?"

No, I thought, but couldn't pinpoint why that was or why it seemed so strange for my father to be in The Midnight Rider.

"Come open your present while we wait for this new guy of yours to get his butt out here and introduce himself."

I followed my father, nearly stumbling when I saw he'd led me to a table where my mother sat waiting. "Mom?

You're here?"

"Well, of course, silly." She looked at my father and they shared a laugh as he pulled a chair out for me before sitting down.

"Here you go, kiddo." He slid a long rectangle-shaped box wrapped in shiny red wrapping paper and a big red glittery bow in front of me and grabbed my mother's hand. "It took some saving up, but Margaret and I feel you deserve it."

"You've been such a very good girl this year," my mother said, smiling wide despite the way her right eye twitched. "Better than your sister, who has decided not to spend the holidays with us this year."

"Kids will be kids, Margaret." My father squeezed her hand. "Our Danni will never let us down though. Open your present, Danni. It's just what you wanted."

Something was wrong, but I couldn't put my finger on it, so I shrugged and carefully unwrapped the present. I nearly squealed in surprise as the wrapping paper fell away to reveal the African-American version of the Midnight Tuxedo Barbie, mint condition in the original packaging. Tears sprang to my eyes as I stared at the beautiful brown face staring back at me with the prettiest painted smile I'd ever seen, afraid that if I blinked, she would disappear.

My father let loose a hearty laugh. "I told you, Margaret. Worth every penny! Nothing but the best for the best daughter."

I forced myself to look up from the beautiful doll and meet my mother's gaze. "You got this for me?"

"Yes, Danni, because you deserve it. You're such a good, sweet, perfect daughter." Her right eye twitched away. "Now, where is that boyfriend of yours? We can't wait to meet him."

"Yes, let's meet your young man and hear all about what the two of you have been up to."

The multi-colored lights strung around the room flickered. Mariah Carey's voice cut off mid-high note, and the atmosphere seemed to darken as I sensed something dangerous enter the bar, and turned to see Rider and Daniel emerge from the rear door.

Daniel only wore ripped jeans, boots, and a rainbow-colored Santa hat, his well-toned pecs and abs on full display. And Rider… my heart skipped a few beats as he crossed the room in his usual attire of dark button-down silky shirt and black pants, but he was covered in blood.

"Oh my," I heard my mother say behind me as I stared, fixated on the two men approaching, one oozing sex with each step while the other carried with him an aura of death and destruction.

They reached our table at the same time. Daniel flipped the empty chair next to me around and straddled it before kissing my neck. Too stunned to move, I did nothing as Rider loomed over me. He stared into my eyes with enough heat to scorch my eyelashes before shifting his gaze toward my parents. "Wrap this up. It's time to feed, and I don't feel like waiting."

"Danni?" The disapproval in my father's voice brought tears to my eyes. Time moved in slow motion as I forced myself to turn my head and face him. "What is the meaning of this? Who are these wildly inappropriate men? Where is your boyfriend?"

Daniel chuckled and slid his hand over my thigh. "A girl with an appetite like Danni's can't settle for one man, Pops. She needs a whole lot more than that to satisfy her thirsts."

"Scandalous," my mother said, her nose turned up. "Your sister would nev… Where is Shana?"

My mother's eyes filled with fear as she stood from the table and scanned the room frantically. Blood poured down the walls as my father slouched down into his chair, mouth hung open in devastated shock while Rider leaned over me from behind and groped me while growling in my ear, "Time to feed."

"Let's go," Daniel said in my other ear before taking

the lobe in his teeth.

"Where's Shana?" my mother screeched. "What have you done with her? What is wrong with you? What kind of monster are you?"

I tried to speak, to move, but my body was paralyzed. I couldn't react at all, not even as Daniel shoved his hand down the front of my leggings and Rider started drinking from my throat. My father sat there, stunned, watching until his skin turned green and he visibly fought down bile. "You don't deserve this," he finally said and reached for the doll. I looked down at its once pretty painted smile to see it staring up at me with an expression of complete disdain.

"You're not a good girl at all," my father said, a tear escaping his eye to run over his cheek before he stood, grabbed my still-screaming and now crying as well mother by the arm. "Let's go, Margaret. I can't stomach any more of this. She's not good at all."

I sat frozen, unable to speak, unable to push away the two men molesting me in full view of the whole room, and watched my parents walk out of the bar. They passed the Christmas tree on their way out and as the door closed behind them, the angel on top winked, and that was when I realized it was the blonde Midnight Tuxedo Barbie. She winked at me and laughed. "You set me on fire because I wasn't the one you wanted. Is this the life you wanted, Danni Keller? Maybe you should set yourself on fire."

I looked down at myself. I sat completely naked, my clothes ripped off by the two men groping and biting into my flesh. A line of men queued up, waiting their turn. A purple-haired woman stepped out of the line, holding her shredded chest together.

"You knew it was hunting, but you didn't stop it. You forgot all about us. You're a monster."

I lurched upright, breath caught on a silent scream as my body shivered violently. The smell of old, dried blood wafted up to my nose, and I looked down to see myself naked, tangled in bedsheets stained with the same blood that had dried into a thin, hard layer of dark red paint covering my torso. A second later, I dropped to my knees in front of the toilet and vomited.

***

I'd awakened shortly before nightfall, unsure whether it was the waning sun or the awful nightmare that had brought me out of slumber. Judging by the amount of throwing up the nightmare had caused, I was leaning toward it being the culprit. I didn't think Rider had ever returned to the room and the memory of his expression as he'd asked me a question I couldn't bring myself to answer caused another round of vomiting before I was finally able to drag myself into the shower and scrub the blood off my body. My torso was redder than a cherry tomato by the time I emerged, but I got it all off. Unfortunately, I didn't succeed in scrubbing away the dirt I felt beneath my skin.

I dressed in jeans and a navy blue Polo Ralph Lauren sweater before pulling on semi-dressy brown Merrell boots and brushed my damp hair, which had grown long enough to hang halfway down my back. I ripped the dirtied sheets off the bed and crumpled them into a ball in an effort to hide the bloodstains, and wished I knew where the washing machine was in Rider's building. We always tossed our laundry into a ball and left it outside the door for whoever was assigned to laundry duty to take care of. I could only imagine what they'd think when they saw those sheets. Heat climbed my face, but I had bigger problems. I found a set of fresh sheets in the closet and made the bed before leaving the room to find Rider.

My phone vibrated in my back pocket as I made my way down the stairs and I removed it to check the incoming message from my cousin. I read it and smiled as it appeared he'd come through for me with the part of Daniel's Christmas present I hadn't been sure I'd be able to pull off, but with that surge of excitement came another wave of nausea as I remembered how Daniel had ordered me away from him, then called Rider to send Lana to retrieve us rather than risk being in proximity with me after. I fired off a response to thank my cousin and turned toward the door to the sublevels. Juan, a tall, lanky, but muscular werewolf, stood posted in front of it.

"I'm not allowed to let you pass."

We stared at each other for a moment as I cast my senses out. As my sire, I could sense Rider within close proximity, but I picked up something odd as I sensed for him this time. His signature was muddled, and I got the feeling it was his doing. He was blocking me. "What is he doing?"

"I don't know, ma'am."

A low growl rumbled in my throat as I stepped closer, and I noticed the hard gulp Juan took as he repositioned himself, hands ready to cover his groin. I stopped. I really had to quit castrating men before I scared the hell out of them all. "Where's Kutya?"

"Out for a walk."

"Thanks." I turned and headed toward the bar. I didn't like the fact Rider was clearly hiding something from me, but I wasn't going to force my way past Juan to find out what it was. Also, my stomach grumbled, reminding me I'd thrown up quite a bit of the blood I'd drunk the night before and I should probably worry about replenishing that first.

I pushed through the door leading to the narrow hall that ran the length of the building behind the bar and froze as Mariah Carey sang about all she wanted for Christmas. The dream slammed front and center into my brain, carrying a wave of nausea with it. I shook my head. It was December, and we'd put that song on the jukebox two weeks ago. It was just a coincidence, I told myself, but as I pushed through the second door and revealed the twinkling merry wonderland beyond, I had to blink.

Multicolored lights had been strung all over the room

to light every corner. The seven-foot-tall Christmas tree we'd picked up at Wal-Mart the night before stood near the entrance, all decked out in ornaments and tinsel. To my relief, a star topped it instead of an angel that could turn into the Barbie doll from my childhood that clearly still haunted me, and although Marty stood just where he'd stood in my nightmare and he did happen to have an elf cap on, his feet were covered with his usual shit-kickers.

He saw me staring at him and stopped sucking on a candy cane long enough to wave at me. I waved back and continued my bewildered scan of the bar. Garland, tinsel, and lights stretched as far as the eye could see, the windows had been sprayed with fake snow and trimmed in blinking red lights, the tables all held poinsettia and holly centerpieces, and the bar itself had been lined with red garland and a string of clear lights that reflected off tinsel with every blink. What really surprised me were the Santa and elf hats the servers wore. Everything and everyone had been all decked out for Christmas, everyone except Tony, I noticed as he served drinks behind the bar sans holiday hattery.

He caught my eye as I moved across the room to the bar and placed a red reindeer beer stein on top before I'd fully settled my bottom on the stool. "I'm supposed to make sure you drink this down. It's still warm from the source."

Still warm from the source meant the body it had been taken from probably hadn't had time to cool yet, which made me wonder what Rider was up to in the sublevels that he didn't want me to know about. "Any idea of the source?"

"Sick motherfucker who took a job as a mall Santa just so he could touch the little kids while they sat on his lap," he answered low enough only I could hear as he glanced at the pair of human women sitting closest to me, sipping on cute little drinks with miniature candy canes.

I lifted the stein and drained every last drop without an

ounce of regret. I didn't know how Rider went about finding all the pedophiles and rapists he took off the streets, how he caught wind of them in the first place, or how exactly he managed to recycle their blood for our use so effectively after he ended their reign of terror in his interrogation room, but it was in those moments that I felt a little less vile, that my love for the man grew, regardless of the darkness I'd witnessed in him. Maybe we were all monsters inside, but we could use the beasts we kept caged for good use sometimes.

Glass clinked from the other end of the bar and we both turned our heads to see a man cussing as he quickly righted the drink he'd just spilled. Tony grabbed a rag from under the bar and released his own naughty-list eligible words as he plucked a strand of shiny tinsel from it. "Fucking Christmas crap. This shit is everywhere, and I do mean *everywhere*."

"I think it's nice," Jadyn said, swooping in to grab a tray of drinks he'd set out for her already.

"Yeah, well, let's see how nice you think it is when you're the one to go to the bathroom and discover a long strand of that sparkly shit lodged in *your* ass crack," he muttered and walked away to clean up the spill, leaving Jadyn and I to share a laugh at the image he'd left us with.

"It really does get everywhere." Jadyn plucked one of the strands off her shoulder. "But I like it. The customers seem to as well. I've noticed we're getting a lot more women and they're a lot less moody than our usual crowd."

She grabbed the drinks and delivered them to a booth close to the front of the room. I noticed the ladies there had ordered food and from the look of it, it was something new and holiday-themed.

"I blame you for this," Tony grumbled once he returned to my side of the bar and slung the snowflake-printed towel over his shoulder.

"What did I do? Ginger was the one who suggested the

Christmas décor would be good for business."

"All I know is this is the first time this bar has ever looked like we all got sucked inside some North Pole fantasyland and I doubt it was done for business. Rider's never given a shit about this Christmas stuff before and I'm not buying that a suggestion from Ginger about this crap being good for business would cause this."

The pair of women sitting toward the other end of my side of the bar raised their glasses and called out for seconds on drinks whose names I'd not heard before. Tony groaned in response.

"Holly Jolly and Warm Merry? Are those new drinks?"

"Yes, and I'm losing testosterone every time I have to make one," Tony grumbled, and set to work on the drinks while muttering, "Peppermint, white chocolate, pumpkin mocha bullshit. Kill me already."

I chuckled, and the dark glare I received in response only made me chuckle harder. "And Ginger thought my Christmas spirit needed a lift. Say, any idea what to get Rider for Christmas if he hasn't ever celebrated it before? I have to get him something, and it's not easy figuring out a gift for a man who can afford anything he wants."

"Get him something money can't buy," Tony suggested with an undertone that hinted he really didn't care about such things as Christmas gifts.

"Like what?"

"How the hell would I know? What are you good at? Use your skill sets."

"Most people would say I'm only good at causing trouble and cutting off men's testicles."

"Well, there you go. Give him the balls of his enemy." Tony plopped little candy canes and cinnamon sticks into the rather feminine-looking drinks he'd just prepared and delivered them to the women at the end of the bar, leaving me to shake my head in his wake. I was pretty sure he'd been serious. I was one hundred percent sure he was tired of discussing anything Christmas-related.

I glanced up as the front door opened and Daniel stepped in, reporting to work. He wore jeans, shit-kickers, and a black leather bomber jacket open over a dark blue T-shirt bearing Clark Griswold's face. Not the usual all-black attire for bar security, but he kept a change of clothes in a locker downstairs so I didn't know what he'd been told to report for, and if he had been told to report to work bar duty with me, he'd be getting reassigned soon enough because I'd already decided I wasn't working in the bar. I had something far more important to do, whether Rider liked it or not. I only hoped I could convince him because I really, really didn't want to fight with him, not after the early morning we'd had.

Daniel's eyes locked with mine across the room, and I watched his jaw tic. My stomach rolled at the thought of speaking with him, but I knew I had to, no matter how uncomfortable. We needed to clear the air, but first I had to speak to the woman I saw behind him.

She moved past Daniel, slid an appreciative glance at him (who could blame her?) which reddened her already rosy cheeks, and smiled at me as she approached where I sat at the bar. "Danni Keller?"

I nodded and shook the hand she offered before leaning over the bar to place my stein in the tub of dirty drinkware kept there rather than risk leaving it on the bar for some human to find before Tony could finish with the man he was speaking to on the opposite side of the bar and retrieve it. "That's me, and you must be Rabea McGhie," I said, recognizing her friendly face framed with a stylish, dark chin-length bob from the picture on the website I'd hired her on and the accent which identified her as originally hailing from Scotland as stated in her bio. "Let's go over to that booth in the corner where it's a little less loud."

She glanced at the jukebox currently blaring another Mariah Carey Christmas song and nodded. I led her to the booth in the farthest corner from the jukebox and rowdier tables of people around it, and looked up as I slid in to my side to see that Daniel had slid into a booth on the opposite side of the room where he had a clear view of me, and he watched me curiously.

"This was a very interesting project," the ancestry specialist said as she took off her coat and removed a scrapbook from her tote bag. She placed it in front of me on the table and opened it, slowly flipping through the pages to reveal charts, hand-drawn portraits, letters, and photographs ranging from old sepia, black and white, to full digital color. My breath hitched as she flipped back to reveal a print of a very old and faded black and white portrait of a black woman whose bone structure and large eyes full of fire looked very familiar. "It's not easy finding slave records, especially with such limited information available, and portraits of this time period are harder, but I managed to find this. It's in great condition considering the age. I think this is exactly the lineage you were looking for, although I'm sad to say the woman whose name you gave me seemed to have just disappeared off the face of the earth." She frowned. "Sadly, I see that often when records in your country go back this far and the subjects were born into such dire circumstances, but I do feel confident I've traced the family down to the youngest living descendant. I hope this is acceptable."

"You did very well," I said, staring into the familiar eyes in the portrait. "In fact, I think you gave me something greater than I could have hoped for."

I need to see you in my office now, Rider's voice said in my mind. I looked across the bar to see Daniel stand and knew he'd received the message too. Great, I thought. This little meeting wouldn't be awkward at all.

CHAPTER SIX

"Thank you so much, Rabea." I shook the woman's hand and waited for her to retrieve her coat. "You've really come through for me with this."

"It was my pleasure." She started to pull on her coat, then paused. "You know, a nice drink might help me fight off the cold long enough to get to my car. It looks so festive in here, I just love it. Is there a drink you'd recommend?"

I cut a look in Tony's direction to see him muttering under his breath as he plopped a candy cane into a dainty little glass and forced down a scowl before turning toward the woman waiting to be served the drink. The poor guy was working hard for his tips and hating every minute of it. I turned a big smile toward Rabea and directed her attention toward the big, irritable kitty. "You're in luck because that bartender right there makes an amazing drink called the Holly Jolly. Make sure you ask for an extra little candy cane."

"Oh, that sounds just too adorable!"

"It really does, doesn't it?" We shared a girlish giggle, and I prodded her toward the bar. I stayed behind, out of the reach of the tiger's claws, but made sure to send him a little wink as he looked up to see me watching Rabea's approach.

Rabea slid onto a stool in front of him and made her request with far too much excitement for the cranky tiger-shifter. He offered her a stiff smile, but the dark look he shot my way once he turned his face away from her to make the drink promised retribution.

With that little moment of much needed amusement out of the way, I grabbed the scrapbook off the table and headed toward the back door. Daniel had made sure to catch my eye and raise his eyebrows in question while headed that way, but I'd continued my business with Rabea until he'd gotten the message and went back to Rider's office by himself. Hey, if he wanted to tattle on me to Rider, I might as well let the two have a bit of privacy in case he hadn't gotten it all out of his system yet.

I tried to hold on to that righteous indignation as I walked down the hall to Rider's office, but I get a little more anxious with every step. All things considered, giving the two men private time probably wasn't the best idea.

I pushed through the door and found myself under immediate attack from an overexcited and oversized pup. I scratched between the big guy's ears and gave him belly rubs as I assessed the situation.

Rider sat behind his desk, dressed in a black sweater. His near-slouch and steepled fingers made him appear relaxed, but the look in his eyes bore into me with an intensity that said otherwise. I didn't want to stare too hard so that it would be noticeable, but the quick assessment showed he still appeared on the tired side, but his color was good. He appeared well-fed, which wasn't too surprising given I was pretty sure I'd been blocked from the sublevel while he killed a man. If he'd gotten drenched in blood in the process, he'd had the decency to clean up this time before calling me to the office.

Daniel sat in one of the chairs on the opposite side of Rider's desk, which meant I would have to sit next to him, something I really didn't want to do. Judging by the stiff set of Daniel's shoulders, he probably didn't want to be so close to me either. Too bad, I thought. He picked that seat so if he had to risk rubbing elbows with me after I'd so obviously repulsed him with my filthy succubusness, that was on him.

"Okay, boy." I gave Kutya a few firm pats on his flank, his signal that he'd gotten enough lovin' for the moment. The whine I received in return suggested he didn't give a rat's patootie about the signal.

"Kutya, lie down," Rider ordered in a tone so firm I nearly went to Kutya's bed to lie down myself.

The big dog whined, but one look at Rider was all it took for him to lower his head and sulk over to his big, plush doggy bed before dropping his head down onto his massive paws with an exaggerated sigh.

"How nice of you to fit this little meeting into your schedule," Rider said dryly, and gestured toward the empty chair next to Daniel. "If you would be so kind as to take a seat."

"I was in the middle of something," I explained as I grudgingly took the seat and did my best not to look Daniel's way. "I figured if you needed me for something urgent, you would have barked much louder. Besides, I gave you and Daniel some time in case there was anything you two needed to discuss."

Rider's eyes narrowed, the blue orbs smoldering, and I caught the slight hint of a nostril flare as he controlled his breathing. "What's with the book?"

"It's a gift for Nannette."

His eyebrows raised a fraction, no doubt surprised by the fact I'd thought to get the surly nurse practitioner a gift at all given the fact I'd once been positive she intended to kill me just as soon as she could figure out how to do so without facing Rider's wrath.

"The two of you are getting along much better these days."

"I guess that's what happens when a couple of women get together every now and then to beat the shit out of each other," I replied with a tight smile. "Bonding is an odd beast."

"That it is." He drummed his fingertips along the surface of the desk and continued to bore his dark gaze into me. Something in his eyes shifted, and I got the impression he was studying me, trying to figure out what thoughts rolled around in my mind. Good luck with that, I thought. I was keeping my mind locked up good and tight. I barely understood the jumbled mess of thoughts rolling around there myself these days. I wasn't about to give him a look at all that mass confusion and risk the fallout from however he interpreted it. "Good timing with the present. You'll be seeing her tonight."

"I don't have a session scheduled with her until tomorrow."

"That's been changed. She'll be coming here since we still haven't located Pacitti's whereabouts and can't risk that rodent tracking you to the hospital and discovering the ward we operate there."

I felt the backs of my eyes burn and sucked in a breath before I grit my teeth against the urge to snap out a knee-jerk response. I knew Rider wasn't rubbing my face in the fact I'd been the reason a human detective had managed to get video evidence of our existence or make me feel like even more of an out-of-control monster by bringing Nannette in ahead of schedule for what I knew would be more of an emergency checkup than our usual training session. That didn't mean it didn't feel exactly like that anyway.

"Your session will be before your shift working security in the bar, so—"

"No."

Rider blinked. "No?"

"No."

"Danni, you're the reason for all this merry and bright

Christmas stuff. I think you'll agree that letting Nannette work with you and take care of any violence needs you need to have met before starting your shift would be really helpful to keeping the merry vibe out there, so you'll see her before you start your shift."

"I'm not going out there, not to work anyway." I squared my shoulders as his eyes darkened. "I'm hunting the monster who killed Angela LaRoche."

I felt Daniel's gaze swing my way, but kept mine locked on Rider. The vampire took a deep breath, reminding me of an overworked, under-rested parent mentally preparing himself to go to battle with a defiant child.

"I'm hunting the monster and I'm not going to argue about it. I already spoke to the relative of the first victim. I established a connection. I'm going to see this through."

"You don't even know if that was the first victim, or the only victim," Rider said. "Because you're not a detective. You wanted to work for me so I'm allowing you to do so, but I pick the jobs you go on and tonight you're staying in the bar where—"

"Are you prepared to use your sire power over me to keep me here against my will so I don't hunt that thing?" I asked, louder and angrier than I'd intended, but my temper was full blown. "Because that's what it's going to take."

"Daniel, you can leave now," Rider said, but didn't bother to glance the dragon-shifter's way. All his fiery-eyed attention stayed locked on me.

I saw Daniel get up out of the corner of my eye and waited until he'd left the office and pulled the door closed behind him to speak. "Gee, I hope the two of you had plenty of time to chat about me before I came in to interrupt."

"Are you mad he did the right thing last night and called me, Danni, or are you mad he didn't take advantage of the situation?"

I barely held back a snarl. "How dare you? Is that why you want me to stay in the bar? So you can make sure I don't attack anyone like the demon whore I am?"

"I've never called you that or anything close to that. I've never thought it either and you should at least know that much about me by now!"

Kutya whined and buried his head under his big paws, clearly upset by the heated emotions and tones being thrown around the confined space.

Rider blew out a breath and raked his hand through his hair. "Daniel called me because he could tell your succubus side was rising and knew it wasn't safe for you to be near any man, and your eyes were red before we…"

"Before I attacked you," I finished for him, my anger transferred into self-loathing. I sank back into the chair and sucked in a breath, held it inside until the desire to cry passed.

"You didn't attack me, Danni. That was nothing like what happened during the Bloom."

"I lost control. I blacked out and when I came back to, I could tell you'd done that thing. You used your sire power over me to calm the succubus." Heat climbed my face, and I averted my gaze. "I was like a wild animal."

"No, you were like a woman who happens to be half succubus and wasn't meeting her dietary needs to keep that part of her manageable, and that's the most upsetting part out of all of this." I heard him sigh, and the sound was so sad it pulled at my heart, threatening to crack the organ in two. "I have been here all this time, Danni, yours for the taking. First, you didn't want to drink from any other live male source and that was fine. My blood would have taken care of that need, but you didn't want it either. You didn't want me."

I winced. "I didn't … not want you."

"That might be easier to believe if not for the fact the only time you haven't recoiled at my touch in the last several weeks was while under the influence of your succubus side's thirst, and once that passed and you came back to yourself, you *cried*."

That reminder and the thought of how he must have felt in that moment brought out another wince. "I wasn't crying because of … You didn't do anything wrong. That was all me."

"Really? You're giving me the old 'It's not you, it's me' line?"

"It's not a line, and no, that's not what I'm doing. I'm…" I growled in frustration as I came up empty for words to explain what my problem was. "I don't know what's wrong with me. I love you. I've loved you probably since the first time I saw you, even though I thought you were a psychopath with a vampire fetish, and I'll probably love you to the grave and beyond, but… I just… I…"

"You what? Damn it, you can't even look at me right now. If you still love me, why can't you even do that anymore?"

"Because you scare the hell out of me!" I snapped, raising my gaze to meet the stunned hurt in his. Regret hit me like a sledgehammer. "I didn't mean—"

"Yes, yes you did mean that." He made a sound in his throat, something between a growl and a mirthless laugh, and ran his hand down his face. "Ah, that's great. That's really great. You're scared of me. You're not afraid to go chasing after something capable of ripping a person wide open and snatching them up a chimney, but me, you're afraid of. I would never hurt you, Danni."

"I know that." Tears came fast and ugly. "I know you wouldn't ever hurt me. I'm not afraid of you hurting me."

"Then what are you afraid of? How else do I scare you?"

I shook my head, again struggling for words that just flat out refused to come. "I don't know. I don't know how to explain what it is. It's just something you have to let me work through. And you have to let me hunt this thing killing people. You have to let me stop it."

"How do you know it's still—"

"Because I *know*. I just know, like I knew Eliza was

taken, and I knew Lovefest was connected. I know it in the same way I knew Angela LaRoche was dead the moment I saw her face in that picture." I sniffed. "I know it's still killing and it'll keep killing if I don't stop it. I have to stop it. Not Grissom. Not any team you send out after it. I have to kill it."

"You really got all that off a picture?"

"Yes." I nodded, wiped the back of my hands under my eyes. "I feel it deep in my gut, just like I feel that eventually I'm going to get through whatever it is that's wrong with me. I'm sorry I'm putting you through this while I sort it all out. I just need some space, some time… and I need to stop that monster. I really, really need to stop that monster."

I forced myself to meet Rider's gaze through the blurry sheen of tears. He stared at me as a parade of mixed emotions ran through his eyes, then took a big sniff and gave a firm nod. "All right."

"All right, you won't try to hold me back from hunting this monster?"

"All right, I believe you believe whatever killed that woman isn't done killing and you need to make sure it stops. I'll call Grissom and look into it while you meet with Nannette, and you do have to see Nannette. Your eyes were red this morning, and you had venom. You need to see her and get her okay to go after this thing." He raised his hands to silence me when my mouth opened, knee-jerk response at the ready. "I'm really not trying to clip your wings here, but you know yourself you are not stable right now. Speaking of which, did you drink the blood I told Tony to give you?"

"The sick pedophile-Claus blood?"

"He was a predator, and he needed to die. I will not apologize for removing that bastard from this world."

"I wouldn't either. There wasn't any reason for you to bar me from the sublevel while you were taking care of him." His eyes widened a little, and I caught a flicker of something there before he averted his gaze, something that set off my suspicion radar. "That was why you had Juan stationed to keep me out of the sublevels, wasn't it?"

"You've been pretty distant since the last time I took care of someone," he said, but I noticed he didn't lift his gaze back up to mine until he finished saying it, nor did he directly answer my question. "Did you drink the blood?"

"Yes."

"Good. It wasn't straight from the source, but it was male and it hadn't been out of the host very long. Hopefully that helps while you're…" He blew out a breath. "You need to drink live male blood, Danni. You need to feed your other thirsts too."

"I know. I should be good now. I drank from you this morning. I drank a lot from you, maybe too much." I shuddered at the memory. "I'm sorry. It was violent."

"Look at me, Danni."

I gritted my teeth and forced myself to lift my eyes to meet his gaze. The minute our eyes met, I wanted to look away, but there was a steely strength in his gaze that refused to allow mine to escape.

"I am yours," he said. "Blood. Body. Heart. Soul. It's all yours whenever and however you need it, and you never have to feel bad about that. I need you to understand that."

My heart hitched with the sincerity in his words, and I wondered how I could ever deny him. Then the memory of that morning after returning from Pigeon Forge and all that blood covering him flooded back, bringing a chill with it. The connection broke and my gaze fell away because all I saw when I looked at him was blood and violence. And fear. The fear was too much.

I felt the disappointment as it left Rider's body on a sigh, and knew, despite the best attempt to block him from my mind, my thoughts had slipped through. "Nannette has arrived. You can meet her in the training room. You'll be allowed down there now."

I nodded, and stood, wanting desperately to say the magic words to fix everything, but I didn't know what they were, so I just turned for the door.

"Don't forget Nannette's gift."

"Oh." I turned and picked up the scrapbook I'd set on the desk at some point and forgot all about. "I want to get you something too. You're not the easiest guy to shop for though. Is there anything you want for Christmas?"

"All I want is to have you back again."

I frowned. "I'm here."

"No, you're about as far from here as you could possibly be." He gestured toward the door and reached for the phone on his desk. "Go. Check in with Nannette. I'll see if I can get Grissom over here by the time you two wrap things up."

My throat burned as I swallowed past the hard lump that had lodged there after seeing the dejected look in Rider's eyes. I didn't like causing the people I cared about pain anyway, but it was harder with Rider, and not just because despite whatever was going on in my head, I knew I loved him, but because of the type of man he was. He wasn't a pushover, a softie. Yes, I got by with things I knew no one else could and I'd been told by more than a few of his people that he'd become less snarly since I came along, but he was still formidable. Strong. Unbreakable. Yet… I felt as though he were breaking, and I was the one who'd put the big crack in him, right in his heart.

He glanced up at me and paused, his hand over the buttons he'd been about to press. "Is there something you need?"

You, I thought, only to be assaulted with the image of him covered in blood, pure violence in his murder-darkened eyes. I shook my head as I tore my gaze away and yanked the door open, desperate to escape.

What the hell was wrong with me?

CHAPTER SEVEN

True to his word, Rider didn't have any shifter guards or other obstacles in my path to block my access to the sublevels. To my relief, I hadn't had to interact with anyone as I made my way to the stairwell that would take me down below The Midnight Rider. I was especially relieved not to run into Daniel. I still didn't know why Rider had called us both into the office. Normally it was because Daniel was my personal guard and wherever I went, he went, so I assumed that was it. Maybe Rider had wanted to see how Daniel and I reacted to each other, see if there was still something there shouldn't be between us after my succubus side had been sated. I wouldn't put it past him, but he didn't have to worry. The fact Daniel had called him should have assuaged all his fears. I'd obviously repulsed the dragon-shifter and I couldn't help but be upset by that.

I reached the sublevel the training room was on and placed my hand over the security panel next to the door, waited for my handprint to be scanned, and pushed through. The tech team, a mostly paranormal version of a geek squad, was the first thing to greet those allowed into the sublevels when stepping out onto that first floor below the building. Men and women, some of whom were shifters, some vampires, even some humans sprinkled in, studiously ignored me as they tapped away at the computers taking up the long tables in their space. I glanced at the large plasma screen that took up the wall before them and saw multiple screens of numbers, random code, and various security cam feeds all projected onto the space. None of it made sense to me, so I strolled past.

I glanced into the gym as I walked down the hall leading to the training room and noted some shifters using the equipment inside. Daniel wasn't one of them, and I wondered if he ever was. I knew he kept a change of clothes in a locker and he'd gotten bigger since he'd started working for Rider. Some of that size was because of the dragon soul inside him still transforming his body, but some had to be good old-fashioned working out. I wasn't sure when he'd have the time. He seemed to always be nearby when Rider called him in, and he was called in a lot, at least while I was awake. Wondering how much time Daniel did or didn't spend in the gym brought forth the memory of his half-naked state in my dream and the feel of his hands as he'd fondled me, sharing me with Rider in front of everyone. I shook my head, wished I could shake the memory of that nightmare right out with it. The last time I'd been having such vulgar dreams, there'd been a trickster demon to blame. Before that, Selander Ryan was the culprit. Now I only had my own warped mind to blame for the nightmares I'd been having since returning to Louisville, and that made it a thousand times worse.

I stopped in front of the training room door and took a moment to collect myself. I could use someone to talk to, a girl friend to confide all my troubles to, but as close as I was with Ginger, and despite how far Nannette and I had come along in terms of not hating each other, they were still Rider's people. The only person I'd ever really felt I could talk to with one hundred percent certainty of not having what I said repeated back to Rider … was Daniel.

And he was one of the last people I'd be comfortable talking to now.

I held the scrapbook to my chest, took a deep breath, and stepped into the training room. Nannette sat in a chair in front of the floor to ceiling mirrors that ran the entire length of the wall to my right. She wore a blood red off-the-shoulder sweater with skinny jeans that molded to her slender thighs, and black suede ankle boots. She kept her black hair shaved close to her scalp, which complimented her big brown eyes, nude-glossed lips, and cheekbones which were sculpted to fit her face perfectly. The woman exuded poise and confidence, even when she was kicking ass, and something about that never failed to make me feel as if I were in the presence of royalty when I met with her.

"Sit," she said, eyeing the scrapbook I still held close to my chest as she motioned toward the chair diagonally in front of her. "I heard you had one hell of a morning."

"Red eyes and venom," I admitted as I settled into the chair. "I suppose Rider told you he handled it, reined my succubus side in."

"Yes." She angled her head sideways, studied me. I could tell by the set of her mouth she was annoyed with me. "He also told me that this morning was the first time you've drank from him since before he sent you to The Cloud Top, that you refused to drink from any live male. You know that's too long."

"I drank from Grey while I was at The Cloud Top, and I drank from Jon. I had live male blood since Rider left and sent me to Pigeon Forge."

"Fine, so you drank from live males while you were there. That doesn't change the fact that before this morning you hadn't drank from a live male since then. You've been back almost four weeks, Danni. That is too damn long to go without live male blood and I distinctly remember telling you that you were pushing it when we met last week."

"I know. I remember." I remembered the ass-beating

I'd taken too, and the one I'd delivered back. Judging by Nannette's clothes, tonight's session wasn't going to be physical, which was a letdown. I'd much rather do the pummeling and physical sparring than the verbal smackdown I sensed coming.

"Good. Do you also remember telling me you were going to drink live male blood after our session?"

"Yes," I muttered.

"Then what the hell happened?"

"I couldn't do it."

"What do you mean you couldn't do it? You're a vampire and a succubus. You crave blood and you crave testosterone." She'd been sitting with one leg crossed over the other at the knee, and straightened to bring both feet down to the floor as she leaned forward, hitting me with the full weight of her pissed off gaze. "How often have you fed from your female donor during these weeks?"

"A few times," I said. "Maybe four times. I've mostly been drinking bagged or bottled blood."

"So you've had access to blood from males and you've had access to sex, but you've simply chosen not to partake of either, yet you somehow forced yourself to take blood directly out of a female's vein at least four times without any live male blood at all in between?"

"I didn't choose not to drink from them," I snapped. "I can't!"

"What do you mean, *can't?* You're half succubus. You should be forcing yourself not to take too much blood from men, not forcing yourself to take it. Have you even tried?"

"Yes!" I blew out a breath. "I've tried. I just…" The image of Rider standing in his room covered in blood hit me, along with images of every man I'd ever drank from. I saw the fear in their eyes, the flinching, and my stomach rolled.

"Why have you drunk from your female donor so often?" Nannette asked, her tone a lot softer.

"I needed blood?"

"You needed blood, but you know drinking from the girl is only to balance out your diet or in case of an emergency. Drinking from her more than once without taking in blood from a man's vein seriously unbalanced your diet and you are way too smart not to know that. I haven't heard anything about any incidents that would cause you to require blood from her."

"You know why I did it," I said, ready to confess and get the mental poking and prodding over. "If Rider told you what happened this morning, you already know."

"Yes, but I'd hoped you'd tell me. I'd hoped you'd tell me long before this morning happened. You should have called me and told me what you were feeling. Even if, for whatever reason, you didn't want to talk to Rider about it, you could have come to me."

"You tell Rider everything, and I didn't want him to know. I thought I could handle it."

"Wow, Danni. Thanks for that."

I raised my eyes to meet her gaze, but she'd already turned in her chair and bent to pick up a black bag that had been sitting on the floor behind her. She stood and deposited the bag on her vacated chair before unzipping it to remove a set of needles. "Yes, you need to feed your succubus side sex, but nearly a month of abstinence seems a little short to be bringing out the red-eyed monster to this degree so I'm going to draw some blood and do some tests when I get back to the hospital."

I slid the book between my body and the back of the chair and rolled up my sleeve, familiar with the process. I inhaled and held it, braced for the needle's sting.

Nannette kneeled next to me and slid the first needle into my flesh. "What's that book?"

I felt warmth climb my face, suddenly feeling a little foolish about the present, especially now that I'd seemed to offend her. "Do you celebrate Christmas?"

She glanced at me before returning her attention to the

syringe filling with my blood. Once it reached the amount she needed, she withdrew it and went to work with needle number two. "I haven't in a very long time. I have no relatives, don't know any children. It's often just another day at the hospital for me."

"Oh."

"Why?" She capped the second syringe of blood and moved on to the third one.

"I celebrate it. Well, at least I did, being human at all, even if it hasn't been the same for me since my father died." My father's disgusted and disappointed expression from my nightmare surfaced in my memory and I quickly shoved it down before the rolling ball in my stomach gave way to full-blown nausea. "I thought I'd still celebrate it, but with you guys."

"Who guys?" She finished the blood draw, capped the syringe and licked the minor wound left behind by the needle, which instantly caused my estrogen-hating half-succubus body to shudder, and moved back over to the other chair to seal the syringes in a plastic baggie before dropping them into the black bag.

"You guys," I said. "Rider, Daniel, Ginger, Rome… You. My friends and… new family."

She stilled completely for a moment and I wondered again if I'd gone too far with the gift. Maybe I'd read too much into our sessions and mistook Nannette's tough love for genuine care. Maybe she really was just doing her job, obeying Rider.

She took a penlight out of the bag and moved to stand before me. "So you thought enough to put me in the friend and family category, but didn't think enough of me to come to me when you were in trouble?" She tilted my head back and sent a ray of light directly into my eye.

"It wasn't personal. I know you have to tell Rider everything, and I thought I could handle it."

She moved the light to the other eye before clicking it off and returned the instrument to her bag. She turned toward me and folded her arms. "First of all, I tell Rider what is necessary for him to know to help you, not every damn thing you tell me in private. This sudden onset aversion to sex and live male blood is dangerous given your hybrid makeup. If whatever is causing it is something you can't talk to Rider about, or if it's Rider himself, your ass needs to tell me. Are we clear?"

"Yes, ma'am."

She narrowed her eyes at the *ma'am* and I couldn't help grin. "You can trust me, Danni. I can keep what you tell me private, even from Rider… unless, of course, you reveal intentions of doing anything to hurt him, obviously."

I nodded. "Yes, obviously that you'd have to tell him."

"No, in that situation, I'd just kill you myself." She grinned. "Now, I've taken blood to be analyzed in case something's off in your chemistry, but I have to say this whole thing is sounding like something mental and the 'I don't know' and 'I can't' responses aren't going to cut it. Rider doesn't blab your business to me unless it's vital either, but I do know you had sex right before your trip to The Cloud Top and nothing between then and this morning when you had the red eyes and venom. Clearly you were in need of sex or live male blood or both, and you had easy access, but you still denied yourself enough to bring out the succubus in all its red-eyed glory. Do you want to tell me why?" She raised her hand in the air. "And so help me, if you say you don't know or shrug those shoulders, I'm going to slap a whole new set of vocabulary words into that annoying-ass head of yours."

"Careful or you're getting coal."

She frowned and lowered her hand. "What are you talking about?"

"Coal in your stocking. For Christmas." I grabbed the scrapbook from behind me and settled it in my lap. "The book is your gift."

She stared down at the scrapbook and blinked. "You

got me a Christmas present?"

I nodded.

Nannette picked up the bag and carefully set it on the floor before lowering herself onto the chair, never lifting her eyes from the scrapbook in my lap. She shook her head slowly from side to side. "I haven't gotten a gift in… I haven't gotten a Christmas gift in over a lifetime." She suddenly straightened and shook her head faster. "No. I didn't get you a gift."

"You don't have to get me a gift."

"I have to get you a gift if you got me a gift. I haven't had Christmas in ages, but I know that much. Wait." She held her hand out, palm toward me. "It's not Christmas yet. Keep that until then. I have a little more time."

"Nannette, you don't have to get me a gift. I got you this because I wanted to, not because I expect something in return. Honestly, I'm not expecting much at all this year with my family issues, and I know most of you in Rider's nest don't celebrate at all." I held the scrapbook out toward her. "And I want you to take this now. It's not Christmas yet, but depending on how you feel about this gift, I hope for it to be the first half of the gift, the part that leads you to the really great second part of the gift."

Her eyes had started to gleam with moisture and she blew out a slow breath as she took the book, but instead of taking it from my hands, she held it between us. "I have to get you a gift."

I rolled my eyes, then realized the opportunity I'd been given. "I want to hunt a particular monster killing people in the area, but Rider said I'd need to get that okayed by you. If you really want to give me a gift, that would be a really great one."

Her brow scrunched. "That's what you want, a permission slip to go out and hunt something down for Christmas?"

"Hey, it's a gift I need and only you can give."

"Girl, I haven't celebrated Christmas in longer than

you've been alive and even I know that's the most lame-ass thing you could have come up with for a gift." She sighed. "But I'll make you a deal. Talk to me, honestly, make a real effort to give me the information I need to figure out what is going on with you, and I just might tell Rider to allow you to hunt whatever it is you're wanting to hunt."

"Deal."

Nannette took the scrapbook and ran her hand over the cover, feeling the leather under her fingertips. I held my breath as she opened it to reveal the first part of the records Rabea had found. She frowned, turned the page, revealed the picture Rabea had miraculously found, and gasped. "Mama!"

Tears filled her eyes as she covered her mouth with one hand and used the other to reverently trace the face that looked so much like her own.

"I know we aren't really supposed to ask each other's ages or dig around in each other's pasts, but you know I have no intention whatsoever of challenging you to anything or trying to take you out. You let enough slip in our sessions, just enough for me to have a rough idea of when you and your mother were brought to America, and … I know it sounds crazy but I had some hunches on a few other things, put it all together, and called in a specialist. She's human and has no idea about the existence of vampires."

"You found a picture of my mother. How?"

"The woman I called is good, but even she said she got really lucky with that. Slave records are hard to find in detail. She was able to trace your mother's whereabouts her whole life, even after she escaped and had that picture taken."

Nannette's stunned eyes left the image of her mother to snap up to me. "She escaped?"

I nodded, and couldn't fight the smile that stretched wide across my face as my own eyes filled with tears. "Your mother and your sister escaped to the North four years after her oldest daughter, Nani Etana, was declared a runaway. Rabea couldn't find anything else on Nani Etana though. That was when you were turned, wasn't it?"

Nannette nodded as tears slid silently down her cheeks. "My younger sister never could say my name. She called me Nannit, and it stuck, so after Rider freed me, I started to go by Nannette. I'd lost everything of my family and so much time had passed I knew I'd never find them, so I could at least keep the name my little sister gave me, and my mama's face. That has always been with me."

"Yes, it has. You look so much like her."

Nannette wiped her eyes and sniffed. "I never thought I'd see her again."

"Turn the page, and then the next. Keep going. Rabea tracked your lineage."

Nannette grabbed the edge of the page and stilled for a moment. I wasn't sure whether she was bracing herself for what came next or afraid of losing her mother's image again, but she eventually took a deep breath and turned the page. Rabea had filled the book with printouts of every record she'd found, every news article, and every picture of every family member.

"Oh, my…" Nannette sobbed as she flipped to the page with her sister's obituary and saw the picture of her aged to eighty-three-years-old, surrounded by her children and grandchildren. "I was an aunt."

"And a great-aunt. You still are," I said, and flipped to a page toward the end of the scrapbook. "There are empty pages here for more memories you may want to add, but if you want to, you can see your family again. Rabea found your living descendants. They don't have to know who or what you are, but you can still know them."

"Is that the second part of the gift you were talking about?"

I nodded. "If you're creative, maybe you can spend Christmas with your own family."

"You gave me back my own flesh and blood family,

and you gave me so much more than that. I never knew what happened to my mama or my sister. I thought they died working in that bastard's fields." Then Nannette did something I thought I'd never see in my lifetime. She started sobbing. Full chest-heaving, nose running, bawling.

I didn't know what to do. My heart said hug her, but the succubus inside me didn't want to do that at all, and the part of me that had gotten to know Nannette fairly well during our sessions thought it best I run away before she realized she was crying in front of me. If Nannette had ever cried before, I highly doubted she'd left a living witness to tell the story.

"If I wasn't wearing these suede ankle boots, I'd stomp your ass into a bloodstain," she wailed, wiping at her eyes. Then she looked at me and we cracked up laughing. "I'm going to hug you just because I know you hate it."

I grimaced as she leaned forward and wrapped her arms around me, but the succubus side of me would just have to suck it up. All things considered, I was lucky hugging me was all the punishment the vampire wanted to inflict on me. "So, does this mean you're not going to kill me for digging into your past?"

She pulled back, sniffed several times and wiped at her eyes a while before giving up and using the bottom of her sweater to absorb the aftermath of the waterworks. "I really should, but you gave me back my family. If you ever tell anyone what you've learned about me—"

I raised my hands. "Hey, not even Rider knew what I was up to. The human I had dig this all up has no idea our kind exists, and no one knows who Nani Etana was. You do, however, look the spitting image of your mother, so you might want to lock that scrapbook up tight somewhere if you don't want anyone finding it and putting two and two together."

She nodded and a hint of a smile ghosted over her lips. "Thank you, Danni. I have no idea how you knew what to look for, but thank you."

"You're very welcome."

"Rider doesn't know how old I am."

"And he won't," I said. "I really don't understand the big deal with not revealing our age. I mean, I understand the reason. I just don't see that many vampires running around throwing down challenges, but I'll keep yours secret, even from him. So… Can I hunt?" I batted my eyelashes.

Nannette laughed. "You need to have your violence needs met so hunting something couldn't hurt there, but you're not stable and that's a problem."

"Hey, I drank from Rider and got all good and sexed up. I am ready to go." I placed one hand over my heart and held the other up. "I solemnly swear."

Nannette's eyes narrowed. "What have you had since waking up?"

"A mug of blood, but it was fresh from a male Rider killed in interrogation. It didn't even need to be warmed up."

"It's not the same." She folded her arms and sat back in the chair, careful not to dislodge the scrapbook in her lap. "I'll give the okay for you to hunt if you drink from a male before you leave here, and only if."

I wasn't sure what face I made, but my unease must have shown because it drew a huge frown out of Nannette. "This shouldn't be a problem for you, Danni."

"Yeah, it shouldn't." I dragged my hand through my hair and fought back an irritated groan. It really, really shouldn't have been an issue at all, but it was, and it was a huge, fucking problem.

"So why is it? What happens when you try to drink from Rider?" Her frown deepened when I looked at her, and I could tell by the way her nostrils flared I was hedging onto her nerves. "I won't tell him a thing. You can trust me. I can only help you if I know what's happening, and that's only going to happen if you tell me, because right now, this shit isn't making any logical sense."

"Welcome to my world." I blew out a breath. Screw it. If she did tell him, it couldn't hurt him any worse than I'd already hurt him. I told her everything. I told her how nausea rolled in my belly when I thought of drinking from him or another man, except for the previous morning when all I'd wanted was to drain Rider and Daniel of blood because I was so damn thirsty for it. I told her what had happened with Trixell, how her screams had been so piercing they'd cut right through me and stuck in my head long after, how Rider came to our room covered in her blood, and how that image flashed through my mind almost every time I saw him now. I told her how I could only see flinching, fear, and revulsion in any other man whose blood I was offered. Then I told her about the dreams that had plagued me since the night Trixell was killed, dreams that were steadily getting worse.

"Damn, girl." Nannette shook her head. "You're a hybrid so there's always the potential for all kinds of surprises with you so I'll still run the blood and see if anything strange shows up there, but I really don't think there's going to be any physical cause for this. I think there's something psychological going on with you, some sort of trauma brought on by witnessing Trixell's death."

"But I didn't even witness it."

Nannette's brow furrowed in thought. "True. You heard the screaming, you saw the bloody aftermath. Your mind put together a lot of pictures to fill in that huge blank in-between though, didn't it? Hell, you probably conjured up something way worse than whatever happened. You had to have. You've seen Rider in interrogation before. That never scared you, did it?"

I thought of the times I'd witnessed Rider kill in and out of interrogation. I'd seen him rip hearts and spines out, even behead people with just his hands. It had never bothered me before, but it sent a chill down my spine now. "It didn't then, but it all bothers me now."

"Shit. Eliza needs to get herself together so she can

help with this. This is out of my zone." She stood and collected her bag, carefully placing the scrapbook inside it first. "Drink from Rider or some other man, but that's the only way I can okay you hunting anything, or for that matter, leaving here at all. And you're taking Daniel with you. I don't need to tell you that if he or any other man starts looking real good to you, you need to get to Rider and take care of your business. Your sister's carrying the Bloom for you, but when the succubus side flares up in you, like I said, there's always potential for surprises."

"I know." I stood and straightened my shoulders. "I have things handled. I'll do what I have to do. If I can force myself to drink from a female, I can … I can drink from a man and take care of my needs."

Nannette raised an eyebrow. "Good, but just in case, I'm walking your ass up to Rider right now and watching you drink. I'd have you drink from Daniel or another male, but with all that's off with you, the blood of your sire is best."

Nausea rolled around in my stomach, but I gritted my teeth and gave a firm nod with far more confidence than I felt. I'd drink from Rider no matter what it took because I had a monster to kill and my Spidey senses had just started to tingle. "Let's do it."

CHAPTER EIGHT

"And just so you know, I never cry. It's very important that you remember that fact," Nannette said as we cleared the stairwell. "I'd hate to have you tell a fib about me and have to get hurt."

I looked over to see her giving me side-eye with just enough of a lift at the corners of her mouth to know we were good. "No one would believe me if I told them you cried."

"Of course they wouldn't. The whole idea of it is ludicrous." The corners of her mouth twitched as she pushed through the door to the hallway. "I still hate you."

"I hate you more."

This got a full smile out of both of us. Our friendship was weird, and there was once a time I swore the woman wanted me dead by her own hand, but I was glad to have her in my life.

Unease grew as we continued down the hall toward Rider's office. I sensed him inside and my stomach clenched in response as, once again, his blood-covered image assaulted my mind.

Nannette grabbed my arm and moved in front of me, forcing me to stop. "You're looking a little green and I can tell you're gritting your teeth. What's happening right now?"

I took a deep breath in through my nose and waited for the wave of nausea to roll along on its way before I answered. "I see him in my head."

"Covered in Trixell's blood?"

I nodded, swallowing hard past the ball that had formed in my throat.

"Okay." She nodded, nibbled on her bottom lip a bit as she thought. "Okay, I've got an idea. Do your best to just clear your mind right now. There's no sense thinking about drinking from him until you actually have to. Try to relax."

She gave my arm a squeeze, and we continued on. Nannette rapped on the door and pushed through after Rider called us in.

Kutya was nowhere to be seen, and Rider sat behind his desk, looking apprehensive. "So?"

"I'm going to recommend you give Danni permission to hunt this killer she wants to go after," Nannette said. "Danni needs to have her violence needs met and I think having such an activity to focus on could help her, so I have no problem giving my consent to do that, but only if she feeds from you first. This may seem awkward, but I want her to do that now while I supervise."

This brought up Rider's eyebrow. "Supervise?"

"*I want to watch her drink from you* sounds a whole lot creepier."

"True," he said, and looked at me. Myriad emotions flitted through his eyes before he let out a big sigh full of doubt and rolled up his sleeve. Every one of those emotions was negative, and I couldn't blame him. He'd tried to give me his blood often over the past two weeks. Rejection sucked, and it sucked being the one to do it to someone you loved and knew you should be happy to be with, but your own mind was screwing with you, telling you to fear him instead.

I looked over at Nannette to see her watching me, her

eyes narrowed a bit. Suddenly, I had a pretty good idea what it felt like to be a bug under a microscope. She nodded her head in Rider's direction.

Showtime.

I sucked in air and released it slowly as I walked around the desk, willing my nerves and the sea of nausea in my stomach to calm. I remembered throwing up that morning, and it nearly triggered my gag reflex. Rider's eyes held mine as I approached. There was so much hurt in them, so much… He was nervous, I realized, and in fear of being humiliated when I refused to take his blood in front of Nannette. It would make him feel powerless, emasculated. Tears burned the backs of my eyes. I couldn't do that to him, but as I looked down at his exposed wrist… all I saw was Trixell's blood covering his skin and the nausea intensified. I felt dizzy.

"Danni, I want you to stay right where you are and close your eyes."

Both our heads swiveled to look at Nannette. "What?"

"Humor me. Stay there and close your eyes."

"All right." I did as asked.

"Rider, stay seated, but turn all the way around. I want your back to Danni."

I heard the chair swivel.

"Now, Danni, I want you to keep your eyes closed and only listen for blood. Don't imagine it, don't smell it out, just listen for it."

I inhaled, released the breath, cleared my mind, and focused on listening. I heard the vibration of music coming from the bar, muffled by the walls, and I heard the zing or whatever it was called, the energy pulsating through wires connected to Rider's electronics in the office, I heard breathing, and I heard heartbeats.

Nannette didn't breathe. I knew she was there, but she didn't make a sound. My heart raced, but Rider's raced faster. I saw him covered in blood and shook my head, shook the image out. I wasn't seeing. I was listening. I was listening to heartbeats and to the blood pumping through arteries to make those heartbeats. I moved closer to the sound, the call of living, life-giving blood. I pictured only it, flowing through those arteries. There was no flesh. Everything was inside, protected.

I was so close now. I reached out, placed my hands on shoulders covered by fabric. Not flesh. I opened my eyes. I saw Rider, but he sat facing away from me. His blood pumped inside his body, raced through his arteries. It wasn't on him, and I didn't have his beautiful face to distract me or his eyes, normally breathtaking, but sometimes dark and cold. I gripped his shoulder with one hand and used the other to tilt his head, avoiding the distraction of his face and eyes, and all the bloody images they could conjure. I focused on the pulse point in his throat, the fountain of delicious nectar mine for the taking.

I yanked the neck of his sweater aside and plunged my fangs into the flesh over that pulse point. Rider hissed out a breath as I took my first big draw, a hearty gulp of rich, powerful blood that ran hot over my tongue and slid down my throat with satisfying ease.

"I'll see myself out," Nannette said as her heartbeat came back online. A moment later, the door opened and closed.

I drank my fill, drinking more heavily than usual due to how long it had been since I'd truly drunk from Rider and enjoyed it, and the fact I'd thrown up that morning. I took until I couldn't take another drop without feeling sick and sealed the small wounds I'd made.

Rider groaned as my tongue washed away the evidence of the feeding and turned the chair around to pull me onto his lap. Eyes closed the whole time, I straddled his lap and our mouths joined. He tasted better than the blood. It had been too long since I'd connected with him intimately, not counting the previous morning while I'd been too starved for physical contact to really focus on anything more than quelling a near-painful need to be sated.

"I don't know what she did, but I think I'll give her a bonus," Rider said against my mouth during the small window we came up for air. "I've missed you."

"I missed you too." I really had, I realized. I'd been with him, but not with him, for weeks, haunted by a never-ending nightmare that made no sense. I reached down to where I felt him already hard behind his fly and opened my eyes … to look straight into rage-filled so-blue-they-were-almost-black orbs of pure violence. Blood covered his face and hair. A small cry lurched out of me as I jumped back, hit my hip against the edge of the desk, and nearly fell before backing all the way up to the opposite wall.

"Damn it!" Rider's face fell as he brought his fist down on the desk and released a string of angry curses before bending forward to bury his head in his hands. "What the fuck is wrong with you?"

I tried to answer, to say something, anything, but I only sputtered as tears filled my eyes.

He lifted his head, looked straight at me. "What do you see when you look at me?"

I closed my eyes and shook my head. I'd hurt him enough. I couldn't keep hurting him. "I'm sorry."

"Sorry about what? Not wanting me anymore? Being terrified of me?"

"I still want you."

He laughed, the bitterest sound I'd ever heard. "Yeah, you want me. As long as you don't have to look at me. I'm the luckiest bastard in the world."

Someone knocked hard three times on the door, and it opened. Kutya barreled in, only made it three quick steps before he completely froze to stare right at me and growled low in his throat.

Hank stood in the doorway. His low brow furrowed as Kutya continued growling, and the shifter looked between the dog's neck where short hair had risen to spiky points all along the back, and where I stood still, pressed back as far into the wall as I could get. "Uh… I walked the dog real good, boss. About to grab a shovel and clean up after him. I saw Grissom park in the lot."

"Thanks, Hank." Rider stared at his dog. "You can go now."

"Sure thing." Hank did another curious glance between me and the dog, and backed out of the room, closing the door behind him.

The minute the door clicked shut, Kutya advanced. Head low, lips pulled back in a snarl, fur standing on end.

"Kutya, stop!" Rider stood from his seat and came around the desk to stand between me and the dog.

Once Rider's back was to me, the fear that had held me in its grip dissipated, and the dog calmed down. He plopped onto his bottom and barked before pawing at Rider, wanting to be scratched and petted.

"What was that about?"

"I have no idea," Rider answered. He reached down to scratch Kutya between the ears. "He's never done that before, especially with you."

Cold engulfed me. "I'm so awful, even Kutya hates me now."

"No one here hates you, Danni. Believe me, I wouldn't feel so fucking bad now if I didn't love you as much as I do. It's hell."

I approached him from behind, and after a moment of hesitation, wrapped my arms around him. He stiffened so fast I couldn't even find comfort in the warmth of his body as I pressed my cheek into his back and held on tight. I was too busy holding in tears from the emotional sucker-punch. Rider shoved his hands into his pockets and released a broken sigh. "You should go on out there and talk to Grissom, find out what he knows so you can be on your way."

"Rider."

"Don't, Danni. Don't tell me you love me, not when you can't look me in the eye and say it." He shrugged out of my arms and walked away far enough to be out of my reach, his back to me the whole time. Kutya whined and followed him, pressed his massive head against his thigh to offer his master comfort. "Take Daniel and Ginger with you, and be careful. Pacitti's out there somewhere and I shouldn't have to warn you about whatever this thing is you're going after."

"I don't want to leave with things like this between us."

"I don't want you to stay here with things like this between us," he replied, a trace of bitterness and enough hurt to gut me in his voice.

"You don't want me to come back?"

"No, damn it. That's not…" He turned and ran his hand down his face, sucked in a breath, and that's when I saw the wetness in his eyes. He wasn't covered in blood, but I knew that wetness was hot, fiery anger. "I don't want you to stay here right now, forcing yourself to look at me just because everything's fucked up. That won't fix it. I want you to go do whatever the hell it is you need to do to be able to look at me again without wanting to run away. Go hunt something, kill something, whatever. I don't care. Just be careful and when you come back to me… *come back to me.*"

"I'm so sorry, Rider."

"Yeah, me too." He flung his hand toward the door as he rounded the desk to drop back down into his chair. "Go. I need to get back to trying to find Pacitti anyway and about a million other things. Just go. I trust this morning was enough you won't—"

My breath left me as he clamped his mouth shut and winced. That was my cue. I squared my shoulders and crossed the room to yank open the door. "No worries, Rider. The sex demon got what it needed. No community dick necessary tonight."

"Danni, I didn't mean that."

"Yeah, you did, and the real shitty thing is I can't even blame you for saying it, so don't sweat it."

"Danni."

"I said it's fine, Rider. Just consider us even on hurting each other for the night." I stepped out and pulled the door closed behind me with a definitive slam. Then I took a moment to will the traitorous tears stinging the backs of my eyes to stay in place, sucked in a cleansing breath, yanked on my figurative big girl panties, and stormed down the hall and out into the bar.

Dolly Parton's voice hit me as soon as I pushed through the door and her wish for a Smoky Mountain Christmas nearly sent me to my knees. Had I stayed in the Smokies, I wouldn't have witnessed the screams of the evil witch or the bloody aftermath left on Rider afterward. I wouldn't be hurting him every time I couldn't bear to hold his gaze longer than a few seconds before being assaulted by that nightmare image. I wouldn't have become something repulsive to Daniel. I wouldn't have become someone so heartless and vile, a big sweet pup like Kutya had turned against me.

"Hey." A hand rested on my shoulder and I looked over to see Nannette the same instant I recoiled from the touch. She raised her hand. "Sorry. You were spaced out. Come to the bar for a moment."

I looked around, saw Grissom sitting at a booth across from Daniel. Both watched me as they spoke, most likely talking about me. Great, because that was just what I needed.

"Come on, girl." I let Nannette lead me to the bar where she'd left her bottle of blood guarded by Ginger. She picked it up and moved down a stool, offering me the one between her and the spiky-haired vampire decked out in her usual leather jacket, jeans, and boots. This time Ginger had paired the ensemble with a T-shirt featuring a really odd-looking red-nosed reindeer.

"Is that a uterus?" I asked, squinting to make sense of the image.

"Yep." She took a drink from her bottled blood and looked past me at the booth where Daniel and Grissom convened.

"You appeared to be drinking very well when I left," Nannette said, voice low, because it was looking like the making of a busy night in the bar. "So well I ducked out before one thirst led to another. What happened?"

"Not what you must have thought was going to happen before you gave us privacy," I answered. Greg, the new vampire bartender, caught my eye and reached under the bar for a bottle. I raised my hand, motioning I was good. "I drank well, and yes, other thirsts were awakened, which is usually the case when I drink from Rider, but then I opened my eyes. Once I looked at him everything went all kablooey right in my face. How did you know I'd be able to drink if I didn't look at him?"

"From what you told me, you seem to be affected by looking at him or thinking about drinking from him. I had a hunch." She looked over at me and grinned. "You're not the only one with hunches, you know. The good news is we know how to make sure you get your diet needs met until we find a way to get you through whatever this thing is. As for your other needs, there are positions—"

I jammed my index fingers into my ears. "Stop. I think I can figure out where you're going without you actually getting there and scarring me for life."

Nannette rolled her eyes, chugged the last of her blood before setting the empty bottle on the bar, and stood, lifting her big black bag. "You sure are a priss for someone of your makeup. I need to get these vials to the lab and test them. Call me if you have any issues."

The look she leveled me with brooked no room for negotiation so I promised I would and we shared another look, a private look of true appreciation for the gift I'd given her, and for the help she'd given me, and then she walked away, exiting through the back.

"So your diet's back on track?" Ginger said. "Are you feeling better?"

"As good as one can feel after hurting the person they

love more than anyone in the world, and being so damn scummy, they got growled at by a dog."

"What?" I looked over to see Jadyn had appeared next to me to retrieve a drink order. "What dog?"

"Kutya."

"Kutya growled at you?" She frowned. "He loves you."

I shrugged, felt a hitch in the vicinity of my heart. "I guess I'm just not very loveable these days."

"That doesn't make sense. I'll check in with the big guy and see what's wrong with him." She picked up the tray of drinks she'd come for and turned. "Later though. These folks are thirsty tonight."

"See?" Ginger nudged me in the shoulder with her bottle. "I bet that dog just has a splinter in his paw or something. Dogs act weird sometimes and get all growly and stuff because something's bothering them and they can't tell us what's wrong. Well, they can't tell most of us. Jadyn will figure out what's wrong with the mutt and you'll see it has nothing to do with you."

I started to nod, but stilled as I locked on to a woman across the bar. She was of average height and build, with wavy light brown hair that just barely reached her shoulders. She wore a red flannel shirt, minimal makeup and glasses with thick black frames. She was pretty and seemed well-liked by the man and woman she sat with. I watched her laugh at something the woman said and felt a wave of dizziness roll over me.

"Hey." Fingers snapped in front of my face. "Danni, what's up?"

I blinked, glanced over at Ginger's concerned face, and sucked in a breath before nodding toward the woman. "That woman is going to die very soon if I don't stop it."

CHAPTER NINE

Ginger's jaw dropped. She followed my line of sight and swallowed. "You can see that? Like, actually see her dying?"

"Something like that." I slid off the barstool and crossed over the room to where Daniel and Grissom sat nursing large frosty mugs of beer. No frou-frou holiday specials with cute little candy canes or cinnamon sticks for the badass shifters.

"Hey, Danni." Grissom started to smile, but it became a frown as I slid into the booth next to him. "Rider said you wanted to talk to me, but he didn't say anything was wrong."

"What is it?" Daniel asked as Ginger caught up and slid in to his side of the booth. Apparently, I was projecting my emotions.

"Danni just had a vision," Ginger told them.

"You have visions?" Grissom's eyebrows rose.

"No. I mean, I have before, but… No." I looked over at where the woman continued to chat it up with her friends. "What did Rider tell you?"

"Not much, just that you had a feeling about whatever took Angela LaRoche and you wanted to track it. He didn't say how you were intending to do that, but I assumed you were using Daniel's sense of smell."

"I don't need Daniel to track anything for me," I said, a lot harsher than I'd intended. Both shifters raised their eyebrows and shared a look.

"I didn't mean any offense. I assumed that was what you were intending, because my sense of smell from my wolf side is what helps me track demons."

"I have my own ways of tracking," I told him. "And I didn't mean to snap. I'm guessing Rider didn't tell you what led us to Angela LaRoche's house to begin with. Her cousin came here looking for her and showed us a picture. I knew Angela LaRoche was dead the moment I looked into her eyes in that picture, just like I know that woman over there in the red flannel shirt is going to be killed by that thing if I don't stop it first."

Grissom looked across the bar and watched the woman for a moment. "You just saw her and knew this?"

"Yes. I need to know everything you know or think you know about what killed Angela LaRoche. I don't have a lot of time. I think it might happen tonight."

"I know whatever it was left a demonic signature… along with the scent of cookies." Daniel groaned, bringing out a sympathetic look from the wolf. "Yeah, it was pretty gnarly. The scent of sweet baked goods doesn't mix well with blood and viscera. Just off what I could get from the scene, it appeared to have slaughtered her right there in her living room, but it only left blood there. I think it's big and powerful. It moved in quick, sliced her open with enough force to cause blood to splash all over the room, then yanked her up the chimney. It would have been moving really fast, judging by the amount of flesh and muscle that got rubbed off by the bricks on the way up."

"Fuck," Daniel muttered, squirming in his seat.

"I think he's gonna blow," Ginger said and scooted closer to the edge of the seat, ready to jump out of the way.

"Sorry," Grissom apologized. "That's as gory as my information gets, so you're good."

"What do you think would kill like that and take the body up a chimney?" I asked.

"Please say Krampus, please say Krampus," Ginger practically begged, then froze when she saw the three of us staring at her. "What? Who doesn't want to say they killed Krampus? It's like killing Freddy Krueger or Jack the Ripper. Major street cred."

"I don't care about street cred," I told her. "I just want to stop the thing before it kills others."

"To my knowledge, Krampus is a myth," Grissom told us.

"That's what we thought about Cupid until Danni sliced his junk and one of his snake-minions nearly killed Daniel."

Grissom sat there, blinking for a moment as he processed this new information. He took a drink before continuing and I got the impression he really needed it. "You castrated and killed the big baby with the arrows?"

"Cupid was an archdemon," I explained. "A big one."

"With wings and Van Halen hair," Ginger added.

This information received more blinks and a headshake. "Okay. Well, all I can say for sure at this point is whatever it was that killed Angela LaRoche, it was fast, big, and possibly demonic. Clearly not human. Once it reached the rooftop, I lost its scent pretty quick so I wouldn't have a clue how to track the thing, but if you can sense its next victim, maybe you can track her and get it when it tries to swoop in for the kill."

"That was my plan."

"Good." He lifted his mug. "Man, being able to see victims pre-attack would really help me do my job. Do you do this often? If so, you'd make a great detective."

"Hey, do you think this is left over from what Jon did?" Ginger asked. "Did he leave some of his juice in you?"

Grissom had taken a swig from his mug and now choked on it. I gave him a few smacks on the back and shot a look at Ginger, who held her hands up, palms out. "I swear I did not mean that to sound so pornographic. My bad."

"Are you all right?" I asked the werewolf after he quit choking and wiped his eyes.

"Yeah, I'm good, I'm good. That just took me by surprise. Who's—" He held his hand up and shook his head. "You know what? I don't even want to know."

"Jon—"

"No, no, no. I'm good." He let loose one last hearty cough to clear his throat and carefully took a drink. His cell phone vibrated, and he muttered a curse before picking it up to read the incoming message. "I have to make a call."

I stood to allow him to exit the booth, then sat back down. Daniel, who'd been far more quiet than usual, glanced at me before quickly looking away to study the woman whose life I hoped to save.

Ginger looked between the dragon-shifter and me and pulled a face I was sure matched my own general thought. It was going to be a long, fun night, and by fun, I didn't even mean a little bit.

"So," the vampire said. "What's the plan? Are you going to go over and introduce yourself?"

"Sure," I said, shooting her a look. "I was thinking something along the lines of 'Hi, I'm Danni and I'm going to follow you home and wait for a demon to crawl down your chimney and attempt to repaint your living room with your blood so I can kill it, what's your name?' would work pretty well."

"Eh, needs to be tweaked a little."

"Ya think?" I looked back over at the woman, trying to keep an eye on her without getting caught staring. "We will have to follow her home, though, right? She's human and so are her friends, who, by the way, we have no idea if they live with her or either is spending the night or what. This is complicated."

"Well, if you're sure she's going to die soon—"

"I'm sure."

"Then we have to follow her home." Ginger looked at Daniel and I forced myself to look at him too, but he seemed to contemplate some deep thought while staring into his bottle of beer.

Grissom returned to stand by our booth, chugged down the last of his beer and left a few bills beside the empty bottle. "I have to go. Caught a case. I'd wanted to help on this thing, but with this new load dumped on my plate…"

"You're already helping us with Pacitti and have my supposedly missing sister among the rest of your workload to handle," I told him. "We'll take this one off your hands."

"Just don't add any bad shit to my conscience by getting hurt, or worse." He gave me a stern look that suggested he wasn't joking. "Whether you kill the thing or not, if anything happens to leave behind a scene like what remained at the LaRoche house, call me directly. It's a lot easier keeping these situations contained from the non-paranormal when none of the humans in my department visit the crime scenes."

"Got it."

Grissom stared at me for a moment, seemed to want to say more, but eventually just glanced over at the woman and looked back at me. "Be careful, Danni. Work with your team here and don't let that gut talk you into making any hero moves."

"I'll be careful."

His eyes narrowed, but he didn't give me any further warning. He nodded a goodbye toward Daniel and Ginger and left.

"So how are we going to do this?" Ginger asked, right back to business. "Are we just going to stare at her all night, follow her out the door and … oh shit. She's on the move."

I looked over and sure enough, the women were hugging each other goodbye. Then the man helped the demon's prey into her coat.

"Move," Daniel said. "We don't know where she's parked and we don't want to all follow her out at the same time anyway."

Ginger slid out of the booth. "So what's the plan?"

"I'll head out first, watch from across the street in case she's in one of the parking garages," he said as he slid out. "The two of you can follow them out discreetly. Head to the bar lot. We'll take my truck if she's parked there. If she's in a garage, take your Mustang. I'll follow her from the sky and give you directions."

"He speaks," Ginger said as we watched him move swiftly across the bar, beating the trio outside.

"Yeah, but not to me," I muttered as I stood.

"Well, in all fairness, you didn't give him any friendly looks."

"What? I barely looked at him at all."

"Exactly. While I'm happy to not see you making hoochie eyes at the guy, this whole frosty air thing you two have going on right now isn't all that better. We don't know what we're dealing with yet, so you need to keep your head in the game."

"My head is in the game, and I don't make hoochie eyes. That's not even a thing." I watched the woman head toward the front exit with the man. Their friend had already departed ahead of them. "Let's go."

We made sure not to rush so our exit looked casual, and I even made a little small talk with Marty as I grabbed my brown leather jacket off the rack by his post at the front, glad I kept a spare there since I'd left the one I'd worn last night at the apartment. Of course, all talk with Marty tended to be small talk. The guy didn't seem to hold enough information in his head for lengthy philosophical conversations.

By the time I shrugged into the jacket and we pushed outside into the frigid December night air, the pair we followed were already crossing the street toward one of the covered garages.

I have them, Daniel's voice filtered into my head. I sensed him near, somewhere inside the parking garage, but didn't see him. *Take the Mustang and I'll guide you.*

"I should have parked in the covered garage," Ginger muttered. "It's snowing."

"It's not even enough to count as snowfall," I said as we walked through the flurry of white fluff that fell to the pavement like a light powder only to blow away. "Just a dusting. It's not sticking."

Ginger fired up the heater as soon as we slid inside the Mustang and she'd turned over the engine. "What do you have in terms of weaponry, Miss Head-In-The-Game?"

I reached into the inner pocket of my jacket and pulled out the pure silver switchblade Rider made me carry everywhere I went while outside of The Midnight Rider.

"That's cute. Is that all?"

I shrugged. "A GED and a give 'em hell attitude?"

"You stole that line from Dean Winchester, and you're a college graduate." She waited until the wipers got rid of the thin layer of fluffy snow on the windshield and pulled out of the lot. "I have some goodies on hand, and Daniel should be packing something. We need to be careful. This thing could be an archdemon like Cupid. He was a bitch to kill."

"Yes. Very inconsiderate of him how hard he made it." I stared up into the sky as we hung a left, watching the impossibly large bird flying high in the moonlit winter sky. "I guess he's just giving directions directly to you now?"

I felt Ginger's eyes on me as I continued watching Daniel with an ache in my chest. "Get it together, Danni. Whatever is going on between you and Rider, and you and Daniel, get it together and get your head in the game so you don't lose it."

***

"Oh, for fuck's sake, screw or get off the pot."

I turned toward Ginger, nose scrunched.

"What? It's an expression."

"That's not the expression."

"Well, it fits."

"I'm not sure it does." I shook my head and returned my attention to the red Taurus we'd followed to a two-story bi-level brick house on Southern Parkway. The couple had pulled into the driveway ten minutes ago, but had yet to emerge. The shocks weren't rocking, but the windows were fogging up and the multitude of Christmas lights decorating the house cast enough light for us to see the man trying to swallow the woman's head. Or kissing. It was a little hard to distinguish, but the woman wasn't screaming, so we assumed she was all right with what was happening.

"The bar looked nice," I said, desperate to talk about anything other than what was happening in the Taurus, or think about Daniel flying high above us in circles, silent. "Did you wake early to decorate?"

"Nope," Ginger answered, and I picked up a miffed undertone. "It was all done before I woke up."

"Oh. Sorry, I know you wanted to do it."

"I got to decorate and bake with Angel." She grinned. "Honestly, I'm more annoyed I wasn't there to see Rider hanging garland and ornaments. Oh man, and the lights. I can just imagine the expletives flying out of his mouth if he got a string with a bad bulb."

"What? Rider? Rider did all the decorating in the bar?"

Ginger took her eyes off the parked car to look at me. "Yeah, that's what Jadyn said. She arrived early for her shift so she could get in some studying. Hank was hanging lights around the windows and doors outside, and Rider had just finished putting the tree up. She helped him out, but yeah, Rider did all that."

"We were supposed to do that. Why would Rider—" I remembered the sound of the door closing behind him that morning. He'd asked me if I wanted to love him and I hadn't said a damn thing, just let him wallow in heartache and walk away. It was morning. He had to have been tired as hell, but instead of sleeping in his own bed, he'd given it to me and left… to put up Christmas decorations when he could have gone anywhere else to sleep.

"I guess he thought it would be a nice surprise." Ginger shrugged. "Trying to do something nice for you."

After I'd pretty much slammed his heart in the door. I was the worst.

Are they going inside or what? Daniel asked through our mental link.

Eventually, Ginger responded through the link. *Then again, maybe their tongues got frozen together. It's getting nipply out here.*

Nippy, I corrected her.

Speak for your own body, she replied. *Mine's definitely getting nipply.*

I'm going to see if I can get in the house, scope it out before they go inside. For all we know, this thing waits on its prey from inside their own homes.

Then we need to go in with you, I said, ignoring my childish desire to not speak to him since he hadn't spoken directly to me. I bit the inside of my jaw as I sensed him sigh.

Come around to the back door. Without being seen.

"Like he actually had to tell us that," I muttered as I reached for the door handle. "What's he think we're going to do? Walk right past her car and tap on the window, ask for the key?"

We got out of the car to immediately be slapped in the face with icy cold wind and quietly closed the doors behind us. Ginger locked the Mustang using her key fob and glared at me when it beeped and I shot her a look.

"Hey, I'm not leaving my baby unlocked, and look at them. He's still sucking her face off. Are you sure he's not the predator that's supposed to kill her tonight?" She asked as we sprinted around the side of the house, keeping to the shadows. "Maybe she dies by suffocation."

"Well, she must like it because she seems an active participant," I answered. "I know whatever happens to her happens because of the thing that killed Angela LaRoche."

"What a sucky night for her. First she gets her face sucked off, then a chimney demon ganks her."

"No one's getting ganked but the demon," I reminded her as we hopped a fence to get into the backyard. I didn't see Daniel waiting there for us or flying circles above us in the sky, so I reached out, sensing for him. "Damn it. He already went inside all by himself like some kind of hero. Is he trying to get killed again?"

"Hey." Ginger shot me a concerned look. "That was scary as hell when he got bit by that nalkrim. I understand the fear, but you have to let that go now. You can't be worrying about him if that thing shows up here tonight. It could be another archdemon. We have to be ready for anything and stay very alert. That means you worry about you. Daniel will be all right."

I sucked in a breath and nodded just as Daniel opened the back door and gestured for us to enter. He didn't hold eye contact with me and I found myself gritting my teeth as Ginger and I entered the kitchen, annoyed I had been worried about him when he couldn't even look at me. Then I realized I was doing the same thing to Rider, and the annoyance turned into full red-hot anger mixed with a good-sized heap of self-loathing.

"No one's home," Daniel said, voice low. "So what are we doing, hiding inside her home like a bunch of stalkers, hoping this thing shows up?"

"It will show up," I growled. "Whether you believe in me or not."

Daniel gave me a dark look and stepped directly in

front of me, but looked over my shoulder just as we heard a keychain jingling outside the back door. *Hide.*

Ginger zipped away, using her vampiric speed, and Daniel evaporated into rainbow sparkles. I looked around, frantic. Thanks to my vampire abilities, I could see decently in the dark, but I had no idea the lay of the land. "Shit," I muttered as I picked up the unmistakable sound of a key sliding into the lock.

Up the stairs, came Ginger's voice in my head. *To your left.*

I started in that direction and felt a hand come over my mouth as I was lifted off my feet and whirled around just as the back door opened.

Daniel moved me across the room and pulled a door closed without making a whisper of sound, and suddenly we were alone together in a pantry that seemed way too small for the both of us.

Great.

CHAPTER TEN

"Merry smexy Christmas loves and lovers, this is Danielle Muething and you're listening to *Talk Smexy to Me* on WDNI, your official station for Christmas lovin'."

I groaned as the radio personality's obnoxious voice spilled out of the stereo the woman we'd followed home had turned on.

Quiet, Daniel admonished me through our mind-link.

I glared at him, not sure if his dragon eyes could pick it up in the dark space like my vampire eyes could, but refrained from saying what I wanted to say because he had a point. Light could still be seen under the door, and I heard the sound of the refrigerator opening.

Where are you? I asked Ginger through the mind-link, rather than focus on how damn close I was with Daniel in the small space or how screwed we were if the woman decided she needed any of the foodstuffs on the shelves around us. I made sure to include Daniel in the conversation, in case Ginger relayed anything we both needed to know.

I think her in-home office, she responded. *I figured this was a safer bet than the bathroom or bedroom, considering it's nighttime and things were getting steamy in the car.*

I think she's alone. I only sense her.

I guess Suckface McSuckerson struck out. I sensed Ginger's amusement through the link. *Maybe she had an asthma attack.*

Sounds like this stupid DJ is about to have an asthma attack.

"Having love troubles this Christmas?" Danielle Muething's ridiculously fake sexy voice asked over the sound of liquid pouring into glass. "No heat in your holiday? No well-hung stocking filled with surprises?"

I think I just threw up a little in my mouth.

Ginger's laughter came through the link, but Daniel's mood was harder to discern.

"Call your best gal pal, Danielle, and let me talk you through it. The heart specialist is in and ready to cure all that ails you."

Her voice is ailing me, I complained. *I wish she'd shut up and cure that.*

Try not to pay her any attention, Ginger suggested. *Focus on why we came here. I'm going to look around the office and see what I can find out about our victim.*

Potential victim. We're here to prevent her death, remember?

Right. Potential victim. Got it.

"You have the number and I have the time. Pick up the phone. Give me a call, and for those not ready to talk, here's Wham! with 'Last Christmas'."

I sighed in relief as the nauseating, fake sexy voice disappeared, replaced by the opening music of "Last Christmas", and soon George Michael's voice delivered a soothing balm to my ears.

I heard the woman's voice coming from the living room, muffled and low. "Is she on the phone?" I whispered.

"Yeah." Daniel's voice was gruff, his body tense. Clearly, he was as excited about being stuck in the pantry with me as I was with him.

"Relax. You won't have to have me delivered to Rider tonight. No need for a barf bag."

Through the darkness, I saw him frown. He shifted,

standing straighter, and opened his mouth.

Guys, her name is Joanna Jaskowick, Ginger said through the mind-link, cutting him off before he could respond to me.

Okay, I said. *Anything useful?*

Like?

I shrugged, although she couldn't see me. *I don't know. Anything suggesting why this demon thing would be coming for her tonight?*

Like a plate of flesh cookies left out for monsters or a stack of virgin sacrifices? Sorry, didn't see anything like that.

You're in her office, Daniel cut in. *Are there any books that look satanic in nature? Does she have any charms, bones, Ouija boards? Can you get into her computer, see what she's been browsing online?*

Ginger was silent for a moment. *The computer is password protected. All I know is she pays her utility bills and credit cards on time, I didn't see any purchases from Satanists-R-Us on any of the bills, she has a book on serial killers, but who isn't interested in serial killers?*

Daniel and I looked at each other and both just shook our heads.

She has a Jack Skellington wallpaper on her lock screen, a Kent State University coffee mug, a Pride ally button… She's cool. We definitely shouldn't let her get killed.

Obviously. It would defeat the purpose of us being here. I rolled my eyes. *So nothing strange?*

No. This looks like the office space of a normally functioning human. No weapons, organs in jars, or spell books. Lots of paranormal romance books. Man, these pen names on some of these are ridiculous. Crystal-Rain Love. Good grief, sounds like a hippie stripper.

"Well, that was all useful," Daniel muttered.

"That was Wham! with 'Last Christmas'," Danielle Muething's way-too-breathy voice blasted out of the stereo, "and I have a caller in need of Christmas lovin' on the line. Are you there, Joanna?"

"Yes," I heard the woman say a moment later as again, liquid sloshed into a glass, and a second later I heard her voice come from the radio.

Wait, did our girl call in to that Smexy show?

Daniel nodded.

Ginger, are you hearing this?

Huh? What? Sorry, I was browsing these vampire books. This chick in this series is so annoying. Whine, whine, whine, but I don't want to be a vampire, I want to eat cupcakes and be told how beautiful I am by my two hot boyfriends. Ugh. Who could stand somebody that needy?

Ginger! Think you could pay attention to me?

Of course, sweetcheeks. Anything for you. A brief moment of silence passed, and I imagined Ginger putting away whatever book she'd been skimming. *I'm paying attention now. I can hear her.*

"Merry smexy Christmas, Joanna. What's got you down this holiday season?"

Joanna released a long, drawn-out sigh. "I've been seeing this guy, a friend from work."

"A hot friend from work?"

"I think he's hot. Well, I think he's attractive, and he's nice. We've been dating a while."

"Oh, a nice guy," Danielle said, and her voice thankfully lost some of the breathy quality. "My smexy secrets detector is sensing the trouble here. Is he too nice, Joanna?"

"I just want to have sex!" Joanna blurted out. "It's been so long I can feel cobwebs forming over my vagina."

Ah, geez. Daniel grimaced. *There's something one should share with the whole world.*

"So, what's the problem?" Danielle asked. "You're dating. He's nice. Sometimes you just have to be direct with the really nice guys, bless their hearts."

"I've done everything except insert him myself like a tampon and that's only because he won't let me. He thinks he's…"

"Gay?" Danielle prompted.

"No, he's not gay," Joanna said. "He thinks he's ... He thinks he's too small and he won't let me see it."

This is so wrong, Daniel said, as Ginger's uproarious peal of laughter traveled through our link. I pulled my lips in, struggled not to laugh as I watched Daniel lower his head and shake it. *I shouldn't be hearing this. This is breaking bro code listening in about another dude's dick issues. It's just wrong.*

How can you break bro code with a guy you don't even know? I asked.

Bro code is universal, and I saw him. That's good enough.

"How old is this man?" Danielle asked.

"Thirty."

"Well, thirty years is an awfully long time to be that insecure," Danielle replied. "Surely he's had sex."

"Oh yes. He was married."

"Oh? Recent divorce?"

"Yes, it happened shortly before we started dating."

"Well, divorce can make people doubt themselves, wonder why their partner left them. Do you think maybe the divorce is the reason he feels so inadequate and he just needs some reassuring?"

"Oh yes, definitely, especially since his wife said she left on account of because he was too small."

Are we sure he's not the killer you sensed, Daniel asked, *because if he listens to this and hears her telling the world how small his junk is, he's definitely going to come right back here and murder her.*

"Joanna, I have to ask. If he's so small and unsatisfying, why do you want this so bad?"

"I don't know that he's small and unsatisfying. He won't let me near it," Joanna wailed. "His ex could have lied just to hurt him. I don't know what to do. I really like him, but how long do I have to wait for him to man up? I've blown out the batteries on three vibrators."

Maybe you should tell her where you got that one Gruff threw away, Daniel muttered through the mind-link as he rested his head back on the shelves behind him. *It could fly and everything.*

I glared at him even though he'd closed his eyes and wished Ginger was in the pantry with us so I could shoot her a look too as I sensed her laughing down the link.

***

The call seemed to last forever and only grew in tediousness as it drew on. By the end I was so thankful to hear anything other than a grown woman nearly crying over the lack of penis in her life, I didn't even care that the next Christmas song played was that annoying one by Alvin and the Chipmunks. And not even gonna lie, I was left with a real hankering to see the boyfriend's pecker, just for the sake of curiosity. I figured it had to be one heck of an odd one for the man to be so afraid to share it because if I'd learned anything about men in my lifetime, it was that they'd generally whip those things out at any given moment whether you wanted to see them or not.

From the sounds and smells I'd picked up on, Joanna had finished a bottle of wine, shed quite a few tears, and polished off a pint of ice cream, something minty, before finally turning off the non-stop Christmas songs and calls in to Danielle Muething which fortunately hadn't been as bad as Joanna's. She released an inelegant belch and headed up the stairs, where I suspected she intended to pass out in bed and sleep the deep sleep of the inebriated.

"Nothing's come for her yet and it's been hours," Daniel said, his head still leaned back against the shelves behind him, eyes closed, hands shoved into the front pockets of his jeans.

"And?"

"Angela LaRoche was killed in front of her fireplace while decorating her tree and dragged up the chimney. No evidence the demon entered the home any farther than that. Joanna Jaskowick just went to bed."

"So what, you think the thing knows when people are standing in front of their fireplaces?"

"No, but I think maybe you got the wrong night or maybe you got it right but the thing can sense us. Maybe it's been somewhere nearby watching. Us being here in the house might make it not show its face."

"If you don't believe in me—"

"I have always believed in you, Danni. You know that."

"I used to know that," I said and felt the knife in my back twist. That was the part of what he'd done that killed me. Daniel had never doubted me, never held me back.

"What the fuck is that supposed to mean?"

I glared at him and refused to let the tears burning my eyes fall. "I get it, okay? You think I'm a nice girl, but the sex-demon thing is too much. I'm trash. I'm disgusting. If you're so sickened by the fear of me jumping you that you have to run away and make sure Rider takes care of me so I don't go after you, then get out. Joanna's gone to bed. You can go out there or hell, you can leave altogether. Ginger and I will handle this. I know how being this close to me repulses—"

Daniel lurched forward, invaded my space. His big hand wrapped around the back of my neck as he pulled me flush against his body, the two of us so close we took in each other's breath. "Is that what you think? Being close to you repulses me?"

As he spoke, his head lowered. He was so close, his lips tickled my neck just under my ear. He kept his voice low and the angry sound of it came out as a rumble. It did weird flippy things to my stomach which was pressed against him so tight I felt the very hard length of him behind his zipper strain against the denim.

"I feel a lot of things when I'm close to you, Danni, but repulsion has never been one of them, and that's why I had to leave your apartment the way I did." He pulled back, looked into my eyes, his own burning hot. "You have no idea how hard it is to be so close to you, to want to protect you, especially when I can tell that hunger in you is rising."

As he spoke, his fingers started to massage my neck, sending tingles of awareness down my spine into every nerve ending in my body. He rested his forehead against mine and closed his eyes. His free hand gripped the shelf behind me, his entire body taut. "I'm trying to be a good guy, but it's been a real long time for me, Danni. It's so hard to walk away from you sometimes. It makes it even harder when I can see you so hungry, know that I could easily… but I can't do that. I won't do that. You love him and I won't ever take advantage of you like that." He groaned. "Push me away."

My mouth moved, but it took me a moment to actually form words and voice them. "What?"

"Push me away. Now."

We were so close I didn't have to reach to place my palms on his chest, but once they flattened over the hard pectoral muscles, an electrical charge ran down my arms straight into my core. He was so hard, so perfect. I had no will to push him away and couldn't think of a single good reason to.

Instead, my hands moved down, felt his muscles clench everywhere I touched as my fingertips continued their slow, languid journey lower.

"Danni?" He raised his head, opened his eyes, and I saw raw hunger there. Rider flashed before me on a wave of guilt, but then blood covered his body. Blood didn't cover Daniel's body. Daniel only wore a halo of golden light. "Danni."

I placed my finger over his lips, then wrapped my other hand around the hand he'd wrapped around the back of my neck. I watched him gulp as I slowly moved that hand down the front of my body and pressed against him, filling his palm with my breast.

"Is this really you?" he asked in a hoarse whisper as he squeezed the fabric-covered mound of flesh tenderly.

I nodded and dropped my jacket to the floor. Daniel chucked his, grabbed the hem of my sweater and freed me of it before unclasping my bra. The moment my breasts sprang free, he took one in his mouth. I arched my back, savored the electric tingle he sent through me.

"I've wanted this for so long," he growled as he moved to the next breast, giving it his undivided attention as I grabbed a handful of rainbow-colored hair and held him tight against me.

Needing more and knowing time was short, I pulled him up, freed him of his shirt, and took a moment just to marvel at the sculpted perfection of him before I unsnapped his jeans and pushed him against the back wall. I licked and kissed a trail down his chest until I worked my way back down to the large bulge straining behind his zipper. I dropped to my knees, lowered the zipper, and took him in my—

"Damn it, Danni. You have to push me away now."

What the—I was still standing fully clothed against Daniel, one of his hands wrapped firmly around the back of my neck as the other gripped a shelf behind my shoulder so hard it creaked. His forehead rested against mine.

"Damn it, I tried." He raised his head, our eyes locked, and his lips hovered just over mine.

The door opened and Ginger reached in, grabbed Daniel by the neck of his T-shirt, and yanked him out. She glanced down at the bulge in his jeans and growled. "You're damned lucky you kept that locked up because if I opened that door and saw anything hanging out, I would have cut it off and slapped you with it, you dumb fuck. And as for you—"

Ginger froze as she turned to see me stumble out of the pantry. I didn't know what I looked like, but I could imagine, given I'd just had a total out-of-body experience, and struggled to wrap my mind around it. It was so real I couldn't even figure out at what point the alternate reality

I'd just lived had started.

"Hey." Ginger grabbed my arm and instead of recoiling from the female touch, I leaned into her. At that moment, I needed the frigid cold of another woman's touch. The reaction wasn't lost on her, judging by the way she looked between us and swallowed before blowing out a breath, calming herself down. She'd been snarling at us in a harsh whisper, but when she spoke again, the harsh quality was gone. "I don't know what the hell happened in there just now, but I know it can't happen again. Both of you know that if Rider had been the one to open that door, there'd be a dead man in this kitchen right now. You have to stop this. Just fucking st—"

Something thumped directly above us, drawing our attention to the ceiling. The house was bi-level, so the kitchen and living room area were on the first floor, which was one-story. The bedroom and office area were upstairs on the second level. If anything was on the roof over Joanna Jaskowick's bedroom, we couldn't hear it, but we knew something was definitely on the rooftop over us and we were the ones on the side of the house that came equipped with a fireplace.

"I'm guessing if that was the boyfriend dropping by to chew her out for telling the WDNI audience about his puny pecker, he'd use the door," Ginger whispered.

Big footsteps that sounded like they belonged to something the size of a Clydesdale clomped toward the chimney and I knew whatever was about to come down it wouldn't come down it with a sack of gifts for good little boys and girls unless good little boys and girls wanted to be gutted and dragged off to hell knew where.

"Let's keep this fight out of the house," Daniel said, then disappeared into rainbow sparkles that quickly flew across the room into the fireplace and up the chimney.

"Fuck!" Ginger and I said at the same time and nearly bowled each other over as we ran for the door and struggled to unlock it while getting in each other's way.

"Wait! You're supposed to save the woman," Ginger reminded me.

"Duh, that's why we're here."

"Okay, but you're running away from where she is and whatever's up there could get past Daniel and come down that chimney, then what?"

"Shit." I ran over to the fireplace and reached inside my jacket for my knife. Ginger grabbed the fire iron and crouched by the hearth. "What are you doing?"

"I figure if it comes down the chimney, having this shoved up its ass will slow it down, assuming it has an ass. Is that blade salt-fired?"

"Yeah." I still thought it completely weird that something like salt could hurt ghosts and demons, but wasn't about to complain. Besides, I was too worried about Daniel. "I'll stay here. Go help Daniel."

"No way, sweetcheeks. We're your bodyguards, remember?" She nodded toward the front window where we could see bright orange flashes of light in the sky right over us. "That's dragon fire making that light. He's probably roasting that fucker to a crisp as we speak. He's got this."

No. He didn't have it because, according to my gut, I had to kill whatever was hunting. Yes, I had to protect Joanna Jaskowick, but I had to do it by killing the demon or monster or whatever it was, not Daniel, and if he wasn't the one destined to kill it, then … "Fuck."

I ran for the door and, without Ginger in my way, quickly got it unlocked and dashed through. I looked up and my jaw dropped open at the scene.

A tall bearded man in long robes of some sort of animal fur stood shielded behind a wall of massive winged creatures. His head was thrown back, his mouth wide open, and the creatures flew out of him to attack Daniel, who'd shifted into dragon form and hovered in the sky, flapping his wings as he released a steady stream of fire at the army of flying creatures.

I heard tires squeal behind me and a car door slam, but didn't turn from the sight above me. The flying creatures kept erupting from the tall man-thing's mouth and I was sure Daniel couldn't breathe fire forever.

Out of the corner of my eye, I saw Ginger exit the house after me just as the man-thing turned his head. The winged creatures coming from inside his giant face hole kept flying out to attack Daniel, but he looked at me, then looked past me as I heard Ginger gasp.

A gunshot cracked behind me and suddenly the man-thing himself exploded into what looked like a storm of giant bats that twisted into a cyclone shape and zoomed off into the night. Daniel quickly dove in my direction, disappeared in a shower of rainbow sparkles and reappeared in his human form at my side just as I'd finished turning to see what I was sure had to be an illusion.

Six feet, one inch of bow legged perfection stood behind me. He had light brown hair cut short with a side part fade, bow-shaped lips set into a triangular face with a strong jaw covered in stubble, and wore jeans, a flannel shirt over a black T-shirt and a well-worn brown leather jacket, and the only thing that looked more dangerous than the shotgun in his hands was the set of hazel eyes staring back at me.

"I have to be hallucinating because there is no way that's…"

"Dean Winchester," Ginger finished for me.

I nodded. There was no freaking way the man was Dean Winchester… except he looked just like him.

CHAPTER ELEVEN

Once the shock of seeing Dean Winchester, or his twin, rolled over me, I was hit with another. Some sort of inner alarm had gone off inside me. I'd thought the surge of fear had come from the scene above me, but with that monster gone, I realized the alarm came from the Dean Winchester doppelgänger. The man was dangerous, far more of a threat than whatever the hell I'd just seen shooting flying creatures out of its face hole.

Apparently, the same alarm triggered inside Ginger because she stood in front of me, gun in hands, aimed, and ready to fire. "If you're who I think you are, I'll warn you one time: You're going to have to go through Rider Knight and his entire nest to get to her."

Daniel stepped forward, also aiming a gun at the man while I stood frozen in place. That inner alarm screamed danger, but as I stared into the man's eyes, it grew quieter. Those hazel orbs shifted over us, and slowly, he lowered the shotgun. "You're all Knight's people?"

"That's right," Ginger said, her gun still trained on the man. "Are you who I think you are?"

"Who do you think he is?" I asked. "Because all I see is Dean Winchester, and I don't know when the hell I tripped into a portal to another dimension."

The man rolled his eyes. "For fuck's sake, not another one. The name's Jake Porter. I'm not that pretty-boy actor, not a TV character, and I won't draw blood as long as everyone stays cool."

"Jake Porter, the slayer?" I remembered Christian laughing at Rider's hesitancy to tell me anything about the man and his explanation that the slayer bore an uncanny resemblance to Jensen Ackles. Clearly, Christian hadn't been lying.

He nodded, a quick jerk of the head. When his gaze landed on me again, he frowned and, for a moment, it almost felt as if he were staring through me, dissecting me with his eyes. "And you must be Danni Keller."

Oh great. I meet the spitting image of the man I've lusted after for fifteen seasons, and he's heard the rumor that slicing balls is my favorite pastime. I groaned and shot a dark look at Ginger. "Really? The legend of Danni the Teste Slayer has got to stop."

"The legend of who?" Jake Porter's eyes reflected enough surprise, I realized he hadn't, in fact, learned of my name the way most people seemed to have learned of it before meeting me. Before I could utter out a response, his gaze shifted past my shoulder and he muttered a curse.

"What's going on out—" Joanna Jaskowick stumbled into the open doorway, in the process of tying the belt on her robe, and froze. Her mouth dropped open as she stared past me. A few stunned blinks later, it curled into a come-hither smile and if her eyelashes batted any faster, they'd fly off her face.

"Ugh, she thinks she's dreaming about Dean Winchester," Jake muttered. "It happens sometimes. Annoying as fuck, but sometimes it can actually be kind of helpful."

I noticed lights coming on in windows in the surrounding houses. "I think a lot more people than her heard the noise."

"No doubt," Jake said, moving past me. "But she's the one with the full view of the slayer, vampire, dragon, and hybrid standing in her backyard. Surely someone's called in the gunshot. Get out of here. I'll use the dream thing to get her to go back to sleep and think nothing happened for real, then meet up with you at The Midnight Rider."

Ginger kept her gun trained on the slayer until he reached Joanna, then grabbed my arm and pulled me along as the three of us cut around the side of the house to where she'd left her Mustang parked along the street across from the front of the house. I caught sight of the big black car Jake Porter had left idling in the alley that ran behind Joanna Jaskowick's house. It wasn't an Impala, but the older model Malibu was close enough. "He looks just like…"

"He's a slayer," Ginger reminded me without an ounce of gentleness. "He's genetically designed to kill us and don't you ever forget it, no matter what he looks like."

Daniel didn't say anything, but he didn't have to. His eyes spoke volumes as we got into the car and he shot a glare in the direction we'd left Jake Porter. The dragon did not like the slayer at all.

"He knew what we all were," I said.

"Again, he's a slayer." Ginger started the car and peeled out. "He knew what we were before he ever laid eyes on us, and he knows how to kill us. He was born able to track and destroy us all."

***

Rider stood in the center of the room when we entered The Midnight Rider, looking very out of place in the festively decorated room full of bright color and merry ambience. His hands were shoved deep in his pockets, his back ramrod straight, and I'd never seen his jaw set harder. A faint golden glow shone around the dark blue of his eyes as his dark gaze rolled over me.

I caught a flicker of the nightmare image, but as soon as I saw the blood cover him, the image changed to what I'd been about to do with Daniel in that pantry, or what I thought I'd been about to do before I'd snapped back to reality. I threw up a mental wall to ensure Rider never saw what had or hadn't almost happened, and forced the image out of my mind before it could make me vomit from the wave of guilt that crashed into me like a tidal wave.

I forced myself to focus elsewhere as we made our way to Rider. Greg, the mustached vampire, still tended bar, but Tony was on the other side, sitting at one corner, every inch of him primed for a fight. Lana, dressed all in black, was on security duty along with Juan, the wolf shifter. Christian sat at the bar, dressed in a cream sweater and faded jeans. The white stripe in his hair stood out in stark contrast to the rest of his short, nearly black locks, as did his demeanor. Everyone in the bar was tense, even the humans who had no idea what was going on, but must have sensed the unease on some level.

Everyone except Christian. He offered me a small smile and sipped the soft drink in his hand before he glanced toward Jadyn and winked. The guardian stood behind the bar, watching us enter just like every other person in the room.

We reached Rider, and he ran the back of his hand down the side of my face, gentle but territorial at the same time. "Are you all right?"

I nodded, aware why everyone was so on edge as it had been explained to me on the drive over, and Rider had been warned in advance of our uninvited guest, but still a little caught off guard by it. Yes, being in the slayer's presence had triggered an inner alarm, but he'd shot the weird-ass creepy entity on the roof, not us. And Christian seemed to be friends with the man, which jelled with what I felt in my gut. He could be trusted, and despite what Ginger thought, I wasn't basing my thought off of how hot he was.

Rider's gaze shifted over to the front of the room and I turned, noting the already tense atmosphere went up several notches as I did. A moment later, Jake Porter appeared in the doorway. He shot a vaguely curious look at Marty, the oversized troll posted on door duty, before scanning the room.

With a slightly amused sparkle in his eyes, he covered the distance between Christian and himself, and pulled the former angel-slash-vampire into a hug, which caused a mix of confused looks and massive ease of tension.

"I heard about the new skunk 'do,'" Jake laughed as the brotherly pair stepped apart. "Only you could pull that look off, my brother."

Christian laughed and gestured for Jadyn to join them. "How's the family doing? Well, I pray."

"We're all good," Jake answered as Jadyn stepped around the bar and approached him. "Hey, sweetheart. Taking good care of my boy?"

"We're taking care of each other," she answered as she stepped into the slayer's arms.

With most of the heavy tension no longer hanging over the room like a thick fog, I noticed the human patrons went back to what they were doing. A few women pointed toward Jake and whispered, most likely picking up on the strong resemblance to Dean Winchester, or just noting how incredibly attractive the man was in his own right. The paranormals, however, still hadn't completely let their guards down, which didn't seem to go unnoticed by Jake.

His gaze did a quick scan of the room, and the slayer shook his head before he approached Rider with a crooked, and incredibly charming, nearly wicked grin. "Ah, GQ McFang, your people never fail to make a man feel welcome. You can draw back the mega vamp power. I'm not here to slay your people."

"Why are you here?" I felt the heavy weight of Rider's power subside, but his eyes still shone with a hint of it. He clearly didn't have the same gut instinct about Jake Porter that I had.

"I thought that would be fairly obvious considering I showed up just in time to shoot a krackling before it overpowered your pet dragon."

"I'm nobody's pet," Daniel growled, disdain dripping from his voice and etched into every plane of his face. "And I had the demon handled."

"Sure you did, Rainbow Brite, because a stream of fire you could only maintain for a finite amount of time against an infinite stream of kracklings was a great idea. And it wasn't a demon. It was a krackling."

Daniel stepped toward Jake with a growl. I raised my arm and blocked him, sure he was about to go for the slayer's throat. "What's a krackling?"

Jake let loose a heavy sigh and swung his hands my way as if to say *See?* "You obviously need my help here."

"They'd probably be more willing to take it if you weren't acting like such a dick," Lana said. She stopped next to Jake and folded her arms under her chest.

Jake made a show of placing his hand over his heart as if he were in pain. "Ah, I'm wounded. After all we've been through, Lana? I thought we were such good partners."

"Refer to my previous dick statement."

Jake smiled. "Hey, my job is stressful. I have to get in my shits and giggles wherever I can, and it's not like stepping into this bar doesn't feel an awful lot like stepping into a den of vipers." He winced. "My bad. I actually didn't mean any offense that time."

"None taken. I know what I am, and I know what you are." The curvy anaconda-shifter relaxed the set of her shoulders. "He fought well with me, Rider. He never tried to hurt me."

"Yes, but he nearly went to battle with me," Rider said. "If not for Jadyn, events would have played out very differently."

"Put a slayer on a battlefield full of paranormals and eventually you all start blurring together," Jake said, "but unless you're planning on starting shit, there's no danger in having a conversation. I have no problem with Jadyn being at my side if you're more comfortable having her near in case the beast in me decides to get a little murdery."

Rider shifted his gaze past Jake's shoulder to where Christian sat. The minister nodded his head, giving his approval, before he gestured for his wife to join us.

"Let's take this into my office," Rider suggested. "You're drawing too much attention from the human customers."

"No wonder," Ginger said. "He really does look just like Dean Winchester."

"Yeah, maybe if you ordered Dean Winchester off of Wish," Daniel muttered.

Jake grinned. "Aw, I'll let that slide, dragon-breath. I know you're upset you just got called into a meeting after you just had your hair done up all pretty for the JoJo Siwa concert."

"I'm not sure who JoJo Siwa is," Daniel replied, but the growl in his voice suggested he did and he was pissed. "I'm a man. I'm sure you're a big fan though, got all the lyrics and dance moves down. You can catch me up at your next slumber party."

"Wow, you just met me and already trying to get into bed with me?" The comment brought out another growl from Daniel and the shifter lunged forward, this time to be blocked by me, Ginger, and Rider, which brought out a bark of laughter from Jake. "I like him. This job is going to be a lot more fun than I thought it would be."

"I told you to stand down," Rider growled, and I realized he'd been giving Daniel instruction through the mind-link without including me in the conversation. Once Daniel got himself under control, Rider pinned Jake with a glare that could probably burn the flesh off a lesser man. "Are you done fucking around yet?"

Jake made a show of bowing politely and gestured toward the back door. "After you, Count Gucci."

"The next time you think about uttering one of your little nicknames, you might want to consider the fact that while you have Jadyn to hold back your beast, there is no one holding mine back, and I do not find you amusing."

Instead of a witty response, Jake held his hands up in surrender and smiled broadly, enjoying himself entirely too much for Rider's comfort. I got the fact that Jake Porter was a slayer, someone whose sole purpose was to kill any and all paranormal beings he crossed paths with, but I also got the sense that wasn't the only reason for Rider's clear hatred of the man. Slayer or not, I'd heard enough about what happened while I was in West Virginia to know Jake Porter actually was one of the good guys, as long as he had someone nearby to keep him under control.

Figuring out that Rider wasn't going to go first, wouldn't dare take his eyes off the man, Jadyn guided the slayer toward the back door.

Rider walked directly after them, with me tucked into his side. I felt a range of volatile emotions come from him and Daniel as the dragon-shifter and Ginger fell into step behind us. By the time we reached the back door and pushed through, the bar went back to business as usual and someone requested a Motown Christmas song on the jukebox.

"Left," Rider barked, although Jadyn knew the way to the office. She didn't point that out though. You didn't have to be a fanged member of Rider's nest to feel how very sour his mood was with the slayer in his presence.

"There." Rider pointed toward the set of chairs in front of his desk and waited for the amused slayer to drop into one before he rounded the desk, bringing me with him. He positioned me behind his chair before settling into it, his posture anything but relaxed.

Kutya wasn't in the office, but the sight of his plush doggy bed reminded me of the earlier incident with him. I caught Jadyn looking at the bed before she frowned in my direction and quickly settled into the chair next to Jake.

Ginger closed the office door and took a seat on the couch set against the wall next to it while Daniel crossed over to the bookshelves running the length of the side wall and leaned back against them. Like Rider, there was nothing casual in his stance. His arms folded over his chest, muscles bulging, and heat seemed to roll off of him.

"Talk," Rider ordered.

The corner of Jake Porter's mouth lifted as he stared back at Rider, his eyes showing a hint of amusement and a whole lot of dare. He glanced over at Daniel for a moment before turning that hazel gaze on me. Our eyes connected and my belly did a flip. I wasn't sure if it was a gut thing or not, but I got the overwhelming sense Jake Porter could see me in a way no one else could. I wished I'd put on a little more makeup than lip gloss.

"The monster on top of that house was a krackling. It's the monster a lot of the Krampus myths originated from. Very ancient. Very strong, and very, very rare." Even though Rider had been the one to demand he talk, Jake's eyes never left mine. It was as if no one else in the room mattered to him, and I could sense Rider's ire growing with every word that tumbled out of Jake's mouth while his gaze stayed locked on mine. "The last known sighting of a krackling was over a century ago. They hibernate for long periods of time, awake when called, and then feast on whatever prey they are led to. They're like minions, killing for the one who controls them."

"Minions for who?" Rider asked.

"That's the million dollar question," Jake said. "Anyone with a deep enough knowledge of dark lore could discover kracklings and how to bind one. Hell, an idiot with the right book could do it."

"So you're saying someone is siccing that thing on specific people?" I said.

Jake nodded. "The krackling feasts often, but it doesn't go after just anyone. It attacks who it is sent to kill… and anyone who gets in its way, as you discovered tonight."

"What were those things flying out of its mouth?"

"Also called kracklings," Jake answered.

"I thought those were pig intestines," Ginger said.

"That's chitterlings," Rider said, his tone harsher than I imagined he'd intended, but Ginger didn't seem to take the tone personally. Anyone in the room could tell both Rider and Daniel were using all their willpower not to attack the slayer right then and there.

"They kind of looked like big, chubby bats," I said to move the conversation along, hopefully get to a point soon where everyone could calm down, wave a white flag, and play nice. And okay, I liked talking to the man who looked like Dean Winchester. He even sounded like Dean Winchester, his voice deep, gravelly, and sexy as sin.

"They're not that far from it, except they're an extension of the krackling. It can release a shitload of them and those blood-thirsty fuckers are mean as hell. They'll suck a human dry."

Angela LaRoche's blood-sprayed living room came to mind. "The first woman we came across who was killed by that thing had blood all over her walls. Her body was gone, from the looks of it, dragged up the chimney. We thought something big gutted her forcefully enough to make her blood burst out of her body before yanking her up there. Was that the krackling or its ... oh this is confusing. The winged things have to have a different name."

Jake grinned. "As you saw when I shot the krackling, it can turn into a swarm of those things. That's how it flies. It likes chimneys, but doesn't need to use them. It'll enter a house through a window or door if necessary."

"It flew away after you shot it so you didn't actually do any real damage to it," Daniel said, a little smug.

"My shot stopped the endless stream of freaky winged mini-its from spewing out before you ran out of fire and they ate your face off or worse, attacked your partners." He returned his attention to me. "I noticed you only had a knife."

"I thought we were going after a demon. I've done well against demons with just a few blades."

He grinned. "Not easy going up against demons with just blades, so I'm impressed, but I still suggest carrying a gun. Some of them are quicker than even you."

"Bullets will kill this thing?" Rider quickly snatched back control of the conversation. I didn't need to see his face to know he didn't like the slayer and I talking to each other.

Jake shifted in the chair, getting comfortable. "A krackling can only be killed when it is whole. You can stab it or shoot it a billion times while it's releasing winged kracklings and you'll do nothing but waste ammo and wear yourself out, and if you're going to shoot or stab it, you should do so with iron. Unlike shifters or your basic demons, silver doesn't do much. UV doesn't affect it even though it prefers to hunt at night."

"Wait. You're saying once it starts spewing those bat-things out of its face, it can't be killed?" My stomach churned. This was going to be a lot harder than I thought.

"No, it can be killed after that, but it'll be damned hard. A krackling is considered whole when it is completely in either form, so if you shoot it in the heart while it is in the form that looks like a man, you'll kill it. If you manage to destroy *all* the winged kracklings when it completely breaks up into those, you'll kill it, but it generally won't do that unless it's flying away. It knows it can't be killed if it's in two separate forms, so it tends to stay that way while under attack."

"This is going to be difficult." I bit my lip, feeling a lot less sure of myself than I had when I'd followed Joanna Jaskowick out of the bar earlier, and to think I hadn't even been armed with the right weaponry.

"You have a slayer with you, sweetheart. This is what I was designed for."

Rider growled low in his throat, no doubt because of the sweetheart reference, and another blast of heat rolled off of Daniel. I started to worry the shifter would go full dragon right there in the office.

"Why does it smell like cookies?" I asked, moving the topic back to the monster itself before Daniel or Rider could let their hostility grow to the boiling point.

"I have no idea the reason for that, but I assume it's part of why the Krampus myth came from it. This thing smells like the spices used in cookies and other baked goods generally made this time of year and it can only be called to hunt in winter, lending to the whole Christmas tie-in. It's a little backward in its hibernation that way, but given it hibernates for decades, not just seasons…" He shrugged.

"Last I knew, you were still operating out of Maryland," Rider said. "We've come across one death by this monster so far, here in Louisville, and Danni followed another woman out tonight who was prey. How did you know it was here?"

"It's killed in Indiana. I came across a police report and put two and two together." Jake's gaze had bore into me when Rider mentioned I'd followed a woman and again I felt like he was looking at more than just what could be seen on the outside. "I wondered how you knew where to be. You followed that woman home?"

I nodded.

"Coincidence? You were following her for some other reason?"

"No."

"Danni followed her gut," Rider said. "If you learned of a krackling kill in Indiana, what led you here to Louisville? I know it wasn't a report on the woman Danni found because my man on the inside wouldn't have let enough details into the report for you to link it to that kill. How did you know where to be tonight?"

"I'm a slayer. You're aware I can sense monsters." He looked at me again. "I can't sense who their prey is going to be, though, which would come in very handy. Your girl is going to be my partner on this."

I may have gotten flutterings where I had no business getting flutterings, but they shriveled up as Rider's power filled the room and another blast of heat came off Daniel.

"You are not to be anywhere near Danni."

"Well, that's going to make my job here very complicated."

"Like you said, you're a slayer. I'm sure you'll figure out a way to hunt this krackling down and kill it without her help."

"Yeah, except I wasn't actually sent here for the krackling." He pointed at me. "I was sent here for her."

CHAPTER TWELVE

"To help her," Jake quickly clarified as Rider came out of his seat, and I had to hand it to the slayer. He was brave, or just stupid. He had to be one of the two to sit there grinning as Rider glared at him, fangs bared. "We've worked together before, vampire. Seta is one of your most trusted friends and she trusts me, as does Christian. I don't recall us having this much friction the last time I was here, even after my moment of instability on the battlefield. What are you afraid of?"

"I don't fear you, slayer, no matter your reputation."

Jake glanced at me, at Daniel, whose jaw was clenched tight enough to chip a tooth, then returned his gaze to where Rider still stood with his hands fisted, fangs dropped, and power simmering. Jake leaned back casually, fighting a bigger grin. "You didn't have any problem at all sending your snake-shifter through a portal with me, completely out of your view. I do remember a very direct warning from you, however, before that. *Stay away from Danni Keller*, or something along those lines."

"That warning still goes."

"I remember now. You said that to me after Jadyn said…" He looked at me. "Let me guess; you're a Dean

Winchester fan?"

I felt heat rush to my face and quickly averted my gaze. Rider growled and this time, I wasn't sure if the growl was because of Jake or because of me.

Jake raised his hand and wiggled his fingers, showing off the band on his ring finger. "Yes, I hunt and kill monsters, drive a big black car, and from what I hear, bear a strong resemblance to some Hollywood jackass, but I am not Dean Winchester. I'm Jake Porter, a very happily married man with no interest in your woman whatsoever."

"Hey!" I said the same moment Rider said "I'm not worried about—" only to stop mid-sentence and deliver a chilling look my way.

I rolled my eyes and fought the urge to smack him. "Oh, what? That was just plain insulting."

"No offense, sweetheart." Jake raised his hands and gave his best innocent look when Rider's glare turned back to him and the vampire growled. "I call lots of women sweetheart. It doesn't mean I want to get to know them a whole lot more intimately. Calm your fangs, vampire. You have a very pretty girlfriend."

Dean Winchester's doppelgänger called me pretty! I used every ounce of control in my body to fight the smile and happy dance threatening to break free, knowing if I couldn't hold my reaction in, I'd set off World War III right there.

"I'm sure she's an even lovelier person, but that's not what I'm here for."

"Get the fuck over yourself, Porter." Rider drew his power and fangs back in, but remained standing. "Lana is a trained Imortian warrior. I know you can tell Danni's new. No sire in their right mind would let a slayer near a fledgling so young."

I swallowed past the lump that formed in my throat and looked down at my feet rather than look at anyone else in the room after Rider had belittled our relationship to something as diminutive as just a sire-fledgling relationship for all to hear.

Sweetcheeks… Ginger said through our mental link, and I shook my head, stopping her from going any further. The sympathy in her mind-voice was hard enough to take. I couldn't stand to be consoled by her at the moment. It would feel like pity, and the only thing that felt worse than being demoted to just a fledgling newbie in front of Jake Porter, Jadyn, and… oh man, Daniel, the dragon I'd rather die than look a fool in front of, was pity.

"As I said, I was sent to help her."

"By who? And why?"

"You're asking questions I can't answer in mixed company."

Rider's jaw clenched. "Everyone out. Except for him."

Rider grabbed my hand as I moved to leave. I quickly snatched it back and kept walking. Ginger waited for me at the door and Daniel fell into step behind us, his heat cloaking me. If not for the awkwardness of our previous interaction, I would have welcomed it since Rider's words had left me cold.

"Do you want me to stay?" Jadyn asked.

"You may go too. The slayer knows to behave, and if he doesn't, I can handle him."

"I'm glad we were excused," Ginger said after we filed out of the office and started down the hall. "That whole office is probably about to smell like piss from all the marking of territory about to happen. You know he said what he said because even vampires are stupid about that macho bullshit and he couldn't let the hot slayer dude who looks just like your biggest celebrity crush know he was intimidated by him, right?"

"It's fine," I said and kept walking, wanting to get as far away from the office as possible.

"Want to go down to the armory and see what we have by way of iron?" Ginger suggested.

"Do you really think Rider's going to let us keep hunting the krackling now that there's an actual slayer in town to do it?"

Ginger stepped in front of me as we reached the two doors and had to decide whether to go out into the bar or take the door on the left and head toward the armory on the first sublevel. She planted her feet and stood, hands on hips, forcing me to face off with her. "First of all, you said that you had to hunt the monster and kill it. Did that strong gut feeling just disappear all of a sudden?"

I shook my head, the feeling still there. "No. I still feel it."

"Exactly. Also, that slayer said he wants you to be his partner, so he doesn't seem all that likely to go out hunting it on his own. He has super slayer senses and all, but you can see who the prey is. I don't think he's leaving this building without you."

Heat rolled over me and I turned to see Daniel looking very pissed off about the whole idea. I started to ask why he was reacting so strongly to the man given Jake Porter hadn't attempted to harm any of us, but the incident in the pantry flashed front and center and I couldn't bring myself to say anything or interact at all as my face burned from the memory.

"So?" Ginger folded her arms.

I sighed and chose the door on the left. We stepped through as Hank and Kutya stepped out of the garage. I turned to ask Jadyn if she'd had a moment to check in with Kutya and see what had caused the pup's strange reaction earlier in the evening, but she'd left us to return to the bar. Judging by the dog's excited spinning and yapping, whatever bothered him earlier didn't seem an issue at the moment.

Hank's body was tense, and he seemed to be sensing for something. "The slayer is still here."

"Yeah, he's in the office with Rider," I said, and bent to give Kutya a belly rub. "Think you can watch Kutya a while longer, keep him occupied elsewhere in case things get tense? They're not at each other's throats yet, but they're not exactly chummy."

"Sure." Hank tugged on the leash. He was one of the few shifters who would walk Kutya on a leash. The werewolves tended to get snarly about putting the leash on the dog, and they absolutely would not bag the pup's poop. "We'll be playing in the alley."

"I'm not sure what Hank intends to play with Kutya," Ginger said after the shifter disappeared back into the garage with him, "but if he runs, he's probably going to make a hell of a lot of potholes."

I pictured Hank running and could see what she meant. The man was built similar to Juggernaut. I imagined all wererhinos were.

I placed my hand over the panel next to the door leading to the stairwell, waited for my palm to be scanned, and pushed through. The armory was located on the first sublevel, behind the area where the tech team did their thing. I hadn't actually been in the armory before, but knew its location because I'd seen Daniel and other members of Rider's security staff go in and out of the room, stocking up on weaponry. Any weapons I'd ever used had been picked out for me.

I didn't know any of the tech team members by name, had never actually spoken to any directly, but there was always a team of them working around the clock. From the images I saw on the giant plasma screen, they were trying to track Pacitti down through his financials.

"How is one human detective so hard to find?" I asked as we passed behind the tech team to get to the armory.

"Well, he had all the characteristics of a rat," Ginger replied, "and those fuckers are really good at burrowing. Don't worry, we'll find that bastard or he'll find us when he decides how he wants to use his leverage. Either way, we'll kill him eventually."

Daniel had stepped around us to place his hand over the scanner and enter the armory first. Ginger and I shared a look, noting his silence, and I was sure she'd felt the blasts of heat coming off him as well as I had. She, however, didn't have the memory of being wrapped up in that heat in the pantry, dangerously close to crossing a line no good girlfriend would ever cross. I was the unlucky one with that weighing on my conscience.

"Let's see what we have of the iron variety." Ginger gestured for me to enter the room before her.

My first thought as I stepped inside was *holy cow*. I'd thought the armory was a small room with maybe a table or a few racks of supplies, but the room was much bigger than it appeared from beyond the outside door. Rows of tables showcased a variety of blades ranging from pocket knives to longer swords. An entire back wall was filled with guns and crossbows. Rows of shelves held various types of ammo, throwing stars, whips, vials, and what looked like potions, even bombs.

"Where do we even begin?"

"Let's check the ammo," Ginger suggested. "Daniel's already checking out the blades. The ammo is alphabetical, so if we have any iron bullets, they'll be back here."

I followed her to a row of shelves stacked high with small boxes, but once we reached them, I realized she'd only wanted to get me alone. "Girlfriend, you need to talk to your dragon. If I could feel that heat coming off of him, I know Rider could too. Maybe we can spin it to seem like being in the presence of a slayer drew that much volatility out of him, but you and I both know that rage came from *you* being in the slayer's presence."

"Yes, but I don't know why. Jake never tried to hurt me. He didn't try to harm any of us."

Ginger rolled her eyes. "Danni, you are not that thick in the head. That man was so jealous his blood was boiling, just like Rider's was. I didn't know which one of them was going to go for the slayer first and the man did nothing except sit there and look like your dream guy."

"What? No, that can't be what's wrong with him." I glanced over to where the blades were kept, not able to see them or Daniel through the rows of shelves stacked with weapons, but I sensed him. His energy almost seemed too big for the space. "I'll agree Rider was definitely behaving like a jealous jackass. I even expected it after all the jokes I've made about how hot Dean Winchester is, and Christian told me Rider was jealous because the slayer looks like Dean, but Daniel? Why would Daniel be jealous enough of him to react like that? He doesn't have that strong of a reaction around Rider, and he would actually have a reason to be jealous of Rider if he were actually going to be jealous."

"Rider and you were a thing when he met you," Ginger pointed out. "As long as he's known you, you've been Rider's property, out of his reach… or supposed to be, anyway." She gave me a look that brought the pantry incident front and center in my brain, along with a massive wave of guilt. "This guy just popped up on us, your biggest fantasy in the flesh, and in the dragon's head, he's been standing in line too long to let some other asshole cut in and take his place."

"It's not like that. Rider and I are together, and Daniel knows that. He's not waiting in line for me."

"Then what exactly did I intrude on in that pantry tonight?" Ginger raised a knowing eyebrow, grabbed boxes of ammo, and turned away. "I got ammo that'll work with our guns, Daniel. Solid iron."

I followed Ginger back to the tables of assorted blades, where Daniel stood leaning back against a shelving unit. He held a dagger out to me, handle first. "See how this feels."

"I'll go check out the guns, see if there are any new toys that catch my eye." Ginger looked pointedly between the two of us before walking to the guns in the back of the armory, giving us a bit of privacy.

I took the dagger and tested its weight. The blade was six inches in length and extremely sharp at the tip, double-edged. Judging by the weight alone, it was made of pure iron. The handle was tubular in shape and fit my hand perfectly. "It feels all right."

"Good. Stabbing with it will be more effective than slicing, but it'll work. Ginger and I will have guns. We should get you trained to shoot sometime soon." Daniel looked over at where Ginger took her sweet time perusing the gun collection and took a deep breath. "Look, about what happened back at that house tonight…"

"Nothing happened."

"Danni."

"Nothing happened." In my mind, I saw myself drop to my knees in front of Daniel, watched myself lower his zipper and free him from his jeans, then snap right back to where we stood close together, close enough to kiss barely a breath of time before Ginger swooped in to save us from making that mistake. "Or maybe something did. The thing is, I don't know what was real."

His brow creased in a frown as he angled his head to study me. "You don't know what was real? What do you mean?"

"I mean… I saw things, things I know didn't happen. Things that maybe I wanted to happen, or I don't know. Maybe I had some bad blood and hallucinated. I don't know. I just know nothing actually happened and if it almost did, it doesn't matter because it didn't."

"What are you talking about?" His frown deepened. "You're not making a lot of sense right now."

"Nothing is making a lot of sense right now." I set the dagger down on the table and raked my hands through my hair. "I'm not making sense right now, not even in my own head. I don't feel right."

"Hey." He stepped forward and reached for me, pulled me into his arms. I flashed back to the pantry, the feel of his mouth on my heated flesh, and jumped back. "Whoa. Danni, I'm just… you have to talk to me, explain what's going on."

He was right. I wasn't entirely sure when reality and

fantasy had collided in that pantry, or why, and in case something did happen or something was said that shouldn't have been, he needed to know it wasn't me in that pantry. I shook my head, not even making sense to myself.

"Danni?"

"I think something is wonky with me," I confessed. "I've felt strange since we returned from Pigeon Forge."

A knowing look flitted through his eyes, and he nodded. "Yeah, I know. We've all noticed the tension between you and Rider. Did he do something?"

I quickly shook my head, noticing how Daniel's nostrils flared. "Rider would never hurt me. I know that. *You* know that."

His eyes narrowed. "If he ever did, you know you could come to me, right?"

I looked into Daniel's gray eyes and found myself frozen in place, stunned by the depth of emotion there. I noticed a red blinking light in the corner of the room beyond him, and a cold chill skated the length of my spine. As long as I was in The Midnight Rider, I was always under some form of surveillance.

"You would be the first person I would come to," I lied, knowing damn well that if, on some off chance, Rider did hurt me, I would never let Daniel know it. The dragon would do his best to kill Rider, and Rider would do his best to kill Daniel. I couldn't stand the thought of losing either of them.

He peered at me for a moment. "I've noticed you've been having trouble looking him in the eye for longer than a few seconds. Ever since that morning. He's a lot moodier than usual too."

"It's been rough," I admitted.

Daniel nodded. "Is it because he killed Trixell?"

As if triggered by the name, the witch's screams shrieked through my cranium and a flashing image of Rider covered in her blood filled my mind. I must have reacted physically, because Daniel reached out to steady me. "Danni, I was there with him, remember? I'm the one who burned what was left of her."

What was left of her. A wave of nausea rolled through my stomach. "Were you drenched in her blood too?"

Daniel's eyes widened. I hadn't meant to ask the question, but once it had slipped out, there was nothing to do about it. "Is that why you're having trouble? You think he was too violent with her?"

I looked away. "I know what he is, what we all are. You know I've done things too."

Daniel nodded. "So why is this thing he did bothering you so much?"

I shook my head and shrugged. "I really wish I knew. Maybe I could fix it then, stop feeling this way."

"Yeah." Daniel studied me for a moment. "Do you remember what Jon told us before he left? About what Selander Ryan was planning?"

"Yes. He said he's planning on some kind of magic spell or ritual or something to bring Katalinka back once he finds her. Trixell was supposed to keep her eye on me, screw with me and make me weak because he planned to grab me when the time was right, to bring her back through me."

"And Katalinka was Rider's mother."

I nodded.

"Rider's mother, who his half-brother turned into a succubus and forced into a disgusting sexual relationship with himself."

I grimaced at the image that thought provoked. "Yeah, Selander Ryan is a very vile creature."

"Yes, he is, so why do you think he wants to bring Katalinka back through your body, Danni? What do you think he will do if and when he succeeds? Do you really grasp the vileness of his intentions?"

"He wants to hurt Rider, and he knows I'm his soulmate, so killing me to do this spell would hurt Rider."

"You're right that he wants to hurt Rider, but you don't realize just how bad." Daniel raked a hand through his hair and I noticed the mix of pity and fury in his eyes. "Selander Ryan has no intention of killing you to do that spell. If he can find a way to bring Katalinka back, he can do that with any body. He wants to use *your* body because you would still be alive, but trapped. You know the twisted desire he has for Rider's mother. Now, imagine you're Rider. You know how depraved your half-brother is, and you've just been told the sick sonofabitch intends to bring your mother back from the dead inside the body of the woman you love, knowing what he intends to do with Katalinka once he does … and the woman who intended to help him do that to another female without batting an eye is standing right in front of you."

A sea of nausea rose and twisted in my stomach as I started to understand. "You mean…"

"You would still be alive and aware. You and Katalinka would share the same body while that evil sack of demonic flesh made you both his sex slave."

I slapped a hand over my mouth as I bent forward and gripped the table. Daniel's hand rested on my back. "Like I said, I was there with Rider when he killed her. I watched everything he did to her, and I didn't lift a finger to stop him because that bitch knew Selander Ryan's plan. She was helping him. Trixell was a woman, and frankly, in my mind, that might actually make her worse than him. She understands a woman's fear of that kind of torture and didn't give one single fuck about helping that demon inflict such depravity on two innocent ones."

"Everything okay over here?" I turned to see Ginger approaching us, her concerned gaze shifting between the two of us.

"She'll be all right," Daniel said. "Rider and I made sure of that, and we're going to keep making sure of it."

I sucked in a full breath once I could and straightened back up. "I knew it was bad, but I just… I didn't understand …"

"I know, but now you do. If you're going to give Rider hell about something, this shouldn't be it." Daniel blew out a breath and a small, rough laugh tumbled out with it. "That bitch deserved everything she got, and then some. I give the guy a lot of shit, and you know we have our moments where we both struggle to play nice with each other, but that morning we were partners and you haven't had any trouble looking at *me* since. Is that going to change now that you know I stood there and let him tear her apart?"

CHAPTER THIRTEEN

I shook my head as I struggled to wrap my mind around the horror of what I'd just learned. I'd always known Daniel had stayed behind and was there with Rider when the screaming began, but whenever I thought of the incident, it was only Rider I saw inflicting the pain, causing the terror-filled screams.

"No," I finally said. "I knew you were there, and even before knowing just how horrific Selander's plan was, I knew Trixell was evil. That hag used my own sister to lure me into a death trap. I know she needed to be stopped permanently. I don't know why I just have this trouble looking at or drinking from Rider now because of it."

"I'm going to grab some blood up in the bar and let you two finish talking," Ginger said, shoving a box of ammo into her jacket pocket before setting the ammo she'd grabbed for Daniel on the table before us. "Keep in mind there's cameras down here."

I felt heat climb my face as she walked past us to exit the armory and could tell by the way Daniel averted his gaze, he felt the awkwardness too.

"It's not just Rider I have tension with," I said, seeing no point in avoiding the big-ass elephant in the room.

"You and I are a little messed up right now too, aren't we?"

Daniel closed his eyes and expelled a rough breath before reopening them. "Danni, I don't know what you mean about not knowing what was real tonight, but anything I said, I meant. You mean a lot to me and I would never think anything bad of you or betray you. Coming to Rider wasn't easy, but it was necessary. I would never, ever let you do anything you would hate yourself for." He raked his hand through his rainbow locks, leaving his hair messy. "Sometimes I have to step away from you to make sure that stays true, and that doesn't say anything bad about you. It says something bad about me."

"No, it really doesn't." I was more certain than ever that Daniel had been in the dream realm with me when we'd fought the trickster demon in West Virginia. He'd kissed me and told me he loved me. He'd been about to kiss me in the pantry before Ginger arrived just in time to put a halt to that terrible mistake. I would not hold those things against him, because I hadn't stopped him. "Hell, you just defended Rider. The two of you have your issues and you didn't have to say anything to clear up what happened in that cell, but you did. That says you have honor, and you're a good man."

Daniel's mouth curved into just a hint of a forced smile as he stared at me, so much longing in his eyes it made my chest ache. I knew he wanted to say something, something that would make our friendship even more complicated, and I wondered if I'd been leading him on in some way.

You wonder if you want him too, a small voice inside my head corrected me, a voice that sounded far too much like my own to be any of the mind tricks Selander Ryan and his minions had played on me in the past. With the memory of what I'd imagined in that pantry clear in my mind, there was no sense arguing with it, but I couldn't entertain it either. Things were already too dangerous inside The Midnight Rider.

"This Jake Porter guy seems like a good man too," I said gently, doing my best not to provoke any anger. "Even if he's a slayer."

"A slayer who happens to look like Dean Winchester." A little growl slipped into Daniel's tone, and a whole lot of disgust. "Don't let that cloud your judgment."

"You know, I'm not some braindead twit. I know Dean Winchester is a fictional character and Jensen Ackles is just an actor. Do I think he is a very attractive actor? Yes. Do I think Jake Porter is a very attractive man?"

Daniel's eyes burned as heat whipped out of his body.

"Obviously, yes," I answered truthfully. "Do I intend on lowering my guard because of that? No. Am I going to throw myself at him? No. Jake Porter is a married man, and a slayer. For someone who has repeatedly told me he believes in me, and he thinks I'm smart, you're really acting otherwise."

He frowned. "I haven't said anything about you—"

"You're throwing off more heat than a five-alarm fire," I cut him off, "and you and Rider are both acting like jackasses. I'm not going to do anything stupid just because a good-looking man is in my presence. If you care about me, at least give me that much credit."

He had the decency to look ashamed. "It's not that. It's just…"

As his skin grew a little pink, I realized he wasn't ashamed. He was embarrassed. The man had revealed his feelings more than once, but in ways we could pretend to ignore, act like they hadn't happened or had gone unheard. First, the kiss in the dream realm, then the heart-to-heart on the cliff at The Cloud Top. And tonight he'd asked me to push him away while he'd clearly struggled not to give in to what he felt. That much had been real, I was sure of it, but I'd told him nothing had happened. I didn't remember any of it. I'd given him an out. I decided to give him another one.

"I know, I know. Jake Porter comes off as a complete

ass and you don't like him. I get it, but your irritation with him could be misinterpreted."

He swallowed and his shoulders relaxed a little as he brought his gaze up to mine.

"If you keep getting so irritated by him and the thought that this slayer guy is going to get the drop on me and do something to us, Rider's going to think you're jealous or something, and you know that's just a bad idea."

"Yeah." Daniel seemed to force the response out before swallowing hard. "Yeah, he's paranoid enough in that area."

"Yes, and he's already champing at the bit to take a chunk out of Jake, even though the thought of anything happening between me and a slayer, a *married* slayer at that, is ridiculous. How about we not give him anything else to get worked up about, and maybe even try to play nice with Jake? You two throwing insults at each other isn't doing anything but fueling the fire."

Daniel's jaw ticked as he thought about it. "The guy's a jerk. I'm not taking any shit off him."

"You didn't exactly roll out the welcome mat for him. I can't blame him for being defensive. You never gave him a chance to give any other kind of first impression."

Daniel's jaw ticked again. "Fine. I'll play nice as long as he does, but if he does anything that puts you in danger with this krackling or so much as looks like he's about to turn on you, I'm killing him."

"Of course. I would expect nothing less from you." I grinned. Rider and Daniel were both overprotective, but Daniel's way wasn't as suffocating, so it generally didn't annoy me. "So I take it you're still coming along even if I end up being the slayer's partner?"

"Hell yes, I'm coming along. Why wouldn't I?"

"I don't know." I gave a half shrug. "Because you hate him?"

"Yeah, well, I'll manage. I go where you go. Nothing changes that."

My heart did a little flip, and I caught myself before I stepped right up and wrapped my arms around Daniel's big shoulders. Even an innocent hug could appear very wrong on camera, and things were tense enough between Rider and me already. The memory of what I'd imagined in the pantry hit me, followed by a surge of heat, and I was suddenly very glad I hadn't hugged the man in front of me, afraid it wouldn't have ended very innocent no matter the intention.

"Are you all right?" He frowned. "You look a little flushed."

I bet I did, but I shouldn't have. "Yeah, I just… I'm going to go grab something from the bar."

I turned to flee, but his hand wrapped around my wrist, holding me captive before I made it a few feet. Without a word, he placed the iron dagger in my hand. "You should get used to carrying it. It's heavier than what you're used to. We don't want anything slowing you down if we get a face to face with that thing."

"Yeah, good idea." I grabbed the sheath the dagger had rested on, slid the weapon inside, and headed for the door.

"Hey, Danni?"

I stopped, fought a groan as I turned. I needed to get away. "Yeah?"

He stared at me a moment, almost seemed to be searching for something. "You said you didn't know what was real while we were in the pantry. Something about hallucinating?"

I took a deep breath, not that it did much to calm my suddenly jittery nerves or stop my palms from sweating. "Yeah. I know, I sound crazy. I think I just need blood. I'm going to go grab some now."

"What did you see?"

Ah, crap. I bit my lip, chewed it while he stared at me, waiting. There was no way in hell I could tell him what I saw. Fortunately, one of the wolf shifters who worked for Rider, but I didn't know well, chose that moment to enter the armory.

"Hey guys. Just coming to grab some more ammo."

"Hey." I smiled too wide, grateful for the interruption, and turned for the door. "Just on my way out. Bye!"

The wolf's brow furrowed as I pretty much fled the room, expecting to see Rider's tech team waiting for me, but of all the information and images I saw on their various screens and the big plasma, none appeared to be the footage from the camera in the armory. I wasn't sure who watched the video feeds or how often, but even the techs whose screens I couldn't see didn't seem concerned with the time I'd spent alone with Daniel.

I took the stairs up to the first floor and sensed for Rider. He was still in the office, the slayer with him. Now that I was aware of who exactly Jake Porter was, the feeling I got from him was odd. I still felt an alarm, but it was almost muted, more a reminder that a slayer was in the vicinity than a direct alert to imminent danger.

Knowing better than to stick my head into the office occupied by the surly vampire and slayer who were no doubt both in there making demands from behind tightly gritted teeth, I headed out to the bar. Paul McCartney's voice rang out from the jukebox as I stepped through the door and headed over to where Ginger sat at the bar talking to Tony, who'd returned to tending with Greg. The tiger-shifter's body gave the appearance of it being any regular night, but I knew him well enough to know he was ready to spring over the bar and start doling out pain at a moment's notice.

He grunted a little as I slid onto the barstool in front of him, next to Ginger.

"I'm happy to see you too," I told him as I set the sheathed dagger on top of the bar between us.

"What's with the dagger?" the tiger asked.

I shrugged. "Feeling cute. Might kill something later."

Ginger snorted out a laugh, but the tiger-shifter didn't seem as amused, although if I peered really close I thought

I might have seen the teeniest fraction of a grin.

"A regular?" Greg asked, noticing me.

"Yep."

A moment later, an open bottle was set in front of me. No mug of brand-spanking-fresh this time. After so long, it got bottled and lost some of its appeal. I raised it to my lips and took a pull anyway. "Why do you look so sour?" I asked the shifter. "I mean, more than usual."

He didn't bother with a facial expression. "There's a slayer in the building. Do you need any more reason than that?"

"When the guy is on our side? Yep, more info would be helpful."

Instead of replying, he looked at Ginger, shook his head, and walked away.

"I think I give him a headache."

"I think the kind of pain you give him is more in the ass region," Ginger said. She waited until Greg moved out of earshot and turned toward me, voice lowered. "Did you settle things with your dragon?"

"There was nothing to settle."

Now she gave me a look very reminiscent of the ones I was accustomed to receiving from Tony.

"Look, I know we were… close… when you opened the pantry, but nothing happened in there. I talked to him about how his reaction to Jake could be perceived. He's going to try to get along with him."

She just looked at me for a while, said nothing, and lifted her bottle to her mouth. She seemed to consider her next words as she drank.

"You have something more to say?"

She gave a light shrug as she set her bottle down. "Nope. I just hope none of this blows up in our faces."

"None of what?"

"You. Daniel. Rider. Jake Porter." She looked around the bar. "It'd be a shame to get blood all over this festive décor."

"Hey Greg, can I get a Holly Jolly, a Warm Merry, and a vodka martini?" Jadyn called out to the bartender as she came up alongside me and set her tray on the bar. "Hey, Danni."

"Hey." I looked for Christian, realizing I hadn't seen him since I'd returned from the sublevel. "Did Christian leave?"

"Once he discovered we'd been told to leave Jake and Rider alone, he went back to the office. I assume whatever those two didn't want to discuss in front of us was related to that thing I told you about that Christian knows but won't discuss with me either. Either way, he hasn't come back out, so they must not mind him being part of the discussion."

"Well, that's a comfort, in a way. Rider was pretty snarly with the slayer. Christian can referee if they go for each other's throats."

"I hope so." Jadyn glanced toward Greg as the vampire worked on the drinks she'd requested. She seemed antsy to grab them and go. I looked toward the table she'd come from and the group of ladies there didn't seem to be very demanding. Then I remembered the way she'd looked at Kutya's doggy bed in Rider's office and hadn't quite met my eyes after. "Hey, did you get a minute to check in with Kutya tonight?"

Jadyn nearly winced and my stomach took a dive. The big breath she had to blow out before forcing herself to meet my eyes didn't do it any favors. "I did."

"And?" I prodded after she clammed up. "Obviously, whatever you got from him is bad. I'd rather you just go ahead and tell me."

She glanced over at Greg again and I could practically hear her cursing out his slowness in her mind. "I don't want to upset you, but I did check in with him. I asked him why he growled at you and the only thing I got from him was, 'Bad in Danni'."

"Bad in Danni?" I looked over at Ginger to see her

fully invested in our exchange. She shrugged as if to say she didn't know what to make of it and drained the last of her bottled blood.

"That's all I could get. He kept saying 'Bad in Danni.' But I've told you before, I often just get feelings, sometimes images and a few words. Animals can't always speak in complete sentences and they might word things odd. I asked if Kutya was happy with you and he made it very clear he loves his daddy and his mommy, so try not to look too deep into whatever happened earlier. He might have been in a mood."

Greg finished Jadyn's drink order, and she offered a consoling smile before she grabbed the tray and stepped away from us.

"Hey, you heard her." Ginger gave Greg her empty bottle to take care of. "That dog loves you."

"He didn't seem very loving when he was growling at me." I looked at the bottle in front of me, but couldn't drink it, afraid I'd just throw it up.

"Hey. It's nothing." She squeezed my shoulder, then quickly pulled her hand back when I cringed. "Sorry. Geez, you're even touchier than usual lately. Are you out of whack or something? I assumed you and Rider…" She did a little shimmy dance in her seat.

"What was that?"

"My bow chicka wow wow moves."

"I think the wow wow part is broken." I grinned as she flipped me off. "Rider and I … *did*… and I drank from him then, and before we left tonight."

"So you had blood from your sire, blood from a live male, and you've had sex within the last twenty-four hours." She scanned the room, making sure no one was within earshot and the bartenders were too busy to snoop. "So what happened in that pantry? And don't tell me nothing happened because the only thing separating the two of you was a single breath."

"You're like a dog with a bone, you know that?"

"Only when I care, and when it comes to you, sweetcheeks, I care a lot. I don't have to be your sire to know something is wrong with you. I can see it all over your face and so can anyone else who's paying attention." She looked toward the back door. "And believe me, I am not the only person paying attention. You can keep struggling through whatever's going on all by yourself or you can lean on me. I guarantee you, whatever you have to get off your chest, I'll handle it a lot better than either of those two."

"Nothing happened in the pantry," I said, "but I imagined something happening."

Ginger sat there, blinking at me as she processed. "What do you mean? I opened the door and the two of you were all smooshed together pretty tight. That happened."

"Yes, but only that." I picked up the bottle and forced down a swallow before I returned it to the bar top. Damn, I wished it was a chocolate milkshake instead of a bottle of blood. "We were close, but he told me to push him away, and I went to… but the moment I touched him, I didn't want to take my hands off him. Then clothes were coming off, I was on my knees in front of him… I had him in my hand, Ginger."

"Him?"

"*Him.*"

"Ohhh…" Her eyes nearly popped out of her head. "Little him."

"It wasn't little from where I was at."

Her eyebrows shot up into her hairline and she held her hands out in front of her about eight inches apart. "Are we talking Rome-sized or…"

"I'm not giving you his measurements." I blew out a frustrated breath. "It wasn't real anyway. One second I was on my knees with him against the wall, the next second I was right where you found me with him, close together, but clothed, with him telling me to push him away.

Nothing happened."

"Wait. Hold on, hold on." Ginger did a lot of blinking and frowning as she appeared to replay everything I'd just told her in her mind. "From everything I just heard, it sounded like a whole lot happened."

"But it didn't. It felt like it did though. It was like a total out-of-body experience. It felt so real, but it was all in my head." I reached for the bottle, but didn't pick it up, opted to just spin it around in my hands. "I had sex with Rider this morning before I went to sleep. I can't even blame the succubus side of me, unless…"

"Unless?"

"Unless it's taking over me. What if Rider's mark isn't strong enough? Shana's carrying the Bloom for me, but she's not carrying all of what's inside me. What if the succubus side of me is just too much to control? What if I'm insatiable?" Images of Rider covered in blood flashed through my mind, along with memories of things I had done myself in his interrogation room and the memory of what I'd imagined doing in the pantry with Daniel. "What if I'm a real monster, and getting worse every day?"

"Girl, you are not a real monster." She reached for my hand, then stopped herself. "But you might be confused."

"What do you mean?"

Ginger bit the corner of her lip, seemed to weigh whether answering would be a good idea. Finally, she closed her eyes, took a deep breath, and pressed forward. "From what you just told me, it sounded like you were the aggressive one in that little fantasy, and it was a fantasy, not a dream. You were awake." She took a quick glance around the room, checking we were still in our own private little cocoon. "You risked your life to save his back in that realm with Cupid, and it was clear to everyone in that space why you did."

"I didn't do anything he wouldn't have done for me."

"Yes, he would have done the same thing for you and he would have been just as distraught at the thought of you dying, because that man is head over heels deep in love with you." She leaned closer. "And you love him too."

I automatically shook my head. "I love Rider."

"Fantasies are things we want, Danni. You had a fantasy so strong you thought it was real, and be honest with yourself. While you were caught up in that fantasy, did you want Daniel?"

"The succubus—"

"Your eyes weren't red when I opened that door and you didn't bite Daniel in your fantasy, did you?"

I shook my head.

"Of course you didn't, because if you'd lost control of your succubus side, that would have probably been your first move, but you didn't lose control of it. The succubus is half of what you are. Blaming it for what happened is like blaming your hand for stabbing someone. The Bloom is gone. Your blood diet and moments of violence may help keep your succubus side in control, but it can't get rid of it because *you're* it. What happened earlier tonight… That was all you, girlfriend."

The blood I'd drunk curdled in my stomach. I was a monster, a horrible, disgusting, cheating monster.

"Fuck." I lowered my head onto the bar with a thud, already so nauseated, Ginger's hand on my shoulder didn't bother me, but the shift in the atmosphere sure did.

"Slap on your game face, sweetcheeks. Here come all three of them."

CHAPTER FOURTEEN

I sucked in a breath as I straightened up and turned. The air left me in a whoosh as my gaze settled on the four men who'd just entered the room.

Christian immediately branched off from the others to go to his wife, but he wasn't one of the three men troubling me. I couldn't look at Daniel without remembering what I'd imagined in the pantry and wondering how close to the truth my imagination had been, and now thanks to Ginger's truth bomb, I also couldn't look at him without feeling like I'd stabbed Rider in the heart.

Rider's eyes narrowed as they held me in their sights and I knew the perceptive vampire sensed my unease. I managed to look him in the eye without seeing the flashes of him covered in blood, but couldn't relish the fact. My brain had simply replaced that terrible image with another: me in the pantry with Daniel, betraying him.

And then there was Jake Porter. I'd meant what I said to Daniel. I had no intention of throwing myself at the happily married slayer, but he looked, talked, and hell, he even moved like Dean Winchester. A girl couldn't help but fantasize. Right then. Right there. As my boyfriend and best friend I'd happened to think very naughty things about approached me.

Pass the Ho Ho Skank Ho lipstick, I told Ginger through our link. *I might as well be the new cover girl.*

Don't be so hard on yourself. It was just a fantasy.

I'm trash and I'm going to hell.

Aw, sweetcheeks, you're not trash, and we're all headed to hell anyway.

I turned and looked at her. "You think so?"

"We drink people, and sometimes you stab them in the balls. The odds aren't looking so great."

Daniel and Jake split off to grab a dark booth in the corner. Rider glanced between Ginger and me as he covered the distance to stop before us. "Are you all right? You look a little green."

"I'm fine. I guess this blood just isn't sitting right. I probably don't need it since I drank from you earlier. I was just trying to do what you're supposed to do at a bar."

Rider studied me for a moment, intently enough I could tell he was searching for a lie. Normally, that would make me mad, but now it just made me nervous. It would have taken a lot more audacity than I had to get mad, given my traitorous hormones and guilty conscience.

I must have lucked out because he reached past me, picked up the bottle and sniffed it. "Smells all right, but you drank from me recently enough. You shouldn't force it if it's making you queasy. Both of you come on over here. Since Jake managed to enter the room without being the focal point of it this time, he's not attracting everyone's attention. We can talk out here."

"Well, he's not attracting any of the humans' attention," I pointed out as I scanned the room, noticing the looks the slayer received from every paranormal within range.

"Yeah, well, the ones staring at him aren't the ones we care about overhearing as much," Rider said. "Come on."

Ginger and I slid off our barstools to cross the room.

Rider noticed the dagger as I tucked it inside the jacket I had yet to take off, figuring that was more discreet than fastening the thigh holster on inside the bar. Halfway to the table, Rider spoke directly into my mind. *You pulled your hand away from mine.*

You made me sound like I was nothing more than your fledgling during your pissing match with Jake. It didn't exactly give me any romantic feelings.

The look Rider delivered my way was dark, but vulnerable. *Slayers always go for the kill shot. It's wise not to show them where your heart is.*

I almost choked on the lump in my throat.

And it wasn't a pissing match. You can't trust him just because he looks like—

Oh, don't even go there. You act like if Dean Winchester was a real person, I'd run right up to him to get slayed just because he's hot. If I trust Jake at all, it's because Christian is his friend and I know Jake helped you fight an army of evil bastards while I was in Moonlight.

The dark look I received then had no vulnerability whatsoever, but even though he looked mad enough to snarl, Rider said nothing.

Instead of sliding into the booth, Jake had grabbed a chair and turned it around beside the booth before straddling it. I was a little surprised he'd sit with his back to all the paranormal beings around him, but if what I'd heard about slayers was true, he knew where every single one of them was without looking. It was hard to sneak up on a slayer.

Daniel had slid into the side of the booth that faced the front, and had to scoot over when Ginger slid in next to him. He glanced at me when I approached with Rider, but didn't hold eye contact long.

Rider gestured for me to sit first on the opposite side of the booth, not surprising, considering sitting last would have put me closer to Jake. I slid in until I reached the wall, which put me directly across from Daniel. My feet bumped his, his long legs stretched out under the table, before Rider slid in beside me. He set my half full bottle of blood on the table in front of him.

"We'll be hunting the krackling," he said.

Ginger and I shared a look. "We'll? As in…?"

Rider pointed to every member of our small group, then himself. Jake smirked as he caught my expression, which I imagined must have looked like shock. Rider caught the look too, but didn't seem as amused. "What? You look surprised, as if I haven't been hunting and killing monsters longer than any of you."

"I know, but I thought you were busy with other things right now."

"I have time. This monster is killing people. It's far more important to end its murder spree."

And keep tabs on me. I looked at Jake to see the slayer watching me curiously. "You kicked us out after Mr. Porter here said he'd come here for me. Care to clue me in on what that was about? I think I have a right to know."

Jake grinned. "She's feisty."

"You have no idea," Rider said before facing me. "You recall I helped Seta last month."

I nodded.

"Helping her was part of something bigger, something I can't go into, but apparently it made an impression. Jake was sent here to help you as repayment for that favor."

"Sent by who? Seta? How would she know I'm hunting the krackling?"

"Not Seta, and that's all I can say."

I rolled my eyes. This secret prophecy stuff was annoying. "So whoever sent us a slayer thought I was worth helping, but not worth sharing your secret with."

"It's not my secret to share."

"Are you going to drink that?" Jake nodded toward the bottle in front of Rider.

"That's blood," I said as Rider slid the bottle toward him.

"I know." The slayer lifted the bottle to his mouth, tilted his head back, and chugged it all down before grimacing. "Ugh, should have pilfered that before it started to cool down."

"Did you just—" Ginger looked at me. "Did he just drink that?"

All I could do was nod. My mouth had dropped open and didn't want to close long enough to manage speaking.

"If you want more, just order a very bloody mary at the bar," Rider told him without a trace of the surprise showing on the rest of our faces. Even Daniel appeared taken aback by the slayer's choice of beverage.

"Nah, I'm good. I just need a boost now and then." Jake looked at me, caught sight of my still-hanging jaw, and grinned. "All right, so even though I think Danni and I are more than enough to handle this krackling, it looks like we will be hunting this thing as a team. It's best you all know as much as possible about these monsters and about how I operate."

"Who said you were in charge?" Daniel asked.

"Whoever decided I was to come out of the womb a slayer," Jake answered. "You do know I'm biologically designed to hunt and kill paranormal beings, right? That kind of naturally makes me the leader."

"That kind of naturally makes you our enemy," the dragon-shifter responded.

"I think Jake's made it clear he isn't here to kill any of us," I said, and nudged Daniel's foot with mine as I speared him with a look. *I thought we came to the agreement you would play nice with him,* I reminded him privately through our mental link.

I'm trying, but he's a bossy doucherocket.

Try harder, I suggested. "Go ahead, Jake."

"Thanks." Jake caught the attention of Hazel, a fae server on shift. "Hey, sweetheart, can I get a double cheeseburger and a basket of onion rings? Oh, and some of that pumpkin pie."

Hazel looked at Rider for approval. He nodded. "Anybody else want anything?"

Ginger and Daniel passed. Ginger rarely ate in my presence, and Daniel tried to be considerate and skip, although his appetite was growing with his body thanks to the dragon soul inside him changing his physique.

"You can eat," I told them. "I don't mind."

"Not hungry," Daniel said, his jaw ticking as he watched the slayer, waiting to hear what he had to say.

"I'm good, sweetcheeks."

Rider passed as well, and Hazel left to put in Jake's order, after he added a beer to his request.

"All right." Jake clapped his hands together and got comfortable. "Here's what we know. A krackling has been awakened and called upon. You don't awaken a krackling to kill just one person and then go about your business. Once someone awakens one of those shitbags, they're stuck with it, and they have to feed it or else it will turn on them."

"And by feed it, you mean sic it on people?" I said.

Jake nodded. "Exactly. The person commanding the krackling has to give it a target to kill every night while it's awake. If they fail to do so, the krackling will kill them instead and go back into hibernation until it is called upon again by someone else."

"The krackling didn't eat tonight," Daniel pointed out. "We kept it from its target."

"Right," Ginger said. "So will it go after the one who called it since they failed to give it someone to eat?"

"Or will the krackling return to finish the job?" I felt my heart skip a beat. "We left Joanna there unguarded."

Jake raised his hands. "Whoa. The woman will be fine. I left some warding in place before I left her, and besides, I shot that thing dead center in the heart. A blow like that's going to take time to heal. It won't be up to hunting until tomorrow night. It'll go back for the woman then, unless the person who called it gives it another target before it gets to her. The krackling wouldn't go after the person commanding it just because it missed one night's meal. It was given a target, and it still has one. Fortunately for us, we know who that target is and we'll be waiting for it to show its ugly face if it returns tomorrow night."

"You said the last known sighting of one of these things was a century ago," Daniel pointed out. "You're nowhere near a century old, so how are you so sure you know what you're talking about?"

"Killing monsters is literally my reason for existing. What I don't instinctually know, I know where to find. When not actively tracking something to kill, I'm tracking knowledge. I'm very good at research." Jake turned his attention to Rider. "I wouldn't mind a look through your bookshelves. I noticed some pretty old texts in there."

"I'm not sure giving a slayer more knowledge about the paranormal community is in our best interests," Rider replied.

"Man, you've got trust issues."

"I wouldn't be here now if I didn't."

Hazel dropped off a cold bottle of beer and a slice of pumpkin pie. "The rest of your food will be up soon," she told him before moving away.

Jake watched Hazel leave, caught Lana's eye from where she'd taken up post near the jukebox, and winked at her. The snake-shifter took her watchful eye off the room long enough to flip the slayer off and grin before resuming security mode.

"She's awesome," Jake said, and picked up his beer bottle. "Disgusting, but awesome. I hear you Imortians come in all different shapes and sizes. I gotta say, you're the first dragon I've come across. Pretty fucking cool."

Daniel didn't say anything, but his demeanor softened a bit.

"You said someone was killed by this thing in Indiana," I prompted.

Jake took a long draw off his bottle and nodded. He

dug a cell phone out of his pocket, pulled up a picture, and slid the phone toward me. "The woman's name was Shannon Jacobs Valdez. Young mother. Her husband and children were out of state at his parents' house, but she was feeling sick, so she stayed behind. The family came home, found the bedroom looking like that, and she hasn't been seen since."

I enlarged the picture of the macabre scene. It was just like the scene we'd found at Angela LaRoche's house. A massive pool of blood and splashes of it up the walls. Only for Shannon, it looked like she'd been killed in her bed. "When was this?"

"Estimated to have happened about three or four days ago," Jake answered.

"How did you not get a report of this?" I asked Rider. "I thought your tech team monitored law enforcement for this type of stuff."

"Depending on how things are reported, we miss some."

"I know a guy on the force over there," Jake said. "He's tight with some fellow hunters, so when stuff like this comes his way, he knows how to bury it so media or feds don't get involved and make the hunters' jobs harder."

"Hunters. You associate with them?"

"Not nearly as many as I used to," Jake answered. "Long before I knew I was an actual slayer, I was just another hunter. A badass hunter, if I do say so myself, but yeah… I've gotten to know quite a few crossing paths on hunts and I've stayed in touch with the ones who aren't just psychotic killers. They can be useful when tracking monsters like these."

I remembered an arrow soaked with hawthorn oil whizzing past me, narrowly missing me in Rider's garage from when a hunter had decided I didn't deserve to live and hunted me down like an animal, and that bastard's hunter brothers had picked up the hunt after Rider had killed him. They'd sought help from a local gang, sent the men to track me with an order to have their fun passing me around before delivering me to them for the kill. I knew what a slayer was, and that Jake was far more dangerous than a hunter, but learning he associated with them sent waves of red hot anger coursing through my veins.

Jake must have picked up on my thoughts, because he paused mid-chew and set his fork down before swallowing the large chunk of pumpkin pie he'd loaded into his mouth and looked over at Rider. "I heard you took out Barnaby Quimby and those other Quimby nutcases."

"You heard correctly."

"Good." Jake took a drink of his beer. "That whole family was a pile of shit. I heard good things about some of the older ones before my time, but every Quimby I ever actually met was a lunatic, some of them bigger monsters than the ones they hunted."

Hazel appeared with a double cheeseburger and basket of onion rings, bringing the scent of fried deliciousness with her. Daniel's stomach growled loud enough to cause every head at the table to swivel his way.

"Want your usual?" Hazel asked him with an expression that said she already knew he did.

"Yeah," he said. "Make it a double-double."

Hazel shook her head, but left to put in the order.

"A double-double?" Ginger *tsk*ed. "Keep it up and you'll be in the hospital with Rome next."

"I can handle my meat and grease."

Jake choked on the onion ring he'd shoved into his mouth and started to swallow. "I'm sure you get lots of practice."

A wave of heat rolled out of Daniel as he glared at the slayer.

"Just fuckin' with ya, dude." Jake grinned. "That one was too easy. I had to take it."

"So what do you know about Shannon Jacobs..." I

couldn't remember the rest of the woman's name.

"Shannon Jacobs Valdez," Jake said around a mound of cheeseburger.

"Yeah, Shannon Jacobs Valdez." I glanced at Daniel, relieved to see he'd cooled back down a little, and steered the conversation back to our case. "How did you know this was the krackling, just the blood? I don't see a fireplace."

"Again, kracklings don't need fireplaces. You're thinking of Krampus." Jake scarfed down the rest of the cheeseburger with a swallow that looked almost painful. I was pretty sure he'd eaten the entire double cheeseburger in four bites. "That amount of blood and no body left behind, plus no bloody footprints or any other evidence of a break-in or body being moved, all pointed to a krackling. My contact knew whatever took the woman, it caused her to bleed with way more force than a human could inflict, so he sent me the info and once I was on the scene, I had its scent. I knew what it was. Not a lot of monsters smell like fresh baked goodies sprinkled with just a hint of sulfur."

"So is that how you tracked it to Joanna Jaskowick's house tonight? Off its scent?"

"In a way." He took a moment to down an onion ring, then continued. "According to the lore—"

Ginger and I both snorted and quickly covered our mouths to hold back laughter.

Jake looked between us. "What did I say?"

"Something a Winchester would say," Ginger told him, "and I haven't even watched that show enough to memorize every line like Danni has."

Jake dropped the onion ring he'd been about to pop into his mouth and rolled his eyes. Rider sat stiff in his seat, a dark and very unamused look aimed my way. Daniel didn't appear any happier.

"I do not talk like that stupid Dean character."

"Actually, you really do, but I think that was more of a

Sam line." Ginger sat back as Hazel delivered a four-decker cheeseburger and basket of fries to Daniel along with a frosty mug of beer, and left. "But please, go ahead. *According to the lore…*"

Ginger and I shared another laugh at her Sam impression, further annoying the men. In fact, I was pretty sure Jake was imagining his beer bottle was one of us when he wrapped his hand around the neck and raised it to his mouth, and if Rider's jaw tightened any harder, something was going to snap. Daniel appeared to be taking his emotions out on his tower of beef and cheese.

"According to the shit I came across on this fugly bastard," Jake continued after setting his bottle back down, "kracklings are believed to burrow in heavily wooded areas, but there's a lot of debate on whether those heavily wooded areas are in the same plane as where they hunt or if they're actually called from some other plane of existence and magically poof their asses back there once they've collected their prey."

"Other plane? You mean like another realm?"

Jake nodded. "There are a few stories of hunters finding dens full of the krackling's leftovers, mostly bones and such, but it's hard to tell if those tales are actually true or just myths. Back in the day there were a lot of made-up tales about kracklings passed down from parents to children because, I don't know, they actually thought terrifying the little crotch-goblins was good parenting."

"Kids weren't always as soft as they are now," Rider commented.

We all turned our heads to stare at him.

"What? In my day, children weren't coddled. We didn't play with toys or have naptime, and we didn't cry at the thought of a monster under the bed. If something was under our bed, we'd kill it like we'd kill any other predator, then go back to sleep because we had livestock to tend to in the morning."

"So much about you makes a lot more sense now,"

Daniel said.

"So anyway," Jake continued, still staring at Rider as if he wanted to say something, but had no idea where to start so he was moving along instead, "I knew the krackling was in the area and would keep hunting. There was another missing woman reported with just a ton of blood left behind, this time in Louisville, but she had been in a really heated dispute with some asshole neighbor with a record of violence against women so that didn't get a lot of attention in the news either, just a mention because of the missing body. Cops thought the case was pretty open and shut. That vic's name was Joan Rowland. I didn't get any decent pictures. Apparently, the neighbor's big-ass bloodthirsty dog got into the house through a door that was left open and rolled around in the blood before tracking that shit everywhere. I would have never thought to connect it to the krackling if not for the fact I already knew about the woman in Indiana just across the bridge."

"So that's how you knew it had crossed over here to Louisville."

Jake nodded. "And since I knew there was a possibility the thing might be holing up in heavily wooded areas during the day, I checked out local parks. I was checking out Iroquois Park when I felt its presence within my radius, jumped in my car, and chased down what I sensed, to find a dragon in battle with it."

"And then you shot it, making it flee," Daniel said, pausing in his annihilation of the tall burger. "Good job."

"Exactly how much longer could you have held that fire before those things were on you?" Jake asked. "As long as you were only burning them, the most powerful part of him was standing there untouched and when I pulled up, I only saw Danni with a silver knife that wouldn't have done anything but tick him off, so I took a shot at him. He turned just as I pulled the trigger and I nailed him right in the heart, not to the right of it as I'd intended. That shot wouldn't kill him, because he wasn't whole, but it would have made him weak, possibly make it harder for him to keep releasing kracklings. So he fled. Things don't always go perfectly, but that outcome was a lot better than the one where he would have killed all of you because none of you had iron bullets or blades or even knew what you were going up against, let alone how to kill it."

"If the krackling flees every time it gets a serious wound, how are we going to kill it?" I asked.

"Beats the hell out of me." Jake finished his last onion ring and looked straight into my eyes. "You're the one who's supposed to kill it."

CHAPTER FIFTEEN

Had I been drinking, I would have choked. "What? Are you joking?"

"The only reason I'm all the way down here this close to Christmas is to help you gank that sonofabitch, but I'm not the one who's actually going to kill it. I'm here to help *you* kill it."

I looked at Rider to see his reaction. He sat still, watching me, but he didn't seem shocked at all which really made me wonder what the hell the two had spoken about in his office after he'd kicked us out, and how he'd come to agree to me hunting with the slayer at all. Yes, he'd decided to hunt with us, but still. The man used to want to lock me away for my own safety for lesser threats.

My mouth had gone dry, but I somehow managed a hard swallow before I turned my attention back to Jake. "Who sent you?"

"Someone you've never met."

"But you have?" I asked Rider.

He nodded, but didn't offer any more detail.

"I can't get a name?"

"It's safer that you don't," Jake said. "Believe me, sweetheart, I know this top-secret shit is annoying as hell, but be glad you're on this woman's radar. She sees things no one else sees, and she's someone you want in your corner when shit gets serious and you need someone to help you out of a jam, however irritating her secretive and mysterious bullshit can be."

"But it's not Seta?"

Jake shook his head. "And there's no use asking me again because I'll only reveal her name if she tells me to herself. And she hasn't told me to."

"This is insane. You're a slayer and you're sitting there telling me you know how to kill one of these things, but you don't actually have an actual plan to kill this one, yet you expect me to be able to kill it?"

"You were all gung-ho to kill the thing earlier," Daniel said. "You had total confidence you could do it and knew in your gut you had to be the one to do it. Nothing's changed."

"Nothing's changed?!" I swept my hand out toward Jake. "I thought we were going after a demon, not some evil giant hobo-looking thing that shoots bats out of its maw, and Dean Friggin' Winchester over here can't even kill the damn thing. That's a whole lot that's changed."

Rider shot me a look that threatened to burn off a layer of my epidermis as Jake threw his hands up and growled. "For the hundredth damn time, I am not some stupid TV character. I really do not look that damn much like that guy."

"Honey, do you not own a mirror, or are you just delusional?" Ginger asked. "You could have been cloned from Jensen Ackles."

"Well, he's right about one thing. He might look and talk and even walk like Dean Winchester, but he's no Dean Winchester. He's not even a Sam Winchester. Or a Bobby Singer. They would have known how to kill the krackling. Garth would have known how to kill the krackling." I huffed out a breath and sat back in the booth. "Daniel knew what he was talking about. No one sent him here.

He was shipped off of Wish."

"Now that's just being mean," Jake said as Daniel laughed. "And I know how to kill it. I just haven't yet figured out how we keep it in one form long enough to kill it."

"Same difference."

Rider squeezed my thigh under the table. "We'll figure it out. You may not have to kill it directly. If we figure out who called it out of hibernation in the first place and prevent them from giving it a target, it will kill them and go back into hibernation, correct?"

"That's what the lore says." Jake glared at Ginger, causing her to swallow down the chuckle his word choice had caused.

"So we can track the person down, prevent them from giving it a target and let it effectively get rid of its own self."

"But that won't actually kill it," I reminded him. "It would only go into hibernation until some jerk calls it back and we might not even know about it then. I'm supposed to kill it, not give it a nap. Of course, if no one knows how to make it stay in one form long enough to do that, I guess we're kind of screwed."

Rider looked over at the bar, thinking. "You saw some random woman in here tonight and you knew she was that thing's prey. You had no reason to think that, no reason except for your gut. You have a gift and for whatever reason, you have been chosen to kill this thing. Maybe Jake doesn't know how to get it to stay in one form long enough to be killed because only you have that answer, and you'll see it or feel it when you're supposed to."

My heart must have swelled to three times its size in the short moment it took to turn my head toward him. "You believe that?"

"Of course I believe that. I believe in you." He looked me straight in the eye. "Don't you?"

And suddenly there was no room left in my chest for

my swollen heart. I leaned forward to kiss him stupid right there in front of Jake the slayer and everybody else, only to come to a crashing halt before I'd moved a hair. Blood covered him until the only thing I could see were his glowing eyes reflecting my own blood-covered image.

I jerked back and closed my eyes by reflex before turning my face away. Rider removed the hand that had been resting on my thigh and I immediately felt cold without his touch, but I suspected a lot of that chill came from knowing he'd sensed my fear as I'd jerked away and I'd just hurt him again.

"I'll have my tech team look into the krackling," he said, dejection clear in his voice, although I could tell he was trying not to let it show in front of the others. "And I'll look through some books I have in my office."

"I can help with that research," Jake offered. "I'm a fast researcher."

"I'm not giving you access to those books, Porter. You were lucky to get into my office at all earlier. You are not to ever step past this area."

"So I guess that means you're not going to offer me a room for the night?"

Rider managed a laugh. "You don't want to go into the only room I would consider putting you in."

I forced myself to turn toward them then, picking up on the threatening undertone in Rider's voice. The blood was gone, and hopefully it would remain gone as long as I didn't look him in the eye. However, if things escalated between the two, I might end up seeing them both bloody for real.

Jake held Rider's glare for a long, anxiety-inducing stretch of time before giving a sharp nod and standing. "I appreciate the food. I have some contacts who can help with the research, so we'll compare when I come back tomorrow." Then Jake looked at me and narrowed his eyes. Again, I got the feeling he saw more than just what lay on the surface when he looked at me. "I'll see you tomorrow night, Danni. I hope you have only good dreams."

Then he turned and walked out of the bar, leaving me with the oddest feeling in my stomach that he could see inside me, right down to the nightmares plaguing my dreams.

"Of all the slayers who could have come over to our side, why did it have to be that jackass?" Rider muttered. "Ginger, Daniel, there's no reason for you to hang out here any longer. Danni's in for the night, and security is covered. It's been a quiet night anyway and we don't have much longer left until close."

Ginger glanced at the clock that hung above the bar. "I have enough time to swing by and see if Angel has any decorating left and lend her a hand."

"You're swinging by to see what she's baked," Daniel said.

"Well, duh." She grinned. "She's getting better and better the more she practices, and what can I say? I love the smell of cinnamon, nutmeg, vanilla, and—"

"When I throw up, I'll be sure to do it all over you," Daniel warned her. His eyes were closed, his skin faintly green.

Ginger laughed, winked at me, and slipped out of the booth. "You've got to work on that weak stomach. Just don't think of the cinnamon-scented chunks of bloody—"

"Ginger." This time it was Rider who cut her off, showing his merciful side as Daniel groaned and clamped his mouth closed.

"I'll behave. See you tomorrow, sweetcheeks."

Rider watched her leave, shaking his head the whole time, and returned his attention to Daniel. "Rome's getting released at noon tomorrow. Will you be all right to pick him up or do I need to send Hank?"

"I'm good." Daniel opened his eyes and waved off Rider's concern. "Ginger just knows what buttons to push to trigger my gag reflex. I'm not sick."

"All right. You're officially off duty until after you pick him up and then you can swing by here. Try to get some rest. I have a feeling Rome will make rest very difficult for you after he's released."

"No shit. That room downstairs still available? I may just sleep there for a while and leave him to fend for himself in the apartment."

"It's available, but Rome will probably need someone watching him to ensure he doesn't eat something that causes him to go right back into the hospital," Rider pointed out. He started to grin, but looked over my way, and any amusement he'd felt seemed to be replaced with something a lot less happy. "Stay in the building tonight, Danni. If anyone needs me, I'll be in the office working."

If anyone needs me. I knew that meant if I needed him. If I could bear to be around him. I hated that he had to say that, worse, that he had to feel the pain of rejection I kept hitting him with. I watched him walk away, the usually proud, confident set of his shoulders not quite as high. "Have you ever wanted to beat the hell out of yourself?"

"My fiancée was murdered right in front of me," Daniel said. "I'm the king of wanting to inflict pain and suffering on myself. The only reason I even looked for a way out of Hades after getting tossed in there was to get out and make Fairuza pay for what she'd done. Otherwise, I would have just figured I deserved the abuse."

"Losing her was enough pain and suffering, and it wasn't deserved," I told him. "You can't blame yourself for someone else's evil."

"Seems you could take your own advice." He lowered his gaze to the remaining fries in his basket, but didn't move to finish them. Instead, he shoved the remaining food away as if he'd lost his appetite.

"I wish I was blaming myself for someone else's evil." I felt the backs of my eyes burn and looked away to collect myself before the burning gave way to the actual shedding of tears. Looking away only brought the Christmas décor to my attention, the décor my brooding sire had put up himself in an effort to please me. I refocused on Daniel's discarded fries, let myself mentally gripe at my inability to eat such fried goodness. It beat crying. "The reason I want to kick my own ass has nothing to do with anyone else. It's all on me."

"I saw you jerk away from Rider earlier, and as much as he's trying to hide it, I know that vampire is a wounded man right now. If you're upset about whatever is wrong between you two, work on it. You can't blame yourself unless you just give up."

Wow. Direct hit to the heart, and a surprising statement coming from one of the last people I'd figure to give advice on how to strengthen and repair my relationship with Rider, but that was Daniel. He was just the kind of guy to put aside his own feelings to ease the pain of the ones he loved. "You definitely did not deserve a single second of the time you spent in Hell. You are one of the best men I've ever known."

"For all the good it does me," he muttered. Daniel drained the last of his beer, set the mug down, and slid out of the booth. "Maybe one day it'll finally all pay off. Go talk to your vampire. Get your mind right before we go out tomorrow. I'm going to go home and crash, get some rest before they release that giant baby from the hospital tomorrow."

I grinned despite the fresh pain in my heart that came with the knowledge that not only had I been hurting Rider, but Daniel as well. Still, they both would give their lives for me, a fact that both touched my heart and filled me with indescribable guilt. "I'm sure it won't be that bad."

"The man just had to have a giant chunk of shit surgically removed from his colon," Daniel said. "There's no way he's getting released without dietary restrictions. Can you imagine living with that man while he's under dietary restrictions?"

Yikes. That really wasn't a pretty picture. "Maybe he'll

be groggy from the anesthesia?"

"Oh good, so he'll be a giant, tired, cranky baby."

"Does he have family other than Auntie Mo? Can he stay with them?"

"He has family, but the way I see it, his poor mother had to birth that giant mountain. She's suffered enough." He sighed and raised his hand in a goodbye wave. "Get some rest. Don't beat yourself up. I mean that literally."

I sat in the booth a while longer after he left, just watching as the bar steadily emptied out. I watched Christian help Jadyn into her coat when her shift ended and walk her out into the cold, his arm around her shoulders. I watched Greg talk to lonely souls as they nursed their beers until the cool liquid grew warm, watched Lana continuously scan the room for trouble, not seeming to mind when Juan appeared to do more chatting with single ladies than actual security work. I watched Tony appear to lose a little piece of his dignity every time he had to plop a miniature candy cane or cinnamon stick into a cute alcoholic beverage.

I watched time tick by as I sat there knowing I needed to make things right with Rider, but had no clue how to when my own mind seemed to be attacking me. How could I face him while afraid my mind would show me a horror show? How did I stop it?

"Hey."

At some point I'd rested the back of my head against the wall and closed my eyes, lost myself in questions I had no answer to. I hadn't even heard or sensed Lana slide into the opposite side of the booth. "You snuck up on me. Very snake-like."

She winced a little, and I recalled other times she'd reacted similarly when anyone spoke of her particular brand of shifter. "You really don't like that you're a snake-shifter, do you?"

She shook her head. "Fairuza got her perfect revenge on me. Even with her dead, I'm still sharing my body with the soul of a giant snake."

"And sharing *its* body sometimes."

"Yep. Never liked them and now I am one from time to time." She gave a little shrug, as if to say there wasn't much to be done about it now. "Couldn't help but notice you're just sitting out here all alone, and you don't seem all that thrilled with your own company. Everything all right?"

I looked around the room, noted how only a few drinkers remained. Greg had been relieved of duty and only Tony remained to tend the bar, or stand in the corner of it staring at the remaining drinkers until he made them uncomfortable enough to decide to head home, which was what he appeared to be doing. I cast my senses out and picked up on Rider, still in his office, all alone, working on something for me when I couldn't even seem to bring myself to work on us. "Yeah. I'm just really bad company."

"Really?"

"Yeah. I need to hang around better people. Ones that don't suck as much."

"That's not even a vampire pun, is it?"

I shook my head. "No. It's just the sad truth."

"Wow. You don't even have to drink to start sounding like these boo-hoo losers."

I blinked. "You are terrible at pep talks."

"I didn't come over here to give you a pep talk. I came over here because I'm bored and it was either talk to you or yank one of these remaining saps out of here just to have something to do. I figured Rider wouldn't like the latter."

"You could play another Mariah Carey Christmas song on the jukebox and see if Tony finally loses it."

She grinned. "Maybe. Or I could play therapist and tell you to get over whatever the hell has you sitting over here imitating a kicked puppy. You're bringing down the atmosphere in here. Go. See if Rider has something for you to do. Take Kutya for a walk. Do something."

I felt a stir in my gut and shook my head. "Sonofabitch. Daniel called you, didn't he? Asked you about me?"

The expression on her face answered before she did. "He didn't call. He texted. He's concerned."

"He's a jerk. A meddling, overbearing, sweet, kind, absolutely wonderful jerk."

"He is." Lana smiled softly, seemed to remember something. "He really is."

I felt another stirring in my stomach region, but this one had nothing to do with hunches. Lana and Daniel had history, shared the kind of experience that bound people in a way no one else could understand. She'd been there with him at some of his worst moments of existence, and as ridiculous as it was, part of me was jealous of that shared experience.

"If I don't text him back soon and tell him you've moved from this spot, he's going to come back here. You know he will."

I blew out a sigh. "So text him and tell him I've moved from this spot."

"I won't lie to Daniel."

Another surge of jealousy hit and I recalled Daniel's mouth hovering just over mine in the pantry. Jealousy turned into guilt faster than I could blink.

"I will, however, drag your ass out of this booth myself."

I lifted my eyebrows. "I'd tell you to bring it, but you'd probably eat me."

"Not until the humans leave." She grinned. "Look, I don't know what your issues are, but everyone here can tell something is off between you and Rider. Do you want to fix it?"

I nodded, words not coming easily.

"Then get off your ass and go fix it."

"You think it's that easy, huh?"

"I didn't say it was easy. I said that's how you do it. Now, go do it." She leveled a determined stare my way.

"Unless you'd rather just throw a pity party, but I have to tell you it's not a cute look."

"You know, I never knew snakes had claws."

"I never knew vampires had yellow bellies."

I fought a grin. She fought a grin. A connection was made. "I think we just became actual friends."

"We'll do each other's nails later. Go deal with your shit."

Ah, damn it. She was right. I was just bitching and avoiding my problems, and if I felt as bad as I felt, Rider probably felt a lot worse. I'd screwed with the man's emotions enough. "Tell Daniel I said to go to bed."

"Will do."

I slid out of the booth, imagined what I'd say to Rider, came up empty and got stuck standing right there by the booth.

"I will drag your ass in there."

"I already have doubts about this friendship," I muttered and forced myself to put one foot in front of the other, then continue until I ended up in front of Rider's closed office door. I found myself frozen in place again, afraid I would see him covered in blood again and react as poorly as I had in the booth and every previous time, afraid I'd keep digging that knife into his heart deeper and deeper until there was nothing left.

The door swung open on its own, revealing Kutya snoring in his plush doggy bed and Rider sitting behind his desk, working on his computer. He didn't bother looking up when he spoke. "You seemed to be having trouble with the door."

Kutya's eyes opened at the sound of Rider's voice, and he lifted his big head to investigate what had caused the disturbance. I felt my body tense as he focused on me and barked, but it was a friendly bark.

"I seem to be having trouble with a lot of things lately," I said as I crossed over to the doggy bed and kneeled down to scratch the big pup in it. Kutya leaned in as I scratched between his ears, kicking his leg with glee as I hit the sweet spot. "Kutya told Jadyn there was something bad in me."

"What?"

I sighed and moved over to the bookshelf, perusing the books, looking anywhere but directly at Rider. "I told Jadyn about how Kutya growled at me earlier, asked her to check in with him. So she did. He told her 'Bad in Danni' when she asked why he growled at me."

He was silent for a moment. "What did he mean?"

"She didn't know, that was all she could get, but he couldn't have meant anything good. You heard him growl at me. There's something bad in me, Rider."

"He's a dog. Maybe he didn't know the right word for what he meant."

"You heard him growl at me. I think he had the right word. He sensed something bad in me and he reacted."

"He's not growling at you now." I heard the chair groan as Rider leaned back. "You're not a bad person, Danni."

"Then why am I hurting you?" The words came out barely above a whisper, but I knew he heard me from the way his breath stilled in his lungs. "Why can't I look into your eyes?"

"Only you can answer that one, Danni, and if you're willing to, I'd really love to know the answer."

"I don't know why. I look at you and… I'm so afraid. I have to look away."

"Sounds like you need to face it, whatever it is."

"How?"

"Don't look away." He stood from the chair. "Look at me, Danni. Look at me until you can get through whatever it is that's scaring you."

I shook my head. "I can feel what it does to you when I recoil. I can't keep doing that to you."

"Then stop." He covered the distance between us and turned me around to face him, held my face in both hands so I had no choice but to look into his eyes.

The blood poured over him immediately. I couldn't turn my head, so I closed my eyes.

"We will never get through this if you don't fight it. Open your eyes, Danni. Tell me what you see."

He was right, but that wasn't enough to make me open my eyes. I opened my eyes because of the desperation in his voice and the low growl that had just started in Kutya's throat. I opened my eyes and forced them to stay open as I stared straight into Rider's, watched them burn with red-hot rage and eventually bleed to black. In that black, I saw an image that chilled me to my bones. Tears spilled from my eyes, but still I didn't allow myself to so much as blink.

"What do you see, Danni?"

I tried to speak, and a sob came out instead.

"Talk to me. What do you see?"

"Me," I managed to get out. "I see me, and I'm a monster."

CHAPTER SIXTEEN

I couldn't bear it any longer. The reflection of me, of what I was evolving into, was too much. Rider's hands fell away from my face, and I lowered my head as I fell forward into his arms and let the tears pour out of me.

"Sit, Kutya! Lie down." Rider's voice was quiet, but authoritative. It effectively silenced the dog. Kutya whined, but did as ordered.

"Kutya can see it too. He sees the evil in me."

"There is no evil in you." Rider's arms tightened around me as I cried against him, my tears soaking the front of his sweater as his cheek rested against the top of my head. "I don't care what you saw or what you think the dog saw. You're not an evil person."

"I will be."

He pulled back enough to allow him to look at me, and sighed when I lowered my head, unable to deal with another repeat of the horror I saw in his eyes when I'd forced myself to hold his gaze. "What did you see? Describe it to me."

"Ever since the morning you killed Trixell, I haven't been able to look into your eyes without seeing you covered in blood, like you were when you came upstairs after. Sometimes I hear her screams."

"Shit," he muttered.

"I know why you were as violent with her as you were. I didn't understand your brother's full intent at the time Jon told us, but Daniel explained it to me. I get it now, and I don't blame you for what you did to her, whatever you did to her."

Rider backed up until he reached his desk, taking me with him, and sat on the edge. "I should have waited until you were upstairs before I started on her. I was just so full of rage at what she'd willingly been a part of. All I could see was his intentions with you, what he would have done if she'd accomplished helping him get to you."

"I know. I understand."

"I should have at least washed off before coming up here, used the showers downstairs and had someone bring me a change of clothes."

"It's all right."

"No, it's not, not if you're pulling up that image every time you look at me, and can't look at me longer than a second because of it. You should have never seen me like that."

"But it was you, wasn't it?" I started to look at him, but thought better of it. This conversation was long overdue, and I needed to get through it. "The real you? The way you were before we met?"

He cocooned me in his arms, my back to his chest, and rested his cheek against mine. "I have had many dark days, times my temper has led me to spill a large amount of blood. I've changed since you came into my life. I'm less angry, less volatile, but as I've explained before, that beast is always inside me. I never meant to terrify you with it."

"I thought that was what frightened me. It certainly shocked me that morning, so when I kept seeing it, I thought it was what you'd done that made it hard looking at you, but it wasn't." I took one of his big hands in mine, entwined my fingers with his. "It wasn't looking at you at all that has been bothering me. It was seeing myself in you, what I'm becoming."

"What do you mean?"

"When I see you, I see you covered in blood, and your eyes burn with rage. I usually look away, unable to bear what I see forming there, but I forced myself to keep looking this time until the truth was revealed. I saw me. Me, covered in the blood of my victims, my eyes burning bright red. Venom dribbling down my chin. Murder in my heart."

"Danni."

"I saw it, Rider. The beast you speak of living in you lives in me too. That's the part of you that was given to me, but I wasn't only given that beast that night. Your brother gave me the beast that lives in him too. I have two horrible beasts inside me, fighting, clawing… starving. They fight with each other and they fight with me, and all the fighting just tears me further and further. I'm losing. They'll win. They'll win and they'll destroy whatever was left of me after that night."

"Danni."

"You should have let me die. I shouldn't have been saved."

"You are not evil, Danni, and you're never going to be evil." Rider turned me around and held me close against him. "I will never allow anything to hurt you, not even yourself. I might not be a hybrid. My struggle might be different than yours, but I promise you this: you are not fighting your beasts alone. I will always be right here fighting with you."

I believed him, and that made me feel even worse because I didn't deserve it. One of the most monsterish things about me was that I hurt the one who loved me most. I'd wanted Daniel in that pantry. I'd wanted his lips and hands on me so badly I ached, and worse, I'd drawn him in. I was leading him on and deceiving Rider at the same time. I couldn't be any more selfish if I tried, and eventually I would have them both without a care because Selander Ryan lived in me as well as Rider, and one day the part of him that had become part of me would take control of me.

"What do you need? Are you thirsty?"

I shook my head. I was so sick of blood and the whole blood diet I'd been given. It was just a Band-Aid, only delaying the inevitable. I couldn't keep my succubus side under control. I was already struggling. "I just want to sleep. No dreams, no thinking. I just want to escape for a while, to actually, finally, get some real rest."

"You've been having nightmares."

I nodded against his chest.

"Do you want to talk about them?"

"No." Tears spilled down my cheeks. "I just want to sleep. I want to go to sleep and not think about a single thing."

"I can give you that." He rubbed my back. "Do you want me to make sure you don't dream today?"

"Please."

"Come on." He took my hand and led me out of the office, Kutya trailing behind.

By the time we reached his bedroom above the bar, the sun had started to rise, and my energy drained, but still the thoughts remained in my mind. The knowledge of what I was becoming mixed with the nightmare images that had been haunting me over the past four weeks.

"Do you want to go to sleep alone or—"

"I don't want to be alone," I said, adamantly. I already felt cold enough.

Kutya jumped up on the chaise and lowered his big head onto his massive paws before closing his eyes. Rider undressed as I shed my clothes, trading them for one of Rider's T-shirts. Once finished, I turned to find Rider under the covers, waiting for me.

I crawled into the bed and turned on my side so Rider could spoon me, allowing his warmth and midnight rain scent to wrap around me like a blanket. He tucked the covers around us and kissed my temple. "One dreamless day of sleep coming right up."

***

I opened my eyes to see Rider looming above me. He sat on the edge of the bed, using a gentle touch to brush my hair out of my eyes. He smelled of fresh, clean midnight rain as he watched me. The dark blue sweater he wore brought out the sapphire blue of his eyes. I looked away as blood poured over him, the nightmare image not cured by my revelation earlier that morning. I'd slept well, without dreaming, as promised, but it was not nightfall yet. Something was wrong. He wouldn't have awakened me otherwise.

"What's happened?"

"Your mother is downstairs in the bar, refusing to leave until she sees you."

I groaned. Even when I avoided nightmares in my sleep, they found me while awake.

"Say the word and I'll get rid of her and put you right back under so you can rest until night falls. I wanted to give you the choice instead of just making the decision for you."

"I really don't think I have a choice." It wasn't the first time she'd shown up at the bar, or at my apartment, since she'd left the letter with Tony telling me she was sorry, that she loved me, and that she needed to tell me something. I'd spent over two decades wanting that woman to say something along those lines and now that she had, now that she seemed to want to make an actual effort at being a loving mother, I didn't trust it. "She's just going to keep coming back, and poor Angel has to listen to her banging on the door when she shows up at the apartment."

"You have a choice. You don't have to see her until

you're ready to, if you're ready to. I can make her go away if that's what you want."

I reached for his hand and gave it a squeeze. "I appreciate that, but I know how she can be and I don't want everyone to suffer because I'm beating around the bush about meeting with her. I'm sure Tony's having the damnedest time refraining from eating her."

"Tony's having a hard time not taking a bite out of damn near everybody. He doesn't appear to be a fan of Christmas music."

"Or tinsel lodged in his ass crack."

"What?"

"Nothing." I sat up and sighed. "Thanks for keeping my nightmares at bay. I needed a good day of dreamless sleep, even if it was interrupted."

"I can give you that any time you need it. You only have to ask."

I grabbed him by the nape of his neck, pulled him in, and kissed him long and deep. Eyes closed, there were no blood-covered images of him flashing through my mind, no fear causing my heart to either seize or try beating its way out of my chest, and no tears to fall. It was just me and Rider, and things felt as close to normal as they had in weeks. When I finally came up for air, I kept my eyes closed and rested my forehead against his. "All right. I need to get dressed now or else I'm going to pull you into this bed with me and doing the hippity dippity with my mother downstairs is just too weird for me."

"The hippity dippity?" Laughter coated his words.

"Shut up." I pushed him away with a laugh and tossed the covers aside before swinging my legs over the side of the bed to stand.

"You still can't look me in the eye, can you?"

I nearly stumbled on my way to the dresser, but managed to get there. "I still see the blood. I'm sorry."

I sensed him stand as I dug clothes out of the dresser. I grabbed a pair of jeans and a black rib-knit long-sleeved sweater before his arms wrapped around my waist from behind and he kissed my temple. "I wish I could take those images away from you."

"I don't think anyone can make them stop." I leaned back into him. "What I'm seeing is about me, not you. I'm sorry if I'm making you feel like I don't want you. I do. I'll always want you." I might not deserve him given my recent thoughts and behaviors, but I wanted him all the same, selfish creature that I was.

"That's good to hear." He said the words, but the disappointment in his voice couldn't be hidden. I knew him well enough to know he needed to see that I wanted him, not just hear me say it. He needed me to be able to stare into his eyes and convey all the love in my heart, and it absolutely killed me that I couldn't do it.

That childhood Christmas flashed through my mind, the memory of such bitter disappointment when I'd found that blue-eyed blonde Barbie doll under the tree. It was just what I'd wanted, except it wasn't. I imagined my words were the same for Rider. They were nice, but not what he'd hoped for, and I hated disappointing him because I knew how some disappointments could be so strong they followed you for the rest of your life.

He dropped a kiss on top of my head and let go of me. "I'll go rescue Tony and let your mother know you're coming down. I need to feed, but I'll be right back after. Don't leave the building."

I watched him leave, wanted to call him back, to tell him I loved him while looking deep into his eyes, but just the thought of doing that triggered a flashback of what I'd seen that morning, the horrible image of me fully giving myself to the two beasts I carried, an image so terrible I didn't even think of Rider feeding from one of his donors, something that usually still caused me to wrestle with jealousy. By the time I forced that nightmare back into the recesses of my mind, he'd left.

MERRY FANGIN' CHRISTMAS

***

Once I'd cleaned up and dressed, I headed downstairs, noting Kutya's leash was missing from the peg on the wall next to the garage door. His food bowl was empty, so I knew whoever had been tasked with taking the big guy for a walk was going to need to use the shovel kept on hand just for cleaning up Kutya's messes. It wouldn't be Rider. I sensed him in the sublevels, but couldn't tell what he was doing. Not that Rider ever cleaned up Kutya's messes, or ever would as long as he could pay someone else to. I couldn't blame him. A person could throw their back out shoveling up Kutya's mess.

I realized I was standing in front of the door leading to the hall that ran the length between the bar and the other half of The Midnight Rider, giving way too much thought to Kutya's bowel movements and recognized what I was doing. Procrastination wouldn't do me any favors, and it certainly wasn't nice of me to leave my pushy mother unattended out there with people I actually liked.

"Suck it up, buttercup," I whispered to myself before straightening my shoulders and pushed through the door, then took another deep breath and pushed through the one that opened into the bar.

Kelly Clarkson belted out a Christmas song on the jukebox as I stepped into the room, something about being wrapped in red. Night hadn't fallen yet, so we weren't in our busiest hours, but the bar was already starting to fill up. Everywhere I looked, I saw the cute holiday-themed drinks, including the table where my mother sat.

She looked like a big pink Hostess Sno Ball in her fuzzy cashmere sweater, pink khakis, and big pearl earrings in a matching shade. Her hair had been recently touched up, her gray roots dyed to match the rest of her blonde mane, and her lips and cheeks were as candy-colored as her outfit. She'd just lifted the small drink with the cinnamon stick in it to take a drink when her eyes collided with mine and I felt like a deer in headlights, unable to run away. Not just because she'd seen me, but because Tony was behind the bar glaring at me with a look that said, 'Do something with her'.

I could run from my mother. I had years of practice doing that, but I wasn't about to press my luck trying to run from the tiger-shifter, especially after he'd been subjected to an encounter with my mother. The nicest person in the world could turn murderous after being subjected to an encounter with the woman, and as much as I liked Tony, I wouldn't ever put him in the running for nicest person in the world.

I forced one foot in front of the other and kept moving until I reached the table and sat across from my mother. "Mom."

"Danni." She took a drink of her frou-frou beverage and glanced over at the bar. "I had hoped after reading my letter you would have accepted my invitation to talk instead of making me track you down. Honestly, the people you have chosen to associate with here can be so rude. That Chinese man growled at me."

I fought a grin at the picture in my mind of Tony growling at my mother, but cringed at her choice of words. "Did he tell you he was Chinese, Mom?"

She looked at me like I'd gone crazy. "Why would that have come up in the time it took to order a drink?"

I took a breath, tried to not let her upset me already. "I'm just saying you shouldn't automatically assume all Asian people are Chinese."

"What's the difference?"

"The same difference between Americans and Mexicans. We share the same continent too, but not the same culture."

She waved her hand dismissively. "None of that has anything to do with anything important. We really need to talk, Danni. I know you hate me and probably tore my letter apart, probably didn't even read it."

"I read it, and I don't hate you." I sat back in my chair and sighed. "We're never going to be the Gilmore Girls, but I don't hate you."

"Who are the Gilmore Girls?"

I shook my head. "Nevermind. Why did you want to see me?"

"Because I'm your mother, obviously." Her voice had raised a little, and held a bit of bite. She seemed to realize this and looked around, always concerned with decorum, before continuing, making sure to soften and lower her voice first. "Like I said in the letter, it really hurt me when you yelled at me in your apartment, when you said such awful things."

"Right, because you don't say awful things to me every time we speak."

"Danni, I am not here to argue with you." I saw her jaw clench as she appeared to gather herself. She took another drink of the frou-frou concoction and closed her eyes on a deep inhale. When she reopened them, she seemed to have calmed. "I am your mother, you are my daughter, and naturally, I have loved you since the day you were born. I've loved you both, but I know I failed to show you this. I know I have been hard on you, at times distant, maybe even cold."

At times? Maybe? It took every ounce of willpower I had not to roll my eyes.

"It's important that you know there was a reason for this." Her eyes grew wet. "I loved my baby girls, but I knew you didn't need me."

"I was a child. You were my mother," I snapped. "Of course I needed you."

She shook her head. "You never loved me like you loved your father. You followed him around, wanting to be just like him, but I was your mother. It was my job to make sure you acted like a girl. Not some grubby tomboy." She dug through her pink Louis Vuitton purse until she found a tissue and dabbed her eyes. "And I tried. I bought you the prettiest dresses, the makeup, and I encouraged you to diet. I know I was pushy, but I knew you had the potential to be so beautiful, to have so much, and you just fought me tooth and nail."

My mouth dropped open, and I sat there and just stared, completely flabbergasted. My mother was a piece of work, I knew that, and I had listened to her criticize me for over twenty years, but this? This was insane. I laughed out loud. I laughed until tears poured from my eyes and Hazel, the fae server, shot me an odd look as she walked by. I was pretty sure Tony and Greg would be giving me similar looks too if I looked their way, but I didn't. I wiped my eyes, got myself under control, and glared at my mother. "You really are something else, you know that? You said you owed me an apology and an explanation in your letter, and this is what I get? 'I'm sorry I couldn't make you beautiful, but I tried'? And you really wonder why I put this off."

"No, you don't understand. That is not what I'm saying at all." She threw back the last of her drink and raised the glass to wave it impatiently as she stared at Hazel. "I swear the service here is intolerable," she said loudly as she tapped her hand on the tabletop until she got Hazel's attention. Nevermind the fact that Hazel was busy with customers at another table.

I mouthed an apology to Hazel as she walked over and took the glass. "You'd like another?"

"That would be obvious, dear. You really must get better at your job if you hope to move up into something better. I can't see tipping well when not getting excellent service."

"Hmmm." Hazel gave the biggest, fakest smile I'd ever seen. "I can't imagine you tipping well at all."

"Why, I nev—"

"Mom." I snapped my fingers, grabbing her attention before she could cause more of a scene or antagonize

Hazel any further. "You came to talk with me, so talk. Or are we done here?"

"No, we're not done, not if all you got from what I said is that I never thought you were beautiful."

"I'm sorry, but if there was anything else in that spiel, I sure missed it. And for the record, I tried to make you happy, but nothing was ever good enough. I was never good enough. If it seems I love Daddy more than I do you, it's because he loved me. He really loved me, just the way I was. I was beautiful enough for him just because I was his daughter. I didn't need to starve myself or go under the knife to make him proud of me."

"You didn't need to do any of that to make me proud of you either," she snapped.

"Oh really? Then why were you always pushing for it? I swear you cared more about the numbers on the scale than you did the ones on my schoolwork. You tried to get me into a plastic surgeon at sixteen. I wasn't even an adult yet. You wore me down until I almost did it. I almost had surgery to make myself look like you wanted. You drove me to hate myself."

"I wanted you to love yourself!" She quieted as Hazel returned with another Warm Merry. The fae set the drink down with a flourish and I noticed the drink seemed to sparkle, and those drinks didn't sparkle. Hazel's eyes sparkled too, with pure mischief, and I considered telling my mother to order something else, but she'd opened old wounds and I knew whatever the fae had done, it wasn't lethal. And let's face it, my mother probably deserved whatever indigestion or bad night's sleep she was about to get. Who knew what she'd said to the staff while waiting for me. She couldn't even be nice to them in my presence and she knew I knew them personally. Well, most of them.

"Accepting me as I was would have gone a long way in doing that," I told her after Hazel left us. "Actually giving a shit about me would have been nice. Whenever anything happened, it was always Shana you worried about. Never me."

"I know I was wrong, Danni. Believe me, after the way you spoke to me at your apartment, after the way Shana just ran off to Vegas to…" She dabbed her eyes with the tissue again and took a big gulp from the sparkly drink. "Who even knows what Shana is doing or why. I failed with both of you. She was the good child who loved my attention, and I spoiled her. I see that now. And you, you were the one who didn't need me. You were always so headstrong, so smart. You seemed so opposite me, and I thought that was why you didn't like me. You resented me, and you resented Shana, and well, that made me resent you sometimes. I wasn't a great mom, but I tried."

"You thought criticizing me in every possible way was trying to be a good mom? That constantly comparing me to Shana would create some sort of bond between us? That's insane."

"I raised you the way I was raised, and I was raised to believe a mother's job is to make her daughters the most beautiful and close to perfect as they can be so they can marry a good man who will take care of them. I was only trying to give you a good life."

"By completely wrecking my self-esteem? I only wanted to be loved as I was, to not feel like I was born wrong, like I was the ugly, unwanted child with the hideously deformed body."

She squirmed in her seat. "I didn't—"

"You wanted me to get a boob job. You bought me breast enhancing pills and Grandma bought something to electrocute my chest. All I ever heard from either of you was how bad it was I wasn't built like you, and how no one would want me because of it."

"I'm sorry." She squirmed a little again, pulling a face, and I wondered what Hazel had put in her drink. She wasn't spontaneously combusting or bleeding though, so I wasn't overly concerned. "That's the way I was raised. Beauty and a profitable marriage were the two main goals, and I didn't have the most profitable marriage. I wanted better for you girls, and if I was hard on you, it was because you just wouldn't listen. I was only trying to give you more than I had myself."

My hand tightened into a fist. "My father was a wonderful man, and you were lucky to have had him as your husband. If you thought your marriage was a failure because the medical bills took all his money, I pity you. And I pity him for having such a heartless wife."

She gasped. "I loved him. I could have waited, married someone my mother found for me, a much better catch, but I married him for love. There's nothing wrong with being disappointed he didn't plan for us better."

Images of my father lying in the hospital bed, wasting away from the ravages of cancer, entered my mind and bloodlust flooded my body. I needed to end the conversation or not even the knowledge that she was my mother would stop me from tearing into the woman across from me, ripping her limb from limb. "This wasn't a good idea. I can't deal with you right now."

"Danni, please. I'm trying to make amends." She squirmed in her seat again. "I'd like for you to spend Christmas Eve with Mother and I. I can't imagine Shana will be home for it."

"Your private investigator hasn't found her yet?" I asked, remembering that the only reason Pacitti had been following me in the first place was because he thought I'd lead him to Shana. If he was still in contact with my mother, she might have information on where to find him, although Rider had already had his tech team go through her phone records and hack into her email account, turning up nothing of use.

"Oh, I fired him. He wasted so much time trailing you while Shana was off on the other side of the country, the moron."

I wanted to remind her he'd followed me because she herself had told him I was hiding Shana, but I didn't want to continue our visit any longer than necessary.

"Please, Danni. It would mean a lot to me if you came. I really do want to work out our differences and have a better relationship with you."

She actually looked sincere despite the squirming, sincere enough that I felt a little bad for not being very willing to make amends myself. "I'll see. I may have plans with Rider."

"You can bring him too," she said with a tight smile as she looked around the bar. "He clearly isn't as rich as he made himself sound, but he does own this… establishment. You could certainly do worse. He is very attractive, I'll give him that." She squirmed again and grimaced. "I am so sorry to cut this short. I need to go, but Christmas, yes? Call me."

I bit back a grin as she grabbed her purse and coat, and nearly knocked over Jake Porter as she fled the bar.

CHAPTER SEVENTEEN

"She sure went somewhere fast," Hazel said with a devilish gleam in her eye as she stopped by the table to pick up what remained of the drink my mother hadn't even finished half of.

"So I noticed." I stood from the table and pushed in my chair. "What did you put in her drink anyway?"

Hazel studied me, seeming to debate with herself whether actually admitting to the mischief was wise of her.

"If you overheard any of that conversation, you should probably be able to figure out I wouldn't get my panties in a twist over a joke played on her. I'm sure she deserved it, and whatever it was, it wasn't as bad as what I know Tony probably wanted to do to her before I came down here to occupy her attention."

Hazel grinned. "Let's just say I made sure she'd have a few good itches in her britches for the next few hours."

I barked out a laugh as the fae walked the discarded drink back to the kitchen.

"Someone is in a good mood," Jake Porter said, reaching my table.

"Surprisingly so," I replied, and quickly picked up on the tension that had filled the room. It had started when

Jake stepped inside, but escalated to an uncomfortable degree once he'd approached me. Every paranormal being in the room was staring right at us. "Boy, you sure aren't a popular guy around here, are you?"

His mouth turned up in a lazy smile. "It comes with the territory. Why do I get the feeling you're like their queen or something?"

"Their queen?" I laughed harder than I'd laughed at the prank Hazel pulled on my mother. "I am so far from that."

"Then why are they all ready to gut me if I so much as breathe on you too hard?"

"Maybe they're more concerned about what I'll do to you," I teased. "You're not the only one with a reputation." I picked up on the husky tone in my voice and noticed I was twirling a strand of hair around my finger, and groaned inwardly. Was I seriously flirting with a slayer? Fine, he looked like Dean Winchester's twin brother, but he was still a slayer and we were standing smack dab in the middle of The Midnight Rider. I'd clearly lost my mind.

I decided to move over to the bar before I had the chance to make an even bigger fool of myself. I'd just slid onto a barstool when someone decided to put their money in the jukebox and select Mariah Carey's "All I Want for Christmas Is You."

"Sonofabitch," Tony growled, reaching under the bar for a dark mug. "They couldn't even wait another hour or two before awakening the Christmas siren."

I felt for the guy, but still had to laugh a little. "You need a break."

"Yes, I do." He placed the mug under the tap just for vampires and filled it with warm blood, keeping a watchful eye on Jake the entire time as the slayer took a seat right next to me. Fresh blood. We'd had another guest in interrogation while I'd slept. "There's nothing I'd like more than to go home and sleep until December twenty-sixth, when Mariah goes back into the crypt until next year."

"Now that's just uncalled for," I told him as he set the mug in front of me. "She's not some kind of evil monster."

"She created a monster with that song. It's the song that will not die." He glared at the jukebox. "Then again, I haven't shot that damn thing yet."

"Man, you must be fun at parties." Jake raised his hands innocently when Tony growled at him. "Whoa there, big kitty, just makin' small talk."

Tony's eyes darkened into two black orbs as his top lip peeled back from his teeth. "What do you want, slayer?"

"Uh, a beer, for starters." Jake looked around. "And if I can grab a girl to take my order, those onion rings I had last night were killer. I could go for a double bacon cheeseburger and some tots too. Ooh, and some pie."

You should keep your distance from him, Tony spoke directly into my mind. I wasn't used to speaking that way with Tony, so the unexpected intrusion caused me to jump a little. *Especially with Rider out of the building. He can't be trusted.*

Christian says otherwise, so I think I'll be fine.

Tony growled low in his throat, clearly irritated with both of us, grabbed a mug and filled it with beer before slamming it down as hard as he could in front of Jake without breaking the glass then moved over to the other side of the bar to tell Hazel what Jake wanted to eat.

The slayer grabbed a napkin and wiped where the beer had sloshed over the edge of the mug. "Was it something I said?"

"Judging by the grin on your face, you know it was, and you knew it when you said it."

Jake's grin expanded into a full-blown smile and he brought the mug to his mouth.

"It's clear you enjoy being a smartass, but you might not want to try your luck with Tony. Of all the paranormal beings in here, he's probably the most likely to eat you."

Jake took a big drink from his mug and set it down. "Hey, big kitty wasn't so bad. I was going to call him a big pussy, and no matter what I say, he's going to still want to sink those teeth and claws into me. That's the way the slayer-prey relationship works."

"Keep referring to us as prey and you're going to make it extremely hard for me to keep defending you."

"You defend me?" He placed his hand over his heart. "That's so sweet. I'm touched."

"It's not really defending you so much as just reminding everyone you're a friend of Christian, so we should give you a chance before ripping off your limbs." I raised my mug and took a drink. "But the more you talk, the more I see why so many people here want to hurt you. You really are a wiseass."

"I like to call it charm," he said, and moved his mug out of the way for Hazel to slide a slice of pie in front of him. His eyes lit up as he grabbed the fork and plunged in.

"Gah, you really are so much like Dean Winchester it's crazy," I commented, watching his absolute merriment as he enjoyed the pie while sitting there in his worn jeans, T-shirt paired with an open flannel shirt and brown leather bomber jacket.

He grunted. "Stop it. I'm trying to enjoy my pie."

"Hey, Jensen Ackles is a gorgeous man and Dean Winchester is like the awesomest character in creation. Why does it bother you so much when people point out the extremely obvious likeness?"

Jake took his time finishing the massive chunk of pie he'd shoved into his mouth and washed it down with a big gulp of beer before looking at me. "What I do requires a bit of anonymity. I like to keep a low profile, which has been damned hard to do since that stupid show started airing. And the fans…" He rolled his eyes. "Fucking insane. Grown women screaming in your face is just nuts. Hell, I've almost shot a few by reflex. They sound like harpies, and some of those nutcases have no concept of boundaries. Had some dumbass ask for a selfie and an autograph while I was in the bathroom last week. Standing at the urinal. It's just common courtesy that you don't ask a dude for selfies when he has his dick in his hand, but it doesn't stop those crazy-ass fans."

I grimaced. "Yeah, that's a little inappropriate."

"Ya think?" He stabbed his fork into the pie and speared off another chunk. "So why are you up in the day? You're not an old vamp, and succubi tend to be nocturnal too. I would have figured you'd sleep in as much as you could before we venture out to kill that fugly krackling."

I'd been taking a drink of blood when he asked me the question, and nearly choked on it. "You know I'm half succubus?"

He looked at me as if I'd just asked him the world's dumbest question. "I'm a slayer. I knew what you were and how long you've been it before I ever laid eyes on you."

"Right, but... I knew you could sense paranormal entities, but most people can only tell the vampire part of me."

"When you're a hybrid, it can be hard to pick up the other half, but again, I'm a slayer. It's very rare that I can't tell what someone is right away. And generally when I can't, that person is, in fact, a hybrid. I can sense you though. I can sense everything in you."

A cold chill ran down my spine, but before I could ask what he meant by everything, Hazel arrived with his small feast. He gave her his empty pie plate, thanked her, and grabbed the double bacon cheeseburger.

Lana arrived as he took the first bite and slid onto the barstool next to his. "Hey, Danni. Jake."

I greeted her, and Jake nodded, his mouth far too full of meat and cheese to speak. I noticed Tony still keeping me and the slayer under his watchful eye from where he tended to a customer on the other side of the bar. "Did Tony suggest you come over here to keep an eye on us?"

"Yup," Lana answered. "I told him I fought with our boy here and he's a good guy, but that tiger really doesn't like him. Also, Rider was notified about Jake being here, and that prompted the order."

Jake swallowed the chunk of burger in a big gulp that sounded painful. "I told you. You're their queen. You still haven't said why you're awake and hanging out in the bar so early."

"I could ask you the same thing."

"I don't generally sleep all day, and I had nothing else to do until that fugly bitch shows his face at nightfall, so why not come here and grab something to eat?"

"Uh, I don't know, maybe because there are lots of other places where the people wouldn't be so rude to you." I looked at his food. "I'd think you'd be afraid to eat the food here."

"Maybe if this was just any vampire-owned bar. Rider doesn't trust me, but he's not the type to have his people poison me or screw with my food."

"Because he has honor?"

"I was thinking more along the lines of he'd want to yank out my intestines and choke me with them himself, but sure, let's go with that." Jake popped a cheesy tater tot into his mouth. "No, he's not some bloodthirsty animal and although he talks a lot of shit about not trusting me, I suspect it's just to keep me on my toes. He trusts Christian, Malaika, and Seta. All three can vouch for me, and I really only need Seta's good word. She doesn't vouch for a whole lot of people."

"I can imagine. She doesn't seem the type to get along with many people."

"Oh, I'm sure she's killed people just for looking at her wrong." Jake chuckled and grabbed another tater tot. "She's actually one of the good guys though."

"So how does a slayer, someone genetically designed to kill all paranormal beings, end up becoming friends with a bunch of them?" I reached for my mug to take a drink of blood and had a lightbulb moment. "You drank blood last night. Does that have something to do with it?"

"Nope. I'm just special."

"Wait. He drank blood?" Lana looked at my mug, then watched Jake take a massive bite out of his burger. "That's how you came back to life after you got killed, isn't it? It has to be the blood. It keeps you alive like it does vampires."

"Came back to life?" My mouth dropped open.

Jake dropped the remainder of his burger onto his plate and rolled his eyes as he chewed.

"He actually died and came back to life?"

"I wouldn't have believed it if I hadn't witnessed it with my own eyes," Lana said. "He got stabbed through the back with a sword. It went all the way through, right through major organs. He died, but maybe fifteen or so minutes later he comes back minus the cavity in his torso and gets right back into the battle like nothing happened."

Jake swallowed down the big hunk of cheeseburger, winced a little and raised his finger at me where I sat with my mouth still hanging open. "Don't even say it."

"Dude. You love pie, you eat like a pig, you're a smartass, you drive a black older model Malibu that looks very similar to a '67 Impala, you're like a hunter on steroids, you look just like him, you dress like him, sound like him, even move like him, and you come back from the freaking dead? You're Dean Winchester."

"You said it." He groaned and looked over at Lana. "Thanks for that. Now she'll never stop."

"I simply asked a question," Lana said. "So, is that how you keep from dying?"

Jake sighed and took a swig of beer. "Yeah. Long story short, I had a run-in with a mad scientist and now I can't die permanently as long as I drink blood from time to time, but I am not a vampire."

"He's Dean Winchester," I said and scooted a little closer to him.

Tony suddenly appeared in front of me, reached over the bar to grab my shoulders and slid me back to where I had been. "Boss's orders."

Oh, right. Rider. My boyfriend. Love of my life. I looked over at Dean Winches... *er*... Jake Porter and smiled sheepishly. Hey, at least I hadn't humped the guy's leg. Considering he was Dean Winchester's twin in looks and damn near everything else, I'd consider that a huge feat of self-control.

"I swear one of these days I'm going to hunt down those actors and everyone who had anything to do with that show and gank the whole lot of them," Jake muttered and went back to his burger. Tony hadn't moved. He stood still, staring right in Jake's face as he ate, so the slayer stared right back at him and opened his mouth, revealing the half-masticated burger inside.

"You really think that bothers me?" the tiger-shifter said. "I've eaten people."

Jake closed his mouth and continued to chew while smiling, amused. He swallowed the burger, reached into his pocket, and pulled out some coins. He kept eye contact with Tony as he handed the money to Lana. "Do me a favor, sweetheart, and go put that in the jukebox. I want to hear that Mariah Carey song."

Tony growled so deep and powerful I thought he was going to shift shape right there, and he might have, if not for the knowledge there were humans in the bar. He glared at Jake as Lana left to request the song. "You're a fucking asshole."

"Aww, big guy, it gives me a tingle when you talk so sweet to me like that."

Tony growled again, baring teeth as Mariah Carey's voice filled the air. "Greg, you handle this guy before I kill him."

Tony stormed off to the other side of the bar and Greg came over, picked up Jake's mug. "Want a refill?"

"Sure thing, Greg." Jake laughed until he was red in the face.

"Okay, so I know you're Dean Winchester and all—"

"Seriously, stop with the Dean Winchester already. I'm

Jake. Call me Jake."

"Whatever, you're like a badass slayer and stuff, but I really wouldn't keep teasing or laughing at Tony. You wouldn't want to cause a major incident, would you? Besides, the man's had to listen to that song like a hundred times a day this month. Cut him a break."

"I'm not laughing at him." Jake pulled back on the laughter as Greg delivered his refilled mug. "So you're Greg, huh?"

Greg looked at me, then Jake, seeming a little uneasy around the slayer. "Yeah."

"I gotta say, Greg, I haven't seen a lot of vampires with such a thick mustache. Haven't met a lot of 'em named Greg either."

Greg raised his hand slowly, and brushed his mustache with his fingers, appearing a little self-conscious about it. "I've always had a mustache."

"Oh, it's a good mustache," Jake said, but couldn't keep a straight face. "It's a mighty dad-stache. The name though… Greg? Greg's an accountant. Greg plays tennis with his boss and lets him win, hoping for a raise. Greg with a dad-stache, well, he's just about the furthest a dude can get from a vampire. Tell me your last name kills, Greg. Greg Darkmore, or Greg Blackheart, or maybe it's short for Gregori? Give me something to work with here, Greg."

Greg shuffled uneasily and dropped his gaze. "My name's Greg Bennett."

Jake had been in the process of taking a drink and choked, shooting liquid out of his nose. Greg's mouth pinched like he'd taken a big bite out of a lemon and red climbed his face.

"You have a perfectly fine name for a vampire," I told him, "and your mustache makes you look very mature and put together." Jake snorted while choking. I smacked his back to help him along. "Unlike some other morons that hang out around here."

"Thank you, Miss Keller." Greg speared Jake with a withering glare, wiped up the mess he'd made, and strolled off to the other corner of the bar.

"You really can be a jackass," I snapped as Jake pulled himself together and grabbed a napkin to wipe his face.

"Oh what? You don't think he's the blandest vampire you've ever seen? How could I not make fun of that?"

"Easy. Just quit trying to piss off everyone." It hit me then that I was probably doing such a good job of not humping the guy's leg because even though he was a dead-ringer for Dean Winchester, the Dean Winchester character was hilarious and sexy while being a wiseass on TV. When the lookalike did it in reality, it wasn't as cute, but then again, maybe that was because the more he acted that way, the more I feared having to jump in-between him and one of my friends who wanted to kill him.

I looked around for Lana, checking why she hadn't returned to us, and saw her speaking with a small group of women in the corner. She was on security duty, so even while keeping an eye on me, she had to do her actual job.

"Fine. I'll be nice, but you should be nice too and answer my question." He lifted a soggy onion ring he'd snorted beer on and dropped it back to the plate before pushing it aside to be picked up. "What's a nice vampire-succubus like you doing wide awake at an hour like this? Bad dreams?"

Again, I got that weird feeling that Jake Porter knew way more about me than he should, and I remembered his parting remark the previous night. "Why do you seem so interested in my sleep quality?"

He opened his mouth to answer, but seemed to get stuck before he could think of the first word to even begin.

"I'm back, y'all!" A boisterous, deep voice I was very familiar with boomed through the room, ricocheting off the walls, and almost drowned out Mariah Carey's high note.

I turned to see Rome walking toward me, a huge smile on his face. He was dressed in U of L sweats and a big, black puffer coat. Daniel followed behind him in jeans, shit-kickers, and a black leather coat zipped all the way up.

"Welcome back, big guy. How are you feeling? Shouldn't you be home, resting?"

"He won't," Daniel said. His dark gaze locked onto Jake as the pair finished approaching.

"Girl, I got all the rest I'll ever need in the hospital." Rome did some complicated bro handshake with Tony, bumped knuckles with Greg, and gave me a big bear hug. "I can't take any more rest, and I want to show y'all my shit. Y'all won't believe this."

"Your—" My heart skipped as he reached into one of his coat pockets, and I turned to Daniel. "He's not talking about his—"

"His actual shit that they took out of him? Yes, yes he is. He wanted to keep the physical shit as some sort of trophy, but had to settle on pictures."

"Man, who wouldn't be proud of this? This is some Guinness World Record shit." He turned the picture my way, and I nearly broke my neck, turning my face away before I jumped off of the barstool to hide behind Daniel.

"Tell me when he's done," I said, and looked around Daniel's shoulder to see Jake, Tony, and Greg checking out the picture. "Oh, gross. How can you even want to look at that?"

"That's some impressive shit," Jake answered. "How can we not want to check it out?"

"Gross. Did you look at it?" I asked Daniel.

"I wasn't given a choice, and sweetheart, I live with the guy, where he clogs the toilet pretty much daily. I've been seeing and smelling his shit for months."

I shuddered at the thought, recalling how often Rome had clogged the toilet when we stayed in Pigeon Forge, and remembered a fart he'd released that nearly took us all out. However, his gas had saved us from demons so I didn't give him too much grief, but I drew the line at looking at pictures of his actual crap.

"It was too big to get out in one piece so they had to hack it into chunks," Rome told the guys, and the human women sitting at the table behind him shared a disgusted look before dropping money on the table and gathering their belongings.

"Okay, can we talk about anything else?" I pleaded. "I don't think Rider would approve of this type of discussion around his customers."

Tony looked over at the women, saw them shoot disgusted looks their way as they headed out, and pulled a face. "Yeah, man, let's put those away. You can tell us more about it outside of the bar."

"Cool, man. I understand." Rome put the pictures back in his pocket and took the coat off. "Hey, Daniel, hang my coat up, partner? I'm supposed to be resting, you know."

Daniel turned to look down at me, rolled his eyes, and grabbed Rome's coat before walking back to the front of the room to hang it on the coat rack.

I took my seat back, and Rome sat around the corner. "Give me a beer, man, and I think I'll keep it light, start off with some cheesy tots. Then you can fill me in on why this slayer is back. Last time he was here, there were angels and lycanthropes and all kinds of crazy shit involved."

"Are you supposed to be drinking alcohol already?" I asked him. "I know cheesy tater tots can't be good for you so soon after the surgery you ha—" I'd noticed Daniel walking back towards us, having shed his coat and sat there in quiet confusion, wondering why in the world he had on a red sweater with Rome's giant face on it surrounded by little Christmas trees and what I assumed were reindeer butts.

Noticing I'd gone silent, Rome turned his head to see what had caught my eye just as Daniel reached us. "Why is my face on your sweater?"

"Oh, this?" Daniel looked down at the monstrosity and

when he looked back up, his smile stretched from one ear to the other. "It's my ugly Christmas sweater."

I burst out laughing. Greg and Jake, who to my knowledge, didn't even know Rome that well, joined in. I thought I even saw Tony's lips twitch, which was saying a lot for Tony.

Rome glared at all of us before fixing the dark look on Daniel. "I hate you, Puff."

This made us all laugh harder, and we continued laughing until the air shifted in the room and everyone grew serious. The boss was back.

CHAPTER EIGHTEEN

Other than the humans talking and Nat King Cole crooning "The Christmas Song" on the jukebox, there wasn't a peep as Rider crossed the floor to stand directly in front of me. He kept his gaze on Jake the whole time, and I didn't dare take my eyes off him to see how Jake reacted to the dark glare.

Once he stopped in front of me, he looked over to where Daniel stood on his left and stared at the sweater for a while. "Ugly Christmas sweater?"

"Yep." Daniel fought back another round of laughter, reading the room.

"Children. You're both children." Rider shook his head as he lifted his gaze to look over at where Rome sat at the bar. "Do not give him anything to eat or drink except for water."

Rome's face fell, and he immediately started to protest, but thought better of it and clamped his mouth shut. I thought I even saw a tear or two in his eye. The man did not deal well with food deprivation.

"I suppose you want to come back to work already."

"Man, I've done enough resting in bed to last me a lifetime. I can do door duty without hurting myself."

Rider stared at Tony for a moment and I got the sense the two were silently conversing through their own private telepathic link. Then he directed his stony look at Jake. "Porter."

"Hasselhoff."

Rider's nostrils flared as he clamped his jaw tight.

"It's like having two Daniels when this guy's around," Tony muttered. "Can I just snap one of them in half? Either one. It can be my yearly bonus."

"Hey!" Daniel frowned. "Not cool, man."

Rider growled, his eyes shone with a hint of golden color, and I got the impression he was more angered by the comparison between Jake and Daniel than the fact the slayer was there. I slid as far away from the slayer as I could without actually leaving my barstool.

"Daniel, Rome, Danni, and Ken Doll, corner booth… now."

With exception to Jake, who only smirked, all the men laughed as Rider stepped closer to me. Even Tony managed a full smile and what passed as a chuckle for him: a silent, subtle shaking of his broad shoulders.

"Guess I'd be Slayer Ken." Jake downed the last of his beer, stood, and straightened his bomber jacket. "Still a badass."

"Still junkless," Daniel said, pulling an approving smile out of Rider and more laughter from the other men as he led them over to the booth in the darkest corner of the bar, minus the two bartenders who resumed their duties.

Rider hovered over me and held my face in his big hand. He tilted my head back, so I had to look straight at him. It didn't last long before I saw him covered in blood, eyes ablaze, and heard Trixell's screams echoing off the walls. I jerked my head, breaking off the eye contact.

"Still?"

"Yeah. I'm sorry."

He reached past me, picked up the mug of blood I'd only drank half of. "Do you think you could drink from me before we head out tonight?"

"I can try, but I think I could if we do it like Nannette had me do it yesterday."

He set the mug back down. "Did you and the slayer talk about anything of use, anything other than how much he reminds you of your fantasy man?"

The jealousy in his voice was crystal clear and the guilt it birthed in me was just as strong. "He mostly just ate and antagonized Tony, and hey, Dean Winchester's just a character. You're my dream guy."

"More like your nightmare guy," he murmured as he took my hand and pulled me to my feet. "Hence why you can't look at me. Come on."

His comment brought back images from my last nightmare, and as we walked toward the booth where three men sat waiting, a filmy haze washed over them. Suddenly, they were all watching me in anticipation. Daniel licked his lips, drawing up images of the vivid fantasy I'd had in the pantry, and Jake Porter delivered a sultry, inviting look that weakened my knees to the point they nearly gave out.

"Danni, what is it?"

I shook my head, and realized I'd came to a complete standstill halfway to the booth. Rider stood in front of me, blocking me from view of the men waiting for us. "Nothing. I'm fine."

He placed his fingertips under my chin, started to tilt my head up, but thought better of it, knowing it would only trigger another bloody nightmare image. He released me and shoved his hands into his pants pockets. "How are you feeling? I can better help you the more honest you are."

I nodded, knowing he could, but still, how did you tell your boyfriend you were having sexual fantasies and nightmares about other men? It would be a hard enough thing to do if I'd been dating a normal guy, but my boyfriend was a centuries-old vampire who could kill people without touching them. And he had a jealous streak that those two men tap-danced all over. "Honestly, I feel really wonky."

"You've had sex recently, and your last two live drinkings were from me. Let's get some violence in. I've got someone waiting in interrogation. I'll let you handle that before we head out. Think that'll help you feel a bit normal?"

Normal. The word rubbed me the wrong way in that moment, but I nodded like a good girl. "Yeah, wouldn't hurt."

"Okay. Are you going to be all right to talk with these guys?"

Wait. Was he asking me if I was going to start humping them or something? "Of course I'll be all right talking to them. Why wouldn't I be?"

We stood there for a while, Rider not answering, and me not looking directly into his eyes. Finally, he sighed. "Let me know if anything changes."

He led me over to the booth as a Bing Crosby song came from the jukebox. The three men waited for us, but fortunately there was no filmy haze covering them any longer. Daniel and Rome sat together on one side of the booth, facing the back wall. Jake once again had commandeered a chair from a nearby table and sat straddling it at the edge of the booth. They all looked my way, but innocently, no lusty thoughts filtering through their eyes, much to my relief. Jake, however, peered a little too intently my way, studying me like a specimen under a microscope. Something about the way the slayer often studied me made me uneasy. Despite what he was, I didn't get the feeling he was studying me for any weaknesses he could use to his advantage should he decide to off me, but still, it was unnerving.

Rider made sure I slid into our side of the booth first, then took his seat next to me. This placed him with a clear view of the entire room and put him closer to Jake. And it put me in the corner away from the slayer and the other two men.

"Did you fill Rome in?" Rider asked.

Daniel nodded. "All up to date."

"You're going to be our driver," Rider told the big guy, "but you're staying out of the action while you finish healing."

"Man, I can handle Creepy Santa, boss. I'm good to go."

"You're either our driver or you're staying here, and you won't be on door duty. That's covered for the week. You'll be on janitorial duty."

"I'll drive," Rome mumbled. "I'm supposed to keep my energy up though. I gotta eat something."

"My techs got your medical records and release forms. The kitchen has been notified of your restrictions and they're preparing you something to eat now."

"Oh." I'd never seen a man look so disappointed in my life. "Thanks."

Rider looked over at Jake, who'd been sitting silently, listening and observing. "I wasn't able to find much on this krackling thing that you didn't already tell us last night."

"It's older than shit and has rarely been seen, so that's not much of a surprise. I had my contacts look into it, but with such short notice, they didn't find anything new either. As I've stated before, I'm great at research. I'd be willing to give those books in your office—"

"No," Rider cut him off. "So we know iron can kill this thing, but only if it is entirely in one form long enough. We have the iron covered. Danni's got her blade. We have blades and bullets. What we don't have is a plan for keeping that thing in one form."

"Or how to track it if we don't manage to kill it tonight," Daniel said. He looked at Jake. "You said it should return to Joanna Jaskowick's house tonight, but if it gets another target it'll go after that target instead. How sure are you of that?"

"Pretty damn sure. There's not a ton of information on these things, but they're similar enough to controllable demonic entities that they follow much of the same rules. Any demon that can be controlled and given targets will drop one target for a newer one. Since the fugly bastard didn't get his target last night, he'll return tonight for sure. We just have to hope he does it before a new target is given. I have no idea if the person controlling it will know the target survived or not."

"Wouldn't the person choosing targets know who they are?" I asked. "You wouldn't just randomly sic a monster on someone you don't know."

"You're thinking like a rational person," Jake told me. "Anyone willing to sic a krackling on anyone isn't a rational person. We don't know why they woke the thing to begin with. If it was intentional, they might have been desperate enough to kill one person then got stuck having to assign more targets to avoid getting killed by the thing themselves. They might have woken it by accident while screwing around with shit they had no business screwing around with, and now they have to supply targets to save their stupid selves."

"If the krackling doesn't return to the house you fought it at last night, we'll know the person who woke it doesn't know the target personally," Rider said. "At least we'll know that much."

"Maybe," Jake said. "If the person is in fact sending the krackling after people he or she knows, maybe that person watches. Maybe they saw the krackling get stopped last night and rather than risk their weapon get permanently neutralized, they'll give it another target to shake us off its trail."

"So if the krackling doesn't return to Joanna Jaskowick's house tonight, we're stuck waiting for a report of a bloody murder scene to come in," I said, and felt my stomach roll. "There has to be a way to track this thing without allowing it to kill more people just so we can find it."

"Hey, you knew where it would be last night and were in place," Jake reminded me. "You saw the target ahead of time. You can do it again."

"I saw the target because she was here in the bar," I pointed out. "This thing already hit a target in Indiana so I doubt all the targets are just going to come through here where I can see them and predict they're next on the list."

"They might." Jake looked at Rider. "There has to be some kind of common denominator between the targets tying them to the person in control of the krackling. So far, we know at least two targets frequented this bar."

"What are you implying?" Rider's eyes shone with the gold color.

"Ease back on the vamp juice, GQ. I'm just pointing out that two of them frequented this bar. It wouldn't be totally wild if the woman just over the bridge in Indiana stopped through here too. I'm not saying you or your people have anything to do with this, but maybe you have a demented regular here who scopes out the bar for prey because they'd rather sic it on strangers than friends. Maybe the person doing the target assigning is some loser who can't take rejection, so if he or she hits on somebody and doesn't get any action, that person gets a visit from the krackling. Maybe it's some nut who thinks women who go to bars are loose harlots and they're saving their souls by killing them. There's a lot of scenarios where your bar could play an integral part in this."

"That's not a bad theory." I looked at Rider. "Can the tech team run receipts and see if all the targets we know about have drank here?"

Power poured out of Rider, filling the room with energy, then faded back into him. "They're on it now. I've already requested they pull everything they can on the targets and look through it all to find anything they have in common. That's going to take time though."

"I'm not doing anything until we head out just before nightfall," Jake said. "I can help them."

"Not necessary."

Jake rolled his eyes. "Man, you have got to work on your trust issues. I am Malaika's brother-in-law and I know you work with her. If you can't trust her opinion of me, or Christian's or Seta's then at least trust why I was sent here." Jake glanced at me before returning his gaze to Rider. "You weren't as hostile with me the last time I was here and the only thing different I can think of is she's here. I am not going to hurt her. You know the person who sent me to help her wouldn't have sent me if she thought I would either."

Well, color me curious because that definitely grabbed my attention.

"The tech team has it handled," Rider said, each word clipped. "They'll work more effectively without anyone screwing with their process. If you want to help, you can help us brainstorm how to keep that thing in one form and plan our method of attack while the techs do their thing, trying to find similarities between targets."

"Fair enough." Jake threw his hands up and sighed, clearly not happy, but not willing to push the issue any longer.

Ginger Marie, a new werewolf server who only planned to be with us for a short while, thankfully, given it could be confusing having two Gingers around, set a plate of food and glass of water in front of Rome and quickly left without a word, sensing we were in a meeting.

"What is this?" Rome looked down at the plate with an expression that almost made me laugh. I'd never seen someone appear so offended by food.

"It's peas, white rice, salmon, and apple slices," Rider told him. "From the list of approved foods while you recover."

"Apples are fruit," Daniel told him. "Peas are green vegetables. I know these are foreign to you, but don't worry. They won't hurt you."

Rome shot a look at Daniel and used the fork on the plate to poke around at the food. "Where's the seasoning?"

"There's seasoning," Rider assured him.

"White people seasoning and black people seasoning are two very different things," Rome muttered.

"Eat it or starve."

"Dang, boss. Sounded just like my mama when you said that." Rome mixed all the food together, minus the apples, and scooped it up with the fork. He dutifully took a bite and looked like he'd just eaten a bug.

"Can we trap him?" Daniel asked, getting back to business. "If we trap the krackling, he'll have to eventually tire out from spitting all those bat-things out so he'll be forced to take solid human form, or whatever that form is where he looks like Demon Santa."

"I imagine it's possible," Jake said, "but damned hard. Any portable trap would most likely have to be made of iron or something it can't just break out of. It also couldn't be impenetrable because we'll need to get a bullet or blade through to its heart to kill it."

"And we'd have to have access to it now," Rider said. "We don't have a lot of time to put together something big if we're hoping to kill that thing tonight."

"Shit on it," Rome said around a mound of food.

Every head at the table turned toward him, but it was Daniel who spoke. "What?"

"Shit on it." Rome swallowed and looked at Daniel. "It's a really big dude you need to keep in one place and you're a really big dragon. You have to have really big doody in that form, bro. Fly over and drop a load on him. He'll be stuck in one form under there, and it's not hard enough to stop a blade or bullets from going through."

"I'm not going to shit on it. You shit on it."

"How am I supposed to shit on it? You're the dragon."

"Yeah, and you still have the bigger shit, so you can do

it. I'll give you a lift and let you release the mother of all loads on it."

"No one's going to shit on the krackling," Rider snapped, then pinched the bridge of his nose as he sighed in exasperation. "I cannot believe I just had to say that."

"I can't believe it actually kind of makes sense." Now every head turned toward me. "What? I'm not suggesting we do it. I'm just saying … I could see how it would have worked."

"Keep thinking," Rider said. "Stay away from any ideas that involve shitting on anything, and Daniel, you're in charge of Rome. Don't let him eat or drink anything that's not right there in front of him. He can eat again after we return tonight. He's on a schedule."

"But—"

"Do you want janitorial duty?"

"No." Rome stabbed a chunk of salmon so aggressively one would think that fish had done something to him personally.

"Danni's going to handle an interrogation. See what you geniuses can come up with before we come back and fill Ginger in if she arrives before then."

"Are you interrogating a human?" Jake asked as Rider stood and helped me out of the booth. His tone held a warning.

"Yes," Rider answered. "A human with a hell of a lot of child pornography on his computer."

Jake stared up at Rider for a moment, then waved his hand. "Kill away."

"That's the plan, and I did not need your blessing." Rider grabbed my arm just above the elbow and led me out of the bar and into the restricted back area.

We pushed through the doors to find Kutya gobbling kibble from his doggy bowl while Hank stood watch next to the garage door. The big pup saw us and ran over for pets and scratches.

"I get that he's a wiseass who likes to push buttons, but

is there really any need for such hostility?" I asked Rider as I rubbed Kutya's belly.

"Would you defend him so much if he didn't happen to look like Dean Winchester?"

"Would you be so nasty to him if he didn't happen to look like Dean Winchester?" I shot back.

"Probably not," he answered with a bit of a growl, "but it's hard to say."

"Uh, do you still need me to watch the dog?" Hank asked, shifting uneasily from foot to foot as he watched us.

"Yes," Rider answered. "If he just ate, he'll need to go out soon."

"Don't I know it," Hank grumbled. "Have you ever considered toilet-training him? I've seen videos of dogs who can do that."

"If you feel you can teach him, you're more than welcome to give it a go. Danni, we need to get moving."

I gave Kutya one last good belly rub, patted his flank, and stood. "Who do we have?"

Rider guided me to the stairwell door. "Child pornographer who just so happens to hang in the same circles with Pacitti. You're going to find out what he knows about the detective, then we can do the world a favor and kill him."

CHAPTER NINETEEN

"His name is Jeff Brinley," Rider told me as we stood in the observation room, watching the man in interrogation from behind the one-way mirror. He was middle-aged, overweight, with shaggy brown hair, a bulbous nose, and heavy jowls. His eyes were big and round, and they darted all over the room as he paced back and forth. He wore jeans, ratty old sneakers, and an Indiana Hoosiers sweatshirt.

"I'll spare you the pictures and videos the tech team found when they remoted in to his computer, but will tell you he is very fond of child pornography, the younger the better. He fancies himself a writer, but what the techs found came off as more pornography and the crazy rantings of a man who clearly fits the incel profile. He loves guns, zombie apocalypse fiction and detective novels, and playing online poker, which is where it appears he met Pacitti. According to the extended email and text history between the two, he's been friends with Pacitti for a few years now, using him for research purposes as he writes a seriously bad series of zombie detective novels."

"Zombie detective?"

"Like I said, they're seriously bad." Rider opened a file

folder lying on the table in front of us to reveal a small stack of paper.

I picked up the stack and saw it was from a manuscript titled *Breff Jinley Saves the World*. "He basically named the main character after himself?"

"He sees himself as an action hero or some sort of savior."

I looked through the glass at the husky man pacing the other room. He had a long way to go, considering I was pretty sure none of his girth was actual muscle. I set aside the manuscript's title page and read a little from the beginning:

Breff Jinley leaned back in his chair, feet planted wide apart, a necessity for his amply endowed manhood which always got in the way. It was a chore to pack such an enormous package, but Breff bore the weight, knowing just like his large brain and sharp cunning were vital to the safety of the world in his quick ability to solve cases his massive lightning rod of pleasure was a vital service to the many women he rescued of loneliness or boredom from their less than stellar affairs with pretty boys who had all the looks and bank accounts but lacked the pelvic generosity of which he was so blessedly granted and of course there were the diseased who needed his miracle nectar most of all— "What the actual hell is this even saying? This is like the world's longest run-on sentence. There's hardly any punctuation on this page."

Rider laughed. "It doesn't get any better."

I flipped through a few more pages and started in the middle of what looked like a very long paragraph:

Breff struggled to get his zipper past the huge mound of flesh the beautiful woman awaited eagerly, a problem he'd struggled with since elementary when he discovered none of the other boys tired from hefting such heavy balls, balls made for planting generations of strapping males of well-breeding while also curing the cursed. The woman licked her lips. Despite having been bitten, the stink of rot had not set in. She only smelled of desire and want as she sat on the edge of the bed, legs spread wide in anticipation, inviting Breff's throbbing penile missile into her aromatic vixen garden, her buoyant tits bouncing gaily in desperation for his— "How are her breasts bouncing if she's sitting still? How is it possible to write anything this bad? What the hell is a vixen garden?"

"That's just the first book," Rider said. "According to the techs, there are three so far, and Breff Jinley works his way through quite a few zombie lovers. Apparently, his sperm is what cures them of the zombie virus, and that's just his side mission while working cases because he's a detective."

I almost lost my lunch at the mention of sperm so close after the name Breff Jinley, who I, of course, pictured as none other than the undesirable lump in the next room. "This is satire, right?"

"No. There are several emails and social media posts of him ranting about how publishers wouldn't recognize real talent if it pissed in their mouth. His exact words."

"Gross. What a loon."

Rider pulled out screenshots of the man's Facebook and Instagram accounts. "The whole timeline of both looks just like this, going back for years."

I looked at the screenshots and saw that Jeff Brinley lived with his mother, who seemed to be the only woman he could get any alone time with. His Facebook posts showed an unhealthy obsession with meat that rivaled Rome's. At least Rome's obsession was just simply eating the stuff. Based on the captions of his Instagram posts, which were one hundred percent just pictures of huge slabs of uncooked meat, he seemed obsessed with the juiciness and firmness of the stuff.

Other than meat posts, there were many pictures of guns, including assault rifles, and a few posts painting himself as some sort of action hero because he flashed them to other men in various scenarios who backed down after seeing his steel. "Are we sure he's not a serial killer? This dude is majorly weird."

"Didn't dig that up, but the full report on what the tech team found is here," Rider said, handing me a one-page report. "I wouldn't be surprised if he was, except for the fact I'm pretty sure he lacks the testicular fortitude to actually take a life."

I scanned the report, which included medical records, financials, and a psychoanalysis. Jeff Brinley hated animals, had an obsession with guns and meat, wanted to be a writer, did not handle rejection well, had a gambling addiction, couldn't hold a job for longer than six months, had never moved out of his mother's house for any length of time, was a pedophile, currently had under one hundred dollars in his bank account, his cholesterol was off the charts (gee, I wonder why), he'd received a mountain of rejections from numerous publishers (again, gee, I wonder why), had never been busted on child pornography but did have a restraining order from a woman he'd gone to high school with and apparently never got over obsessing about, and he'd also received restraining orders from a handful of well-known authors he'd harassed over the years.

"And I'm supposed to get him to tell me what he knows about Pacitti?"

"I'll be with you. I can help with questioning, but you can take care of smacking him around and ultimately taking him out so you can get your violence needs met."

I placed the papers back in the file folder on the table which also contained chat transcripts between Brinley and minors that Rider had already warned me I wouldn't want to read, and looked at the man in the other room, noting the sheen of sweat that coated his bloated flesh. "I don't know if I'm going to be able to touch him. He's absolutely repulsive."

"Do you have your knife?"

I'd left the iron blade on the dresser in Rider's room, but carried a switchblade in my boot. "Never leave home without it."

"You haven't left home, babe."

I rolled my eyes. "I have a switchblade."

I sensed him looking at me intently, but didn't attempt to meet his gaze. I knew that once I did, the blood would cover him.

"If you can't bring yourself to touch him with your bare hands, use the knife. You've been pretty tame this past month, in addition to having an aversion to live male blood. I'm sure that's why you feel out of sorts. You're unbalanced."

Unbalanced. Yep, because monsters had to hurt and kill, and succubi had to feast on men. I was an off-kilter monster.

"Are you going to be able to do this?"

I stared at the man, all the information I had on him enough to make me loathe him, but the desire to slaughter did not rise in me. I couldn't even scrounge up a shred of anger. Very odd, considering anger always seemed to be just under the surface with me. "I honestly don't know, but I'll try. I know he needs to be permanently stopped if he's interested in harming children, and we wouldn't want me to get any more unbalanced, would we?"

Rider watched me for a moment before speaking softly. "You know I didn't mean anything when I said you were unbalanced. I was just—"

"I know. It's just what I am." I grabbed the file folder, squared my shoulders, and turned for the door. "Let's get this done."

***

"Sit down," Rider ordered, as we stepped inside the interrogation room.

Jeff Brinley didn't have to be told twice. Like a lot of men who relied solely on guns to protect themselves, he wasn't much when it came to actually facing another man one-on-one. He was a bigger man than Rider, but it was mostly fat, and Rider had a way of looking at scum that shrank their balls all the way up into their stomach.

The pedophile plopped his large posterior into the chair and placed his fisted hands on the table while he stared at me. I watched his gaze roll down my body and tried not to shiver at how icky it felt being assessed by someone who could write such garbage about penile missiles and vixen gardens. Still wasn't one hundred percent sure what that last one even was and wasn't sure I really wanted to find out. Ever.

"I want to speak to my attorney," he demanded after I'd set the file folder on the table.

"You don't have an attorney on retainer," Rider said. He leaned back against the wall next to the closed door.

"I can still get an attorney," Brinley said. "I want an attorney. I have rights."

"Not in my house, you don't."

He looked incredulously at Rider, blinked a few times before deciding to speak to me—the inferior woman—directly, something I didn't think he often did when there was a man to speak to instead. "This is unlawful. You can't hold me without allowing me an attorney or reading me my rights."

"You seem to be under the impression you've been arrested by LMPD and brought to the police department," I said, hands in pockets. I'd seen the way others had been brought into the interrogation room before and, based on that and what I knew from other assignments resulting in criminals brought to the room, I deduced that Rider's people had done a quick grab of the guy. Basically, they'd covered his head with something, trussed him up, and hauled him back to The Midnight Rider to be dumped in the room to await sentencing. Spoiler alert: Sentencing was always death, but the exact cause of death depended on what was said and how much rage it caused.

Brinley's eyes bobbled between the two of us. He licked dry lips and fidgeted nervously. "Where am I?"

"The place you're going to die," I answered, seeing no need to beat around the bush. I still didn't feel the rise of anger or bloodlust, but I knew what the disgusting piece of shit was and I knew what was going to happen to him, whether I would be the one to do it or not. "But first, we'd like you to answer some questions."

His mouth dropped open, revealing small yellowed teeth. He did another look between the two of us before barking out a laugh. "This is a joke, right? This is a prank."

"Does he actually have any friends who'd care enough to have fun with him?" I asked.

"Wouldn't seem so," Rider answered. He sounded bored, but I knew it was an act. Rage simmered under his skin. One thing that would never fail to guarantee a death sentence by Rider Knight and associates was any form of harm to children. If that harm was sexual in nature, it just made for an even more violent end.

"Who do you think would prank you?" I opened the file folder and leafed through the papers inside while Brinley thought that one over. I didn't actually need to read anything in there, nor did I want to again, but I wanted him to know we had way more information on him than he'd thought. "Kind of quiet there, Jeff, and I see why. Your mom seems to be the only person who gives a shit about you, but she doesn't seem the fun and games type. Of course, if I gave birth to a sad sack like you, it would have drained all the joy of life out of me too."

"Fuck you, you cheap whore."

Rider growled and stepped forward. I held my hand up, silently telling him to stop while I watched Brinley watch him. All the color had drained out of his ruddy face. Action hero, my ass.

"You'd like that, wouldn't you, Jeff? Couldn't do it though, I bet. Men like you, men with all these guns, they usually are compensating for something, aren't they?" I picked one of the printouts up and flashed it to Rider. "He's even sleeping with this one on the pillow next to him. Good grief, man. I guess you do know about cheap whores since you clearly can't afford a full night with one and have to sleep with a gun instead. You could never afford me."

He sat there with his mouth opening and closing like a fish for a moment, surprised I'd thrown his comment back at him instead of being insulted by it. Then his lips curled into a smug slash of a demented smile. "I knew you were a whore."

"Yes, I believe you said that," I replied, displaying absolutely no emotional response. "I'm not sure why you appear so smug about it though. I already told you, you'd never be able to afford me. My rates go up the more pathetic the man."

He lunged for me. Before Rider could make a move, I grabbed Jeff Brinley by his repugnant face and held him in place, calling upon all my vampire strength to do so while he swung his meaty fists at me, continuously missing due to the table between our bodies. He grunted as he tried to move closer, but with one strong arm, I kept him in place. I saw tears form in his hot, angry eyes as I emasculated him just by simply holding him back. He continued swinging those fists, resembling a windmill, as he strained to gain an inch.

He'll keep that up all night before he'll admit a woman stopped him one-handed, Rider said through our mental link, then walked behind Brinley. He grabbed the man by the scruff of his neck and slammed him back into the chair, then bent down, putting him face to face with the jackass. "Get up again and I'll bust your head open."

Brinley snarled, but didn't utter a word in response. Rider glared at him for another minute before returning to his post at the door. He folded his arms over his chest, looking every inch the tough guy.

I pulled out the chair across from Brinley and sat down. I still wasn't really angry despite the insults and attempted assault. Oh, I loathed the guy and definitely hated him for the child pornography I'd been told had been found on his computer, but the desire to inflict pain that generally rose in me in these types of situations just wasn't there. It almost felt as if some invisible force was holding me back, similar to how Rider could mentally control me if he chose to, but I knew he wouldn't do that.

"What the fuck do you people want?" Brinley asked. "Who are you?"

"We're your killers," I told him. "And we want information. Where's Pacitti?"

Brinley's eyes goggled as he looked between us. "What?"

"Nicholas Pacitti. The private detective you play poker with. We've accessed your emails and texts. We have everything that was on your personal computer. We know you know him. When was the last time you spoke with him?"

He blinked at me. "You said you were going to kill me."

"I've said it twice, actually. I believe in being honest, but if it makes you feel less like pissing on yourself, I could tell you we're just going to give you a lot of really big boo-boos until you cease to exist."

"You're crazy."

"Says the guy who sleeps with a gun and uses way too many sexually suggestive adjectives to describe slabs of raw meat."

His face reddened to the point I thought it might actually burst. "You have no right to meddle in my business."

"You have no right to prey on children," I replied. "But you did, so here we are. We're going to kill you, Jeff. Whether we kill you fast or slow depends on how long it takes for you to answer a fucking question. When is the last time you saw Nick Pacitti?"

"I don't know what you're talking about. I didn't prey on any children."

Rider walked over and backhanded the man. He held back so Brinley didn't go flying across the room, but he still rang the guy's bell pretty hard. Before Brinley could slide off the edge of his chair, Rider grabbed him by the neck of his sweatshirt and lifted him a good foot or so while he glared directly into his face. "I'm going to do that again if you don't actually answer the question. Last chance, asshole. When was the last time you saw Nick Pacitti?"

"Months," Brinley said, his voice a squeak. "Months ago."

"You expect me to believe that?" Rider tightened his grip, drawing more of the sweatshirt material into his hand until Brinley kissed the edge of strangulation. "We have your emails and your phone records."

"You asked when I saw him," Brinley managed, his voice roughened by the pressure on his windpipe. "I've tal…uh… tkked…"

Rider loosened his hold. "Speak."

"I've talked to him since. On the phone. You said you have records, so you know I'm tellin' the truth."

"Where is he?"

"He didn't say where he was."

Rider growled and brought Brinley close to his face.

"But I know where he'll be!"

"Where?"

"I don't know yet." Some weird wounded bear sound escaped Brinley as Rider snarled. "I'm waiting for his text! He said he's got something big, we're going to make a lot of money, but he has to get somewhere safe first, then he'll text me the safe house."

"What's a moron like Pacitti need a safe house for?" Rider asked, although I suspected he'd already gotten the same inkling I had. Pacitti was running from us, or at least me. "Who's after him?"

Brinley barked out a nervous laugh. "You'll think I'm lying."

"Try me."

"He thinks he caught monsters on film. Blood-sucking,

shape-shifting monsters." The nervous laughter bubbled up again.

"And you have no idea where he's headed?"

"None. He's being all evasive. But he's supposed to text me coordinates when he finds a place and gets everything together, so you need me."

"I've already gotten everything I need from you." Rider dropped him back into the chair. "Including access to the phone he'll be texting you on."

All the red color drained from Jeff Brinley's face, leaving it pasty white. He gulped. "You're not really going to kill me, are you? You're not the kind of person who'd do something like that to a guy you don't even know, would ya?"

"I know a hell of a lot about you, Brinley, and every bit of it makes me sick. Also, I'm exactly that kind of person. So is she." Rider allowed his eyes to glow golden and growled, peeling his lips back to reveal elongated fangs.

Brinley screamed and toppled over out of the chair. He scrambled to his feet, ran to the door and twisted the knob, but it wouldn't budge. Rider had secured the room with his power. Brinley turned toward us, plastered his back against the door and promptly pissed his pants as he blubbered like the cowardly sack of human waste that he was.

Rider drew his fangs back in. "He's all yours. Kill him."

I stood and faced the man. Brinley immediately scampered to the other side of the room where the mirror was and turned. His terror-filled eyes flicked between Rider and me as they spilled over with tears, and eventually he sank to the floor and bawled while pleading for his life.

"Is there a problem?" Rider asked so quietly only I could hear. "You need to get your violence needs met. He's a pedophile. Take care of him."

I watched Brinley cry and beg. I knew what he was. I'd been told. I hated what he was. But every time I attempted to move toward him, I only saw a human begging for their life from me… a monster. "I can't do it."

"What do you mean, you can't do it?"

"I can't kill people anymore. I can't be a monster."

Rider walked to me, grabbed my chin in his hand and forced me to look into his face, but before my reality could warp and show me a nightmare image of him covered in blood, he flooded my mind with the pictures and videos he'd withheld from me.

My heart split open as I saw such innocent faces in such compromising positions and the broken heart gave birth to an all-consuming rage that started in the pit of my stomach and expanded to fill my entire body. By the time he released me and stopped the movie reel, gasoline had been poured on that pool of rage and a match lit. Rider pointed to Brinley. "That all came from him."

I turned toward Brinley and caught my red-eyed reflection in the mirror before a guttural cry erupted from my throat and I leaped over the table to land on the screaming man. Drawn to the pulse point in his throat, I grabbed two handfuls of flesh and tore it open. Blood shot out of him like a fountain and I feasted before ripping him open further, cracking open his ribcage to get to his heart. Then all I saw was red as I continued to break and tear, feasting on blood as I went.

"Enough! Damn it, enough! STOP!"

Rider's voice ricocheted off the walls as I was wrenched off my feet. An eviscerated animal was sprawled out on the floor before me. No, not an animal, I realized as the human head three feet from the rest of the torn apart body stared at me with eyes frozen in pure terror.

"What the hell, Danni? What was that?"

Rider stepped around to stand in front of me, his mouth hung open. His eyes glazed over in shock. Blood covered his arms and the front of his sweater, but it didn't pour over him. I shook my head, feeling as if I were in shock myself, and when I did, I caught my reflection in the mirror and froze.

MERRY FANGIN' CHRISTMAS

The blood hadn't poured over Rider because it had poured over me. Head to toe, it coated me. Not a single strand of hair was dry. I was painted in red from top to bottom. Even my eyes burned red. The nightmare had come true, I realized. I was a monster. I gasped.

And then I lost my fucking mind.

CHAPTER TWENTY

The red demon in the mirror cocked her head and winked before her mouth twisted into a demented smile. She threw her head back and laughed hysterically as screams echoed off the walls, walls that all ran with blood.

"I got you now," she said in a voice that sounded like the wails of a thousand tortured souls. "I am going to tear you apart and put you back together just so you can kill your loved ones with your own teeth and hands."

Then she laughed again, a maniacal sound that chilled the blood in my veins, because she was the most frightening thing I'd ever seen... and she was me.

"I'll kill you first," I growled, raw anger coursing through me, thawing the ice in my blood. I lunged at the woman in the mirror. She laughed, knowing she wasn't physically there, and I laughed right back, knowing it didn't matter because I knew how to destroy where she lived. I bashed my head into the mirror, sending shards of glass flying.

***

Red was everywhere, suffocating me as I sank. I kicked

out, swam up through the hot, metallic liquid to burst free. I drew a ragged breath and wiped blood from my eyes to see. I was in an ocean of blood under a red sky with a red moon. A face came into view. A face I knew. A face I loved.

"Come back! Come back to me!"

I knew that voice. That voice would save me. I reached for it.

Something gripped my ankle and down I went, plummeting through the blood. I opened my mouth to scream but blood filled it, silencing me as I was dragged to what I knew would soon become my grave. I was drowning. I kicked out, clawed for the sky, but I was in the grip of something much stronger than I. Down I want, sinking faster and faster, caught in the vise of something I instinctively knew had the power to completely destroy me.

I broke free of the blood ocean and free-fell until I slammed against a hard, slippery surface with enough force to rattle my teeth. I groaned and attempted to get up, my hands and knees slipping in the layer of blood covering the hard ground beneath me.

I saw red-painted feet and legs walking a circle around me as I finally managed to get to my knees without slipping back down to my stomach or hip. I looked around to see an endless stretch of red. I was in a box, or a room, all coated in blood. Above me, the blood ocean somehow existed without falling. The red, dripping monster circled me, stalking her prey, and I realized I'd been sucked inside a prison cell with her.

"You really thought you could destroy me?" She laughed, that chilling maniacal sound again. It scraped along my cranium, attached itself to my nerve endings and shot pain into my body that left me spasming as if I'd been electrocuted.

I knew I could. Or I thought I'd known it. I wasn't sure what I knew anymore. Shit, I didn't know who I was. Or where I was. I looked at my captor, familiarity mingling with the terror her red-coated gaze shot through me. I knew her.

Distant rumblings broke through the barrier of the ocean, a mighty roar of wind, a roll of thunder. No. Power. Voices. It was voices. Voices of entities mightier than this monster who'd dragged me to her lair.

"They can't help you here." She stopped circling and crouched down in front of me. "You're so deep down inside they'll never be able to pull you out, and you can claw as much as you want, but you can't get past me. Only through me. And you can't get through me and survive."

Who was she? Who was I? Thunder rolled. The walls shook. Something was happening above the ocean. I focused, straining to hear over the blood ocean's waves and the pounding in the walls.

"They can't help you!" she screeched.

I looked at her. She was so familiar, but covered in blood, it was hard to make her out. She was angry, full of hate, but beneath all that, she was afraid. Not of me. She had me right where she wanted me. She was protected by the ocean. It separated us from what she feared, what could break me free.

I got to my feet. We crouched before each other.

"You can't do it," she snarled with a wicked smile, as if reading my mind, and judging by the way she braced herself to lunge for me the moment I moved, I knew she had, but I had to try. I had to try to reach that blood ocean and find my way out.

I leaped.

I managed to plunge one hand into the bottom of the floating pool of blood before she tackled me around my midsection and propelled me backward. My breath rushed out of me as my back hit the blood-soaked wall. The back of my head connected, caused stars to shoot before my eyes, momentarily adding a little light in the blood-coated world, and my action, and what it had caused sparked a little light inside of me. A little spark of hope. I'd snatched a wave of blood and brought it down with me, and on that wave there were voices.

"I am not going to hurt her!"

"You will not touch her! Get him out of here now! Her too!"

"I was sent to save her, you overprotective, jealous idiot! She's hainted and I'm the only one here who can get it out of her!"

Two men. I knew them. How did I know them? I saw faces. Beautiful faces. Long black hair and piercing blue eyes. Short tawny hair and a chiseled jaw covered in scruff. Heat rose in me.

"She needs my blood!"

"*Slayer* blood? One more step and I'll kill you right here and now."

Slayer? *Slayer*…

The tawny-headed man's face became clearer, and I felt compelled to find him. Just before the name formed, another voice came through. "She's not responding to your call, so just try it! I'll kill the motherfucker myself if she so much as jerks after the first drop!"

More heat. The wave I'd pulled down with me snapped back and a fist hit the side of my face, knocking me sideways.

"Oh yes. I have you now. Your loins burn with desire even while on the brink of total madness. You can't fight what you are, but you've tried so hard, so stubbornly. All your fight is what made it so easy to crawl in and tear you apart from the inside. There is no greater weakness than self-loathing."

What was this crazy bitch talking about? I ignored the throbbing pain in my skull and rose to my feet. I slipped, but caught myself, remained standing to hold her glare as she again circled me.

"Who are you? What do you want from me?"

"You know who I am, and you know what I want."

No, I didn't... but I did. On some level, I knew her. We circled each other now. She was a coiled snake, ready to strike at the first hint of attack or escape. There was no leaping for the ocean above us. She'd grab me before I got more than a hand in. If I couldn't go above her... Despite her threat that I'd never make it, I had to go through her.

I tightened my hand into a fist and threw it. She didn't even try to block me and I discovered why the moment my knuckles connected with her jaw and sent my own head whipping to the side.

I staggered, covered my aching jaw with the palm of my hand. She had staggered too, but didn't fall. She stood laughing at me, the excruciating sound sending shards of glass into my brain.

Shards of glass...

That triggered something, but before I could fully recall the memory, she was on me, pummeling me, laughing louder and louder. I blocked the blows as best I could, rage building in me the more blows she delivered, and once I saw my shot, I flipped her and rammed my fist into her mouth, splitting her lips open. Mine split as well.

I scrambled off of her, holding my mouth. She laughed all the way to her feet and spread her arms wide. "I told you, you'd never make it through me. You can't take a piece of me without taking a piece of yourself."

She lunged. I dodged her and kicked out, connecting my foot with her stomach. I couldn't even celebrate the fact I'd kicked the bitch hard enough to make her want to vomit because I was too busy swallowing back bile myself. She was right. Every bit of damage I did to her, I did to myself, but I couldn't stop because we were in the ring now and my only choices were stand there and take a beating from her or beat my own ass while trying to fight her. There was no way I could just let the woman beat the hell out of me and not get any pain delivered to her in return.

Every time my fist or foot connected with her, I felt

the pain shoot through me. Every inch of torn flesh was my own, every painful breath, every spilled drop of blood, every cracked bone. I was going to kill myself killing her. I gasped, realization slamming into me. Then her fist slammed into me and I flew back. My head hit the wall and stars shot out just like the shards of glass had shot out of the mirror. The mirror I'd rammed my head into to kill the monster inside me. The monster who was… I looked at the creature standing over me, imagined her without the blood coating her from head to toe.

"You're me."

She smiled that wide, wicked smile.

She was right. She had me. The only way to get through her was to kill myself. "Have I lost my mind?"

"Yes."

I looked around. So this was insanity. I'd always believed the insane were locked away in padded cells, not blood-painted rooms underneath floating oceans of blood. Tears spilled from my eyes. I was covered in so much blood, the only reason I could tell there were tears was because the blood had cooled after I'd plunged out of the hot ocean. The tears were warm, cooling halfway down my cheeks to get lost in the rest of the liquid covering me. So much red. The room's macabre design mocked me as memories flooded my mind and I fully remembered who I was.

It all came back in a rush. Rider. Daniel, Ginger. Rome. Angel. My heart ached, and the walls shuddered. I laughed bitterly, realizing why. I wasn't in a room. I was inside myself. Lost. Somewhere out there above the ocean, my physical body was in a room, most likely still the interrogation room under The Midnight Rider. Poor Rider. I knew he'd try so hard to save me, but how did you save someone from insanity? Not even a sire could call someone back from that.

He would blame himself. Somehow, he would find a way to hold himself responsible. Daniel probably would too. I hoped they would take care of Angel. I'd never even gotten to take her to Disney World. I'd never gotten to take myself there. More tears flowed. Maybe Ginger would ask her to be her donor. Ginger… She'd wanted us to have a nice Christmas. *Oh no.* The krackling. I was supposed to kill it. I had to kill it.

"I have to go back."

She crouched over me. "You can't."

"I have to go back!" I shoved her, and she grabbed my shoulders, penned me against the wall.

"You'd best get used to this, bitch. I won. I drove you completely crazy and dragged you into your own personal hell. You can't leave here until I say you can or I'm destroyed, and that murdering bastard will never allow what would need to be done for that to happen." My gut clenched, and she growled. "You can kill yourself trying to escape me or you can wait here for Selander to find that whore, Katalinka, and shove her soul into your body. Then we'll both just sit back and watch the show."

Hold up. That so wasn't me speaking. The moment I realized that, the me in front of me flickered and I saw a flash of someone else under all the blood. Someone much older. And much deader. Sonofabitch. I had to escape. But how when killing her would kill me? My gut clenched, and I went over what she'd just said…

That murdering bastard will never allow what would need to be done for that to happen.

Rider. Rider had to allow something to—No, Rider had to allow *someone* to do something to save me. I'd heard the voices. Rider, Jake, and Daniel. They were with me, trying to save me. Jake said I needed his blood.

"I see the wheels turning in your head, you little bitch. Knock yourself out trying to find a way back home, but it won't happen. This is your home now. You're locked in with me, deep inside where no one can hear you scream." She smiled that wide, wicked smile again, and I knew the evil witch was going to lunge, but before she did, I had to prove her wrong.

I wasn't just Rider's fledgling. I was his soulmate. I'd found my way back to him through my many deaths and centuries of time. I could find my way back to him through this.

I closed my eyes and drew every ounce of energy I had left deep into my core.

"No!" the evil me screeched, and I sensed her propelling toward me, but in that fraction of time, I released the energy I'd drawn into me and sent it bursting from my body like a meteor.

Hands wrapped around my throat as the energy raced up, up, to crash through the ocean of blood, speeding to the top like a torpedo. I watched it as I grabbed the evil entity's hands and pried them from my throat. They were locked around me like steel. I was steadily growing woozy, missing my chance. She'd never give me another shot now that she knew what I'd intended to do. I had no choice. I wrapped my hands around the three center fingers of each of her hands and snapped them back, breaking all six of mine in the process.

I screamed through the pain, able to now that I'd broken her grip on my throat, and on the tail-end of that agony-filled scream, I released another, praying it would break through the blood ocean and the red sky, make it up there to the outside where Rider, Jake, and Daniel fought for what was left of me.

"Let Jake save me!"

The back of a broken hand slapped my face hard enough to knock me over, and a booted foot kicked me in the side, breaking a rib on impact. The scream it caused brought a wave of pain so strong I nearly blacked out.

"Nice try, whore, but he won't do it. Even if your pitiful scream reaches him, he will never allow that slayer to—" She jerked back and screamed herself as my throat caught on fire.

My back arched off the blood-coated floor, broken rib

and all, the pain so great I couldn't draw a breath to scream. Then the ocean fell, covering me in blood, and up I went, an invisible force snatching me out of hell.

There was a pop as I burst free of what I could only describe as red darkness and a horrible, raw, ragged sound erupted out of me. A symphony of noise flooded me, too many voices to differentiate, all speaking too fast and too loud.

I forced my eyes open and saw a hazel-eyed fantasy in the flesh hovering right over me. His wrist was held over my open mouth, dripping blood into me. I tried to lurch forward and clamp my fangs into that wrist, but I couldn't get to him. I was in a chair and someone held me back. Women, judging by the cold chill.

"You did it." Rider stepped into view behind Jake, and I saw the broken mirror behind him. "Now get the fuck away from her."

Jake looked at someone next to me, revealing scrapes and the beginnings of bruises. I couldn't see who he looked at. It hurt too much to move. "Malaika, now!"

Green light exploded around us, and I fell onto stone. I cried out as the hard floor jarred my already aching and broken body, and took a quick look at my surroundings. I was no longer in Rider's interrogation room.

I was in what looked like a cell made of stone, lit by torches. Jake held me in his arms so I was half sitting up. Malaika and a slim blonde woman I didn't recognize stood just behind him.

"Sorry, sweetheart," he said as he pulled a switchblade out and flipped it open, "but that vampire would have never let me do this."

Then he slit my throat open.

CHAPTER TWENTY-ONE

Well, sonofabitch, I thought as I started choking on my own blood. I just got slayed by Dean Winchester. That bowlegged motherfucker. I should have been a Sam girl.

He raised his wrist to drip blood into my mouth while I stared into his eyes, thinking what a fucking idiot he was if he thought I could swallow that after he'd just nearly beheaded me, but the blood didn't reach my mouth. It dripped into my throat. The man who'd just murdered me was feeding the new mouth he'd carved into my neck.

Green light filled the room and Malaika stepped into my view, close enough I could tell the light came from her. The blonde hunkered in as if awaiting something, then Dean started speaking something that sounded an awful lot like Latin.

No, not Dean. *Jake.* Jake Porter. The ultimate slayer. Well, he'd sure slayed my ass. I'd call him every bad word I knew if I could still talk. Instead, all I could do was wait to die while I continued to choke on—*I wasn't choking anymore.*

Jake lowered me to the stone floor while the blonde woman quickly bandaged his wrist. He continued speaking in Latin, his voice growing stronger and louder with each word as Malaika held her hands several inches over me, one hand above my forehead, the other now somewhere I couldn't see, but estimated to be around my hips.

Once his wrist was bandaged, he straightened me, lined me up so I stared straight up at the ceiling above us. The ceiling with the giant pentagram that had all kinds of symbolic doodads drawn around it. The Latin continued to flow from him as he backed away from me, out of my view. The blonde knelt next to my head, sliced her wrist, and shoved it into my mouth. I reflexively clamped down and drank, no clue how the hell I managed to swallow anything.

The green light grew brighter, the Latin grew louder, stronger, and then an unholy screech rent the air to echo off the stone walls as black smoke rose from me. Malaika's hands twisted over me, closer to my throat area as the smoke grew. Whatever it was, it came out of me, out of the opening Jake had created in my neck.

Still speaking the repetitive Latin, he stepped into view and held a pale stone jar upside down over the plume of smoke. It had strange symbols on the sides I'd never seen before. He chanted faster, and the smoke flowed out of me quicker. The screeching grew louder, as did Jake's voice, until finally the last trace of smoke was collected in the jar seconds before I was sure my eardrums would have burst.

Jake capped the jar and tossed it up toward the pentagram on the ceiling. He released a quick burst of Latin that sounded a bit different than what he'd been saying, and the jar disappeared in a ball of fire that quickly vanished.

"Heal her up quick," Jake ordered, "before we lose her."

"On it." Malaika's hands rested over my throat and I saw the green glow of her power as fire seemed to burn across my neck.

"How you doing, Marilee?"

"I'm good," the blonde said, but sounded a little weak.

"No, you're not." Jake walked over to where my head rested and crouched over me to squeeze my cheeks in to the point I had to release the woman's wrist. "Grab a couple of jugs, then go refuel. Hell, grab three. I'm going to need a hit too. Her sire still might kill me."

"Throat healed nicely," Malaika said as warmth slowly flowed over my chest. "She's taken a hell of a lot of damage though. Cracked ribs. Broken fingers. Kidney is messed up. I'll do my best, but she needs a lot of blood and a day's rest."

"The day's rest will have to wait. We have a date with a monster tonight." Jake brushed my bangs back from my forehead, wincing as I hissed from the pain it caused. "How are you doing, champ?"

The man had saved my life. I had no idea how or what the hell had just come out of me, but he'd saved my life. However, he'd saved my life by cutting my throat, so I responded with the first thought that popped into my brain. "Fuck you, Dean Winchester. You can shove your Impala up your ass."

He barked out a laugh and looked over at Malaika. "Yeah, she'll be just fine. Get another pass over her head. She really cracked her melon open."

"That really happened?" So many images were rushing back to me and I couldn't tell what was real and what wasn't. So much of it seemed like a giant, blood-soaked nightmare.

"You bashing your head into the mirror in the interrogation room before Rider knew what the fuck you were doing and could stop you? Yep, that happened. Things didn't get any less crazy after that."

"There was a monster in the mirror," I told him as I remembered. "She was me. I tried to kill her, but I almost killed myself. She sucked me into her prison. It was inside me under an ocean of blood."

Malaika returned to my head and her glowing palm hovered over my brow, easing away some of the pain as my skin tightened, knitting together.

"That wasn't you, Danni. It was a haint. I suspect you've had it a while. I was sent to help you kill a monster, but I don't think the krackling was the main objective. The haint was far more of a danger to you. Do you know what a haint is?"

Malaika raised her hands, drawing her healing power back into herself and moved back, allowing Jake room to ease his arm under me and lift me into a sitting position. A moment later, the blonde appeared at my side with three jugs of blood. She handed me one. My side hurt, my hands were stiff, and I had a migraine from hell, but I was pretty sure nothing was still broken. My fingers worked as I took the jug. "Nope, can't say I've ever heard of a haint. Sounds like it could either be a very personal area of the body or the hillbilly version of a haunting."

Jake chuckled. "Definitely not a taint, thank goodness. That would have been hella awkward to remove. You're not too far off on your second guess though. Just take out the hillbilly part."

I gawked at him as I remembered the black smoke rising from me. "Are you telling me that what I saw in the mirror was a ghost? And I had a ghost in me?"

"Drink. You need to heal." He reached for the jug in my hand, I guess to raise it to my mouth, but he didn't need to. I'd just had my ass beat, my throat slit open, and a squatter evicted from my body. I was thirsty and would have already started guzzling if I hadn't had so many questions in need of answers. I started drinking.

"I can't say what you saw in the mirror, not for sure," he said, and took a swig of blood from one of the other jugs. As he did, Malaika waved a hand over his face, healing scrapes, swollen lumps, and bruises until only a little discoloration remained and it hit me with sudden clarity he and Rider probably really had fought. Jake had a decent amount of blood on his clothes that couldn't all be from what had bled from my head. "But you did have a haint inside you. Like a ghost, a very violent, hate-filled ghost. That's why the smoke was pitch black as it was forced out."

"I know this place is warded, but Rider has witches in his pocket more powerful than me," Malaika told Jake. "Hell, he's probably having someone work a spell to find Seta now so she can find her. Danni needs to contact him before he totally loses it and someone gets hurt. He'll probably blame Lana since she helped you get to her."

Rider. Daniel. They were both probably frantic by now.

Jake grinned at her. "You could pop on back and let him know she's all right."

"Are you crazy? My ass isn't popping in anywhere near him until he's had time to cool down. Hell, that dragon would probably try to eat me before I could get a word out."

Jake laughed and turned toward me, but I was already reaching out to Rider, or trying to. I couldn't get a connection. "Here. You'll have to move out from under the pentagram to connect with him telepathically. Do it quick and then get back under. We don't need him locking onto you and having a witch poof his ass here so he can tear this place apart brick by brick, then start throwing punches at me again. Malaika's right. He needs to cool down before we go back there, so just tell him you're fine as quickly as you can and you'll be back soon."

I set the jug down, now half of the blood it had contained in my stomach, and Jake helped me to my feet. I was stiff, a bit sore, but I could walk. Still, I didn't mind the help. I'd really kicked my ass. Or the haint had. Or me. Hell, I didn't know, but someone had beat my ass.

I found the mental link the moment we cleared the pentagram and immediately sent Rider a rushed message. *I'm fine. Jake saved my life and got some ghost-thing out of me, so just cool down and wait for us. We'll be back soon. I love you.*

I stepped backward and the link immediately died as if I'd disconnected a phone line. "I hope I haven't pissed him off more. I didn't even give him a chance to respond."

"He'll get over that. The important thing is he knows you're safe and can calm his ass down instead of frantically trying to find you." Back under the center of the pentagram, Jake lowered me so I could sit.

The floor was hard rock, but I didn't mind as long as it wasn't covered in blood. I hoped I never saw a room like the one inside my mind ever again. At least I thought I had been in my mind. "Tell me more about this haint business. What was it? How did it get in me? I was in a red world and it pulled me down this ocean of blood until I fell into a room underneath the ocean and the thing looked just like me, and…" I noticed the blonde sitting nearby, listening. She was pretty, with long pale blonde hair and not a lot of makeup. She wore faded jeans, boots, and a light blue flannel shirt under a blue jean jacket. "Who are you?"

"Danni, meet my sister, Marilee."

"Hi, Danni." The young woman I placed somewhere in her twenties offered her hand.

"She's half succubus, Marilee. She doesn't like female touch, probably wouldn't have drunk from you if she hadn't needed it so bad at that moment," Jake explained.

"Oh." Marilee's face flooded with pink color and I grabbed her hand before she finished pulling it back. A shiver of revulsion slid up my arm, but not nearly as bad as it had been over the last few weeks, so I held on and completed the much deserved handshake.

"My succubus side can be a real bitch," I told her. "Thank you for helping me, but you do look a little pale. Please get something to eat or at least drink some juice."

"See?" Jake said, grinning. "It's not just me being the overprotective big brother. Now go rest and eat before I tell your husband on you and he force-feeds you until you puke."

"All right, all right." She raised her hands in surrender and stood. "I'm glad you're free of the haint, Danni. Stay safe."

"Wow. A sister?" I said as I watched the pretty blonde leave through a door that matched the stone walls so perfectly it was hard for even my vampire-succubus eyes to see until she opened it. "I guess you're really not Dean Winchester."

"That's what I've been telling you, repeatedly, over and over again."

"Yeah, yeah, I get it." I grinned. "So no moose-like little brother who actually towers over you?"

"My brother is older than me, actually."

"Does he at least look like Jared Padalecki?"

"No, he looks more like Randall Batinkoff."

"Who's that?"

"The dude who knocked up Molly Ringwald in *For Keeps*." He sat down fully and turned toward Malaika. "You did very good, Wonder Woman. Thanks for the assist. You should go get something to eat too. Give us a moment before we need you to pop us back to The Midnight Rider. Tell Nyla to wait outside."

Malaika looked between us, understanding filled her eyes, and she nodded before leaving us alone in the stone room.

"So, is this like an exorcism-slash-holding cell for demons and ghosts?"

"It's a safe room, and yes, it works very well for exorcisms and as you experienced for yourself, haint vanishing."

I snorted out a laugh before I could stop myself. "I'm sorry. That sounded a lot like some really painful waxing."

He shook his head, but grinned. "Haints are some of the most violent, most evil forms of paranormal entities. They don't actually possess a person's body, which is why you were still haunted despite that soul stitch business you have going on."

"How do you know about the soul stitch attachments?" I asked. "Seta wasn't supposed to tell anyone about what she does for Rider."

"Oh, so Seta carved those into you guys?" Jake grinned and I felt heat flood my face, realizing I'd just told him. "Not surprised. There probably aren't a hell of a lot of witches on the right side of magic powerful enough to do that. As a slayer, I sense magic in many forms. I picked up on Rider's the first time we met, then sensed yours and the dragon's when we met. I found it odd all three of you had them, but when I told Rider you were hainted, explained it as best I could in what little time I had while fighting off his people to get to you, and he was so adamant you couldn't be possessed by anything, I figured it out that those two have them to keep you from being possessed. I'm guessing the incubus that sired your succubus half has something to do with that."

I nodded. "So I wasn't actually possessed, but the haint was inside me."

"Yes."

"That makes absolutely no sense at all."

"She never controlled your body. She couldn't. She only fucked with your mind and emotions to the point of driving you mad, which is exactly what a haint does."

"But it caused me physical pain. I got sucked into the mirror and went to that red world, or… I was in my mind, in a blood-covered room, and I couldn't destroy her without destroying myself. That's why my rib and my hands were broken. Everything I did to her happened to me. How could that have just been a mind thing?"

"Like you said, you were inside your own mind." He tapped my forehead gently. "Everything you saw yourself do in there, you actually did to yourself out here in the real world."

"You mean I…?"

"Broke your own bones?" He nodded, and his eyes were so full of sympathy I knew he was telling the truth.

I gasped and covered my mouth. "Why didn't Rider force me to sleep, or at least freeze me in place?"

"He couldn't. The haint had driven you mad. He

couldn't get through to your mind until I could get some of my blood in you. Slayer blood burns the shit out of a haint, weakens their hold." He angled his head to the side and studied me. "He didn't call his people off or stop fighting against me until he said you told him to let me save you. Did you really manage to find the link to him while that bitch had you?"

I thought back to what I'd gone through, and nodded. "I heard voices. At first I thought it was thunder over the ocean, but it was you, Rider, and I heard Daniel too. I heard something about slayer blood and then there was this thing with my gut. A feeling. Somehow I figured out I'd gone insane and if there was any way out, Rider had to let you save me. It took just about everything in me, but I got through to him."

"That gut of yours is a very special gift, and you are one badass motherfucker, Danni Keller, because you shouldn't have been able to hear us. You damn sure shouldn't have been able to reach Rider, sire or not."

I felt myself blush a little and averted my gaze. "Well, it wouldn't have mattered if you weren't there, since only you seemed to know what was happening. How did you know I was hainted?" That sounded so weird, but I could only describe it the same way he had.

"Slayer, remember?" He grinned. "I saw it the first moment I laid eyes on you at that house."

"What?" I suddenly remembered the intense looks I'd gotten from him, when it had felt like he was looking at more than just me.

"I could see it, a sort of glow deep in your eyes. No one else around you could sense it, but my abilities made it clear right away a haint had attached itself to you."

I balled up my fist and rammed it right into Jake Porter's pretty face.

CHAPTER TWENTY-TWO

Jake's head snapped back and to the side as he toppled over, but he quickly rolled to the upright position, a hard fighter to keep down. He bellowed a slew of cuss words and rubbed his jaw as he balanced on the balls of his feet in a crouch. I simply remained where I was, glaring at him.

"If I was just a normal human, you would have broken my jaw with that shot! What the hell was that for?"

"For letting a ghost live in my eyeballs!" I snapped. "Why didn't you get it out of me right then, before I tried to beat my own ass to death?"

He rolled his eyes and muttered another string of bad words before he moved back over to sit across from me and raised his hands. "All right. You got your punch in. We're not doing that again."

He lowered his hands, rubbed his jaw again, and explained himself. "You were aware through that whole haint removal process." He clamped his jaw and shot me an unamused look when I snickered. "Yes, yes, sounds like waxing. Hilarious, I know. Anyway, you were aware of what was happening during that time. You know what I had to do to you first, before I could expel that thing from you. No one was going to let me slit your throat and see another breath's worth of time after that. Not the sire, not that dragon. Hell, not even the spiky-haired vampire or that grouchy tiger. And they damn sure weren't going to give me permission if I told them what was going on and asked for it."

I started to feel a little bad for slugging him. He had a pretty good point.

"Also, you're not some fragile human. You're a vampire-succubus. I thought we'd have more time before that thing drove you mad. I fully intended to snatch you away to do this right after we ganked that krackling and everyone was focused on that. I had Malaika on standby from the very first night."

"And Lana?" I asked. "I heard Malaika say she helped you get into the sublevels to get to me."

"Lana and I fought together before. She knows that despite being a slayer, I didn't walk into that bar looking to kill any of you so when I sensed the shit had hit the fan and saw Rider's people running toward the shitstorm, I grabbed her and told her I needed to get to you or you would not survive. She took care of the security access on the doors and helped me fight my way to you."

"That had to piss Rider off."

"Oh, he was furious, but it's probably Tony she'll have to watch her back around after this. Have you ever seen two shifters not afraid to eat people fight each other? It wasn't pretty." He scratched his head. "It shouldn't have happened so soon. Haints are powerful, yes, but according to Rider, you'd started acting strange just under a month ago, right after he killed a witch, which would make sense for a haint. You'd have either picked up a haint while running across one somewhere or one had to enter you immediately as it formed, which would be the moment it died."

"It was her," I said, remembering when the image of me had flashed back in that blood world, or inside me. Whatever. It was all so confusing. "When I was wherever I was, I was facing off with myself, but there was a moment the image glitched and I saw her. Trixell."

Jake nodded. "All right, so we know it was her, and we know you'd been hainted by her for about a month. From what I was told about her, I know she was a powerful, very malevolent being, but this was still really quick to drive you mad. The only way that could have happened is if you have a really big weakness. You're a badass, Danni. You proved that when you fought through that hell to reach Rider, but you've got a great big bleeding wound in you, and as long as you let that remain open, you're a walking invitation for this type of shit."

I gulped. "You mean this could happen again? I could be hainted?"

"As long as you leave that wound untended?" He nodded. "So let's patch that bitch up."

"Patch what up?" I looked down at myself. Blood was on my clothes and skin from the damage I'd done to myself in the interrogation room, and to the man I'd pretty much slaughtered before I'd been dragged down into that blood ocean, but I didn't see any open wounds. "I don't know where this wound is."

He tapped my forehead again, then pointed at my heart. "You said you saw yourself in the mirror and you faced off with yourself in that world you created in your mind, a world of blood. You saw yourself as a monster. The wound is you, what you think of yourself. What you hate about yourself, and what you fear, so let's talk about that."

I looked away, the backs of my eyes burning.

"You have to face this, Danni, or you're just risking another incident like this, or something worse. Hating yourself makes you your greatest enemy, and as you've already proven, you can't fight yourself without destroying yourself."

"You make it sound so simple."

I felt his sympathetic stare on me as he studied me.

"The man I thought was my father for over twenty years never was. My mother tried her best to love me, but I can see the pain in her eyes when she looks at me and sees my real father, and I suspect maybe on some level she knows what I am. I was born to kill. That's what I am. A killer. It's in my actual DNA. I even drink blood now so I can wake back up every time I die. Does that make me a monster?"

I looked at him and shook my head. "You save people. Yes, you're genetically designed to kill my kind, but I know there are bad ones among us. You do us a favor by taking them out, and I know you fight against the urge to kill the rest of us."

"I do now," he said, voice soft, "but I didn't for a long, long time. I'm sure I've killed a lot of good people just because they had fangs or shifted shape. I did what I was designed to do because I didn't know any better. The love of my life is half vampire, half therian. I'm married to her. There was a time I would have killed her just for being what she is and I have to live with that knowledge. I could easily hate myself for the sins of my past, but I chose to forgive myself for my ignorance, to accept myself for what I am and use my abilities for something good. And if I stumble, I give myself grace because I am what I am, and I can only do my best with the cards I've been dealt. You need to do the same."

I nodded, sighed. "I know. Believe me, I've been told. I even go to therapy." I laughed at that a little. "Rider and his people, my friends, they tell me all of this, but they don't understand what it's like being two different beasts and loathing everything about one, the one that keeps trying to take over."

"The succubus?"

I nodded.

"I asked you how you were sleeping before. I know haints cause nightmares. What nightmares did you have during this time?" His eyebrows rose as I felt my face flush with heat. "Whatever you tell me, it'll stay safe with me, and I won't judge."

I forced myself to meet his gaze and found only empathy there. He was a slayer, the thing my entire race feared the most, but I trusted him. He'd already saved my life once. "You know Rider is more than just my sire?"

"That was obvious." He grinned. "He warned me to stay away from you before I even knew you existed."

I chuckled, imagining what Rider had thought when he'd gotten a good look at the slayer. "I think he was more concerned with your Dean likeness than the fact you're a slayer, but yes. I love him. I love him more than I can put into words, but succubi are sex demons. My nightmares, my fantasies I had during the time I was hainted could get pretty vulgar, and sometimes those fantasies and nightmares didn't include just Rider."

Jake nodded. "I can see how that would make you feel bad, but you weren't cheating. I'm sure the haint made you feel that way, but you had to have been feeling guilty or afraid for a long time before that witch died and hainted you, and you had to fear something pretty damn intensely to have been driven mad with it so quick. It can only work with the ammo you give it." His eyes narrowed in thought. "You flipped during interrogation, after pretty much ripping a man apart."

I winced at the image that caused. I barely remembered what happened, but I remembered seeing what I'd left of the man.

"That was the final trigger. What happened in your mind to throw that switch, opening the door to total madness?"

"I became the monster," I said. "The monster I've feared becoming since…"

"Since?" he prompted after I went silent.

"Since the first bite."

Jake nodded. "And who delivered that first bite? The incubus or the vampire?"

"The demon. Incubi are demons. Selandar Ryan made me a demon." Hot tears spilled over. "Rider tried to save me, to turn me into something different. He keeps trying to turn me into something different, to save me, but he can't. I'm a sex demon. It's in me, it's in my blood, in my soul, my mind. It's in my heart. I want things I shouldn't and I hate myself for it. I fight it. I fight it so hard and it only gets stronger. The harder I fight, the harder it gets. Blood diets, controlled violence, therapy... It only pushes that part of me down where it stews, until there's a crack and it rises, overflowing. I keep fighting... but I keep losing. I destroyed that man. I tore him to shreds. I thought I could at least respect myself if the vampire side won, but what does it matter when both sides are of the same coin? I'm a monster. One gets covered in blood, the other in shame. Both lose every time."

Jake stared at me for a moment after I ran out of words. I was suddenly so tired, exhausted from the release of so much I'd carried for so long. All I could do was stare back until he reached over and brushed my tears away with his thumbs. "You're gonna be all right, kid." He looked over toward the door, which I realized now had been left open just a sliver. "Babe?"

A stunning violet-eyed woman with long black hair stepped into the room. A soft purple sweater and black leggings tucked into ankle boots hugged her slender but curvy frame.

"I think she needs to talk to you more than she needs to talk to me." Jake stood and walked over to the woman.

"I agree. You might as well grab a shower and change out of these filthy clothes before you take her back." She grabbed a handful of his shirt and pulled him close. "And you'd better finish this job before Christmas or I won't be the only one upset."

"Yes, dear." He smiled, kissed her forehead, and left us.

The woman walked over to me and sat cross-legged in the same spot Jake had just vacated. "Hi, Danni. I'm

Nyla."

I studied her. Not just her beauty, which was impressive, but her energy, which was unlike any I'd felt before. "You're the first therian I've met."

"Half therian," she reminded me. "There aren't a whole lot of us hybrids out there, fewer like us, so if you ever need someone to talk to about what you're going through, what you're feeling, you can call me anytime."

"Like us?" I frowned. "Half vampire?"

"Half something we fear giving into. What do you know about therians?"

I thought back over my shifter lessons I'd gone over with Eliza. "Shape-shifters. Similar to Imortians in the way you shift, but not created by magic. Created by birth, but then there is a ritual. A ritual only the strong survive."

"Yes." She nodded. "I am a pantherian which is exactly the type of shifter it sounds like. I have panther DNA which gives me certain traits. One of the most undesirable of those traits is that I go into heat."

"Oh." My eyes rounded, realizing the implication. "Oh."

"I'm not a sex demon, but believe me, there have been times I felt like one. I will be this way for the rest of my life and, given my vampire side, I have a very long life ahead of me."

I smiled. "But you're married to Jake. You have a husband for when you … have those episodes."

She arched a perfectly shaped ebony eyebrow. "And you have your sire. Rider, right? You can always go to him when the succubus side of you needs its lusts fed?"

"Yeah, but…"

"But when the succubus comes out to play, she doesn't care who her playmate is? Believe me, Danni, that is a feeling I know all too well. I can control myself long enough to get to Jake, but that doesn't mean I don't lust for other men when the heat cycle starts. I don't even have to find the men attractive." She leaned forward and whispered. "The worst was the time I wanted to climb on top of his brother, a shameful secret I will take to my grave and ask you to do so too. I've only told you because I'm sure you've been there yourself. That's why you were an easy target for the haint. You'd already been tearing yourself apart before it ever entered you."

My heart constricted so tight it was hard to breathe. "You understand."

"I do." She nodded. "Pantherians don't have sires, but we served a queen, our version of a pack leader. We made money for her. Basically, she was the madam, and we were all her prostitutes. We became hers after the ritual. Our mothers didn't even protect us because they belonged to her too."

My hand had covered my mouth automatically on a gasp.

"I didn't become a hybrid until my twenties. It was the first night I saw Jake. A voice sent me to protect a boy, so I did. The vampire who would have bitten him bit me instead. I have always been an empath and something about that caused me to draw vampiric traits from that bite. I stopped aging, and the vampiric traits blocked me from the pantherian queen. I was free."

I blinked, soaking in the story. "What did you do?"

"I followed the boy. As a small black cat, of course." She laughed. "He was so lonely, so full of pain. He didn't feel he belonged, and neither did I. We became best friends and as he grew older, became a man, I fell in love with him, even as I watched him hunt people like me, knowing he would kill me if he ever knew what I really was."

I frowned. "He didn't sense you?"

"Long story." She waved her hand dismissively and continued. "He only knew me as Alley, his pet alley cat, until he went searching for a demon-possessed man, a search that actually led him back to the vampire who had changed both our lives forever. I knew he needed my help, so I let him see me as a woman. Not long after that, I went into heat."

My heart ached for her as I saw the light dim in her eyes. "What happened?"

"What happened was I never got the magical, romantic first time I'd envisioned having with the love of my life. The heat made our first time something very different. It robbed me of that moment I'd dreamed of for years, but… Jake still fell in love with me. He continued to love me after learning what I was and what I had done in my past. I've been with more men than I can remember, and he knows that. He still loves me." Nyla tilted her head and gave me a warm smile. "If your vampire loves you, and from what I've heard, that would appear to be the case, he loves you no matter what. I heard what you said earlier about him trying to change you. Is he really, or has he been trying to give you what you want, trying to help you find a way to love who you are?"

I looked down and fiddled with my hands as I thought, hands I had broken myself because I hated myself and what I feared becoming so much. "I don't know."

"Maybe you should talk to him about that when you're ready. Clear the air. You need to love yourself, Danni. You are half vampire and half succubus. That is what you are, not who you are. There are ways you can draw from both sides for good, but you'll never find the good in your succubus side if you keep punishing it just for being what it is, and you'll draw from the bad part of your vampire side the more you turn it against the succubus. That is what's making you feel like a monster."

Everything she said made sense, but there was something she didn't know. Something I was afraid was in me, not the succubus or the vampire. Me. Deep within my own black and crusty, traitorous heart.

"What is it?" She frowned. "Something's rolling around in that head and guilt is written all over your face."

"If I tell you something, I can trust you not to share it

with anyone?"

"The door is closed. No one can hear you but me, and considering what I told you about that disgusting moment Jake's brother looked like a sexual appetizer, you have blackmail on me for life. Yes, you can trust me. We can trust each other. Who the hell else do we have to understand our crazy shit?"

I laughed with her, but it didn't last long, humor bogged down by the absolute horribleness of what I was about to reveal, what I'd been dying to share with someone, but couldn't. "The haint couldn't just make things up, could it? It had to work with what was already there in my mind and heart, didn't it?"

Nyla nodded. "To my understanding, yes."

I sighed. "I was afraid so. It caused me to have nightmares, basically disgusting dreams of becoming something very vulgar, and my succubus side flared up too, but although there were a few times other men became attractive to me, there was one man in particular…"

"One man not your vampire?"

"Definitely not my vampire." I looked down at my hands, unable to look someone in the eye and see judgement while I told them how horrible I was. "My friend, actually. My best friend. Even before the haint there have been moments … I brush them off, but then they happen again. I think he's in love with me, and I sometimes think I have feelings, desires… but I love Rider so much." Tears started flowing down my cheeks. "I had a fantasy so strong while being hainted, I really thought I'd been about to… to…"

"Danni." She squeezed my shoulder, a quick touch before moving her hand away, aware one side of me wouldn't like the touch. Strangely, I really hadn't minded it. "You are half succubus, so you will always have desire running through you. If thinking of this other man and the feelings you've had about him is enough to make you cry, you need to evaluate why. Do you love him, or do you desire him? Lust for someone dies over time as long as you don't feed it, but love is forever."

"What do I do?"

"Find the truth and be honest with yourself and those you care about. The haint amplified your feelings, made fears become real. You need to look beyond what the haint twisted inside you, find the truth, and then you'll know what to do. Whatever you find, give yourself grace. You're not a monster. You're just a woman trying to find herself, a woman who needs to be kinder to herself while she does."

I wiped away my tears and laughed. "You know, it's weird. I normally don't like female touch, but I really, really want to hug you."

Nyla smiled, got to her feet, and opened her arms. I stood and hugged her. I didn't feel the least bit repulsed by her either.

"Aw, I think I had a really great dream that started off like this once."

"You can be so disgusting sometimes," Nyla groaned as we stepped apart to look at Jake. He leaned against the door frame, hair still damp from the shower. He'd changed into jeans, a black T-shirt under a red and black flannel, and grabbed an olive military jacket since his bomber jacket had been doused with blood.

"You shower quick," I said.

"Before he met me, I don't think he even used soap."

"You know I did. You used to watch me shower before I knew you were my cat." He winked at me. "And she says I'm the perv."

I laughed. "You two are a perfect pair."

They shared a look so full of mushy love it would have made me puke if they weren't truly just too freaking great together. Jake finally wrenched his gaze away from his gorgeous wife to look at me. "Are we ready to get back to your vampire and beg for mercy, or do you need anything else?"

"I think you all have helped me tremendously. There isn't anything else you could do … unless you happen to know what to get a very old, powerful, rich vampire who has everything he could ever want for Christmas?" I said, remembering I still hadn't thought of anything to get Rider, and Christmas was so close. After what he'd been put through with my aversion to him the past month, I really wanted to make it up to him.

"Freaky sex," Jake said without a moment's hesitation, and grunted when Nyla backhanded him in the stomach. "What? No man has enough of that, and it's the gift that keeps on giving."

Nyla and I looked at each other and shook our heads. "I keep him because he's pretty."

Jake grinned at her as I laughed, then grew serious. "Rich and powerful or not, no one has everything. Really think about it. What does he want or need more than anything? What would be the gift you could present to him if you could give him anything in the world?"

When put like that, I knew the perfect gift, but it wasn't something I could wrap a bow around and give to him. It wasn't something I could get for him at all.

Jake raised an eyebrow. "Well? I saw a lightbulb blink on in there."

"It doesn't matter. It's not anything I could actually get for him."

"Maybe I can. I have a lot of connections, even know a bitch-angel or two."

"Jake." Nyla's tone was scolding.

"Well, she is a bitch." He grinned at me. "Let me help you out. What do you want to give him?"

"Well… there is one thing…"

CHAPTER TWENTY-THREE

Despite calling ahead through our mental link, every part of my body trembled with nerves as Malaika did her thing and poofed Jake and me into Rider's office. We'd barely appeared there before she poofed herself right back out, and looking into the vampire's dark blue eyes, burning with murderous intent, I couldn't blame her. But then I realized I was staring right into Rider's eyes and there wasn't a single drop of blood pouring on him, and I smiled.

"Honey, we're home," Jake announced in his typical wiseass fashion. "Did you miss me?"

"I missed *her*," Rider snarled, and glared at the slayer. "You can go light fire to your own ass for all I care. What the hell took you so long?"

Jake shrugged. "I had to wax her haint."

Rider lurched out of his chair and I shoved Jake behind me while the idiot laughed. "Haint, not taint, and he didn't wax anything, I swear!"

I elbowed Jake in the stomach when he laughed harder, and he grunted. "Ouch."

"You deserved that. Quit riling him up."

"But he makes it so much fun."

"Get the fuck out of here, Porter, before I forget all about our little truce."

"Right, like you've been pleasant all this time." Jake sighed and moved for the door. "I trust I'm not going to get jumped when I walk out of here? That wouldn't end well."

Rider glared at him. "No. You brought her back alive. As long as you didn't touch her, you can walk away unharmed."

Jake just stared at him for a moment. "Fine. Since it's already nightfall, I assume you have someone posted outside Joanna Jaskowick's house?"

"Daniel and Ginger. Rome's there as a driver. The krackling hasn't shown yet."

"I'll head over, check the warding I left in place after last night, and make sure it isn't too strong. It might not be able to land at all with it there if it is, or it might have been given another target already. We'll see. I'll catch you there later, Danni."

"Are you out of your fucking mind? She just damn near tried to kill herself not more than a few hours ago. She's not going after that thing."

"Yes, I am." I walked over to Jake and escorted him out. "I'll be there."

I closed the door and turned.

"Danni, there is no way I am allowing you to go after that thing tonight."

He looked awful. Beautiful, gorgeous as always, powerful, but still awful. Under all that fiery anger, his eyes were haunted with memories of what I'd done in that interrogation room, to Jeff Brinley and to myself. He still wore the same clothes, and they were covered in blood. He hadn't changed in the hours since it happened, hadn't cleaned the blood off, and because I knew him so well, I knew he'd spent all that time worrying, fuming, wanting to kill someone or something to get me back, but he couldn't… because for the second time he'd already killed the monster trying to hurt me. His killing those monsters was what gave them the power to get inside me, and that was a pretty heavy amount of guilt to carry. He didn't even have Kutya with him, wouldn't allow the animal near him to offer him comfort.

"It wasn't your fault." I crossed the room and grabbed his face, held it between my hands. "It was not your fault. Any of it."

"It was Trixell."

I nodded. "It wasn't your fault."

"If I hadn't killed her, filled her with that much need for vengeance—"

"The bitch would have done this no matter who killed her, and if you hadn't killed her, she would have continued to help your brother until he got what he wanted, what we can never let him have. I am fine. It's over now and we're both moving on, but first we're going to move into the shower and wash all this blood off, then we're going to put on clean clothes and go kill a krackling." I hardened my stare. "You can come with if you want, but I am not staying here. I need to kill that thing and you're going to let me do it because I need to, and you will give me what I need because you love me."

He removed my hands from his face and looked at them. "You were broken just a few hours ago. I thought I lost you. Then that fucking slayer took you and—"

"He saved my life like he was sent here to do. I still don't know who this mystery woman is who sent him, but I'm thankful for her anyway, and we should both be thankful for Jake. He's one of the good guys, no matter what he's done in the past. Now, if I can manage to not give a shit that he happens to look like Dean Winchester, you should be able to do the same." I narrowed my eyes. "I know that's why you're so snarly with him."

Rider fought a grin and lost. "Fine. I'm jealous of the asshole."

"You have no reason to be."

He brushed the hair out of my eyes and stared down into them. "You can look at me again."

"I can, and I'm going to do a whole lot more than look at you in that shower, but we need to hurry. We have a creepy Santa to slay before Christmas."

***

"Merry Smexy Christmas, loves and lovers, this is Danielle Muething—"

"Ugh." I reached for the button to switch the radio station, but something made me decide against it. Besides, it was so close to Christmas and I really did need to scrounge up some spirit, even if I was worried Jake had bitten off more than he could chew when he'd offered to help with Rider's gift. There was no way he'd be able to get it and I had no back-up. My brain was just a big, useless blob whenever I tried to think of something.

"Problem?" Rider asked. We'd taken his SUV after showering, which involved more than just showering, and changing into matching black sweaters, pants, jackets, and boots. We were kind of cute in our matching all-black, looking like Burglar Barbie and Ken.

"Something about that woman's voice just irritates me."

"The way she sounds like she's been bobbing up and down a dick for ten hours and really needs an inhaler?"

"See, you just get me."

He grinned. "We're almost there."

"What's your name, caller?"

"Lori. Lori Hunter-Lewis from Louisville."

I rolled my eyes, wondering what ridiculous problems this caller was going to have.

"Hello, Lori. What problem do you have for The Heart Specialist to cure tonight?"

"The Heart Specialist?" Rider groaned.

"Trust me, it'll get worse."

"Well, you see, it's Christmas season and after working all day, I just want some me time at night. I just want to relax."

"And your partner just doesn't get it?" Danielle tsked. *"I get this a lot, and I always say, blunt honesty is the best medicine for an unsupportive partner."*

"So I just say what I need?"

"That's exactly what you do, Lori. Say it loud and clear."

"Well, then, Danielle… I need you to shut the hell up so I can listen to my Christmas songs in peace and relax."

Rider barked out a laugh as my mouth fell open.

"Wh—what?"

"I said shut up. Shut. Up. Take the vibrator out your cooter or whatever it is you're doing to yourself to sound like that, it ain't cute by the way, and shut up. Just play the music."

"Oops, looks like we lost Lori. We'll be right back after—"

I got that clench feeling in my gut stronger than ever, and it became clear why as we rolled up to Joanna Jaskowick's house. "It must be coming. I feel it."

Rider had pulled up behind Jake's Malibu, which was parked behind the SUV Rome still sat in, in the alley behind Joanna's house. He cut the engine, and we got out. Rider didn't look happy as he scanned the alley. "This is more exposure than I would like, especially after Pacitti already got his hands on evidence."

"Yeah, I know. But we can't let her get killed."

We walked over to where Jake, Daniel, and Ginger had been standing behind a hedge at the corner of the backyard. Ginger immediately threw her arms around me as we approached. I returned the hug despite my succubus side getting a little uneasy about it and looked at Daniel over her shoulders. He stared at me with far too many emotions to deal with at the moment.

"You all right?" he asked, voice soft.

"I'm good."

His jaw ticked, and he glanced at Rider before shoving his hands back into his jacket pockets and went back to watching the house.

Ginger finally released me. "Never do that again. That was scary. And you should be sleeping."

"It's nighttime and I'm half vampire."

"You need rest anyway, after what you just went through." She let her gaze roll down me and I knew she was recalling what shape I'd been in before Jake had snatched me away.

Deciding to change the subject, I looked at the slayer. "You checked your warding?"

"Yeah, just finished. It looks all right. It can't get into her house, but it can land on it or in the yard. If it hasn't been assigned another target, it should show up."

So we stood there and waited, all the while my stomach felt uneasy. Something was about to go bad, but there wasn't anything I could do until the krackling showed.

"Maybe it got another target," Daniel said, shuffling his feet.

"Unless Danni's discovered a new target, we just stay here and wait. You know from last night, it can wait until pretty far into the night before it shows." Jake sighed, but stood firm, resolved to wait as long as it took, but after a while he appeared impatient and bored too. He looked over at Daniel. "So, do you lay eggs?"

"Why do people keep asking me that?" Daniel started to roll his eyes, but stopped when they locked onto something. He gave a light whistle and nodded.

We all looked up at where he'd nodded and saw several chubby bats descend upon the roof. They came together and morphed into a giant, dirty bearded man in long fur robes. He took one step toward the chimney and froze.

"That your warding working?" I asked as I unsheathed the iron blade I'd brought.

"It shouldn't do that," Jake said. He trained his gun on the krackling as Daniel jumped into the air and shifted.

The krackling split apart into bat-things and took off. Daniel chased after it.

"What the hell?" Jake looked at me. "It shouldn't have

done that. Kracklings are focused on getting to their targets to the point they'll only disappear like that if wounded to the point they can't keep shifting forms."

"Unless they were given another target," I said, my gut clenching painfully.

Daniel landed behind me in the yard, shifting to his human form before he hit the ground. "Damn thing disappeared."

"Where is it going?" Rider asked me. He stared at where I'd placed my hand over my side as if suffering cramps. "You have a feeling, don't you?"

I nodded, thinking. "I got it when we arrived. I thought it was because the krackling was about to show, but it had to be something else. We were driving here so I don't know what… *sonofabitch*."

"What is it?"

"Call your techs. Get us an address for Lori Hunter-Lewis now!"

***

Rider's techs got us the address before we'd turned out of the alley behind Joanna's house. They were good like that. Rider didn't say anything as we sped toward the address. Didn't ask questions or voice any doubts, and I loved him for that because the thought of identifying a target just by hearing their name on the radio was pretty damn crazy, but he believed in me.

There was no alley behind Lori's house and we could see the bat-things flying out of her chimney as we screeched to a stop along the curb in front of her house, so we jumped out and ran for the front door.

"Am I crazy, or are they flying away?" Rider asked.

"Yeah, I don't get it either," I said as we reached the door just behind Jake and Ginger. The slayer kicked it down and we poured in. Daniel had already found somewhere to shift and taken to the sky.

A brunette woman in her late thirties or early forties screamed profanities up her chimney. She caught us out of the corner of her eye and spun toward us, brandishing a fire iron. "I just poked that motherfucker full of extra assholes and I'll poke you full of 'em too! Nobody's robbing my house this Christmas! Git!"

Ginger burst out laughing and we all looked at her. "What? She's funny."

Jake grinned and muttered, "The poker is iron. She wounded an ancient monster bad enough to chase it off and doesn't even know what she did."

"Disappeared again," Daniel said, stepping through the front door. "I lost it."

"So we have to wait another night for it to come back here?" Ginger pouted. "This is seriously harshing my Christmas mellow."

"Git!" The woman pointed the poker at us. "I'm not messing around with you…" She appeared to just notice Jake and her eyes rolled back in her head before she hit the floor.

"Does that happen a lot?" I asked.

"More than you'd think. Damn Dean Winchester." He shrugged. "At least she'll think all this was a dream when she comes to. I'll ward the house in case it comes back before we get here tomorrow. Daniel, can you carry Lori off to bed?"

"I'd rather kill a bat-Santa, but I guess I'll do that instead," he muttered and stepped forward to scoop up the woman.

"What is it?" Rider asked, watching me. I'd been piecing together an idea since we'd left Joanna's house.

"Have your techs pull up everything that can on WDNI and Danielle Muething. See if they can pull records of every caller she's had on her show this month and cross reference those names to see how many have been reported missing or dead. We're going back to Angela LaRoche's house."

***

"What are you looking for?" Rider asked.

"Found it!" I cracked open the ugly gnome's ass and removed the spare key.

"Well, that was an unexpected twist," Jake muttered as I slid the key in the lock and swung the door open. "But I could have had the door open already if you'd just let me."

"Shut your pie hole, Winchester."

He grumbled behind me as we stepped inside the house. I went straight for the living room, which had thankfully been cleaned. Grissom wouldn't have wasted time with getting that taken care of, getting all his necessary evidence in one visit and not wanting any human police to come in behind him and take over the case for any reason. "I remembered Tina Sweeney saying the radio had been on when she'd discovered all the blood in here."

I walked over to the stereo and turned it on. My gut clenched as Danielle Muething's breathy voice identified Elvis Presley's "Blue Christmas" and the song started to play. "I had a feeling it would be this station playing."

"Who's in here?"

We turned as a purple-haired woman appeared in the doorway.

"Tina, I can explain."

"Danni? The neighbors called me and said someone was poking around in Angela's garden. What's—" She took one look at Jake, let out a scream, and ran across the room to wrap herself around his leg.

"Ahh! Get it off!" He kicked out his leg, but the harder he kicked, the tighter she clung.

Jake continued to plead, but we were too busy laughing at the sight to help him. Then Rider's cell phone vibrated. He removed it from his pocket and we went into the foyer, away from the distraction Jake caused by hopping one-legged around the room trying to dislodge the Dean

Winchester fan.

"Angela LaRoche called in to the show the night she was snatched by the krackling," Rider said, showing me the list of names on his cell screen. "Your hunch was right. All of these women who called in were either reported missing after and a ton of blood was left behind, or quit showing up to work or school after. Those who haven't been reported live alone. I'll send out some guys to check their residences. I'm sure they'll find blood."

"Okay, wait." Ginger stood there for a moment, wrapping her mind around the concept. "The radio DJ is controlling the krackling and sending it after callers to her show?"

"It would appear so," I said, "and now we know who to go capture because when she doesn't assign any new targets and it can't get through Jake's warding to kill Lori, it's going to come after her."

"Before we do that, do you think we should rescue the jackass?" Daniel asked, pointing his thumb over his shoulder to where Jake still hopped around in the other room.

"Somebody better come get this damn thing off me before I shoot it! It's starting to hump. Yow! Hey, those are for my wife's enjoyment only, lady!"

"He can manage," Rider said with a twist of his lips, and started for the door.

"Stop." I grabbed his arm. "He saved my life. The least I can do is save his testicles."

"I'll save him. You stay here." Rider extracted his arm and went back into the living room, muttering, "I don't want you anywhere near his testicles."

CHAPTER TWENTY-FOUR

"This isn't the way to the radio station."

"I know." Rider stared straight ahead as he continued to drive steadily toward The Midnight Rider. The radio was set to the classical station because I couldn't hear Danielle Muething's voice without getting a cramp. Apparently, my gut didn't know I'd gotten the message already. "According to Jake, the krackling doesn't protect her. It only kills those she names as its targets, one per night, so even if she tried to call it to protect her, it couldn't. She's just a human. Grabbing her is not a five-man job."

I looked in the side-view mirror and only saw Jake behind us. "You sent Daniel and Ginger to get her."

"Let them have this one, Danni. They were worried sick about you. They need to get their hands on someone they can smack around."

"And you don't?" I raised my eyebrow. "I saw you got in some smacking on Jake."

"We all got in some smacking on Jake," he muttered. "For someone who's still human, not a normal one, mind you, but human nonetheless, he's hard as hell to put down."

"Apparently, he can't be put down. Kill him and he'll just pop back up."

"Yes. One of his more annoying quirks." Rider glanced in the rearview mirror, and I thought I saw his lip curl a little bit. "But he did save your life, which wouldn't have happened if I'd let my foolish jealousy stay in the way, so I owe him."

My eyelids grew heavy as we neared home. "I'd argue with you about grabbing Danielle, but I'm tired."

"You need sleep. I don't know what they did to patch you up as well as they did, a lot of that I assume was Malaika, but you need sleep to heal fully."

"I wanted to look into her eyes when she realized it was over."

"You will. Daniel and Ginger might be the ones bringing her in, but you'll be there when her pet comes back to bite her hand."

I almost dozed off before we reached The Midnight Rider, but managed to keep my eyes open. Rider parked in the garage and came around to open my door before leading me into the building through the garage door.

We'd barely stepped through before Kutya was spinning and jumping. I tried to bend down and scratch his ears, but he was way too excited and seemed to want to lick me to death instead. Juan stood by the door leading down to the sublevels, watching with a smile.

"Kutya was a mess when it happened," Rider said, voice low. "Somehow he sensed it. Started shaking, howling, pissed all over the place. Hank had to take him outside and although that man is built like a tank, he could barely do it. Didn't calm down until Jake took you out of here and then he just whined uncontrollably. Jadyn couldn't even do anything with him."

"Oh, my poor baby." I dropped to my knees and pulled Kutya into a hug, putting a pause on all the licking.

Jake Porter stepped through the door leading from the bar, duffel bag in hand. He looked down at me and the dog and smiled.

"Your room is downstairs, Porter. Juan will be your shadow until you leave. Don't make me regret this."

Jake saluted him, winked at me, and followed Juan down the stairs.

"You're letting Jake stay here?"

He shrugged. "I owe him, and he's the expert on this kind of stuff, so we need him here if shit goes sideways."

"Well, there's a comforting thought." Kutya had calmed down enough I could get up without the big pup jumping up on me, knocking me back down, so I stood and yawned.

"No troubling thoughts for you. It's time for you to go to sleep." Rider took my hand and led me up the stairs. "Do you need me to put you under, or do you think the nightmares are gone?"

"The haint is gone. Jake obliterated it, which means Trixell is gone too. I'm safe, but there are other ways you can help me sleep soundly."

"Mmm." He pulled me to him as we stepped into the room. "Have I told you I'm glad to have you back?"

"I might have heard something like that." I pulled away as his lips went to my neck. "I'm covered in doggy drool."

"You are." His eyes warmed. "How do you feel about a second shower tonight?"

"Will it be like the first one?"

He nodded, grinning impishly. "But longer."

I took his hand and led him to the bathroom.

***

I woke up, sensed it was about an hour from nightfall, and stretched. I'd slept peacefully without Rider having to put a mind-whammy on me, and my body had healed completely.

Rider stood over me with a mug. He'd dressed in black pants and a black long-sleeved shirt, and appeared to have been up at least a few hours. "I'd have you drink from me, but we might get a repeat of what happened when you did that last night and as great as that would be, we need to handle the DJ."

"Is she in interrogation?"

"No, but she's here." He handed me the mug as I sat up, keeping the bedsheet over me to prevent either of us from getting distracted.

The blood was warm, fresh, and went down smooth. "Geez. This isn't hers, is it?"

"No. We got another pedophile working as a mall Santa. Those filthy fuckers are a dime a dozen, sadly." He shoved his hands into his pockets and rocked back on his feet.

"I can tell you have to tell me something, but don't want to. Just spill it."

"The krackling will come for her wherever she is. Unlike the targets, he doesn't need to be assigned a name and location. He's connected to her because she called him. He'll come right to her, so we needed to put her in the best place for us to fight him."

Interrogation was small. The gym was full of stuff. That left the training room, but Rider wouldn't seem troubled by that, which meant... "The room with the cells."

He nodded. "Where Trixell was killed. Are you all right with that?"

I recalled the way Trixell had screamed that morning, but it didn't send the same shivers through me as it had the past month when I thought of it. "She needed to be killed. I'll be fine going down there."

"Good. Jake thinks he knows how to alter the warding he's been using to keep it out to actually keep it in once it gets in the room so you'll have your shot at killing it before it escapes, but if you can't kill it and we can't..."

"It'll kill us."

"It's a possibility. Even Jake would probably stay dead

if he resurrects so many times without a blood booster."

"No pressure," I said, and raised the mug to my mouth. It didn't go down so smoothly this time.

***

I dressed in faded jeans and an old U of K sweatshirt that had seen better days, not seeing much point in dressing up for a possible bloodbath, grabbed the iron blade and the sheath that fastened around my thigh, and headed downstairs.

"Jadyn's got Kutya for the night," Rider told me as I met him at the base of the stairs. "Tony's managing operations. It's just you, me, Jake, Daniel, and Ginger. Those three have guns. We have blades."

"You don't have a gun?"

He placed his hand over the security panel to unlock the door to the sublevel stairwell, and we headed down. "No. I prefer hand to hand."

"Even when the thing you're hand-to-handing with can paint a room with the blood of its victim?"

He looked at me and grinned. "I can do that too."

I rolled my eyes. "Why are men so cocky?"

"Not all men, and hey, I'm just stating a fact."

We made our way to the sublevel and moved toward the back of the floor. I noted the demeanor of the vampires on security duty as we passed. They might not be part of the group assigned to kill the krackling, but they knew something big was going down. "Is Lana still on security detail in the bar?"

"Yes."

I looked at him, but didn't note any anger or hostility. "I heard she and Tony fought."

"She helped Jake get to the interrogation room. Tony and others tried to stop them. If Jake had ended up killing you, she would have died too, but much slower."

I gulped. Rider could be scary sometimes. "But since I didn't die?"

"She did the right thing, and it worked out well for her." He looked at me. "I'm sure Tony will look for an opportunity to rematch though."

We'd reached the room at the end of the floor. I forced the thought of Trixell and what had happened to her inside it out of my mind and started to place my hand over the security panel.

"You don't have clearance for this room," Rider said, and did it himself.

"Why not?"

"Your own safety." We stepped into the room to see Jake, Daniel, and Ginger standing just inside, waiting. Daniel and Ginger were dressed in black top to bottom as if working security, and Jake was in his usual attire of jeans and a dark T-shirt. I figured he'd left the flannel and jacket in his room so there'd be less to clean after.

"They have clearance?"

"Daniel has temporary clearance. He let the other two in."

Before I could respond to that, I noticed the woman huddled on the cot in the cell Trixell had died in. The other cells were empty. She had shoulder-length light brown hair and wore jeans and a gray hoodie with Santa Claus on the front.

I'd like to say she was pretty, but she had two black eyes and a swollen lip. I looked over at Daniel and Ginger and raised an eyebrow.

"She tripped," Ginger said. "Repeatedly. Down a flight of stairs. Might have got a door slammed on her a few times too. It's hard to say."

"Glad you decided to leave enough for the krackling," Rider said dryly as we crossed the room.

The room was like a prison. Wide open space on the right, and cells on the left. The last time I'd been in it, only one chair sat outside the first cell. Now there was a small metal table, and I saw why as I walked over to it and saw the file folder. I opened it and perused the contents.

"So you're Danielle Muething, or should I call you The Heart Specialist?"

"Why are you doing this to me?" The woman trembled as her eyes darted from each of us. "I didn't do anything to any of you."

I looked down at the sheet of names in the folder. More had been found while I'd slept. "Charly James-Matthews, Joan Rowland, Angela LaRoche, Amanda Weaver, Tricia Spaulding, Kayleigh Thompson, Amy Summers, Tracy Gollins, Linda Barnette Davis, Angel Sigmon, Karin Stahlecker—"

"Okay, okay, I know what I did was wrong, but I had to give it names!"

"You wouldn't have had to do a damn thing if you hadn't called it to command in the first place. Why did you call it?"

"I already told the cosplayer over there why."

I looked over at Jake to see him raise his gun and aim for Danielle's face. Ginger placed her hand over the steel and pushed it down while shaking her head. "Nope. We have to let the big, ugly guy kill her."

"I want to hear you say it." I looked down at the list, saw a handwritten note I deduced was from Jake, who'd apparently done a bit of interrogation before we'd arrived. "Amanda Weaver was first, and she never called in to your show. She was the personal one, the one you called upon the krackling to kill to begin with. Why?"

"Because she got engaged to my ex!" Danielle snapped. "She deserved what she got. He was supposed to be mine."

"And then you sent that thing after all these innocent people because you were stuck assigning it new names or else it would eat you." I read more of Jake's notes, saw that a small ritual was involved in assigning the targets, one Danielle hadn't completed since giving the krackling Lori's name the night before. I closed the folder. "You should have let Amanda have the guy. The krackling didn't get his last two targets, and we left a little something behind at the last target's house, so he won't get her tonight either. Two nights without a kill makes the krackling a very grumpy boy. He's going to come for you, and we're going to let him get you."

Her face had paled as I spoke. "He didn't get the last two?"

"Nope."

She ran across the cell and shook the bars. "You have to let me out of here!"

"Why, so you can do the ritual and give it another name? No chance, buttercup."

"I had to give it those names!" Her eyes widened. "I can give it any name you want. Anyone you want dead, I can assign it to go after. You look like the type who kill people."

"Well, she has a point there," Rider said, then looked at her, "but we use a more direct approach when we want someone dead."

Danielle gulped, then started shaking the bars again. "Let me out! It's going to rip me open!"

"I'm familiar with its work," I told her. "I've seen the aftermath of what you caused it to do to an innocent woman."

She glared at me. "Then just kill me yourself, Ms. Judgmental!"

"Oh, you'd like that, wouldn't you? Get off easy? No." I moved over to where the others stood and settled in to wait for the krackling to make an appearance.

"If she doesn't stop screaming and rattling those bars, I'm going to kill her myself," Jake muttered an hour later as we paced the open portion of the room, waiting. Daniel stood in a corner, arms folded, seeming to do a lot better with the patience thing than us. Rider stood near the door, watching everything at once, and Ginger played with her knife while sitting at the table. And Jake and I paced in circles, itching to kill.

"At least she dropped that fake sexy voice once she was off the air," I muttered. "What if it doesn't come for her tonight?"

"It will. It'll be hungry. It's got to go to Lori's first and realize it's been screwed over on targets twice now, then when it doesn't get a new target, it'll come for this one."

"There's nowhere for it to get in," I said, realizing the obvious for the first time. "Is it supposed to walk in through the bar and take the stairs down?"

"It doesn't need an entrance to get to her. She's not just a target. She's its tie to this world. It'll appear right in this room, kill her, and then what would usually happen is it would go back to sleep wherever it gets sucked into after doing that, but with this warding I'll place when it arrives, I'll hopefully lock it in so we can kill it."

"So sometime before dawn, basically? We could be down here waiting for hours." I glanced over at Daniel. "It's seriously going to screw up a Christmas gift for me if it takes too long."

"Yeah, well, if I don't get out of here before too long myself, my wife's going to kill me, so believe me, I understand. Two nights without a meal though, and two times it's had to heal injuries means time is on our side. This thing is going to be hungry for a kill."

Three hours later, I was ready to just kill Danielle and let the thing go back to its hibernation so I could get on with my life, but the lights flickered.

"Heads up!" Jake said, and drew his knife over his palm.

I winced at the sight of him cutting himself, but didn't have a lot of time to think about it before the krackling appeared inside the cell in its multi-bat form. Danielle let loose a bloodcurdling scream and crab-walked as far back into the wall as she could before deciding to crawl under the metal cot.

Ginger, Daniel, Rider, and I positioned ourselves outside the cell as Jake ran to the door and started drawing something in his own blood.

Danielle continued to scream as the krackling transformed into its man-shape, tossed the cot against the opposite set of bars, grabbed the woman underneath and ripped her open like a bag of potato chips, sending blood and viscera flying, some of which rained over us.

I screamed and picked something long and juicy off of me as Rider cussed, Ginger wiped a ton of slop off her face and Daniel gagged.

"Now I know what it'd be like to sit front row at a Gallagher show," Ginger muttered before raising her gun. She started shooting into the cell.

The krackling surrounded itself with the bat-things it spewed out of its mouth, grabbed the husk of Danielle's body, and leaped up, but couldn't get past the ceiling. It dropped her body and turned fully into its multi-bat form.

"I think the warding worked," Jake said, and trained his gun on the cluster of bats hitting the ceiling. "It should have disappeared right after it killed her."

And it definitely had killed her, I saw, looking over at the splayed open mess that didn't even look human anymore.

Some of the bat-things exploded as they were hit with iron bullets, but the krackling figured out it was a goner staying in that form and the bat-things swooped down around us before taking shape as the big bearded man right behind Daniel.

It reached for Daniel as it opened its maw, but Daniel disappeared in rainbow sparkles before he could get ripped apart. Before the first bullet could connect to the krackling's chest, it started releasing the bat-things out of its mouth. It was smarter this time and made sure to keep some bats as chest cover to deflect any bullets aimed for its heart.

Daniel shifted shape, taking up a lot of space in the open area and unleashed a wave of fire at the krackling, burning several bats to a crisp while Rider and I moved in behind it, far enough not to get burned ourselves, and Ginger and Jake continued shooting at it from the side.

"How many damn bats can that thing vomit?" Rider asked.

"A lot, apparently."

We closed in from behind and Rider moved in to stab the krackling through its back as Daniel eased back on the stream of fire, but the monster sensed the movement and swung one of its arms out to send Rider flying into the wall behind us.

I heard his head hit the wall and rushed over to where he'd slid to the floor. "Are you all right?"

"Yeah," he said, rubbing the back of his head as he got up, "But this thing's really pissing me off."

"Join the club," Jake yelled as he tossed his now-empty gun aside and replaced it with his blade. Ginger had done the same thing. "All those bullets and the damn thing still isn't weakened enough to stick to one form so we can kill it. Fucking hell, man! We have to get it to stay in one form!"

Rider and I looked at each other, then met eyes with Jake and Ginger. Daniel was still busy blowing a steady, yet diminishing stream of fire at the bat-things the krackling kept releasing. We nodded at each other, raised our blades, and ran full speed at the thing.

The krackling raised its arms and spun its body without moving its head, knocking the four of us back while still releasing a continuous flow of bat-things toward the dragon desperately trying to fry it.

I saw stars as my head hit a wall and I slid down to the floor to see the other three just as stunned as I was. "What the fucking hell? When did it learn to do that?"

"Fuck!" was Jake's only response as he got to his feet and wobbled before shaking his head. I was pretty sure he was seeing stars circling it.

"I thought you said this thing flew away after getting shot with iron once and poked up the ass a few times,"

Rider growled. He got to his feet and helped me to mine. "Why the fuck isn't it weakening now?"

Jake started to shrug, then his face twisted in a horrified expression as something must have dawned on him. "Oh, fuck me sideways. That must be how the damn thing survives hibernation. Killing the one who called it must give it more strength, so it's going to take a lot more to weaken it." He frowned, angled his head to the side as he stared at the creature. "Then again, now that I think about it, it's also possible it just fled those times because it sensed a slayer. Some monsters do that."

Rider's eyes turned into chilly pools of dark blue rage as he tightened his hand around his blade. "I'm going to kill that slayer over and over again until he can't come back."

I grabbed his arm as he lunged for Jake and yanked him back. "Fight later. We have to kill this thing before it kills us."

The dragon disappeared in rainbow sparkles and Daniel appeared in its place, breathing heavily as the bats surrounded him.

"Smear the warding!" Rider yelled. "Just let it go back into hibernation!"

Jake looked at me for my approval or rejection of that order and a trio of bat-things struck him. Then they were everywhere. We swiped and slashed with our blades, taking out as many as we could, but we'd pissed the krackling off and without a dragon breathing fire at it, it was able to focus better on all of us.

I screamed with fury as I slashed out at the flying bastards biting and scratching at me, madder at myself than the damned creatures from hell attacking me. I was supposed to kill the krackling. I knew it, but how? And why me? I wasn't anything special, just a vampire-succubus… "Holy shit."

I remembered my conversation with Nyla, and something clicked. I'd only viewed my succubus traits as bad, always fought against them, pushed them down. I'd never called upon them like I called upon my vampire gifts when I needed to feed, run fast, or see better in the dark. I had to kill the krackling because I was the only one able to make it hold one shape.

I slashed at the bats and fought my way back toward Jake, Rider moving with me about a foot away, using his power to hold back as many of the things as he could. He'd never left my side. "Cover me, everyone! Give me some room!"

Without asking why, apparently trusting I had a plan, all four moved in closer to where I was while slashing at the endless stream of bat-things biting and clawing at them.

"Everyone down!" Daniel yelled and allowed time for us to duck before he shifted shape again and blew out a stream of fire toward where the krackling stood, roasting the bats between him and it.

By doing this, he'd positioned his massive dragon form in front of the rest of us and bought me some time to work. Judging by the thin stream of fire, it wasn't much.

"What are you doing?" Rider asked, and my heart lurched, seeing all the bleeding bite marks and scratches on him and the others, and those were just the ones I could see. I was sure there were more under the Danielle gunk that had splashed onto us.

"Just trust me, and pray this works." I closed my eyes and breathed in deep. I'd never called upon my succubus side before and it wasn't like I found the krackling attractive. It was a monster, and a monster who looked like an old homeless man and smelled of gingerbread and sulfur at that, but I needed to make that monster want me.

I relaxed my shoulders, rolled my neck, and released my breath. I was as much a sex demon as I was a vampire. I could make anything male want me as easily as I could drop fangs. I opened my eyes and walked down the length of Daniel's dragon form until I could see the krackling over his tail. It was a hideous old man with a creepy, unhinged jaw that spewed bats, but it was a male. There was no way I could get close enough to it to inject venom into it, but…

Come to me, a voice in my head far huskier than I had ever spoken called out to it mentally, and I saw the creature's pale gray eyes slide my way. *Come to me. Taste me.*

I ran my tongue over the fangs that had dropped and tasted something sweet I'd never tasted before because I'd never called for it before, had only accidentally injected it straight into flesh. I stepped around Daniel's tail and started toward the krackling. *Come to me.*

"Danni!" Fear laced Rider's commanding voice.

"Let her be," Jake said. "I think I know what she's doing, and she's a fucking genius."

Come to me, the demon voice purred across the mental link I'd somehow created between the monster and me, but the krackling didn't move or stop spewing the bat-things. However, it didn't attack me, which allowed me to grab one of the chubby bat-things outside of Daniel's stream of fire and bite into its juicy belly, injecting it with venom.

The stream of fire stopped, and I heard Daniel say, "What the fuck is she doing?" as the remaining bats were sucked back into the krackling's maw. It snapped its mouth closed and opened its robes to reveal a massive erection stretching the front of its pants, and rushed toward me, eyes drunk with lust. It moved fast, but my iron blade was already in my hand, and before the krackling could lay one gnarled finger on me, it was in its heart.

It gasped out a strange growling sound as its hot, coppery, cinnamon breath washed over my face and it started to blacken and shrivel before my eyes before bursting into a pile of black ash.

I heard the sound of excitement and praise around me, but couldn't make it out clearly. I'd called on my succubus power, but had taken the offering away. Now it had risen, and it was thirsty. My heart beat in my ears as I turned toward the others and watched their jaws drop. I didn't need a mirror to know my eyes were red and I was looking at the three men like they were a meal because I felt it.

Down, I coaxed my succubus side in my mind. *I'll feed you all the sex you want when I get Rider alone.*

Want them all, the demonic voice responded. *Want them now.*

I saw Rider talking, knew from the fierceness in his expression he was commanding me to sleep, but it wasn't working. I'd called up the succubus, and I had to be the one to settle her back where she belonged.

But she wasn't a her. She was me. Half of me was a sex demon, and I had to quit thinking of it as some foreign thing in me. I had to embrace what I was, accept it. I had to love myself. My palms started to sweat as an ache spread in my loins.

"Get out of here!" Rider barked at the two men, his voice finally penetrating through the loud heartbeat in my ears, but the men didn't budge. I'd somehow enthralled them.

Shit. I was all about loving myself, and embracing my succubus side, but I wasn't about to embrace it by having an orgy with men I knew would all kill each other after, and I didn't know how to talk the succubus side of me back down so I looked at the only source of libido killer in the room and did what I had to do.

"I'm sorry," I managed to get out before I grabbed Ginger and shoved my tongue down her throat.

CHAPTER TWENTY-FIVE

"Blech!" I released Ginger and nearly tripped over my own feet running to one of the open cells. Bile rose hot and fast, erupting just as I hit my knees in front of the toilet.

"Well, it wasn't that great for me either!" Ginger said, but even over the sound of my retching, she sounded upset and insulted.

"Wow," I heard Jake say, "that had to be the worst girl on girl action ever."

"Oh shut up," Ginger snapped. "She just sucked on a weird bat-looking creature that came out of some creepy hobo-Santa-looking guy. Of course she's throwing up, jackass!"

I hurled again, the memory of biting into the bat-thing not doing me any favors. It had seemed like such a brilliant idea at the time. So had kissing Ginger, and boy was that a regret. Succubi *reaaaaalllllly* didn't dig chicks.

Suddenly, I heard laughing from the last person I expected to laugh after seeing me kiss someone else. "Look on the bright side, Ginger. If she'd enjoyed kissing you, I'd have to kill you in a jealous rage."

I started to wipe my mouth, but thought better of it. I

had blood and gunk on me. Some of it was Danielle, some of it was the krackling, some mine, and who knew what else I'd picked up. In fact, I was still losing blood from my bites and scratches. Rider, Ginger, and I really needed to seal our wounds before we bled out. With that in mind, I stood and started back toward the others, slamming my shoulder into the cell bars as a dizzy wave hit.

I heard the door open and Daniel yell, "We need some vampires in here to seal up some wounds. Bring some towels and soap and water!"

Twenty minutes later, we were sticky, but wiped down. Daniel had healed through shifting, and the rest of us had taken advantage of the saliva donated by the vampires on security duty in the sublevel, which was a less gross way of saying they licked us all over. Even Jake took advantage of the vampire healing properties on his more serious wounds so he could ensure he didn't get woozy on his long drive home.

"You did good, hybrid."

I took another swig of blood from the jug that had been brought in to us and grinned at the slayer. "Well, somebody had to save the day, since it didn't look like you were going to live up to your legendary slayer status."

He laughed out loud. "Yeah, I'll have to work on my seduction skills in case I run into another one of those things."

"Thanks for your help, Jake." Rider extended his hand and didn't even try to break Jake's bones when they shook. "Juan will see you out so you can get back to your family."

"Right." Jake glanced over at the shifter who'd been with him since his arrival the night before and had waited outside the cell room during our battle with the krackling to escort him out upon completion. Then he looked back at me. "Your girl has some real gifts. I might need to borrow her sometime down the road. Never know what might fall in my lap."

"Not going to happen."

Jake's grin widened as he looked at Rider and backed out of the room. "You know she wouldn't have sent me to save her if she didn't think we might need her someday."

"What is he talking about?" I asked as Jake turned around and allowed Juan to lead him out of the sublevels.

"Nothing we need to discuss today." Rider swung his arm around my shoulders, pulled me to him, and kissed my forehead. "Nothing I even want to think about at the moment."

I started to press for information, but noticed Ginger wiping down her knife, still looking pretty grumpy about our disastrous kiss.

"Ginge, you know the succubus just hates women. I'm so sorry, but it was either kiss you or make a very awkward, humiliating low budget porno in this bloodbath."

"Yeah, I know." She raised her finger and gave very pointed looks to Rider and Daniel. "But for the record, I am a great kisser."

"I don't know." Daniel pulled a face that was something near a grimace. "That was a pretty strong reaction. I mean, her lips had barely left yours before her head was in the toilet."

"Oh yeah? I'll kiss you right now!" She rolled up her sleeves as if she were about to hit him instead of kiss him, and Daniel laughed. "Wanna put money on how good I am?"

"Kiss me and you'll be stuck straight forever." He winked. "These lips are addictive."

I'd had a run-in with those lips in a dream realm once, and I didn't know if they could turn a lesbian straight, but they did pack a powerful punch. I remembered the fantasy I'd had in the pantry with him, the dreams and thoughts that had popped up here and there since that moment in that dream realm, and remembered my discussion with Nyla. I had a lot to sort through, but first…

"Oh, crap!" I grabbed Daniel and pushed him out the

door. "You have to go pick up Angel right now and get on the road. Hit the shower and go!"

"What?" He was walking backward, facing me. "What are you talking about?"

"Your Christmas present! It's all set up, but you have got to get to Nashville on time. Just go! Angel will fill you in when you pick her up. Hurry!"

"Nashville?" He gave me a confused look, then his eyes widened. "The Guns N' Roses Christmas Eve concert? I thought that was sold out."

"I have connections. Go!" I pushed him.

"That's not until tomorrow. Relax."

"I got him," Ginger said, aware what my big surprise was and why I needed Daniel to arrive in Nashville so far ahead of the concert. In about four and a half hours, actually. She grabbed him and pulled him along.

I turned and walked back toward where Rider stood waiting just outside the room we'd destroyed the krackling in, watching as the unfortunate staff on janitorial duty worked on mopping up all the blood and viscera. Halfway to him, I spun back around. I hadn't missed the disappointment in Daniel's eyes when Ginger had dragged him away and he'd realized I was sending him away for Christmas.

"Daniel, hold up!" I ran to him and, despite Rider watching, stood on tiptoe to wrap my arms around his broad shoulders. "I'll miss you on Christmas, but this was a very time-sensitive gift. I know you'll have a great time taking Angel to her first concert for me."

He pulled away and smiled down at me, disappointment in his eyes. "I thought you'd want to be there for her first concert."

"There'll be other concerts. Things have been crazy this month, and I thought it best not to put myself in that kind of environment when I planned this."

His expression grew very serious. "You're better now?"

"I'm much better now." I reminded myself there was

no time for this. "You're going to have a great time, and I can't wait to hear all the details when you get back. Now, go, go, go!"

He looked over my shoulder as I sensed Rider approach and smiled down at me. "Sure. And thanks. I hope you two have a great Christmas."

Rider's hand splayed over my hip as Daniel turned and allowed Ginger to herd him off to the shower so he could clean up, change into something less bloody, and collect Angel for the big surprise. "Everything all right?"

"It is now." I sighed. "I hope they make it in time."

Rider looked down at me and grinned. I'd told him about the plan when I'd first thought about it to make sure Daniel had the time off. "I think they will. We should go shower too, and get out of these clothes. I'm giving us the rest of the night off, what little is left of it."

I looked down at myself. We were both a mess despite being wiped down, and I could tell by the expressions on the faces of vampires posted on security detail nearby, we didn't smell that great. However, wearing all the funk kind of made one just accept it. "Yeah, good idea."

We headed toward the stairs, but I paused as we reached a hall, and looked down it. Rider looked down the hall, then at me. "You want to see her?"

"It's Christmas Eve tomorrow."

"Come on." He took my hand and led me down the hall to the room at the very end. There used to be guards on duty outside it, but the security panel that had been installed since made that unnecessary. Rider placed his palm over the panel, and the door opened.

"She always looks so peaceful," I said as we stepped in and I went over to the side of the bed to take my sister's hand, but decided against it. Although she still wore the clothes she'd worn the night she'd tried to kill me, she'd been cleaned up, and I didn't want to mar her with my hands, which had been wiped down, but could really benefit from a hot shower. "This will be my first

Christmas without her. I think I'll actually miss her turning her snooty nose up at my gift."

On the other side of the bed, across from where I stood, Rider offered a consoling smile. "You'll always have memories."

"Yeah." I sighed. "My mom doesn't even know she's like this. She thinks she's off in Vegas living it up. I know we don't get along, but it really does suck that she thinks her perfect daughter won't be with her on Christmas Eve just because she's run off."

"Is that why she wanted the meeting, to ask more about her?"

"No. She actually asked me to come over tomorrow night. She said I could bring you." I grinned at him impishly before the thought of my mother being without her daughters on Christmas Eve stole all my humor. I looked away and took a deep breath. I didn't want to cry.

"What time do we need to be there?"

I looked up at Rider so fast I nearly put a crick in my neck. "What?"

He raised an eyebrow. "I assume you want to spend Christmas Eve with your family?"

I stood there blinking for a moment, wondering if I'd just imagined what I'd heard. "Well, I mean, it's Christmas…"

"Do you want to go?"

I sighed. "I should. She'll be all alone, except for my grandmother and that awful dog, but that's even worse than being alone. But I can't make you go. I know you don't want to spend any time around them or that little fart machine."

"No, but that doesn't mean I won't do it for you."

The tears I'd done so well hiding a moment ago slid down my cheeks. "You'd really do that for me?"

"Of course. Now, let's go shower and rest, and stop that crying. I'm sure you'll have plenty to cry about after spending time with those two tomorrow," he assured me, causing my tears to turn into laughter. He walked around, grabbed my hand, and led me out. "However, I must warn you that if they start in on you, it's possible I will stab them and give their little rodent to Kutya as a treat."

"Of course you will."

***

"Are you sure you're not hungry?" my mother asked as we moved to the living room area of the condo she shared with my grandmother. "All you had was salad, and you just picked at it. Christmas is when we get to splurge on calories."

"I think you splurged enough for all of us, Margaret," my grandmother snapped before sipping from her wineglass, staring at Rider over the rim as she'd been doing the entire visit.

"I'm fine," I answered as Rider and I sat on the loveseat across from my grandmother, who'd perched on the sofa, leaving the lounge chair for my mother. "I think I've eaten too many sweets this week. So many Christmas treats going around."

"Too many sweets tend to stick to your hips," my grandmother admonished me, but her hard glare was on my mother's hip area. "That's no way to keep a man. Wouldn't you agree, Rider?"

"I would not," he answered smoothly and turned toward my mother. "A woman is always as lovely as she carries herself, and a little extra in the hip area is a welcome softness."

The red hue of embarrassment that had filled my mother's cheeks upon being admonished by my grandmother in front of company turned into the pink blush of flattery, and if I hadn't already loved Rider, I would have fallen for him right then and there.

"Well, aren't you the odd sort of bird," my grandmother muttered as she took another sip from her wineglass, this one more of a gulp. The woman did not like being disagreed with, especially while she was in the process of tearing someone down.

At her feet, Terry the Tiny Terror picked up on her displeasure and growled at Rider. Rider growled low enough my mother and grandmother's human ears couldn't hear, but Terry's canine ears got the message and he yelped before running off, farting along the way.

"Oh, what has disturbed my little precious?" my grandmother said, watching the little stink bomb patter away while the rest of us fanned the air.

"That dog is the only thing on this planet that makes worse smells than Rome," Rider muttered in my ear, causing me to laugh.

"What was that?" my grandmother asked.

"Oh, I was just admiring the décor," Rider said with a pleasant smile.

My grandmother arched an over-tweezed eyebrow, not believing the lie, and took another drink. "If Shana were here, she'd play piano for us. She is so talented, that one. It's such a shame she chose not to be here, but she always was the one going places. I suppose the child with the talent is the one to go off and leave."

"Danni was always a wonderful writer," my mother said, a little loudly. She smiled at Rider. "Oh, she used to play with her dolls and come up with the most imaginative stories. Creativity has always been her talent."

"Pah!" My grandmother downed more wine. "Where did creativity get her?"

"Her own apartment," my mother muttered.

My grandmother opened her mouth to respond, but then it went slack as her eyes glazed over. She slumped in the seat and dropped the wineglass. Rider moved in a flash of speed to scoop it up before it hit the floor, saving the white carpet from the red liquid.

"Oh, finally," my mother all but cheered. "I put enough crushed pills to knock out an elephant in that glass. My goodness, you're fast. I didn't even see you move to grab that."

Rider was kneeling on one knee beside my grandmother's chair, and both of us gawked at my mother. We met each other's eyes and burst out laughing.

"Mom, did you drug Grandma?"

"Oh, you know how she is, and she's been even worse since Shana ran off." She took a big swig from her mug of egg nog that I could smell was more whiskey than egg nog. "You know what we haven't done in a long time is play a good game of Monopoly. Who wants to play Monopoly?"

I looked over at Rider, who was still smiling. He shrugged. "I could play."

I shrugged too. "What the hell? We don't have to be in bed before Santa arrives."

"Speaking of which, would you like me to carry her to her bed?" Rider offered.

"Oh would you, dear? It's the second room on the left down that hall." She watched Rider effortlessly scoop up my grandmother and carry her off before turning toward me. "You know, he might not be the CEO of a more respectable company, but he's not that bad of a catch." She took another drink of whiskey nog and released a delicate belch. "I could take a bite out of that ass too."

"Mom!"

***

Christmas Eve with my mother went surprisingly well. It was kind of fun, actually, once my mother drugged my grandmother and her little farting machine. We ended up playing one of those games of Monopoly that went on for hours and it was the best time I'd had with my mother in… well, ever.

Despite the unexpectedly enjoyable evening, and the texts I'd received from Daniel and Angel detailing just how appreciated my surprise gift had been, I was still full of disappointment when we arrived back at The Midnight Rider, and I couldn't shake it off, not even when Rider started talking in clever innuendo on the way up to bed.

"Everything all right?" Rider asked as he kicked off his shoes and shrugged out of his leather jacket.

I did the same and passed him my jacket to hang in the closet. "Yes. It was a good night. Thank you for coming with me."

"Not a problem, and surprisingly, it wasn't all that bad."

I'd bent down to rub Kutya's belly as the big guy rolled over on the floor at the foot of the bed, and when I stood back up, Rider was behind me with a rectangular box wrapped in shiny blue wrapping paper with white snowflakes.

"What's that?"

"It's just something, probably very stupid, but you've seemed a little down since we left your mother's so I thought I'd give it to you now."

And suddenly I felt even worse. "Oh, Rider, I wanted to get you something really great, but I couldn't think of anything. You can buy whatever you want and you're not the easiest guy to shop for to begin with. I feel so—"

He covered my mouth with his, silencing me, and by the time he pulled back, I'd almost forgotten what I'd been saying to begin with. "I told you the only thing I wanted for Christmas was to have you back. You're back. You looking into my eyes without freaking out is the best gift anyone could have gotten me this year."

"Well, then you should kiss Jake because that was kind of all him."

"Boy, you really know how to kill a moment, don't you?"

I laughed, then groaned. "I'm a terrible girlfriend. I could have at least got you a card. You got me something."

"You might not even like it. I don't know. I just…" He shrugged. "Just open it. If you think it's dumb, I'll take you shopping the day after Christmas."

"I'm sure it's wonderful." I took the package he'd wrapped so prettily with a big silky bow and carefully tore it open to reveal the prettiest brown face I'd ever seen looking back at me. She was gorgeous, from her silky black hair to her beautiful thick-lashed eyes and dark red lips, right down to the little diamond buttons on her tuxedo-styled dress.

My knees gave out, I plopped down onto the foot of the bed and bawled. Rider went down to his knees in front of me. "Shit. I'm sorry. I can get you something else."

"It's the m-m-m-most b-b-b-b-b-b-"

"Honey? I can't make out what you're saying." He reached for the Barbie. "I'll get rid of it."

"No!" I held the doll to my chest. "I l-l-l... I l-love it."

I wiped my sleeve across my eyes to clear the pool of tears and saw Rider staring at me with a look of utter bewilderment. I couldn't blame him after the way I'd wailed that last part. "How did you know I wanted her?"

His face grew a little pink. "I kind of slipped into your thoughts a little, a few times. You got pretty emotional sometimes thinking about this doll. You did it quite a bit over the past month, actually, so I thought maybe if you were thinking about it so much, I should get it."

"But she's so expensive for a doll, and so hard to get! How did you find her?"

"Remember that time you were barred from going downstairs?"

My jaw dropped open. "You killed someone for her?"

Rider barked out a laugh. "No, you goof. I had my techs track it down. There was an auction going on when you were barred from the sublevels. I didn't want you to see what was on their screens."

I laughed with him, then started crying again. "I feel even worse now! Jake was supposed to help me with your gift, but I knew he wouldn't be able to, and now it's almost Christmas morning and I have nothing. You were even nice to my mom!"

"Hey, hey, hey." He took the doll and set her on the dresser. "It's all right."

"No, it's not. I'm the worst girlfriend ever. I got gifts for everyone, but I couldn't find anything good enough for you and you mean so much more to me than anyone else!"

He smiled down at me. "Well, then, you just gave me everything just by saying that."

"It's not enough."

"It is." He leaned me back and trailed his fingers over my collarbone, then started a path down the center of my chest over my shirt. "But you know there's always something else you can give me if you really insist…"

I narrowed my puffy, red eyes that had just shed buckets of tears. "You get that all the time. It's not enough."

"Well, then… I guess you'll just have to use some of that creativity of yours. I heard somewhere that it's a talent you have. I'm sure you can come up with something extra special…"

CHAPTER TWENTY-SIX

I shivered as I opened my eyes to see a blue-tinted world. A cerulean forest spread out around me. Rider stood at my side, his jaw clamped extra tight. "Rider? What is this place?"

"Nowhere you should be," he said. "Damn that Porter. He must have told her she could use you."

"Who?"

A bright ball of pure white light formed in front of us. We shielded our eyes as it expanded and elongated until it stood about six feet tall and three feet wide. As it dimmed, a woman with golden hair and eyes stepped out. She wore a long white gown cinched at the waist with a belt made of pure gold loops. She seemed to glow from the inside out. "Relax, vampire. The slayer called upon me because it seems your beloved wanted more than anything to give you a gift that was far too great for her to give."

Rider looked at me before addressing the woman. "Who are you?"

"My name is Kiara. She who called you to this realm before has not called upon either of you now. I brought you here."

"You're an angel," Rider said. "You're the angel who

helped Christian."

A wave of sadness washed over the woman's eyes, and she nodded. "How is my brother?"

"He's doing very well. He's married to the woman he loves, and he's happy."

The woman seemed to struggle to absorb this, but she eventually nodded and looked at me. "Jacob Porter asked for my help. We've been watching and although we don't meddle in affairs of the outside world unless absolutely necessary, especially affairs of those who are not powerless to help themselves, we felt a gift could be granted in this situation. Follow me."

Rider looked over at me and raised his eyebrows as the angel turned and walked away. I shrugged in response, just as clueless as to what was happening. When Jake had asked what I would give Rider if I could give him anything, I'd asked for the impossible, so I had no idea what the angel was leading us to.

As we followed the angel, the temperature warmed and the blue forest morphed into a beautiful spring meadow full of color. The sun warmed our skin, but not painfully so as we continued on to a cliff.

The angel turned before we reached it. "You know there is no trespassing into this world. Very few are capable of entering, and anyone else must be brought here by one of us. We are aware of the situation and your half-brother must be stopped. You must do that. What we can do for you, as a gift from your beloved because her heart was so pure in its asking of it, is keep your mother safe so he never gets his hands on her."

Rider's body went very still. "Are you saying…?"

"You may not speak with her or interact with her, for it would disturb her peace, but she has been brought here where she will be safe, never to risk being taken by any dark magic your half-brother may work, never to reincarnate and risk falling into his hands again. You may look upon her and know it is true."

Kiara stepped out of the way and Rider rushed forward. His mouth fell open as he stepped to the edge of the cliff and fell to his knees.

"Mother," he whispered. He braced himself against an invisible barrier and stared at something below the cliff as tears spilled silently down his face.

I looked at Kiara and she nodded before tilting her head toward the cliff, indicating I could look. I kneeled next to Rider and rested my hand on his shoulder as I watched the beautiful woman in white frolic in the valley below us, dancing amid multicolored flowers as she played with the butterflies fluttering around her. Her ebony black hair hung to her waist. It and her ruby red lips stood out in sharp contrast to her pale skin and white gown, but it was her eyes that mesmerized, so blue like her son's. "Rider, she is so beautiful."

"She always was, inside and out." Rider sniffed. "Was she in Hell?"

"No."

He released a sigh, heavy with relief. "Is she lonely here?"

"No. She is at perfect peace, which is why you may not speak with her. She was a good woman who had a very bad thing happen to her. Those horrible memories have been taken from her, but one look upon you as what you are now and she would regain them."

He swallowed, and I squeezed his shoulder as I felt it tense under my hand. "Does she remember me at all?"

"She does not know Rider Knight, but remembers her son. She loves you very much, Lovas."

Tears were still on Rider's cheeks when we woke up just before nightfall, which was how I knew what had happened had been real, not just a really beautiful dream, that and the way he immediately kissed me breathless in the most genuine, nonsexual display of love and appreciation.

"Best gift ever," he whispered. "Do you have any idea

what you gave me? You gave me peace."

I sighed. "Again, it almost feels like you should be kissing Jake if you want to thank someone."

"You know, if you suggest I kiss Jake one more time, I'm going to start thinking this is some weird kink you have."

I laughed. "No, but he was the one who got the impossible. I only told him what I would give you if I could give you anything in the world."

"Then it only happened because you asked for it, and like Kiara said, because your heart was so pure when you asked." He kissed me again. "Thank you."

"You're not mad that I told Jake about what happened? About your brother?"

Rider shook his head. "No. You got me a moment with my mother, a chance to see her and know she is safe from Ryan. And hell, the way Ryan keeps staying one step ahead, I might need to bring in the slayer to finally kill him permanently."

I smiled, then realized what day it was, and that the day was almost over. "It's Christmas! Everyone's supposed to be here at nightfall."

"Then I suppose we need to get showered and dressed." He sat up and offered me his hand.

"Why, you're always such a gentleman… Lovas." I raised an eyebrow.

Rider blew out a breath and grinned. "Technically, Rider Knight isn't a fake name. It's a close English translation of the Hungarian name I was given at birth, but no one outside of this room ever needs to know that."

"Understood, as long as I always get to call you *mine*."

"That's an easy promise."

***

I finally felt genuine Christmas spirit, so much I wore my Christmas sweater. Rider did not appreciate the fact that my Christmas sweater was Dean Winchester in a Santa hat, but he only shook his head and muttered under his breath as he finished buttoning his red silk shirt and rolled up the sleeves. The red color was as festive of a fashion choice as he would agree to. However, he allowed me to put a jingle bells collar on Kutya so I was happy.

Once dressed, the three of us made our way downstairs to the bar. Rider kept it open for customers with nowhere to go, but all our friends were there too to get together and celebrate each other's company, even surly Tony.

I did not expect to see Daniel and Angel back from Nashville so soon, having paid for them to stay at Gaylord Opryland through to the next morning, but when we entered the bar, the first thing I saw was Rome, Tony, Ginger, Lana, and even Eliza huddled around Angel as she showed them the video she'd sent me the previous night of Daniel fangirling over Slash.

"So Danni sent us to the Nashville Zoo where her cousin works to see Slash's snake that he gave to the zoo to keep for him years ago. What she didn't tell even me was that Slash visits the snake every time he comes to Nashville and her cousin knew when he'd visit before the concert so he got us in then even though it was outside their actual hours, and we were there when he came. Listen to Daniel!"

The dragon-shifter happened to be standing behind her in the tour T-shirt he'd grabbed at the show under a leather jacket and turned a nice shade of red as she played the clip. Then his eyes met mine, and he smiled.

"Merry Christmas, boss!" Greg raised a mug of blood and the rest of the group huddled around Angel at the bar followed suit.

I got one look at Ginger's ugly Christmas sweater when she turned around to face me and burst out laughing. Rider took one look at it and groaned.

"What?" She winked at me while she stretched out the material to display the sweater's design, which was a perfect replica of her Danni the Teste Slayer T-shirts, only this time the set of cartoonish testicles wore a Santa hat and had been impaled with a candy cane instead of a knife.

"I don't know what I like better," I said as I reached her, "the sweater or the sparkly silver-blue lipstick."

"Isn't it gorgeous? It's called Oh Hoey Night."

I laughed. "Why do all your lipsticks have Ho in the names?"

"Because they're made from The Ho House." She took a tube out of her jeans pocket and showed me the company name branded on the case. "It's like their whole thing. Embracing your ho power, like you did with the krackling."

"So you're not mad I shoved my tongue in your mouth and then threw up?"

Angel's mouth dropped open. "You did what?"

"That's right," Ginger said. "She laid one on me." Then she lowered her voice as she turned toward me. "I'm not mad, but I think we need to work on your technique."

"Trust me, she's a master," Rider murmured and kissed my neck. "All right, can we get the teenager away from the actual bar, please? Move it over to a table, kid."

Angel huffed out a sigh, but did as told, and the party continued with gift giving, drinking—nonalcoholic for Angel, and bloody for quite a few of us—and music although Tony had made it clear that if he heard Mariah Carey one more time, we were all getting shot in the ass so we left it to non-Mariah holiday tunes.

Angel's surprise gift to me was a fleece throw of Dean Winchester's face, which Rider declared would absolutely not be going on our bed. Ginger had gifted me a makeup kit from The Ho House, and Eliza gave me a beautiful leather-bound journal and told me Nannette had gifted me the Swarovski Crystal pen that she'd wrapped with it. "She said she couldn't come because she was volunteering somewhere, but to thank you. She said you would understand."

I smiled, my gut telling me Nannette had looked up her newly found blood relatives and wherever she was volunteering, she was with them.

Ginger loved the *NCIS* DVD set I got her and Rome put on his U of L hoodie the moment he opened it. I'd even gotten something close to a smile out of Tony when he'd opened the noise-canceling headphones I'd gifted him, but I couldn't help but notice the quiet way Daniel watched me the whole night, so once Rider and Tony got absorbed in a discussion, I broke away to join Daniel in the booth he sat alone in near the front of the bar.

"Is everything all right?" I asked as I slid across from him. "I paid for you guys to stay until tomorrow morning so you'd have plenty of time to enjoy Gaylord Opryland. It's so beautiful there."

"It was beautiful, and we walked all through it for hours and ate a ton of gelato, but you surprised me with the trip so unexpectedly, I couldn't even give you my gift." He pulled a small rectangular box out of his inner jacket pocket and slid it toward me. "Remember Donna, the woman I met with here?"

"The Imortian from Australia?"

He nodded. "This is what we were meeting about. I had it custom made by her."

"Custom made?" My eyebrows rose into my hairline.

"I couldn't give you just anything. Go ahead."

I opened the small black box and gasped. A gorgeous silver bracelet was inside with a dragon charm and two additional charms, a brown and green stone in a silver setting that resembled a dragon eye, and a pale bluish-white orb. "It's so beautiful."

"You can't even see its full beauty yet. The silver you see is imortium, which is why I had to have Donna make it." He touched the charm that looked like a dragon's eye. "The stone in this charm that's designed to look like a dragon's eye is actually called dragon eye. The round stone is a moon pearl. It's all from Imortia and maybe one day

I'll take you there so you can see it in its true colors."

"Oh Daniel, this is too much."

"Hey, you gave me Slash."

I laughed. "I think I got the better gift, but I'm glad you liked the surprise."

He smiled. "I wanted to give you a ring, but I didn't think that would go over well with Rider. Then I thought of a necklace, but passed for the same reason. You can wear this on your wrist or ankle, if he doesn't mind."

"I love it just the way it is, and if Rider doesn't like it, he'll just have to get over it." I slid the bracelet on over my wrist and sighed. "Daniel, I know I've been acting unusual over the past month, and if I've said or done anything I shouldn't—"

"We're good, Danni."

I stared at him for a moment, searching for a hint of where his head was at, but I couldn't read him. I thought about what I felt, and it was a little hard to make out clearly too, but I knew who I was in love with. "You're my best friend. I don't know what I'd do without you."

"Same." He smiled, just a small curve of his lips, and glanced over at the bar. "I just want you to be safe and happy."

I glanced over at the bar just in time to see Rider lift Rome upside down and shake him. "Spit it out! Now!"

A blob of something fell out of Rome's mouth and Ginger scooped it up in a napkin before Kutya could gobble it up.

"You're worse than the dog," Rider grumbled as he set Rome back on his feet. "Eat an apple slice."

Rome muttered under his breath as he stormed toward a fruit tray that had been set out, slugging Tony in the arm when the tiger-shifter actually grinned at him.

"I'm happy," I said, meeting Rider's eyes before he turned and started walking toward the back of the bar. "Thank you so much for the bracelet. I love it."

I got up, and after giving Daniel a hug, walked across

the bar. I didn't use my vampiric speed until I was in the back hall, out of view of the few human customers, and then I used it to catch up to Rider and Kutya before he entered his office. "What are you doing?"

"I was going to check and see if Pacitti has tried to contact Brinley yet," he said as he opened his office door and stepped inside. Kutya went straight to his doggy bed and plopped down.

"You're working on Christmas?"

"I'm making sure you're safe, and I never take days off from that, not even Christmas," he said before kissing my forehead. "Is that the bracelet I saw the dragon give you?"

I raised my wrist and ran my fingers over the small charms. "Yes, is that a problem?"

He walked behind his desk, settled into his chair and turned on his computer, taking his time to answer. "Honestly, I would have been very upset if it was a ring or a necklace, but the dragon seems to be respecting boundaries."

I sighed. "You know I love you, don't you?"

He nodded as he tapped on his keyboard, bringing something up. "And I love you, which is why no matter what, losing you is my greatest fear."

"Daniel's a friend, and hey, I controlled myself around Dean Winchester's twin."

"Funny." He shot me a dark look, but grinned before looking at whatever he'd pulled up on his screen. He sighed and sat back in his seat. "No contact yet."

"We'll find him."

"We will." He looked up at me. "You called up your succubus power on your own."

"I did."

"It almost got away from you. I think you actually enthralled Daniel and Jake, and Jake's a slayer who should have natural resistance."

I ran my finger along the edge of his desk, in need of something to concentrate on because suddenly it was hard to look him in the eye. "Are you angry about that?"

"No, but it is worrisome." He sighed. "It was a good thing that you were able to use the succubus venom to your advantage and kill that thing, but apparently you can lure too. That can backfire on you."

"Rider, would you still love me if something happened and I had sex with someone else because of the succubus side of me?" I blurted out the question as my conversation with Nyla resurfaced in the back of my mind before I lost the nerve.

Rider was silent for a long, tense stretch of time. "Have you?"

"No." I forced myself to raise my eyes to meet his gaze and hold it. "But with everything that has happened recently, I realized I've been trying to shove down my succubus half as if it's its own thing, a foreigner in my body, but it's not. It's half of what I am. I'm half sex demon, and I need to know if you love me anyway."

He stared at me for another stretch, then stood and pulled me over to him. "I love you anyway. You might have some things to worry about in this lifetime, but never that."

I leaned against him and released a breath I hadn't known I'd been holding.

"What the—"

I straightened and looked into Rider's eyes to see him staring past me at one of his bookshelves. "What is it?"

He moved me aside and walked over to one of the shelves and extracted a book. "That sonofabitch."

"Is that a Harry Potter book?"

"Yes, and this one's a sex manual." He pulled out another book, one that just the cover of made me blush. "Porter did this. He got in here and swiped books, left these in their place because he's a cocky asshole. I'm going to kill him. I'm going to kill him, wait for him to pop back up, and kill him again."

I laughed, unable to fight it, and covered my mouth

when Rider turned very unamused eyes my way. "Oh, come on. It's kind of funny, and I don't see the harm. He's obviously on our side. I thought Juan was supposed to be watching his every move though."

"He was. He was with him at all times or stationed just outside of private areas like the bathroom."

"So he managed to swipe your books right under your nose while he was in here with you?"

"Of course not, and I would have noticed long before if he had."

"Then how did he do it?"

Rider shook his head, muttered a few more curse words, and frowned, spotting a sliver of yellow sticking out of the center of the Harry Potter book. He opened it, growled, and showed me the yellow Post-It note that had CLEAN YOUR AIR VENTS scrawled across it.

I bent over, laughing.

"Glad you're so amused by—What the hell does this mean, *In case you still need freaky sex?*"

I stopped laughing, looked up, saw the note Rider had just removed from what looked like an illustrated guide to some really advanced sexual positions for the highly flexible, and groaned. "I think that note was for me."

Rider's eyes glowed with a fiery hint of gold. "Why would Jake Porter leave you a note about freaky sex?"

"Um, because it's what he suggested I give you for your Christmas present when I asked if he had any suggestions."

Rider's eyebrows raised a fraction, and he pursed his lips as he flipped through the pages of the book. "You did say you felt like Jake actually got me the two presents I thanked you for earlier…"

I huffed and folded my arms over my chest. "I thought you said I didn't need to get you anything? You were happy with what you got already."

"And I am." He smiled a little as he closed the book. "I'm just teasing. You'd never do anything in this book."

"Excuse you. Why? Are you saying I'm boring?"

"Boring? Never, and I am completely satisfied. There's a lot in here that's just... not your thing."

I grabbed the book, opened it, and tried not to swallow my tongue as the first picture I landed on assaulted my eyes.

Rider barked out a laugh. "Exactly. It's fine, Danni. I love what you got me, and despite Jake's help being involved, the gift was from you and it was the greatest gift I've ever been given."

Mmhmm, maybe so, but he was looking at me like I was some inexperienced, stuffy prude incapable of doing things he was obviously interested in and that just could not be tolerated. I shoved the book into his chest, forcing him to grab it. "Pick one."

"What?"

"Pick one."

"Danni, you don't have to do any of this to prove anything to me."

"Hey, I'm half succubus and you love me anyway, right? You'll love me even if I do all that twisty, bendy, freaky stuff, right?"

He stared at me for a moment with a look that suggested he might be afraid to answer before finally saying a slow, stretched out, "Yeeeaahhhhh..."

"All right then. Pick one and if it's too much for boring little me, I can always use the practice calling up my succubus side and controlling it, so let's do this."

"Danni..."

"I said pick your freaky festivity and let me merry up your Christmas, you stubborn ass!"

He laughed so hard his eyes grew wet, but he took a breath to get himself under control and perused the book. His mouth stretched in a wicked grin, and he turned the book around to show me something that so did not look humanly possible. "There's no shame in bowing out if this is outside your comfort zone."

I snatched the book out of his hands and backed toward the door, hoping we didn't get stuck once we managed to twist ourselves up like the couple in the picture. "Succubi don't bow out. If you can catch me, you can get it until *you* have to tap out."

His mouth dropped open, but as I turned and ran for the bedroom, he was right on my heels.

MERRY FANGIN' CHRISTMAS, Y'ALL!

ABOUT THE AUTHOR

Crystal-Rain Love is a romance author specializing in paranormal, suspense, and contemporary subgenres. Her author career began by winning a contest to be one of Sapphire Blue Publishing's debut authors in 2008. She snagged a multi-book contract with Imajinn Books that same year, going on to be published by The Wild Rose Press and eventually venturing out into indie publishing. She resides in the South with her three children and enough pets to host a petting zoo. When she's not writing she can usually be found creating unique 3D cakes, hiking, reading, or spending way too much time on Facebook. Find out more about her at www.crystalrainlove.com

If you enjoyed this book and want to help the series grow, please leave a review!

Printed in Great Britain
by Amazon